THE
CONFESSION
OF A CHILD
OF THE CENTURY
BY
SAMUEL HEATHER

———

a novel by
THOMAS ROGERS

———

SIMON AND SCHUSTER | NEW YORK

First printing

SBN 671-21266-4
Library of Congress Catalog Card Number: 72-189740
Designed by Edith Fowler
Manufactured in the United States of America
by H. Wolff Book Mfg. Co., Inc.

This book is dedicated to
my dear Chinese people,
Jacqueline, Rebecca, and Susan

Yang is for individualism, which does not recognize the sovereign; Mo is for universal love, which does not recognize parents. To be without sovereign or parent is to be a beast.

—MENCIUS

BOOK ONE

1

There is a novel by Alfred de Musset called *La confession d'un enfant du siècle* which I have never read but which seems to provide an excellent title for this book since my *terminus ad quo* is 1930 and actuarially speaking I am due to cease upon the midnight with no pain at the beginning of the year 2000 when I shall have attained my threescore years and ten. It will have been a purely twentieth-century life, which qualifies me to speak as a child of the century if not as its citizen.

I once thought of calling this book *How It Was,* but the title sounded presumptuous. I'm not sure how *it* was. I thought too of adapting to my era Ruskin's great title *Stormcloud Over the Nineteenth Century,* a very interesting meteorological study, but finally I rejected the idea because my story (this is a story) is really a kind of comical historical pastoral. The worst stormcloud I have seen, to wit a tornado that once chased me up Route 66 for several miles, finally bounced over the car I was driving and did no worse damage than to husk all the corn in a field half a mile away. I've been lucky. So I decided to call this book *The Confession of a Child of the Century.*

You know what the confessions of children are like. They are not meant to be taken very seriously nor should they really end up as big bound books like those of St. Augustine or Rousseau. Ideally this confession should come to you as a loose sheaf of papers perhaps kept together by being encased in the foundation stone of a civic Fun House of the future. Ideally, too, the confession of a child of the century should be anonymous, but this ideal has proved as impractical as the first since my publisher was unable to think of a commercially feasible way to market an anonymous book encased in stone. Hence, Reader, you hold in your hand this volume by Samuel Heather entitled as above.

Perhaps I should have waited. I will have more to confess by the end of my life, yet how would I know when to begin writing? The Venerable Bede expired a minute after dictating the last sentence of his translation of St. John, but how often do you get timing like that? And even if I can be sure of serving out my seventy years, suppose I wait till I'm sixty-nine to start writing and then fall apart physically? Held together by baling wire and chewing gum, would I have the necessary freshness and peace of mind to write a good book? It seems doubtful. Life is short and art takes a long time. To be sure, medical science might keep me going clear up to my *terminus ad quem* and even beyond. I could very well spill over into the twenty-first century with a strong young heart in my chest—that of a freshly slaughtered teen-age motorcyclist. And with fresh kidneys and liver available at the local organ bank, plus imperishable teeth courtesy of Medicaid, I might very well be in splendid shape thirty years from now, especially if vanity triumphs over common sense and I decide to purchase a full new head of hair. Though in that case what would be me and what would be bits and pieces of less fortunate others, only chance and the ravages of time will tell. So, balancing one thing against the other, I have decided to start writing today, when I am forty, and while my organs are all my own and my memory is still intact.

This memory of mine is a wonderful power or faculty which I possess in common with all men. Life, which takes us in hand and makes of us what we never expected to become, kindly leaves us our memories of what we were, so that nothing is ever lost. And please note that memory is the mother of the Muses, so we are all potential artists. In fact I will go further and declare that we are all actual artists continually transforming and re-creating our experiences in the laboratory of memory like so many alchemists stirring the pots and getting smoke in our eyes. My style is not always so metaphorical, but a prologue goes to one's head.

Of course, memory works in different ways for different people. Losers transmute the raw material of their disasters into the pure lead of woe, while winners transmute their triumphs into the pure gold of success. And, to get to the point, this child of the century has transmuted his adventures into a comical historical pastoral, a tricky literary genre which I would like to define except that something tells me it is time to get the story started. I suspect authors enjoy their own prologues more than readers do.

So now to my story.

Father was Bishop of Kansas City. "What is it like to have a bishop for a father?" people ask. Well, it's hell. Most fathers are terrible (most sons are terrible, too) but a bishop father is worse than most. He is a professional father. His diocese is his family. He delivers homilies and distributes advice. He gets into the habit of being a father, whereas most fathers are fatherly only on occasion. Their daily work is to be businessmen or dentists or farmers. My father's daily work was to be a father. It was excruciating.

Dinners had the mixed character of a sacred repast and a gladiatorial combat. The episcopal palace of Kansas City (actually a ten-room McKinley Administration house) was far from cheerful. There was more stained glass than one wants in a home. The downstairs rooms were too lofty for small talk and the halls too narrow for comfort. The bedrooms were like old-fashioned Pullman cars, all green and hard. It was really a terrible place to live.

Our dining room table was round. Suspended above it was a large, branching electric light fixture with fourteen flame-shaped light bulbs that gave off a yellowish glare which contrasted, painfully, with the white tablecloth. The view from where I sat was largely filled by a full-length oil portrait of Bishop Benedict (1845–1923) in mitre and cope, with his left hand resting on a terrestrial globe and his right hand raised in benediction. I identified with the globe. When I looked at the picture—and I could hardly avoid looking at it—I felt my head was being patted.

Naturally when I was young I seldom ate in the dining room with my parents. When I was older I was away at school. But off and on during the years the setting became etched in my mind until even now I can see it as it was on the evening shortly before Christmas in the year 1949 when I was nineteen years old.

There were just the four of us, which was something of a rarity: Mother on one side of me, Father on the other, and Bishop Benedict across. Father, as usual, blessed the food. Emma stood near the pantry door holding a tureen of soup, because in point of fact Father's blessings always took place before there was anything on the table but bread, butter, olives, celery, salt, and pepper. Presumably the real edibles were unsanctified.

His blessing over, Father raised his head and asked me whether I had studied that morning. *One* of our problems at that point was my school record, which was only average. As it happened, I had read Homer that morning, or rather about Homer in a book on archaeology I'd gotten from the public library.

"Yes," I said, "Homer."

Father nodded with approval.

"It appears," I said—*it appears* was one of Father's favorite opening gambits—"it appears there are two historically distinct styles of warfare described in *The Iliad*. The earlier is foot combat, in which warriors use immense oxhide shields like Ajax' and obviously move about very slowly

12

with plenty of time to announce their pedigree and insult their opponent before laying on. In the later form of warfare combatants drive horse-drawn chariots and use bronze shields like Achilles'."

This little speech gives some notion of our domestic life.

"Very interesting," Father said. "Where did you learn that?"

"From a book."

"Not responsive," he said. He picked up legal language from his lawyer friends.

"From *The Celts*, by Childe."

"Oh? Do you call that reading Homer?"

"Roughly," I said.

He looked at me directly. A man does not get to be a bishop without having a direct look. "I consider it reading Childe."

"Father," I said, "I've been meaning to ask whether you would be pleased if I were to become an archaeologist?"

He frowned.

Mother was not always left out of our conversations. She had her own point of view, as a matter of fact, and when so inclined she was perfectly able to make herself heard, as she now was. "I don't enjoy these disagreements," she said. "I love you both. Now can't we have a quiet dinner?"

This made us both cross.

"I cannot see the relevance . . ." Father began.

"What's the point of being quiet?" I asked.

Mother went on eating her soup. Father turned back to me. "In other words, you have not read *The Iliad* at all to-day?"

"No."

"Anyway, it *is* his vacation," Mother said. "Even if he's doing badly he still needs a vacation as much as anyone."

"I am not doing badly," I told her. "I passed all my Hour Exams."

13

"Passed?" Father said. "Passed? Is that your idea of success? To pass? Is that the modest level of your ambition? To get through? How many boys are there with your advantages? And yet you set yourself goals anyone could achieve."

"You exaggerate," I said. "Not quite anyone could pass at Harvard."

"How often have I told you not to quibble?" he asked.

"Anyway, grades are only a superficial indication."

"A stupid answer. Everyone knows it. To scorn superficial indications indicates superficiality." He surprised himself with that turn of speech and so he stopped short to think it over. I wondered if we were witnessing the birth of a sermon.

"Would you be pleased?" I asked.

He waved his hand and turned to his soup, which was getting cold.

"Archaeology is exciting," Mother said. "There is something healthy . . ." she meant digging, I think, "and at the same time intellectual."

At that point, Reader, the ceiling of our dining room opened, a beam of light descended on me, and I had one of my visions of Western civilization. I saw that all our notions of duty, work, and sacrifice are simply rationalizations of a bad climate. In Kansas City, for instance, the mean summer temperature is 80° and the mean winter temperature is 20°. The Midwestern steppes undulate away in every direction. Naturally, in such a spot, who could conceive of life as a thing of joy and beauty? Who could fly in the face of facts and pronounce the great sentence: Be happy. Even the Mediterranean basin where our civilization started is subject to temperature extremes. There are cold winds in Greece, and in Palestine the summers are broiling. So, made uncomfortable by the weather, Western man has rationalized the fact and built up religions, laws, and moral codes that treat discomfort, strenuousness, guilt, and misery as the proper and nec-

14

essary conditions of life. In the South Seas they would not have invented Christianity simply because they have no seasons, and as everyone but people like Father know, the story of Jesus Christ is simply the old seasonal fertility legend all over again. One might as well worship a pumpkin or a string bean. Air conditioning and central heating have obviously been more effective in undermining Christianity with the masses than Voltaire, Huxley, and Anatole France combined and squared. Iron out the seasonal variations and Christianity ceases to exert any real appeal. Even Christians give indirect acknowledgment of the importance of climate. Heaven, you will find, is always moderate and unchanging, while Hell is always extreme. Read Dante. Part of the Inferno is icy and part is fiery, while some poor wretches, like people in Kansas City, are roasted at one end and frozen at the other. And so ended my vision.

Mother was a Clay. Rather, her mother had been a Clay but had married a Jones. The Jones connection was never much talked about but the Clay connection was. As everyone knows, the Clays arrived in Virginia in 1613, seven years before the Pilgrim Fathers made it to Provincetown or Plymouth or wherever they did finally pull in. Those seven years —mystic number—figured prominently in Mother's thoughts. When she heard of a Bradford or a Brewster or a Winslow accomplishing anything she would shake her head slightly as if to imply that newcomers were taking over the country.

Between my Clay mother and Father, who had been consecrated by a bishop who had been consecrated by a bishop and so on back to St. Peter,* I was pretty well fixed with a sense of tradition. As the dinner table conversation reveals, I was made to be aware of my advantages, the strongly implied conclusion being that I damned well ought to be

---

* I've gone into the matter and I think there can be no doubt the Protestant Episcopal Church does have Apostolic Succession.

grateful for all they had given me. The upshot of the particular conversation I have begun by recording is that Father delivered the following speech once he had eaten his soup.

"One day you will discover that life is not a joke. You will be troubled and helpless and all the things you are now throwing away will be unattainable. Without faith, without good habits, without a profession, you will find yourself unable either to bear burdens or surmount obstacles."

As can be seen, Father was at heart a Puritan. For all his fashionable High Church practices, his real vision was gymnastic rather than sacramental. He saw life as an obstacle course to be successfully and effortfully negotiated by those with good habits, a plausible view given the climatic conditions of Kansas City. However, to transport you into the future, Reader, I should now reveal that Father's warnings, though superficially sound, turned out to be as mistaken as his ecclesiastical views and his political opinions. He was— need I say?—a Republican. Out of loyalty to her Clay ancestors Mother was a Whig. I know it sounds odd. I've never pretended my family was ordinary.

2

And that, Reader, is more or less the start of this confession. I have spared you my childhood and the earlier stages of my adolescence, together with my loss of faith and other saga material which does not fit into the rather perfectly classical framework of this story. And now a word about my method.

I have a good memory, but not, I would say, an exceptionally accurate one. I remember, or think I remember, the names of the kings of Judah and Israel as well as the first fifteen or twenty Roman Emperors and how they died, as from eating poisonous mushrooms, sword thrusts, strangulation, and fever. I believe I could tell you, if you wanted to know, the sixteen or eighteen different ways in which Louis XV descends from Henry IV. I can recite, though not here, passages from Shakespeare, Milton, Pope, and Wordsworth, but I am conscious of a certain shakiness here and there, a tendency to transpose and skip. When, or if, Western civilization is totally wiped out, I am not the sort of person who can be relied upon for a literal reconstruction of any particular texts or historical episodes. So don't come asking me. In what follows—for that matter, in what has already come—I aim at the essential truth of the scene. Who cares what we ate for dinner that evening in 1949? Could it have been lamb chops? I have no idea nor does this lapse of memory worry me, just as I am not worried over my haziness about the battle of Manzikert. My current impression is that some time in the year 1076 the Emperor Manuel Commenus led his Byzantine army to a stunning defeat at the hands of the Seljucks. Go look it up if you want to check the accuracy of my memory. The reason I haven't checked is that I believe books should be written straight out of your own head without looking up anything, even the spelling of words. What is remembered is all that counts; the rest is just research. An author who checks everything and quotes a lot is relying on other men's memories and other men's minds. And what is the distinction between such a writer and the next pretty actress who goes all the way and simply hires a hack to write her autobiography? Or what about politicians who have speech writers? What kind of monkey business is that? No, I must play honest with you, Reader. I will write down my story exactly as I remember it, with only such omissions and curtailments as my own sense of tact and artistic economy shall dictate.

Of course, since the events I have begun by recording took place some twenty years ago, I don't pretend those were the actual words we used. Yet like Thucydides I was there, and like him I have made Mother, Father, and myself speak not the words we actually spoke but only such words as in my opinion are reasonable and proper for us to have spoken on the occasion. Just as poetry is more philosophic than history, so memory is more rational than a tape recorder.

And so onward.

Nothing was decided at dinner, nothing ever is, and so after New Year's, back to Harvard I went on the Atchison, Topeka and Sante Fe as far as Chicago and on the New York Central from there to Boston. The world was all before me, where to choose if only I could make up my mind.

My roommates, all three of them, were back ahead of me. When I opened the door of our suite on the fourth floor of Leverett House, there they were, sitting around the table in our living room playing Hearts. "Hey, Sammy," they said. "Want to join the game?"

I stood just inside the doorway with my suitcase at my feet and looked them over before I said, "You wouldn't ask that question if you could see yourselves the way I see you, sitting around that table with cigarettes dangling from your lips. There's a fug in here you could cut with a knife."

"Oh, well, Happy New Year to you, too," Morrison said.

Walker looked at me in his special way. "What's the matter with you?" he asked.

Rather than speak, Bartoldi belched. Bartoldi had been to Exeter.

Then they went back to their game. I picked up my suitcase and walked around them. I went into my room, shut the door, and sat down on my bed with my coat still on. It struck me then, very forcibly, that there must be something more to life than playing Hearts at Harvard. Or wondering whether to become an archaeologist, for that matter, digging through dry soil to find the broken pots of long-dead Greeks. I remember saying to myself in the way one does say to oneself, "What am I doing here?" The question had been coming on ever since I'd climbed the steps out of the subway in Harvard Square, my suitcase banging my legs as I negotiated the turnstile. The question had gathered within me as I walked along Massachusetts Avenue and down Plympton Street, sniffing the raw winter air of Cambridge. And now the question was precipitated by the sight of my roommates playing cards. What am I doing here? I asked myself, sitting on my bed in my overcoat. Am I happy?

And the answer to that was *no*.

One has these moments, Reader. Depressed, still in my overcoat, I remember wondering if the Bishop might possibly be right. Maybe work, discipline, purpose, faith—all the qualities (virtues?) my life lacked—maybe they were the thing. The possibility depressed me even more. I sat there for quite a while wondering why I hadn't been born a happy South Sea Islander diving for clam shells in the clear water and combing my hair in the sun. Maybe I could run away.

Then I took off my overcoat and went out to see how the other three-quarters were living.

They had apparently agreed to ignore me. I circled around the card table looking down into their hands while they went on playing as if I weren't there. "If you think," I said, "that I'm going to spend the rest of the semester playing stupid card games while the Charles freezes over, you have another think coming. Bartoldi has the Queen."

Bartoldi folded his hand and put it on the table. "All right, Sammy," he said. He was the one who always started the rough stuff.

"Pay no attention to him," Morrison said. "I knew you had the Queen anyway."

"So did I," said Walker. And in their voices you could hear undertones of sadness, as if they both expected to have the Queen dumped on them.

Bartoldi picked up his cards. "All right, but I'm warning you, Heather," he said.

I decided to ignore him. I opened the window and put my head out to breathe some more of Cambridge's chemical-smelling cold air. With my head out the window I could hear music coming up from the suite below ours where there were two Bach-and-Before, Stravinsky-and-After music lovers, no favorites of mine. Sounds of Bartok emanating from their windows reminded me of a Christmas present I'd been given by a demented girl in Kansas City whom I used to go around with and who still gave me cultural presents in memory of what hadn't exactly been a grand passion. This year she'd come to the episcopal palace with "Highlights From *Madame Butterfly*" wrapped up in red tissue paper and afterwards we'd gone off to a party together. I'd brought the record with me and I decided now would be as good a time as any to start putting it to use. So, leaving the window open, I went back to my bedroom, got the record out of my suitcase, put it on the phonograph, and turned up the volume as far as it would go. I even opened the door of the suite so the boys downstairs would have a better chance to hear some real music for a change. This, incidentally, created a draft that threatened to blow the cards off the table.

Bartoldi folded his hand, got to his feet, closed the win-

20

dow, and turned off the phonograph. Cio-Cio-San scratched to a halt in mid-aria.

"What are you afraid of?" I asked him. "Why do you huddle around that table handling little bits of cardboard?" Then I opened the window, and turned on the phonograph. Cio-Cio-San zoomed up to high C.

"Shall we get him?" Bartoldi asked.

The others shook their heads. Uninvited, I poured myself a glass of California burgundy from the bottle that was sitting on the floor beside the table. Then I sat down in one of our armchairs and sipped and listened to Puccini. The room grew colder and colder. Presently I got up, went to my room, put on my overcoat, and came back. The card players, like figures from a Cézanne painting, were still immobilized at their table.

Finally, with a sort of mild regret in his voice, Morrison said, "Does it have to be Puccini?"

"Puccini is the Wagner of music," I told him.

"I still think we should get him," Bartoldi said. He was always ready for violence, that one. The perfect prep-school thug.

"Prep-school thug," I said.

Walker went to his room for a sweater. "Get me a jacket, will you?" Morrison asked. They bundled up against the cold. Bartoldi continued to play cards in his shirtsleeves. The scene became somehow more Cézanne-like.

"I have a feeling for life," I told them. "I know things that most people don't know. For instance, that life can be beautiful. Even people like you, sitting there ignoring me, even you have a certain beauty of composition. The planes of Walker's face as he looks at his cards, the square lines of Bartoldi's back, Morrison's profile—maybe I should become an artist. What do you think?"

"If you think we're interested in what you become . . ." Bartoldi didn't finish.

21

"One must love beauty," I said. I got up to turn the record. My depression was lifting. I still couldn't have answered any hard questions such as *how do you plan to spend your life?* or *what is the good for man?* but at least I had successfully negotiated the change from Kansas City to Harvard, always an awkward transition to make. "Look, deal me into the next game," I said.

Harvard, in case you didn't go there yourself, Reader, is the sort of school where everyone is so happy he's gotten into it that no one bothers to gripe about what he's getting out of it. I felt this a few days later—I felt it keenly if you want to know—as I sat in class listening to what the man on the podium had to say to us about A. E. Housman. A. E. Housman, the man seemed to be saying, was a Victorian imperialist whose poems reflected his Victorian imperialism. That *can't* be what he was saying, but it's what I remember him as saying as he sat there behind a table, very upright in his straight chair. He was an extraordinarily upright man. I think most of his height was from the waist up. Short legs and a long, long body. And A. E. Housman was a Victorian imperialist. Not that I had such an investment in what A. E. Housman might turn out to have been, one way or another. It's just that, sitting there in class, I felt a little dip toward despair, as if the floor in Emerson Hall were tilting and we were all about to fall over backwards, pencils and notebooks flying, while the man on the podium grew higher and higher until he too toppled over, crashing down onto us like a colossal statue of, say, Constantine the Great. Those staring blank antique eyes flashed into my mind. Who did they remind me of? Father?

So after class I went straight to the drugstore on Mass. Avenue where they squeezed fresh orange juice right in front of your eyes—sometimes right into your eyes. I drank a large o.j. to restore the situation, and then I went off to meet Martha, about whom something needs to be said.

Reader, if you are masculine, imagine the smallest girl

22

you have ever seriously fallen for. Turn her nose slightly up. Give her black shoulder-length hair and a temporizing expression, as if to say, "I might, or I might not." Not a girl to be sure of, but on the other hand, not a girl to despair about. Stimulated by orange juice, raised to a new energy level, I walked purposefully toward Cambridge Common, where we had agreed to meet.

She wasn't there, of course. Catch her waiting for anybody, but she had her own principles and it wasn't more than the usual twenty minutes before I could see her coming.

"A. E. Housman's a Victorian imperialist," I said, "and how are you this afternoon?"

"So, so." She stopped a few feet away, one foot advanced toward me, the other on which her weight rested turned like a ballet dancer's so that her small hip was slightly thrust out. It was her Degas pose. Her manner, as always, seemed to say, "Well, here I am, now what are you going to make of the situation?"

I looked from her to my watch. "We better get moving if we don't want to be late." I was taking her to an afternoon concert at Symphony Hall in Boston. Koussevitsky was still conducting in those days.

She was never one to waste words where silence would do. She turned and we began walking toward the subway in Harvard Square. "You're always late," I told her, "because you're so small you're afraid you won't be missed otherwise."

"Did you just figure that out?" she asked.

I nodded. "And I also happen to know that you're a lot less cool and collected than you pretend to be."

"You think about me a lot, don't you?" she said.

"When I have the time." Then, reaching more down than out, I put my arm around her waist.

Boy/girl relationships were very different in those days, Reader, from what they have since become. We had to pay court, take them to concerts, flatter them, fall in love, and

23

even then it wasn't a sure thing. Will you believe that I had never more than kissed that half-pint? Not that venery was unknown. Bartoldi, for instance, had personally polluted I don't know how many girls. (His bedroom door closed . . . the *Liebestod* at full volume on our phonograph . . . cries of distress from the boys below . . . and after an hour or so a dazed coed moving shyly through our living room to repair her face and whatnot in the bath.) But Bartoldi was an exception, not the rule. Walker, Morrison, and I looked on, not sure whether it was right, or wrong, or even real.

Martha and I arrived at Symphony Hall in time to see Koussevitsky emerge from the wings, mount the podium, and bow to the applause of his followers before the house lights dimmed. Then came the electric moment when, rigid, facing his orchestra, the maestro began to pump good red, that is to say, White Russian blood into his neck and temples. He swelled, he colored, he raised his arms trembling with the tension of it all, and the concert began—in this case a race between Weber and Koussevitsky's oncoming stroke. It was wonderful and terrible, a more wonderful and terrifying experience than many of the little old Boston ladies could take. They tended to drop out at the intermissions so as not to be present when the maestro finally cashed in his chips. And at their age you couldn't really blame them for not wanting to see it through to the bitter end—the sudden faltering, the dropped baton, the vague clutch at incarnadined temples, the music stand overturned, and then the final fatal plummeting forward into the lap of the first violinist. Actually, the old man retired intact from the Boston Symphony and for a year or so even continued to hold sway at Tanglewood during the summers. Münch took over in Boston, and while he might have been a better conductor than Koussevitsky, he didn't keep you guessing the way the old fellow did. I loved those last Koussevitsky concerts.

Afterwards I took Martha to a tea parlor near Copley Square where we took tea.

"I'm leaving Harvard," I told her. "I'm not getting anything out of the place. I'm going to go to the Far East. Will you miss me?"

She never took my lies seriously. "Will you go?" she asked.

Dull question. Even the most petite charmer can occasionally say the wrong thing.

3

And now a short digression on sex, Reader, a funny business if you want to know.

I was at that time a virgin, through no particular efforts of my own; indeed, rather the reverse. As a child of the century I'd read Auden and had Freud talked at me. I knew virginity was a bum rap which could get you into lifelong trouble. Only I hadn't succeeded in beating the rap, and, at nineteen, time seemed to be running out. It worried me. All of which goes to show that in every age people tend to worry most about the problem that is least likely to beset them. Thus the eighteenth-century skeptics and rationalists spent their time warning each other about the dangers of religious enthusiasm. And thus the Victorians zealously guarded themselves from the dangers of idleness and frivolity. And so now in America, where virgins have become as rare as the whooping crane, young people are made to think that only by getting a good early start on their sex lives can they avoid an immaculate existence. Everyone is on the alert to detect signs of incipient chastity so that it can be caught early, like cancer, and cured. In fact, isn't there an Auden poem in which cancer and chastity are treated as synonymous?

Hence that young man looking across the tea table at Martha knew there was work cut out for him. It was practically his duty not only to lose his own virginity but to rescue her from what in his innocence he assumed was hers. True, this was not the conception of duty which prevailed in the See of Kansas City, where duties were not conceived as potential pleasures, but still that young man, that younger version of myself, was showing some signs of his upbringing as he nerved himself for action.

"Look, what do you want to do tonight?" I asked.

"What do you suggest?" Martha said.

"Well, *Kind Hearts and Coronets* is on at the Exeter. It's supposed to be good." This was said on the principle that if you take them out on the town and give them a good time they're bound to be grateful.

"But it means going all the way back to school for dinner and then all the way into town again."

"We can eat in town," I told her. "I'll take you to the Athens Olympia."

She considered the proposition. Then she said, "We could eat at home if you don't mind eating with my parents."

They were not exactly the folks I most looked forward to hobnobbing with that evening, but there was a certain tactfulness in her suggestion, episcopal salaries being what they were and my allowance being what it was. Also it was a joke. Used to eating with my own parents, how could I be expected to mind eating with hers, civilized types from what I had so far seen of them? Besides, what with dinner and the movies, there might not be enough money in my wallet for anything further.

"Fine," I said.

So while the Kansas City hedonist finished his tea and even downed two English muffins, off Martha went to telephone Mama, or more probably the cook, to say there would be two extra for dinner.

The Sears—they were Sears without being Sears, if you know what I mean—lived within walking distance of Copley Square, so when Martha had come back from telephoning, we strolled off on foot into the evening darkness. She must really be fond of me, I thought, or she wouldn't be willing to spend so much time in my company. Perhaps I fascinated her. It was a theory worth testing, anyway. I stopped in the darkness between two street lamps and pulled her toward me to kiss her. Sometimes this worked, sometimes it didn't. This

27

time it did. And after we had kissed I thought that perhaps, appearances to the contrary notwithstanding, we were really made for each other. I, Samuel, take you, Martha, I thought to myself, and I imagined us living in peace and happiness in . . . Well, I couldn't imagine where, or what work I would come home from or whether our children would be shrimps like Martha or beanpoles like myself. And that thought begot others more nervous and lustful, though sufficiently absorbing to keep me at least in a meditative silence for the rest of our walk. And she, either because she had liked being kissed, or because she had nothing to say, kept her own silence. Probably we looked like lovers strolling hand in hand.

Then we arrived at her house where immediately things began to seem less felicitous. Not that there was anything wrong with the house, quite the contrary. It was a good house as houses go, but it did rather insist upon social distinctions. One flight of steps led up to the front door and another led down to the basement kitchen, thus nicely separating the bourgeois sheep from the proletarian goats. Following Martha upwards as she fished in her purse for her door key, I felt a sort of diminution of being. Goathood receded, and standing under the fanlight beside Martha, I bleated softly to myself.

"What's that?" she asked. The door opened and we entered the hall.

"Nothing," I said. "I was just bleating."

The hall we were in had an Oriental carpet on the floor and one of those drop-leaf tables with its polished skirt hitched up against the wall. Above it there was a Federal-style mirror. These were people with possessions. From a room on our right came a tinkling shepherdess' voice saying, "Is that you, darling?" I bleated again.

"Will you stop making those sounds?" Martha said.

Then we went to greet her mother.

Mrs. Sears was having an evening cocktail or two in front of a fire. Great-grandfather somebody, painted perhaps by Copley, hung over the mantelpiece. This room had another Oriental carpet on which I felt like rolling. All that colored wool began to go to my head, and I barely restrained myself from bleating a third time as Mrs. Sears held out her hand, a kind and welcoming shepherdess. "How are you, Samuel?" she said. "I'm so glad you could come to dinner."

Martha kissed the authoress of her being, and then we all looked at each other more than was strictly necessary.

"Sherry?" said Mrs. Sears, and sherry it was. In that household they reserved the hard stuff for adults. Perhaps they even hoped their lamb would grow another inch if they kept her off the sauce. Anyway, it was sherry we were sipping when Papa Sears came in, fresh and rosy from his bank. Actually, he'd been upstairs washing the smell of money off his hands.

He and I pressed the flesh. "Hello, Samuel," he said.

He was the larger of Martha's two parents, and looking him in his eyes, I wondered if I wanted to get involved even unto matrimony with the daughter of anyone with such very odd, flat pupils. After dealing with the Bishop for all these years, did I really think I was up to having this banker as a father-in-law? Perhaps a short affair with Martha? A passionate seduction and then curtains?

"How does it come that Dartmouth beat us?" Mr. Sears asked. One of the things we had in common was his assumption that I cared about the fate of the Harvard squash team. This banker had swung a mean racquet in his youth.

"I guess Dartmouth is just better than we are," I said.

"Nonsense," said Mr. Sears cheerfully. He poured himself a martini.

"Hasn't the weather been lovely these last few days?" Mrs. Sears said. As a shepherdess she kept a sharp eye on the weather.

29

"We beat Brown, didn't we?" Mr. Sears asked.

"A fluke," I explained.

Mr. Sears laughed again. He could afford to laugh. After all, it was only squash, not money, we were losing. "This fellow of yours doesn't want to admit that we're good this year."

Martha, thus appealed to, said, "He doesn't know anything about squash."

"I was the best player at my school," I said, which was not exactly true but none of them were in a position to disprove it. In fact, you couldn't even be sure Mrs. Sears had heard me. Her mind was still on the weather.

"I walked along the Embankment this afternoon," she said. "All the ice is gone from the basin."

"The Charles is still partly frozen beyond Mt. Auburn Hospital," I told her. It seemed only courteous to show an interest.

"You should have gone out for our team," Mr. Sears said.

It was like playing ping-pong with two balls. So, keeping them both bouncing, we chitchatted our way through our aperitifs while belowstairs the menials toiled over our meal, which presently rose to us in the dumbwaiter to be handed around by a morose retainer named Charlotte whom the adult Searses very probably thought of as a devoted old family servant.

Over the goodies we discussed some first principles of political philosophy.

Marx' ideal of a classless society had not struck a responsive chord in Mr. Sears' breast. "It's all nonsense," he said. "In any social system there are going to be people at the top and people at the bottom," and you could tell where he thought he belonged.

"What about the Eskimos?" I asked. I'd never heard about an Eskimo class system, and I still haven't.

But Pop Sears was not about to be scored off at his own dinner table. These capitalists are no pushovers, my revolutionary friends. "The Eskimos don't have a complex social system," he said. "In any *complex* system, there will always be those on top and those below." We were back to position A.

"Then maybe we shouldn't have a complex system," I said. "Haven't you ever thought life ought to be simpler than it is?"

"As at Walden Pond," said the Shepherdess, getting a look from her Banker telling her pretty clearly to keep out of this. He could deal with my nonsense in his own way.

"I'm afraid I accept the fact that life is complex," Mr. Sears said.

Afraid nothing. He loved it. If life weren't complex, if gravity didn't exist to keep the lower classes in their place, then Sears wouldn't be sitting where he was—on top of the world, or at least such portions of the world as lay around State Street and Copley Square. By God, I thought, I *will* take his daughter away from him. We would live together in holy poverty, cashing such checks as he would send us only to distribute the money among our even poorer neighbors. I would grow a beard. Martha would . . . One look at Martha dissolved that fantasy.

"Well, I don't know," I said, in answer to Mr. Sears' acceptance of life's complexity. "I don't know. I guess I'm really an anarchist."

Mr. Sears' answer to that was to go *ha! ha! ha!*, he being the genial host entertaining his daughter's unsound suitor. Then he came off it. "Anarchy is impossible," he told me.

"If it comes to that," I said, "government is getting impossible, too. Look at the war—" the Second World War, Reader—"fifty million people killed. Europe in ruins from the Volga to the Irish channel. Japan atomized. If that's the best our governments can do, we could hardly do worse ourselves."

There was a moment of silence while Mr. Sears considered how best to dispel this argument, if it was an argument. Then he said, "But people are responsible for what their governments do. You can't just blame the war on governments."

"But, sir!" I said. "Look at Hitler. He wasn't elected. Hindenburg appointed him Chancellor. And even the Germans who did vote for Hitler weren't necessarily voting for war or the extermination of the Jews. Hitler was only able to do that because he held governmental power. Governments are dangerous!"

Got you! I thought, and in my love of argument I felt a sort of dim awareness that there was a fellowship between myself and Mr. Sears, a fellowship which excluded the Shepherdess and Martha, both of whom, I was willing to bet, didn't give a damn whether people were responsible for what their governments did, or vice versa.

"Now just a minute," Mr. Sears said, but did he get that minute? No, sirree.

"Besides . . ." the idea had just come to me . . . "besides, if people are responsible for what their governments do, then governments are responsible for what their people do, so if there are murderers and rapists, and burglars, and poor stupid miserable illiterates getting nothing out of life, then it's the government's responsibility to help them. Your argument really leads to a form of state socialism, Mr. Sears."

Got you again, I thought, and I imagined Mr. Sears and myself going off together to some desert island where we could argue endlessly about the principles of political life while our womenfolk baked pies at home.

"After all . . ." I started to say, when mine host tapped on his wine glass with a spoon.

"Your trouble," he told me, "is that you won't listen." He turned to Martha, "Does he always talk your ear off like this?"

"No," she said.

"With her I'm very humble and eager to please," I said.

"But not with me," said Mr. Sears. You could see he was rather enjoying this.

"Well, but Martha doesn't have your ideas, Sir!"

"Which are all wrong?"

"Oh, I don't say that."

"No, you wouldn't *say* it," Mr. Sears said. He was smiling. That's the nice thing about these Eastern biggies, Reader. You can argue with them without bringing down the house, which is usually so solidly built that only a stick of dynamite can shake it. As a matter of fact I had a stick of dynamite, though not on me at the moment, but of this you shall hear more anon.

"This is fun," said the Shepherdess.

Rather than putting her out of her pain, Mr. Sears said to me, "Now just let me get this straight. If we do away with all government, how is the world going to be organized?"

"In communes, I guess. There'll be factory communes, and teaching communes, and farming communes, and so on. They'd exchange goods and services with each other."

"I see." Mr. Sears sat back in his armchair and nodded his head. I could imagine him going through exactly the same routine in his office at the bank just after someone had offered insufficient collateral for a big loan.

Martha said, "He's not really an anarchist at all."

"What is he?" Mr. Sears asked.

"I'm a student of life," I said, though what I really meant was that I was a child of the century.

"He's a poet," said Martha.

"Oh, do you write poetry, Samuel?" Mrs. S. asked.

And I had to confess, what I have so far concealed from you, Reader. At that time in my life, I did write poems, a practice I have since renounced in favor of the sterner and more exalted work of writing prose.

"Can we hear one of your poems?" Mrs. Sears asked, and Oh! Reader, can you forgive me for what is to follow?

33

"Why yes," I said.

In youth we are more keenly aware of shame than at any other time in our lives, precisely because in our recklessness we do things that wiser, older, and more prudent men would never think of doing. How I died during the following days as I remembered myself reciting this poem to Mr., Mrs., and Miss Sears at their dinner table that evening. The first stanza went:

> No, no, never in the night take refuge
> When envenomed bats spin aloft
> From their deeper dark and dogs howl.
> Pale moonflowers open and newts spawn.
> Darkness is no time for lovers.

And there were three more stanzas, each beginning, "No, no, never in the night take refuge." Even now, twenty years later, I'm still shaken by it all. Dylan Thomas had a lot to answer for when he stood at the seat of Euterpé, the Muse of Lyric Poetry, and demanded admittance to Parnassus.

However, to revisit the scene of my particular crime, when I had finished my recitation, Mrs. S. said, "Why, how nice!" And it is awe-inspiring—is it not, Reader?—to consider that in the scheme of creation there is probably a use and purpose and meaning to everything: Mrs. Sears, my poem, the ice above Mt. Auburn Hospital, and a larch tree growing unobserved in the Canadian wilderness. Existence is too strange to be merely natural. These thoughts, however, are best reserved for later, along with the stick of dynamite and my seduction of Martha, which will have to be put into the next chapter.

4

So we left the Sears' and their rugs and their furniture and their opinions and walked toward the Exeter Theater.

"Do you think your father really likes me?" I asked Martha.

"Do you like him?" she asked.

"That isn't the question," I said. I brooded a bit. "I wish I hadn't recited that poem," I said at last. "I was doing all right up till then." Martha didn't feel called upon to comment on that. I looked at her. "You know," I said, "if I were really trying to seduce you, I wouldn't be taking you to the movies, would I? I'd buy you some drinks in a chummy bar and then suggest a hotel."

"I expect you would," she said.

We walked along in silence after that. Thinking seemed to be going on right and left. Down the block we could already see the lights of the Exeter.

"It seems to me," I said, speaking carefully and thoughtfully, "it seems to me that was a rather unimpressive Beaujolais your father offered us for dinner, not that I want to criticize him in front of you. And he wasn't any too quick in refilling our glasses."

"No."

"So would you like a drink now?" I asked.

She would not have been Martha if she'd answered right away. We strolled, casually of course, for another ten or fifteen feet before she said, "Yes."

I stopped. The Exeter was right ahead of us.

"You mean, *Yes?*" I said.

I got her quizzical look. She still wasn't giving anything away. "I said, *Yes.*"

"You want a drink?" I asked. One gets stupid, you know.

"Yes, a drink. Don't you want one?"

"Oh, yes," I said. "Yes, a drink. Let's go have a drink."

In the snuggery we eventually found I remember saying, "Well, this is nice," an utterance I immediately ranked in its felicity somewhere between a belch and a breaking of wind. I *must* keep from chattering, I said to myself, and then aloud, "What did you think of my poem?" When she seemed about to answer that question, I forestalled her by saying, "No, don't tell me." And then, "Are you sure you don't want to see *Kind Hearts and Coronets*? I mean, what hotel should we go to?"

"Do you want to see the movie?" she asked.

"No, no," I said. "No." And then after a moment, "No." Then, to clarify my position, "I mean, if you want to go I'd be glad to see it, but, uh . . ."

And was she any help, Reader? No. She sat there with her hands on the tabletop, looking as if butter wouldn't melt in her mouth, while I plowed hideously ahead. "What hotel? . . . I mean, I've never . . . I mean, you know Boston . . ." I trailed off and stared hopelessly at her. "We don't have any suitcases," I said at last, and I remember thinking how nice it would be to have several big heavy suitcases and perhaps a trunk or two to tote around. Moreover, why had I recited that poem? If this was living, give me something else. Oh to be an angel, a pure flame of ardency freed from the clumsiness of limbs and tongue.

"Aren't you assuming something?" she said.

And that did help. It gave me grounds for complaint and argument. "Now, just a minute—" her father's phrase—"just a minute. It was perfectly well understood that when we came here instead of going to the movie . . . I mean . . . you know."

"What sort of girl do you think I am?" she asked.

I shook my head. "I have absolutely no idea what sort of girl you are, but you can't deny that you promised."

36

"I certainly did not," she said.

"You came here for a drink," I told her. "You can't deny that. You're drinking right this minute. What do you think that is?"

"It's a drink," she said.

"All right, Martha," I told her. "This is very coy, shabby behavior."

At that she spread her elbows on the table and put her hands on top of each other and leaned forward in a way she'd probably been taught not to. "So you think I promised?" she said.

"You definitely promised," I told her. "At least that's my interpretation of things."

"I see."

"And the question I want answered is what hotel we're going to go to." I was beginning to sound pretty sure of myself.

She lifted her little shoulders and let them settle. "It's up to you," she said, and I found myself right back where I'd been a minute before. Flustered. Then I caught her smiling at me. "All right," I said, "we'll go to the Parker House."

"How nice," she said. A hateful little girl, Reader. I couldn't think why I liked her.

On our way to the Parker House the night air restored my faith in her. "You only behaved like that in there to see how I'd react," I told her.

"I expect you're right," she said.

"You wouldn't be doing this if you didn't love me." I stopped. We were crossing Boston Common by then. "You do love me, don't you?" In the darkness under the trees her expression didn't reveal much. And there were bums and sailors wandering around. It wasn't the ideal spot for the question.

"Do you love me?" she asked.

37

"Don't be silly," I said. "I'm always calling you up, aren't I? I've been taking you out for months. I try to see you all the time. Don't you think it's obvious?"

"No."

"No?" I stepped back, amazed. "But if you aren't sure that I love you . . . ?"

"You're interested," she said. "You like me, but I'm not so sure you really love me."

"This is terrible," I said. I sat down on a bench, which brought me down to her level, since she remained standing on the path. "Terrible."

"What's terrible?"

"But, I mean, we can't just . . . I mean, you've got to be sure I love you. Otherwise . . ."

"Otherwise what?"

"Otherwise . . . Martha, this is a very serious matter. Sit down." I felt like my own father. I felt like her father. I even felt like her mother. I believed, you see, in a double standard. It was all right for a man to go to bed with a girl he was not sure he loved, but I felt very strongly that a girl owed it to herself, if not to the man, to be convinced he was passionately devoted to her. Otherwise where would we be? Just having fun with each other? Even a convinced pagan and hedonist like myself had to draw the line somewhere. This looked like absolute vice. "Look," I told Martha, "you can't just go to a hotel with me unless you're convinced I love you. It wouldn't be right."

"Well, perhaps you'll convince me," she said. She didn't sit down, probably not wanting to dirty her coat. I was beyond caring. I even leaned back on the bench and put my hands over my eyes.

"How long are you going to sit there?" she asked.

I removed my hands and looked at her, realizing I really didn't know what sort of girl she was. I also realized she had perfectly good grounds for being in doubt about whether I loved her. Thirdly, I realized there was a certain discourtesy in keeping her standing there in the dark on the Common. Hadn't I myself written that deathless line, "Darkness is no time for lovers"? Shouldn't we hurry to a nice, brightly lit hotel room to thrash things out? No, not thrash, discuss. Talk. I felt pretty sure of my ability to convince her in candid argument that the feelings I entertained toward her fell under the general heading of love. Uplifted by that thought, I got to my feet and we resumed our walk. Still, it was a pensive and rather nervous child of the century who escorted his young lady friend into the lobby of the Parker House some minutes later.

One advantage of picking the Parker House in a fit of bravado was that the desk clerk displayed a lordly disdain for my explanation of why we had no luggage. Such details were beneath him. One got the impression that nothing could damage the reputation of the Parker House. One felt that taking a girl to the Parker House more or less solemnized the union, at least in the eyes of the Parker House staff. A night at the Parker House was as good as or perhaps slightly better than marriage. One felt such things and a good deal more.

Alone with Martha in our tasteful love nest, however, one began to feel other things.

I went to the window and looked out. It was a clear drop of five stories to the street below. A quick jump and then oblivion. Instead of which I bravely turned to face the situation.

"I do love you," I said. "You've got to believe that."

"Will you stop talking about love?" Martha said.

This is hideous, I thought. She's already ashamed of herself. What have I done to her?

"When you've settled the bill here, how much money will you have left?" she asked, and in my total confusion, Reader, I thought she was going to ask me to pay her.

39

"Why?" I asked.

"Because if you're out of money, I'll stand you a drink. I think you need one."

"Oh." The relief must have shown in my face. At any rate, without further discussion we went down to the bar. We hadn't even taken off our coats in the room, so we had to check them downstairs.

In the bar, however, our age was called in question, a nasty check to our plans. So we retrieved our coats, leaving only a moderate tip, and went to find a spot where more lenient views prevailed. I felt like moaning. And underneath everything, there was . . . Well, no, why explain? But I must. Underneath everything there was—dare I name it?—a certain lust.

Which began to seem more legitimate, more acknowledgeable as we wandered down Tremont Street, hunting for a sympathetic-looking drinkery. We were approaching Scollay Square, where every sailor had his lass tightly clutched in one arm while with his free hand he dug in his pockets for money to spend. It was the sort of scene I needed just then. I pulled Martha to me and tried to imagine that all would yet be well, a thought which might have come easier if there hadn't been that difference of approximately a foot and a half in our heights. Why hadn't these Sears given their only child more milk and vitamins to grow on? They could afford it. Was this the American way of doing things, to bring up a daughter to be only five feet high?

Eventually we found a bar where amid the smoke and noise no one would be likely to notice our age or even our race. I bought us beer.

We sat side by side in a booth at the back, and I continued to keep my arm around Martha. Under the table I moved my leg until I was in contact with her from humerus to femur. It was this fact, I think, which got me started on the story which I presently found myself telling her.

40

"I broke my ankle as a child by walking out of a cherry tree."

"You mean falling," she said.

"No, walking. I thought I could walk on air, the way Jesus walked on water."

"That's peculiar," Martha said.

"No, it isn't really," said I. "I mean, I'd heard so much about my Father in heaven, I thought I was His Son. Of course I knew I wasn't supposed to perform miracles, but I didn't think it would do any harm if I took just three steps on air. Then I was going to walk down to the ground. If anyone saw me, he'd probably just think I was jumping out of the tree."

"And so you broke your ankle?"

"Yes. It was puzzling. I couldn't figure out what had gone wrong."

She looked amused. I often did amuse her. "And so you stopped trying to perform miracles?"

"Not right away. We had an old cat named Anthony who was no use to me at all. I decided to turn him into a red and green parrot I could talk with."

"I like that," said Martha.

"But it didn't work either," I said. "I put him on a grapefruit crate behind the grape arbor and stood back and said, 'Cat, be thou a parrot! Only he just stretched and jumped down and started back to the house. I was terrified he'd start turning into a parrot while Father was watching him. Maybe right in Father's study. So I grabbed him and put him back on the crate and said, 'Cat, be thou a cat!' "

Martha nodded her head. It struck her as sound tactics apparently.

I went on. "And the funny thing is that just the other day, well, last month actually, I came upon the same kind of incident in Bunyan's *Grace Abounding Unto the Chief of Sinners.* He was walking along a country lane meditating on

41

God's extraordinary grace toward himself when he came to a big mud puddle. Suddenly he felt an enormous temptation to test his powers by saying, 'Puddle, be thou dry.' However he resisted. Of course he was older than I was."

"You're really very religious, aren't you?" Martha said, which brought me back to Scollay Square.

This was not an ordinary situation in which any kind of palaver would do, especially palaver about my Christian childhood. "Not at all," I said, and drank some beer. I increased the pressure of my arm. "Martha," I said, "don't you think when two people like each other as much as we do, then it's practically like marriage?"

"No, I'm not sure I do," she said.

"But, you know, desire is holy. Blake said that."

"Did he?"

I leaned away from her, momentarily overcome by a desire to bat her one for not allowing me to pretend that our flesh was more than flesh, as, after all, I was theoretically convinced it was. As I've said, I was a pagan, Reader, not a materialist.

"Well, damn it," I said, "we can't go on seeing each other all the time and just talk."

"Who are you trying to persuade?" she said.

I stared at her, trying to figure out the answer to that one. Was it a riddle? Then, to my surprise, she kissed me.

We were staring into each other's eyes from very close range. "Do you think I'm just a goof?" I asked.

She shook her head. In the negative, thank God. Thank Him indeed, for with His help, or someone's, we seemed to be emerging toward some degree of animal dignity. We kissed more ardently than we ever had. My hand slipped under her right arm and rested on her frail rib cage just below her breast. Her smallness became, for the moment, not so much a matter of comic disproportion between us as a source of something very sweet. It had the charm of difference and physical delicacy.

42

"Do you want to go back to the hotel?" I asked her.

"Do you?"

"Yes," I said. Yet walking back to the Parker House with my arm around Martha, I could feel little of what I imagined I had been promised. There were too many unanswered questions and too many topics we hadn't gone into. When I shot the bolt on our hotel room door, it sounded to me like the crack of a pistol. And that, Reader, is all you'll know, and all ye need to know, of this particular episode in my life.

5

So now, you see me studying feverishly during Reading Period. The heat is on. Back home in Kansas City the February temperature has dropped right through the bottom of the thermometer, but on my desk there is a hot letter from the Bish., whose internal weather is more or less unaffected by the seasons. I keep his missive in sight as a spur to my flagging interest in Immanuel Kant, whose every sentence I seem to be underlining. I've never read a man so difficult to summarize. And after I have finished with this little red book of Kant, there is another little red book full of Spinoza, whom I have also neglected all my life and particularly during the last semester, when we have been studying him in Philosophy I.

The Bishop's letter is torrid not because he knows I'm about to pull some very indifferent C's in my courses, but because I have recently been touching him for more money, the desire and pursuit of Martha, which has now been going on for several weeks having eaten into my allowance to an unprecedented extent. I am insolvent, behind in my courses, and not even particularly happy, love's young bliss being what it is, to wit, an expense of spirit in a waste of shame when it is not just plain anxiety at being discovered.

Bartoldi's semi-public amours are not for Martha and me. We cannot use the suite, we cannot, or at least *I* cannot, afford hotels all the time, the weather has been cold, and so we have had recourse to the Sears' house. There, in Martha's bedroom, in the presence of her very own Pooh books, we have made love several times, jumpy with passion and jitters, for Mrs. Sears' social life has its unpredictable moments, and the servants prowl around that house like the hosts of

Midian. Disaster or at least exposure is just around the corner, and I am not sure how I will shape up as a publicly acknowledged libertine and seducer of bankers' daughters. Added to which I now know what I was incapable of perceiving that night at the Parker House, namely the mystery Martha holds for me is that she is not really a chaste person. I am her fourth lover, I find. This is a very puzzling fact, which I have not yet absorbed, but which makes it all the harder to concentrate on Immanuel Kant.

Indeed, the more I underline him the more the conviction grows upon me that the categorical imperative is a product of the Koenigsburg weather. "This man lived in a bad climate," I tell myself, adding, "And so do I." Though at the moment a mild, almost springlike breeze comes through the open window of my room, for today we are having a brief warm spell. I raise my head from *The Critique of Pure Reason* to sniff the air, and what do I hear but Schönberg, borne to me on the tides of a false spring. The boys downstairs are at it again. I listen for a while and think, Really, why use twelve tones when silence is all?

Such was the scene, such my mood, Reader, when it dawned on me that I had not looked at my stick of dynamite for some time. I abandoned Kant and opened the bottom drawer of my desk. There it lay in its candy-colored cardboard wrapper. I took it out and put it on the desk in front of me.

How and why I acquired this stick of dynamite is not really germane to the story. What concerns us here is that I have now possessed it for several months, and it has been a comfort to me before in moments like this. I have an obscure sense that if an explosion is called for I am provided with explosives. I like the look of the thing. I like knowing it is there. I was still looking at it and thinking dreamily of this and that when the door to my room opened and friend Bartoldi entered, unannounced and uninvited.

45

"What's that?" he said, looking at my dynamite.

"It's a stick of dynamite," I said, starting to put it away. One doesn't like to be surprised gazing at one's dynamite.

"Hey! It *is* a stick of dynamite." Bartoldi reached across and plucked it from my hands.

"Careful," I said.

"Oh, this stuff is safe," said Bartoldi. "I worked on a construction crew all one summer and we used to toss it around."

"That sounds like the kind of construction crew you'd work on. Did you *build* anything?" I asked.

But Bartoldi was happily staring at the dynamite.

Reader, there is a certain kind of person with whom we become friends not necessarily because we like or approve of what they are, but because they represent for us a simpler, cruder possibility of life. How easy to be Bartoldi, how hard to be Samuel Heather—or so I thought then. Hence my pleasure in Bartoldi's company was strongly mixed with condescension and even disapproval.

"Put it down," I said to him.

"Where'd you get it?"

"Never mind."

"What are you going to do with it? You know, we ought to do something with it."

"*We?* That's my dynamite."

"Say!" Bartoldi said. "How about burying it in the riverbank and touching it off at three A.M.? Wake 'em up around here."

"Yes, I've thought of that," I said, which illustrates why Bartoldi and I were rooming together. He always zoomed unerringly toward the folly I merely dreamed about.

"Got a detonator?" he asked.

"Yes."

"Say, this is great." Bartoldi tossed the dynamite in the air and caught it.

46

"Will you put that down?" I said to him.

"Why? What's the matter?"

"You make me nervous juggling with it."

"It won't go off. You could drop it on the floor and it wouldn't go off."

"Well, don't drop it," I said.

"No, look!" And he dropped it on the floor.

In a way, of course, it would have been the perfect answer to everything, including Schönberg whom I could still hear, but as you will have surmised, Reader, the dynamite didn't go off.

"You fool," I said. I picked the dynamite off the floor and put it away in its drawer. Bartoldi sat down on my desk.

"What are you going to do with it?" he asked again.

"I haven't decided yet."

"Look, I'll help you wire it up. We can set it off tonight. There's no moon. Conditions will be perfect."

I didn't much like what was happening, or rather I didn't like it very much. I was feeling challenged. "I don't need *your* help," I said.

"Well, come on. What did you buy it for, anyway?"

"Never mind."

"But think what it'll be like to set it off tonight when everyone's keyed up for exams. It'll go over like a bomb."

"I *know* it will."

"We could plant it on the Business School side of the river and then run the wire over Weekes Bridge. That way we can get back into the House before the police arrive."

"We'll miss the fun that way."

"We can watch out the windows," said Bartoldi. "How much wire have you got?"

"I'm not sure I have enough," I said, so we opened my drawer to examine my stores. After a little while Bartoldi decided he better go out to get more wire, "just to be on the safe side," as he expressed it.

And so, Reader, I was alone again with Kant and the Bishop's letter and a brand-new project that threatened to blow me clear out of Harvard and all the various perplexities of my life there. I wondered what Father would say when I was caught detonating the banks of the Charles. Because surely we would be caught. It wouldn't be right to get away with this sort of prank. I buried my head in my hands.

Bartoldi would not have been Bartoldi if he hadn't invited Walker and Morrison to join in the fun, which of course gave them the chance to argue us into a fixed resolve to carry out the scheme.

"It's crazy," Walker said. "You'll kill someone." Walker had gone to Putney. He didn't believe in killing people, or even making big holes in the ground.

"At that hour there'll be no one on the riverbank but mere vagrant amorists," I said. "They'll never be missed."

Walker shook his head. Morrison said, "What you and Bartoldi both need is thorough psychoanalysis," an opinion with which I totally agreed.

"Nonsense," I said.

"Just tell me *why*," said Walker.

Bartoldi had been listening to this with mounting impatience. "All right, if you don't want to do it with us, don't. No one's making you."

"That's right, no one's making you," I said.

Morrison pursed his lips. "What I'd like to know is, what's making you?"

"Life's full of these mysteries," I told him, and we left it more or less at that, they going off to the movies in disapproval, and Bartoldi and I settling down to plan and wait.

I was beginning to feel elated. It had taken Bartoldi's irresponsibility to get me started, but once started I rather liked the sensation. I had a sort of inkling that there comes a time in every young man's life when he either sets off a stick

48

of dynamite or caves in, and I was slightly impressed with myself that instead of studying for my philosophy exam I was planning to blow up the banks of the Charles. Which is not intended as a denial that the whole plan was essentially nuts.

Bartoldi and I were alone, then, when in the early hours of the morning we made our way across Weekes Bridge with the dynamite and detonator concealed under our jackets. It was an incredibly warm night for February, so warm that we were not even wearing overcoats. There was a moon: Bartoldi had been wrong about that, of course. A bright gibbous moon shone through an occasional hole in the dense clouds overhead. Or, as the *Grettissagga* puts it: *tunglskin vár mikit úti ok gluggaðykkn.* High overhead great winds might be blowing, but down there on the banks of the Charles all was still and calm, for the moment.

We dug a hole with an entrenching tool, which was part of the equipment Bartoldi had come to college with. Then I consigned my gaily colored stick of dynamite to the dark earth and we packed the soil around it. Ah, happy youth, when one has never had occasion to bury anything dearer to oneself than a well-loved stick of dynamite! That rite completed, we began to unpay the wire. The moon came out as we crossed the bridge. Below us the unruffled Charles like a river of ink reflected the moonlight back toward the clouds, which presently closed and obscured fair Cynthia's face once more. It was very dark as we completed our arrangements on the other side of the river.

All this time we had seen no one. An occasional car hissed along Memorial Drive. We could see lights in Dunster and Leverett where students were up late studying. I was glad I was not one of them, but I felt a kind of detached admiration of the scholar's life. How fine to be a good student, to change one's clothes at night as Machiavelli used to

49

do before entering his study where in the ancient courts of ancient men he fed on that food for which alone he was truly born. To courteously ask and receive courteous answers from the wise men of the ages! It seemed, somehow, a more beautiful, graver existence than the one to which I was now committed. It might be worth mentioning that my philosophy exam was scheduled for ten o'clock that morning.

Then, when we were ready for action, a new problem arose. It was too dark to see across the river. "Suppose someone comes wandering along over there?" I said.

"No one will," said Bartoldi.

"We can't take the chance," I said. I mean, dynamiting one's own life is a very different thing from dynamiting the life of a casual stroller. What if said stroller weren't prepared to meet his God, if any? So it was decided at last that one of us should keep watch. The watcher could shelter from the blast behind the solid parapet of the bridge.

"Okay," Bartoldi said, "if you think it's so important, you go watch."

"Nothing doing. It's my dynamite."

"We'll flip to see who touches it off and who watches." And with that Bartoldi produced what was probably his two-headed nickel. He tossed it into the air, called *heads*, and heads it was.

"This isn't fair," I said.

"You lost," said Bartoldi. I stood there a moment prepared to assert my rights, and then it occurred to me that even in an infinite universe it was unlikely that anywhere there would be conditions sufficiently strong to persuade Bartoldi to sacrifice a bit of his fun on the off-chance of saving the life of an innocent bystander.

"All right, I'll watch," I said. "How'll I signal you when it's clear?"

"Light a match," he said.

"I don't have a match." I didn't smoke, Reader.

So Bartoldi gave me a packet of matches and off I went,

50

reflecting that this way at least I'd be closer to the epicenter of the little disturbance we had arranged. It seemed right for me to be at the center.

And once across the bridge I was immediately glad I'd been conned into losing what was probably my one chance of blowing up a portion of Cambridge's sacred soil, for I saw I was not alone. During a momentary period of moonlight, I spotted a figure on the riverbank. I had saved a life. Congratulating myself, my heart uplifted, I stood quietly at the far end of the bridge waiting for this lucky fellow to pass out of the picture, instead of which he climbed the steps to the bridge and came drifting to a halt a few feet away from me. It was a boy I seemed vaguely to recognize from some class I'd been in.

"Hello, you're out late too," he said.

True, I was out late. Undoubtedly it was very late. Yes indeed, it was late all right. Or perhaps it was early. It all depended on your point of view. My answer was, "Yes."

My new friend smiled at me and leaned seductively against the parapet. "Lovely night," he said.

This, it seemed to me, was all I needed. "Yes, lovely night," I agreed.

It seemed to encourage him. He leaned toward me.

"Could you give me a light?" he asked, and I saw the wicked creature had an unlit cigarette in his mouth.

Without thinking, I handed him Bartoldi's matches, and then reason regained her throne, so to speak.

"Don't light that match," I said.

He paused in the act. "Why not?"

"Just don't light it."

He stared at the matchbook in his hand. "Are they some sort of special matches?" he asked.

"No." I reached out to repossess them, but he was not so easily ruled.

"Then don't be stingy," he said, and he struck a light.

51

The explosion was really very fine. A portion of the riverbank erupted with a roar, sending clods of earth heavenward like the souls of the redeemed. My fine friend and myself were protected from the blast by the parapet and by the fact that, shouting "Duck," I ducked while Ronald Nightowl toppled over backwards with surprise. The noise of the explosion went rolling away in all directions. Then bits of winter grass and earth and pebbles began to shower down upon us like the rain of atoms in Lucretius' universe.

It seemed to me I crouched there for some time receiving this atomic baptism. I certainly crouched there long enough to become worried about Ronald, lying flat on the pavement in front of me.

"Are you all right?" I asked.

He didn't answer for some moments, and I remember watching his miraculously lit cigarette roll away down the incline of the bridge until it disappeared over the edge of the step. Then he said, "What happened?"

"There was an explosion," I said.

I got to my feet and began to dust off the debris. He continued to lie on his back. Obviously this sort of thing had never happened before in his sad life. He was not used to God striking so quickly, so prematurely as it were.

"Are you hurt?" I asked him.

"Was it the match?" he said.

"No, it was a stick of dynamite."

He received that calmly enough. We were visited by the moon again, and I could see his eyes were closed. Across the river Bartoldi whooped with manic laughter.

"Can you get up?" I asked.

Ronald opened his eyes. "Is it safe?"

"Yes. We better get away before the police come."

"The police!"

"To investigate the explosion."

"Oh."

You could see that thoughts of policemen asking questions held no charm for him, but on the other hand he didn't seem to want to get up. It was as if he'd found a position that suited him. Here on this bridge I will lay me down and on this pavement make my bed. He closed his eyes, perhaps in prayer.

Bartoldi called to me. Lights were coming on in the Houses. I could even hear windows shooting up. "If you can walk . . ." I suggested. I was anxious to get away, but it seemed wrong to leave Ronald behind. "Here, let me help you."

"We could have been killed," Ronald said.

"Yes, but we weren't."

I had hold of Ronald's arm. He made no effort to rise. "Did you put the dynamite there?" he asked.

"Yes, I'm an anarchist," I said.

Then he said something I rather admired. "Just leave me here. I think I'm safer with the police."

It was tempting. Then it occurred to me that it might be better all around if the only eyewitness disappeared along with the principals of this night's drama. So I hoisted Ronald to his feet and to our mutual relief he appeared to be unbroken.

Bartoldi was not at the other end of the bridge, which didn't surprise me, in view of the fact that a police car was by then coming up Memorial Drive at a good rate of speed. Still, I missed Bartoldi. With his help I might have gotten Ronald across the Drive and into the shrubbery in front of Leverett House. As it was we were still in the open when the police arrived and turned their searchlight onto us. All of which goes to show, Reader, that you can never avoid responsibility for your actions. You can't even avoid the police.

53

6

All art is a question of selection whereby one extracts the needle of truth from the haystack of experience. In life we generally find the needle by rolling in the hay, a painful and time-consuming discovery which the artist can avoid by using the lodestone of memory. This explains why we are sitting now in the office of Dean Pocock some three hay-filled days after the events described in the last chapter.

It is an austere but handsome chamber in University Hall. Pocock is behind his desk, backed up by a portrait of A. Lawrence Lowell hanging above his mantelpiece. They make a reasonably impressive team. Facing them sits yours truly, the all-American anarchist, alone in a chair with a spotlight of afternoon sun slicing through the Venetian blind and hitting him squarely in the eyes. The topic under discussion is my recent behavior:

"That was a very immature thing to do," Dean Pocock said.

"Sir!" said I, "I wasn't trying to prove my maturity."

"Then perhaps it's time for you to start trying to prove it," said Pocock. "You are suspended from College for a year. I suggest you get a job. Work. Settle down. If you wish to apply for reinstatement a year from now, the College will be willing to consider the matter, provided you can give a good account of yourself."

There was a pause.

"Oh," I said. Then, "Is breaking rocks in prison the kind of work you had in mind?"

"You are not going to prison," Dean Pocock said.

"How can you be so sure?" I asked him. "The police are mad because I won't tell them who helped me set off the bomb."

"I'd like to know that, too," Pocock said.

"But Sir," I protested, "I can't betray a friend, can I?"

"It's a matter for your own judgment," and I got the idea Pocock didn't think much of my judgment.

It was not a happy interview. None of them had been happy. If hell is a series of rooms in which red-faced Cambridge policemen and pale-faced Harvard deans keep asking you why you've done what you've done, then I'd spent the last seventy-two hours in hell. And as if that weren't bad enough, the normally discouraging Kansas City returns weren't in yet. It began to look like a landslide for the opposition.

—It sounds well put that way, but since this is a confession I may as well tell the truth when I can. Besides, the intelligent Reader will already have guessed that I skip so easily over these interviews because for me no beery Irishman or martini-raddled Harvard dean could represent true authority. The Real McCoy was out in Kansas City, and shortly I would be hearing from it. I was ten before it dawned on me that this President Roosevelt people kept talking about might be considered to have more power in the land than Father. I was more than thirteen, trembling on the verge of a late adolescence, when I first distinctly perceived that Father was subject to human law. He was summoned to appear for jury duty. Father summoned! It was a revolutionary conception, made more revolutionary by the fact that he neither resented that imperious mode of address nor resisted the summons. Waiving his ecclesiastical privileges he served on the jury. He was chosen Foreman and he jailed his man, but I was still shaken that the People of the State of Missouri had had the temerity to *summon* Father to sit in judgment on them. And even now he was still Authority, though for years I'd risked life and limb in flouting and disobeying him to the full extent of my growing powers.

I left Pocock's office bothered by the question of where to go next. Could I fade far away, dissolve, and disappear?

How? It was no use thinking of New Zealand, I didn't have money enough to buy passage. Maybe I could change my name, grow a moustache, and go underground. It was a better idea than some I'd had. But would Martha like me with a moustache? For that matter, how much did she like me now? Damn! Why was life so difficult, so full of questions? Then, brilliantly, I thought of a solution. I would join the army. I halted in my tracks to size up this inspiration and at once I saw it would solve all my problems. The law certainly would not prosecute me vigorously if I showed it I was burning with desire to serve my country in the armed forces. And acceptance of army discipline might very well convince Pocock and his ilk that I was on the path to maturity. Most of all, if I could get into the army quickly enough, I might be able to avoid a trip to Kansas City. I could do basic training in New England, where I'd be close enough to see Martha on weekend passes. Even the money problem would be taken care of.

Dazzled by this clear thinking, I raised my head and looked around. I had come to a halt beside Widener. Near me there was a pigeon on the grass, dead, alas, killed by a barn owl which had recently taken up residence in the Yard and begun to decimate the local squirrels and pigeons. There had been several indignant letters to the *Crimson* advocating poison, or shotguns, or traps. Silly! With nature red in tooth and claw, should man worry about the fate of a few pigeons? It was *sauve qui peut,* and I had found my salvation. With a gun in hand, and protected by my commanding officer, I could hold the Bishop at bay for years.

I picked up my feet and hurried on down to Leverett House. "Well, I've been suspended," I announced, "and I'm going to join the army."

"The army!" Walker looked and sounded reproachful. And he had cause. It wasn't so long since he and I had worked together to oppose the Universal Military Training Act, but *autres temps, autres moeurs.*

56

"We were all wrong," I told him. "Until philosophers are kings and students are soldiers, we will have no true republic."

"Take his temperature, he sounds feverish," Morrison said.

"Did you tell Pocock about me?" Bartoldi asked. He couldn't really believe I would hold out against the curiosity of police and deans to know who had helped me do the dirty work. They had found out, by questioning Ronald, that I couldn't have set off the charge myself.

"Of course I didn't tell him," I said.

Bartoldi smiled. "Say, that's great!"

"But the army!" said Walker.

"What's the matter with armies?" I asked him. "Aeschylus, Socrates, Thucydides, Gibbon, Shakespeare, Stendhal, Alfred de Vigny, Coleridge, Keats, Mark Twain and P. G. Wodehouse were all in the army, and look at them."

"They were *not* all in the army," Morrison said. He knew too much.

I turned on him. "Do you deny that Aeschylus fought at the battle of Marathon?"

"Anyway, what difference does it make if they *were* in the army?" Walker asked.

"What difference? Being in the army could be the making of me as an artist, or an historian."

"Keats was *not* in the army," said Morrison, still plugging away at the facts. "He had tuberculosis."

"And if he'd been in the army, he might have lived longer. Besides, if I join now they won't prosecute me for blowing up the riverbank."

"Hey, pretty clever!" Bartoldi said.

I felt a momentary chill of doubt. Could any line of action Bartoldi admired be truly wise? Nevertheless my mind was made up, and I maintained my ways in the face of Walker's arguments, Morrison's sarcasm, and Bartoldi's mounting enthusiasm. That evening I walked over to Radcliffe to see what Martha would say when she heard my news.

She was cramming for her last test, but she interrupted her intellectual labors to come down to the lounge for a talk.

"I've been suspended," I said.

"I was wondering what would happen. How do you feel?"

"Fine. I'm joining the army."

She looked at me in a considering way. "Will you like that?"

"I'm bound to. Besides it will mean I can stay around here. I may even do basic training at Camp Devers, so we can see each other from time to time."

"That will be nice."

"Martha." I took her hand. "Let's go out for a little walk."

She smiled. "I didn't bring down my coat."

"I'll keep my arm around you. It's not all that cold outside."

"Besides, I'm studying."

"Just a little walk." I gestured around the lounge. "We can't talk here."

So she stepped outdoors with me. I put my arm around her as I'd promised. Then, drawing her off the path and into the shelter of a pine, I put both arms around her. "Martha, I hope you won't miss me too much."

"I don't know." She looked up at me. "Are you going to miss me?"

"Don't ask silly question." I unbuttoned my overcoat and put it around her. "Martha, you mustn't feel I'm deserting you. You don't, do you?"

"No, I don't," she said.

"I'll write. We *will* see each other."

"Good." She shivered a little. "Look, it is cold out here."

I didn't let go of her. "Martha, you *will* miss me?"

58

"Yes, I'll miss you, Sammy. Let's go in."

"Just a minute." I wasn't satisfied. "You know I'm not a philanderer. I'm not running out on you."

"I know that."

"And I'll be coming back and things will be just the same." There was no answer. "Martha, things will be just the same between us, won't they?"

"I expect they will," she said.

"What do you mean?"

She peeped up from inside my overcoat. "Well, *you* said the situation will be just the same."

Oh, the exasperation she could cause me! "Yes, but what is the situation? Martha, I have to know whether you love me."

"Don't start this, Sammy. I'm getting cold."

"How can you be cold? You're inside my overcoat and I've got my arms around you. Martha, tell me that you love me."

"I love you Sammy."

"I don't believe you."

"Shall we go in?" she said.

"No." I held her tighter. "Martha, I want things to be more definite between us. Shall we get engaged?"

"I don't think that's such a good idea."

"Oh, you don't?"

"No. Now take me in, Sammy. I'm cold and I've got a lot of studying to do."

"First tell me once more that you love me. And this time try to sound as if you mean it."

She kissed me on the chin. "I love you."

Maybe it was the best she could do, but it still didn't sound right to me. However, I had to let her go in.

So that was that, and now all I had to do was get out of Leverett and into the army, avoiding on my way the twin perils of jail and the Bishop.

59

I was packing my clothes two days later when the telephone bell rang. Exams were over. Bartoldi had flown down to Buenos Aires to see his father. Walker was in Concord with his family. Morrison and I were alone in the suite. I let the bell ring several times. I was surrounded by clothes. I seemed to have acquired a disgraceful quantity of charcoal-gray clothing during the last years, plus books and papers and such embarrassing odds and ends as this teddy bear I had unearthed from the back of my closet. It was a gift from the same mad girl who had presented me with "Highlights from *Madame Butterfly*," so I didn't really feel responsible for the thing, yet there it was. I suppose it was a Pooh bear. That girl had a whimsical streak you could turn handsprings on. When the phone began to ring, I was staring helplessly at the bear. Why couldn't Martha love me with the same forlorn passion that seemed to inspire this Kansas City girl? And should I answer the phone?

Morrison answered it. "I'll call him," he said.

I dropped the bear.

This is it, I thought, as I walked to the receiver, and sure enough it was it.

"Samuel?" Father said, his voice sounding as if it came out of my brain. "I have a letter from your dean. Is what he tells me true?"

The manly thing would have been to plunge right in and start explaining, but I did not feel particularly manly. "What does he tell you?" I asked.

"I am informed that because of an irresponsible and dangerous prank of yours, the College has been forced to suspend you for a year."

"Yes, that's true," I said.

There was a brief pause. "Astonishing!" Father said. "You do not sound penitent," he added.

"This connection isn't very good," I said. "Your voice doesn't sound right either."

That didn't go down very well. "If that is a witticism, it is quite out of place," Father said.

I began to feel better. When my admissions were all made and the battle joined, I always began to feel better. He couldn't dismember me over long distance, and I suddenly realized I had another little jolt I could administer.

"Father," I said, "I've been thinking of joining the army."

"I don't want to hear about it, Samuel. We are discussing your recent behavior."

"I think the army is the best place for me right now."

"Did you hear me, Samuel?"

"Dean Pocock himself practically suggested it. He feels I need to grow up and become more mature."

Father tried to cut through this. "I wish to know what motives, what conceivable aim you had in doing anything as idiotic, as dangerous, as pointless as dynamiting the bank of a river?"

"It's hard to explain," I told him. "What I'd really like to know is whether you think I should join the army."

"I have told you I will not discuss it."

There was another pause. Father apparently sensed that he was at a disadvantage on the telephone. "When will you be home?" he said.

"Well, my hearing is on the twenty-third."

"You are to be tried?"

"They haven't decided yet."

"I leave you to imagine our feelings," Father said. "Your mother will speak to you now, but don't hang up."

Then Mother said, "Samuel, dear? We're very upset. When will you be home?"

"Hello, Mother," I said. "How are you?"

"Well, I'm fine. My back hasn't been giving me as much trouble as usual. Are you all right?"

"Yes. I'm thinking of joining the army."

61

"Really?" She sounded interested. She had always had a soft spot in her heart for *la vie militaire*. It was her ancestry showing up again. The Clays and related families had produced a fair number of warriors. Indeed, they had fought in every war the United States had been in, often on both sides as in 1776 when Ephraim Clay remained loyal to his king, and again in 1861 when the family had been much divided. Even in civil life some of them had shown a Napoleonic Touch. When, at age ninety, Cassius Marcellus Clay kidnapped a local girl and married her despite her family's protests, there had been talk of reprisals which he settled by mounting two cannons at the foot of his drive and threatening to give his neighbors a whiff of grape should they try to interfere in his domestic life. Men were giants in those days.

"Cousin John Logan is a colonel now," Mother said.

"I'll have to start as a private."

"I know," she said, "but it does show what can be done. John was such a stupid boy."

In the background Father spoke, urgently it seemed, for Mother said, "Your father has something more to say to you." She apparently felt recalled to duty. "You know," she said, "you shouldn't have done what you did."

"Probably not."

"Well, here's your father," she said, and I could visualize him yanking the instrument from her hands.

"Samuel, you have heard what I said. I expect obedience on this. You are to do nothing about joining the army until you are here where we can discuss matters in the proper atmosphere."

I knew that atmosphere: Father at his desk in his study, Christ crucified on the wall just to remind us, and yards of the Ante and Post Nicene Fathers in glass-fronted bookcases, their gilt backs winking in the afternoon light. I began to appreciate just how much Christian hope Father possessed if he thought he was going to get me in there soon.

"Well, I'm registered in Cambridge. Don't you think I

ought to volunteer before I make any plans to come home?"

"I want it clearly understood—you do not have my permission to volunteer for the army. Is that understood, Samuel?"

"It's a patriotic thing to do," I said. "I think it will help with the judge, if he knows I've already tried to volunteer."

The Bishop brushed this aside. "You seem to have absolutely no conception of other people's feelings. Your mother and I are deeply concerned about you. I will not listen to any further talk about the army."

"Well, all right," I said, "but I've pretty much made up my mind."

"Now when will you be home?" he asked.

"I'm not supposed to leave Massachusetts until the hearing is over."

That baffled him a bit. "You cannot stay in the dormitory," he said. "As I understand it, your room contract has been canceled."

"I'll stay at the Bartoldis," I told him.

Before flying off to see his father, Bartoldi had informed his mother, who lived in Brookline, that she would be having a guest for two weeks. It wasn't an ideal arrangement, but I'd agreed. After all, the Bartoldis owed me something.

"Then, depending on the disposition of your case, we can expect you shortly after the twenty-third?" Father said.

I thought it best to leave them in expectation. "Yes."

"Very well." But he still sounded dissatisfied. "I shall write you a letter. I am not at all encouraged by the tone you've adopted in this conversation. Were I in your position" —what an imagination the man had!—"I would feel some responsibility for the distress I had caused my parents."

He had a point, of course. "Don't worry about me," I told him.

He didn't actually slam down the receiver but it was a near thing.

The talk had really gone better than I expected. It was odd. I'd dreaded his call, but as soon as we'd started to talk, I realized there wasn't much he could do to me. I had him in a cleft stick. I was of age to join the army, and unless he flew to Cambridge and tried to lame or blind me (thus rendering me 4-F), I didn't see how he could stop me from serving my country in uniform.

After we'd hung up, I went back to my room. The teddy bear lay on the floor where I'd dropped it a few minutes earlier. It no longer seemed to present a problem. I picked it up and took it to Morrison, who was reading Heine in his room. "You want this?" I asked.

After a single dispassionate glance, he did not dignify my question with an answer. So I took out my scout knife and plunged it up to the hilt in the bear's sawdust chest. Then I tied a rope around its neck and dangled it out the window where the boys downstairs would presumably see it first thing in the morning. They were still in residence. Perhaps they would take it as a sign and a portent.

Then I went back to Morrison's room. I had just found a formula that solved my packing problem. "I leave my books to anyone who wants them, my clothes to whoever can fit them, my bicycle to he who can ride it (the left pedal was broken), and my wit to he who can get it."

"And the trumpets sounded for him on the other side," Morrison said. "You've been reading *The Pilgrim's Progress* again."

"And Bunyan's a better writer for you to read than that Jewish cosmopolitan."

Morrison put down Heine and looked at me for a while. "You'll probably end up as a religious maniac," he told me.

"And you will become a professor of comparative literature," I told him, which is how we left it.

7

The following morning I went down to my local draft board and asked them to change my status from 1-S to 1-A. "Actually, I'd like to volunteer," I told them, "but I have a legal problem hanging over me." I explained it, and they were quite encouraging. It seemed the army would take me, if prison didn't, and of course prison didn't.

Justice Crombeck, who heard my case, was an elderly man not long for this world, as he himself was the first to admit. "Young man," he said, looking at me over his glasses, "I'm dying of cancer and I don't want to hurt anyone if I can help it. Now what's the case here?" He listened to the facts, tut-tutted once or twice, and then looked at me again. "And you're trying to get into the army now?"

"Yes, Your Honor."

"Well, this court will not stand in the way of any young man who wants to serve his country. Case dismissed." And so I was free to take my great leap forward, or at least my great step forward.

"Raise your right hand," Captain Schiller said, "and repeat after me."

Ten of us raised our right hands and repeated after him in mumbling unison that we did solemnly swear to obey this and uphold that and do the other.

"You are now in the United States Army," Captain Schiller said. The sentence was not delivered with spine-tingling force; nevertheless it gave me great pleasure.

It was March by then. Ten days *du côté du chez* Bartoldi, and another ten days camping out in Leverett House had given me a deep desire to have a place of my own. The House Secretary had promptly filled my old room with a person named Waterbuck, who tended to object that his closet was filled with my clothes and that the couch in the living room had been turned into my bed.

"I'm *giving* you the clothes," I told him.

"They don't fit me."

"Well, I won't be here much longer."

"And what about the clothes?" he asked.

"Give them to the Salvation Army." And since my ex-roommates supported my presence, and helped to conceal it from the authorities, Waterbuck acquiesced, though with ill grace.

And speaking of grace, the letters and phone calls back and forth between Kansas City and my fluctuating abodes had been hot and heavy, but inconclusive. The Bishop was too busy a shepherd to leave his flock and set out with the dogs to round up his strayed black sheep. I did not have to encounter him in the flesh, and when Captain Schiller said, "You are now in the United States Army," I breathed a great sigh of relief. I'd made it across the ice floes.

Later in this narrative we will have military scenes aplenty, so I will skip over the next three months of my life. They were singularly peaceful humdrum days, filled with busy but not demanding tasks. I did KP, learned to march and to box the corners of my bed. I fired an M-1 rifle and swung on a rope over a pit of scummy water. I climbed obstacles and saluted officers, and in the evenings I went to the Post Library and read Walter Scott, whose romances were well represented on those shelves. It was a kind of never-never period in my life.

The one hitch was that we were confined to camp during the entire period of basic training, so I could not see Martha. I wrote her long letters, to which she replied with short letters. I could detect no change in her attitude toward me, but what was that attitude? I could not really be sure.

Did she love me, or didn't she? If I chafed at all during basic training, it was because I could not go to Cambridge to pin her down—in more ways than one.

Sometimes in the evening I would put down Walter Scott (it is easy to put Scott down) and daydream a bit. Forgetting the drab uniform I wore, and the ambiguities of Miss Sears, I allowed myself to imagine that shortly I would embark on a life of passion and glory. I was very conscious of the fact that I had turned twenty. I was no longer a child, no longer in school, beyond the Bishop's control, almost a free man. I felt I was progressing. Soon the dull chrysalis of basic training would be over, and I would emerge into a vibrant existence where exciting things would begin to happen. Was I right!

So work, work your imaginations and picture me now as a young GI in the pink of health setting off for Boston on his first weekend pass. I have written ahead to Martha to tell her I am coming, and after depositing my travel kit in the suite at Leverett House where I intend to stay, I take a taxi to the Sears' and am mounting the steps of their stately home when my fair Martha emerges from the front door accompanied by an overgrown blond-headed young man dressed in a tuxedo. Martha is also in fancy raiment, and it looks very much as if they are about to go off to a dance together in the tricky little MG which is parked at the curb.

"Well, Private Heather!" Miss Sears says.

I look at the overgrown young man and then back to her. "Didn't you get my letter?" I ask.

"Didn't you get mine?"

"I wrote I would be in town this evening."

"And I wrote I would be going to a dance with Richard."

During this exchange the overgrown blond young man —was I correct in assuming he was Richard, or would a sec-

67

ond snake turn up in the grass at any moment?—at any rate this character in his tuxedo had been studiously looking around the horizon as if trying to judge the direction of the wind, or perhaps locate the source of a smell. Martha now introduced us. "Samuel Heather, Richard Shuttleworth."

Shuttleworth withdrew his attention from the wind. Maybe he'd only been trying to estimate what tack to use in navigating his MG toward Copley Square. He looked at me, and then (a perfect gentleman) held out his hand and said, "Hello."

If I had had my rifle with me I would have known what to do. As it was, all I could think of was to shake his proffered hand. A split second later it occurred to me that since he was standing on a higher step, I could easily have jerked him off balance, causing him to tumble down and perhaps crack his fat head on the pavement. But by the time I'd figured that out his hand was withdrawn and the opportunity lost. "Hello," I said.

Martha smiled.

"Well, nice to have met you," said Richard. He prepared to escort Martha around my unmoving form.

"Where is this dance?" I asked.

"It's a private affair," said Richard, giving me the first concrete evidence on which to pin my instinctive dislike of him.

"Maybe he *could* come," Martha said.

"Dressed like that?" said Shuttleworth. He was speaking to Martha, but I felt his remark called for some comment of my own. I also felt it released me from the obligation we must all respect not to hate people simply on the basis of their looks alone. I felt several other things as well, but those two will do. After all, this is a confession of a child of the century, not a *récherche du temps perdu*.

"I am wearing my country's uniform," I told him, "which is more than you can say for yourself." That settled

68

the sartorial issue, as well as the momentary possibility we both might accompany Martha to this private dance for which they were all dolled up.

Shuttleworth didn't answer me. He seemed to be studying the wind again, perhaps thinking that if it freshened he could put up a spinnaker and really make tracks.

"Well, good night, Sammy," Martha said. "I'll see you tomorrow."

She was wrong about that. She frequently made such mistakes. You'll see me tonight after that dude brings you home, I thought, as the MG turned the corner, the wind abaft its beam with Martha delivering a parting wave of her hand.

I did not actually camp on the Sears' doorsteps. In fact, quite calmly, I went back to Leverett. There were hours to pass; I might as well spend my time hobnobbing with Bartoldi.

School was over. Walker and Morrison were already on their separate ways to Europe, Walker to work for the American Friends Service Committee in Dauphiné, Morrison to haunt the Uffizi. *Chacun á son gout.* Bartoldi, at least, was still on native ground, standing in front of the mirror over our mantelpiece, smiling fatuously at his reflection as he knotted his necktie. Seeing me, he postponed the finishing touches to his toilette. "She stand you up?" he asked.

"She's off dancing with someone else," I said.

"Well, for crying out loud!" Bartoldi had a fund of ready sympathy for men without women. "Look, shall I get Alice to find another girl for you? We can double date."

"No. I'm going back to the Sears' later. I want to see Martha when she gets home."

"But what are you going to do now?" Bartoldi asked. He gestured around the room. "You can't just sit around here and read a book."

"I'll find something."

"Come along with us," Bartoldi said. His face lit up. "Hey! We could go to Revere Beach."

"Would Alice like that?"

"She doesn't mind anything," said Bartoldi. He grabbed the telephone and dialed a number. "Alice?" he said. "How about Revere Beach tonight?" He listened for a while and then said, "Yeah, but my old roommate's turned up. He likes to ride the Dodgems." More listening. "No, the tall one with jug ears." He looked at me and explained, "She doesn't like Morrison. Thinks he's snotty." Then back into the receiver, "Yeah? Well, I like the Dodgems, too, so how about it? Pick you up in ten minutes." He put down the receiver. "She had her heart set on some damn foreign movie," he explained, "so I had to persuade her."

Alice, when we eventually picked her up, was a pretty thing who got in beside Bartoldi and immediately leaned over the back seat to say, "Was this your idea, going to Revere Beach?"

"No."

She turned toward Bartoldi, who said, "Come on, now. Let's not keep changing plans. You agreed."

The Dodgems, Reader, in case you have never ridden them, are one of our principal compensations for living in a machine age. They are little electric cars with heavy rubber bumpers all around. You ride them on a sort of dance floor and your aim is to catch another driver from behind and send him spinning out of control into the buffers that circle the arena. It is a worthy and fascinating pastime, which Bartoldi, Morrison, Walker, and I had often indulged in.

That evening I pretended Bartoldi was Shuttleworth. We circled the floor maneuvering to sideswipe each other. Once he caught me a juicy one, and then when I was in position to let him have it, I was sideswiped by a ferrety-looking kid who maneuvered his car with one hand and went dashing off through the crowd before I could retaliate. That sometimes happened. At Revere Beach you encountered a tough element, the hoi polloi, not to put too fine a point on it, and that evening they were out in force. Bartoldi and I abandoned hostilities and teamed up together. The climax came when Bartoldi, unable to catch the ferret in a disadvantageous position, spun his car around and charged head-on. It was against the rules, it tended to jar loose your teeth, but it was satisfying.

Afterwards the ferret and a couple of his friends approached us on the sidewalk. We had just rejoined Alice, who had been watching from the sidelines.

"Hey," said the ferret to Bartoldi, "you a fink?" His pals laughed. "Hey, how come you look so much like a fink if you're not a fink?"

Alice—she was not a dumb girl—immediately crossed the street and got into Bartoldi's car. Bartoldi said to me, "What's that smell around here? Must be these punks."

My own attitude was that this was not how I wanted the evening to end. Was I, with my high hopes, to soil my country's uniform in a degrading scuffle with these yobs? Was I to waste the happy feelings of aggression built up by an hour on the Dodgems? With Martha to be reproached, and Shuttleworth denounced if not actually assaulted, was I to spoil everything by a fight with these perfect, and somewhat menacing-looking, strangers? Who meanwhile had closed in several paces.

The second assistant ferret spat on the sidewalk a scant inch from my shoe, while the first assistant ferret fanned out to the left. Ferret-in-chief faced us. "Me and my buddies don't like your looks," he explained. Coming from whom it did, that was a colossal insult.

Bartoldi said, "Well, you're too chicken to do anything about it."

That seemed disputable. However, Alice began honking

71

the horn urgently, whether to summon us or the police I don't know. Bartoldi gave ground a few feet. Who can resist the call of a horn? I followed him. The ferrets jeered, but did not pursue us. They kept on jeering as, with some loss of honor, we regained the car.

Bartoldi was in an energetic and dissatisfied state of mind. "They had knives," he said to Alice. "They would never have started anything if they hadn't had knives." He was driving north by that time. He looked at me in the back seat. "You're in the army, why the hell aren't you armed?"

I regretted it myself. I hadn't seen any knives, but two of the ferrets had kept their hands in their pockets in what now struck me as a suggestive way. I accepted Bartoldi's theory that they were armed.

"We shouldn't have let them get away with that," I said.

"You're damn right we shouldn't," said Bartoldi. "Shall we go back?"

"Where are we going anyway?" Alice asked.

"My mother's got a house in Marblehead," Bartoldi explained. Then to me, "You want to go back?"

"Oh, well, let it pass," I said.

"Won't the house be closed?" Alice asked.

"We can break in," Bartoldi said.

It was a summer place, a square bubble of glass perched on some rocks sticking out into Marblehead harbor. Bartoldi smashed a window with the crank of his tire jack. Then I climbed through and together we helped Alice into the house. "Your mother's not going to like it when she finds out you've broken in," she said.

"Who's going to tell her?" Bartoldi asked. "We'll make it look like vandals did it. They're always breaking into these summer places."

"But if you leave the window broken, some real vandals may get in."

72

I couldn't think of a vandal more real than Bartoldi, but I let them work things out. I was opening the curtains so we could have some moonshine to show us what we were doing, if anything.

"That's better," Bartoldi said. "Now there ought to be some hooch around."

He found a bottle of Scotch and brought it into the living room where things were brighter. The running water had been turned off as well as the electricity, so we drank our Scotch straight.

"I don't know," Alice said. "I think you should tell your mother about the window."

"What for? She pays a watchman to watch the place. He'll find it."

I was standing at the glass front of the house looking out over the rocks at the moonlit harbor. "Hey, Sammy," he said, "you see anything you'd like?" He explained to Alice, "We'll make it look like burglars."

He kept pressing various objects on us, but neither Alice nor I felt like appropriating any of Mrs. Bartoldi's bric-a-brac. Finally, Bartoldi went off to the kitchen, found another bottle of Scotch, smashed the neck, poured the liquor down the drain and left the broken bottle on the kitchen floor. "There, that looks better," he said. "She's stupid to leave Scotch here anyway. It's what they break in for."

Then, having satisfied his urge to destroy (Freud calls it *thanatos*), Bartoldi dropped onto the couch next to Alice and gave way to the other basic human instinct (*eros*). I felt my presence might not actually inhibit him as much as it ought to, so I climbed out the window by which we had entered and stood by myself on the rocks in front of the house.

The moon, the rocks, the harbor, and the Scotch combined to produce a mood of some depth and subtlety. I decided Martha would be waiting for me when we drove back to Boston. She would be wearing a simple white dress, having changed from her glad rags because, with the intuition of lovers, she had divined that I would be coming for her that evening. She would be at her window, I fancied, and I would climb the vine outside and we would kiss through the opening, before I entered. Or if there was no vine beside her window, she would trip down to the back door and open it to me and we would make love, and afterwards she would confess to me that though she had not been a virgin when we first met, I was the only man she ever had loved or ever would. And we would make love again. And then she would tell me that all evening she had been nauseated by Shuttleworth's hot breath on her neck and his gross paw at her waist. And we would make love again. Then she would tell me that, thinking things over, she had decided we should become engaged to be married. She would wait until I had made my decision on a career, but she would not wait until I had made my fortune. She would marry me, penniless as I was, and work with me, sharing my triumphs and tempering my despairs with the sweetness of her sweet presence. Then we would make love again.

I raised my glass of Scotch, holding it with both hands like a chalice, and tried to look at the moon through its amber liquid. Life, I decided, was okay after all. Then I felt I ought to firm up that insight by quoting something, preferably in Greek if only I knew Greek. I climbed down to the very edge of the water and looked at the wine-dark sea— very black, of course—and decided to make a libation of my remaining Scotch. But what to say as I poured the potent fluid into the waiting sea? I really must learn Greek, I thought.

I was considering which of my store of quotations from the English poets best fitted the situation when I was interrupted by Bartoldi looming up on the rocks above me, his form outlined against the sky. "Hey," he said, "what are you doing?"

"Are you finished already?" I asked, exasperated. "Haven't you read about foreplay and afterplay?"

"Look," he said, "she feels kind of funny with you wandering around out here." (I felt she was to be complimented on the delicacy of her feelings.) "So we're going to go back to the suite, okay?"

"Yes, fine," I said.

"You still going to see Martha?"

"Yes."

"Well, good. Don't hurry back."

I started to climb up from the water's edge, still holding my glass. "What were you doing down there anyway?" Bartoldi said. "Peeing?"

"Praying."

"Yeah? Well I got to pee before we start back." He climbed down—our positions were reversed—and while Bartoldi made water into the ocean, I finished off the Scotch. When he'd climbed back to where I stood I handed him the empty glass. "Here, this is yours," I said.

He tossed it onto the rocks and we went to help Alice climb through the window.

8

It was well after midnight when I found myself once more in front of the Sears' house. There were still lights on in a downstairs front room. I could only suppose that the elder Sears were up late, tippling probably. Martha's windows were invisible from where I stood.

I backed away from the house. Standing on the sidewalk across the street, I straightened my cap and then put my hands in my pockets. The Scotch was still at work on me and I felt ready for love or war, though I hoped for love. Von Flotow's music—there's a composer for you—von Flotow's music began to run through my head. I owned or had owned a recording of Jussi Björling singing "M'appari." I sang a little of it in a low perhaps slightly hoarse monotone, transposing it into the English lyrics we had learned at school.

> Like a flower, pure and fair
> One alone has entered
> Martha, Martha I adore thee
> Oh return and be my own
> Do not leave me, I implore thee
> Once again, oh be my own!

But this would not do at all. I could not stand forever under this lamppost, singing von Flotow to myself.

I crossed the street.

The back yard of the Sears' house was enclosed with a brick wall. One entered the yard through a locked wooden gate set in a brick archway. Or, if one didn't have a key to the gate, one mounted a garbage can and shinnied to the top of the wall. There, balancing oneself carefully, for the wall was narrow, one walked slowly along the top until one was opposite Martha's windows, which were lit.

I stopped, teetered a moment, and then carefully lowered myself until I was sitting on the wall with my legs dangling. I straightened my army cap again.

She was up there in her room. What was she thinking about? Me? Shuttleworth? No one? Was she curled up in bed with a good book—say, *Madame Bovary?* Or was she brushing her black hair? The thing to do was find out. I searched with my hand until I found a loose piece of mortar—this was an old brick wall—which I tossed gently at her lighted window.

It made the most surprising racket in that quiet neighborhood. Her form suddenly appeared—started up, one might say—and was momentarily outlined against the shade as she stood between the window and the source of light in the room. Then the light went out. "Martha?" I called. I did not want her to run downstairs with news for Daddy that there were intruders on the premises. "Martha?"

The shade moved slightly. I was relieved. I could imagine her peeking out into the night to see what she could see, which couldn't have been much. The moon was still up, but this was the shaded side of the house.

"Martha," I called a third time.

"Where are you?" she said.

"On the wall."

"Sammy?"

"Yes."

The shade went all the way up, and my eyes, accustomed now to the darkness, could see her standing at the window looking out at me across the moat between us. She had on some species of white nightie or robe that showed up well in the dark.

Presently she seemed to make me out. "Aren't you afraid you'll fall off the wall?" she asked.

77

"I've come to see you," I said.

"Are you squiffed?" she asked.

I spurned the unworthy suggestion. "I am never drunk. I have a naturally temperate nature."

"How nice for you." She seemed to find some obscure humor in the situation. I wasn't positive she was glad to see me, but I was pleased she seemed willing to talk. She sat down on the floor, resting her elbows on the windowsill.

"Martha," I said, "it was cruel of you to go off with that Shuttleworth after I'd been looking forward to seeing you for almost four months, but that doesn't bother me so much any more."

"I'd written you about it," she said.

"I know you wrote, and it's all right. After all, we aren't engaged. There's only a moral commitment between us."

"What sort of commitment?"

"A moral commitment. Martha, why don't you let me in the back door? Your parents won't hear us."

"It's rather late," she said.

"We have a lot to say to each other."

"We can say it tomorrow."

And then without any transition—it was always happening when I was with Martha—I was suddenly appalled and angry. "Now listen here," I said, "you've spent the whole evening with that chubby Shuttleworth of yours. You can certainly come down to the back door and let me in for a talk."

"He's not chubby," she said. "Those are muscles."

"How do you know?" I asked.

"I've seen a picture of him in his bathing suit."

"Where? Where did you see the picture?"

"In his class book."

I laughed, though it was not a happy pleasant sound. "He's been showing you his class book?"

"He went to Groton," Martha said.

"Ah? Does that impress you?"

"I just mentioned it," Martha said. "You seemed interested in his class book."

"I think you're the one who's interested." I felt this approached bickering, however, so I changed my tone. "Martha, we won't have much time together. Why don't you let me in?"

"I'm tired, Sammy."

"Why? I'm not tired."

"I'm tired because I've been dancing, and it's late."

"You didn't go anywhere with Shuttleworth after the dance?"

She stood up. "Good night, Sammy," she said.

"Just a minute," I said. "I've learned how to scale walls in the army. I could climb right up to that window."

"Then you don't need me to let you in."

"Martha, I'll do it." I made to jump down from the wall I was sitting on.

She peered toward the ground. "Be careful," she said. "I think there's a rose bush below you."

"Martha, why are you behaving this way?" I asked.

"I've told you, Sammy. I'm tired."

"I've never seen you tired before. And don't call me Sammy."

"Sam."

"Samuel! It's a great name. Samuel anointed Saul, the son of Kish, to be King over Israel. Samuel was the last of the Judges."

"You've told me before."

"You see?" I said. "I've told you so many things, and what has Shuttleworth ever said that you remember?"

She leaned against the window frame, as if to think. "Let's see, what has he said?" She sounded definitely amused.

"You can't think of a thing."

"He's told me his father is a director of United Fruit."

"United Fruit!"

"And he's told me what goes on in Porcellian."

79

"How can you be interested in that?" I asked. "And anyway, a bishop outranks a director of United Fruit."

"*You* asked what he'd told me."

"He's a very obvious, shallow kind of character," I said. "Would he accept a challenge to fight?"

"Ask him," Martha said. "I know he boxes."

"What I can't understand," I said, "is how you ever happened to meet such a person?"

"My father knows his father." Martha leaned forward slightly. "Tomorrow you can ask all the questions you want about Richard."

"Don't call him Richard."

"What shall I call him?"

"Shuttleworth."

"All right. Now it's just getting later all the time. Why don't you go home and go to bed?"

"Martha . . ."

"I mean it, Sammy."

"Martha, I have something more to say to you."

"What?"

"You need to have someone like me in love with you. Shuttleworth doesn't know how to love you."

"If you mean he doesn't climb up on the wall at two A.M., you're right."

"I mean a lot more than that," I said. "But I mean that, too. I should think you'd be touched that I'm here on the wall."

There was a brief silence. Then she said, "You know what you remind me of? Humpty Dumpty."

I didn't speak for a while. Then I said, "Martha, you're really a terrible person. I mean, you're not good."

"Good night, Sammy Sam Samuel."

"I come here burning with ardor, and all you do is make jokes. Not very funny jokes, either."

"You're not going to talk your way into the house," she said.

"Without me, you're lost," I told her. "You'll end up a godforsaken suburban matron married to a zero like Shuttleworth. Is that the kind of life you want?"

"I'm going to bed, Sammy." She moved away from the window, disappearing into the darkness of her room.

"You could at least think up a more honorable excuse than tiredness," I said. "What sort of explanation is that?" She didn't answer. I sat for a while thinking things over. Then I said, "If you feel that after dancing with Shuttleworth all evening it would be gross to let me into the house, why then that's a scruple I could respect." She didn't answer. "Is that the reason, Martha?" I had raised my voice slightly. When there was still no answer, I searched until I found another lump of mortar—that wall was really coming apart. I tossed it through her window and heard it land with a thump on the rug. She reappeared. "Is that the reason?" I asked.

"Is what the reason?"

"If you'd been listening . . ."

"You know, you're going to wake the neighbors."

"I may just get down and ring the front doorbell and talk to your father about you."

"You can't," she said. "My parents are in New York."

As that sank in, I said, "You mean you're alone in the house?" Then, at the exact moment when a horrible suspicion reached my mind, I heard a stirring within the darkness of her bedroom, and a male voice said, "Just tell him to go."

"You better go," Martha said before she disappeared again.

You see, Reader, a comical historical pastoral is a complex genre in which one must be prepared for moments like this. Naturally at the time I was not aware of the fact. As I climbed down from the wall and walked back to Leverett House, I believed my life was a tragedy or perhaps a Sicilian melodrama. First I would kill Shuttleworth, then Martha, and then myself. After I had killed us all and was utterly alone in the world, I would enter a monastic order, or perhaps retire to some remote section of Southern France, where amid scenery of striking and lonely beauty I would live to a great age, tending my garden and meditating. A kind of serene and wise happiness would descend so that Martha, seeing me from the window of her chauffeur-driven Cadillac, would have the car stopped so that she could speak to me and learn my secret. A graying thirty-nine-year-old woman by then, she would approach my low walled garden, and I, with gentle courtesy, would invite her into my stone cottage for a glass of water. "It's very beautiful here," she would say, and I would answer, "I love it better each year and I have lived here now for sixty years." (The sudden difference in our ages being due to the relativity of time.) We would not speak of what might have been.

It was three A.M. before I got back to Leverett. There, in my former bedroom (where was Waterbuck and what was he doing?), I removed my uniform and got into bed wearing the olive-drab skivvies to which I had become accustomed as pajamas. Bartoldi had taken his Alice back to where he'd gotten her and was sleeping the sleep of the just while I lay awake thinking about life.

It's boring to have to explain this, Reader, but at that time I was much influenced by a French writer named Henri Beyle, alias Henri Brulard, alias Stendhal, a fly-by-night novelist who wrote *The Red and The Black, The Charterhouse of Parma*, and various other books I thought were just swell. He believed in being in love, and being witty, and various other things I believed in, or thought I believed in, and if I couldn't be William Blake or John Keats, as I obviously couldn't, I was willing to settle for being Stendhal.

Lying in bed that night in my skivvies, I began to think I'd made a bad bargain. Love! What was so wonderful about being in love? I mean, assuming I was in love with Martha, what was I getting out of it except pain, distress, anger, restlessness, and sleeplessness? What was so valuable about that, please? Then it occurred to me that the big proponents of love—Stendhal, for instance—had more or less been admitting, in fact proclaiming, that love led you into the kind of misery I was in. I hadn't really noticed that before.

I noticed it for a while, and began to think that Stendhal was simply a muddlehead, licking his wounds, savoring his distress, and enjoying his predicament. Why had I never before been offended by that unpleasant description of the three days he spent hiding in the cellar of his mistress' castle? Why had I been such a Beyliste? In a sort of anger, I hopped out of bed, found my wallet, and extracted a little slip of paper which I'd been carrying around for several months. On it, just before my birthday, I had written: *Imgo ingt obet wenty*, in imitation of Stendhal who, before his fiftieth birthday, had written on the band of his new English trousers, *Imgo ingt obef ifty*. Now, looking at my slip of paper, it occurred to me that since Stendhal had written in English, I should have written in French: *jeva isavo irving tans*.

But what a sap I'd been to write anything at all. I crumpled up the slip of paper, and then got back into bed and finally managed to fall asleep hating Stendhal.

9

Bartoldi woke me the next morning. "You going to sleep all day?" he asked. I pushed myself up in bed and asked what time it was. "About ten," he said.

"Then we've missed breakfast anyway. Why wake me up now?"

"They're not even serving breakfast. The dining room's closed. We're supposed to be out of here by tonight." He sat down on the edge of my bed. "I've been thinking. Maybe we ought to move over to my mother's. Probably she wants to see me anyway." Vandalizing his mother's summer home the evening before had apparently wakened Bartoldi's filial sentiments.

"Will she want to see me?"

"Oh sure," Bartoldi said. "So get dressed, hunh? We'll have breakfast there."

I had little to pack, and Bartoldi nothing. His way of leaving a place for the summer was to lock the door behind him, leaving his sheets on the bed, his laundry in the bag, his tennis racquet and entrenching tool in the closet, and so on. Once again I found myself thinking enviously and disapprovingly of how easy his life seemed compared to mine.

"How'd you make out last night with Martha?" he asked on the drive to Brookline.

"Not so well," I said.

"Yeah? Well, I always figured she was a tease," Bartoldi said, and we left it at that, I not caring to illuminate him, and he not caring to be illuminated. Besides, I didn't want to start thinking seriously about Martha until I'd at least had some orange juice and milk.

My stay at the house in February had prepared me for the shock uninitiated people sometimes experienced on first catching sight of Mrs. Bartoldi. In the morning, before corsets had closed in on her, she looked like something come out to eat hay. Later in the day she changed shape. A monumental bust appeared from which her figure descended in a more or less sheer precipice of unimaginable geologic complexity. One guessed at folded sedimentary deposits laced with igneous intrusions of elastic and whalebone or whatever these women use to keep themselves together. One reached bottom in a heaped up scree of thighs, knees, and ankles from which protruded two quite well-shaped feet. For a shrewd observer of the human scene, one glimpse of Mrs. Bartoldi was enough to explain a lot about the character of her son.

The Bartoldi household, aside from its resident Earth Mother, consisted of Mrs. Bartoldi's sister and brother-in-law, a third person called Caroline, and a ticker tape. Caroline was used as a fourth for bridge; the ticker tape was for watching over Mrs. Bartoldi's investments. Bartoldi *père* now conducted business in Buenos Aires, a cool six thousand miles from Mrs. B. in Brookline, but he had not been allowed to get away before making over a considerable portion of his wealth to support the dear ones he left behind.

They lived in some comfort, for the establishment was run on broad and easy lines. Money was good to have, food was good to eat, and bridge was good to play—this about summed things up.

It was almost eleven when we arrived. Breakfasted, corseted, Mrs. Bartoldi greeted us impartially. If anything, I got the bigger welcome. "So you're back again," she said to me, and to her son, "Hello."

"We're hungry," Bartoldi said. "We haven't had breakfast yet."

"Well, don't tell me about it," his mother replied. "Gertrude's in the kitchen."

Bartoldi went across the hall to the dining room and raised his voice to summon Gertrude. Mrs. Bartoldi looked at me, beginning with my necktie and going on down to my polished army shoes. "Those clothes don't fit you too well," she said. "How do you like the army, anyway?"

"It's not bad," I told her.

She nodded as if this confirmed one of her own secret opinions. Mrs. Trexler came into the room and looked at me curiously. "Anne, you remember Sam," Mrs. Bartoldi said. "He's the kid who blew up the riverbank."

Mrs. Trexler looked at me again and then sat down. She was a silent woman, her conversation mainly confined to saying, "By me," or, "I double."

"Bill's here," Mrs. Bartoldi said. That news seemed to bring no joy into Mrs. Trexler's life either.

"Well," I said, "maybe I ought to go have breakfast."

Mrs. Bartoldi waved a large arm. "Help yourself," she said.

Bartoldi was already at the table with a glass of orange juice in front of him. Morning papers left by earlier breakfasters were lying about, and it will perhaps give you a deeper insight into this family than any I have so far supplied when I tell you, Reader, that during the meetings and greetings I have limned, no mention was made of the news which now stared up at me in banner headlines as I pulled the *Boston Globe* toward my place.

"My God!" I said. "The war's begun."

How clearly it all stands out in my mind: I gaping at the newspapers, Bartoldi drinking his orange juice, and Gertrude putting a glass in front of me. I automatically took it in my hand before I realized that perhaps one should not drink orange juice at a time like this. Thus, on December 7, 1941, Father pushed aside his plate of roast lamb, remarking that he had no appetite for food, though now the situation was

86

less clearly catastrophic than it had been nine years earlier. As I read further into the *Globe*'s news columns, I discovered that so far our troops were only fighting against those North Korean soldiers who had invaded South Korea. From the headlines it had looked as if we were actually in combat with the Red Army. I suppose the *Globe* editors were making a laudable effort to interest readers in international events.

Bartoldi glanced at the papers in front of me. "Maybe you'll see some action now, Sammy."

"How many eggs do you want?" Gertrude asked.

Nothing made sense. "Two," I said.

On the front page of the *Globe* there was a map of the Korean peninsula with the familiar shaded bulges and slightly curved arrows which represented some staff artist's idea of the line of advance of the North Korean army. How it brought back old memories! I had been visiting my grandmother in June 1941 when Hitler invaded Russia. There, on the porch of her house in Lexington, Kentucky, we had studied the bulges and arrows that represented the advance of the Wehrmacht. Sometimes there were big arrows and little ones. As a bulge stretched out, a big arrow would indicate the ultimate goal of the advance—Moscow, for instance —while two little arrows would circle like fishhooks to gather in the various intermediate objectives. Pinsk and Minsk had both been snared by those fishhooks. Grandmother and I hoped Smolensk would resist them. On the day Smolensk was hooked, Grandmother sighed delicately. "The Russians are just being rounded up in hordes," she said. I was eleven. Her sentence sunk into my mind, and I had a vision of drab hordes of Russians shambling like buffaloes across an open plain while Germans in feathers and war paint galloped along shooting arrows into their flanks. I offer the memory as one of those totally misleading visions which serve to climax our understanding of modern history.

Reading the latest war news that morning in Brookline,

I was aware of a new factor in the situation which hadn't been present on all the mornings of my childhood when I pored over the news from North Africa or Russia or the South Pacific. Even if Bartoldi hadn't mentioned the fact, I was keenly aware that I was now in uniform.

Perhaps as a result of reading that terrible old fraud Stendhal, perhaps as the result of some constitutional romanticism of my own, I had always sympathized with the youth of post-Napoleonic France, those young men who had grown up too late to know the glory of following the Imperial eagles from one corner of the continent to the other and participating in those lightning victories—Austerlitz, Jena, Marengo, Wagram—which had transformed the map of Europe and raised France to the skies. I felt I was essentially like those young Frenchmen, part of a backwater generation, militarily speaking. I had been seeing myself as Julien Sorel, deprived of grandeur and forced to make my way by craft and love.

Now war opened out as a possibility. I bent my head to the *Globe* and began my first serious study of Korea.

It seemed to be a typically Manichaean country divided into a good South and a wicked North. Seoul, it seemed, was the capital of the good half of the country. Pyongyang was the capital of the North, where reigned a tyrant with the appropriate name of Kim Il Sung. The President of the South was Syngman Rhee (Syngman Rhee whaetwudu?). Seoul, which lay close to the border, was already threatened. An important river barrier, the Han, had been crossed by Northern troops. The Southern government was believed to be in the process of transferring itself to a city named Taejon. American troops were defending Kimpo airport in the suburbs of Seoul. It was like reading about Oz under attack by the Gnome King. Glinda the Good, that is to say, General of the Armies Douglas Arthur MacArthur, was unfortunately off in Tokyo, too far from the battle to restore the situation by his magic. Syngman Rhee, who like Ozma

88

was a powerful fairy in his own right, seemed to have been taken by surprise.

That much I grasped in a few minutes. The subtleties of the situation, its true inwardness, was still hidden from me, as much as from the reporters who were off in Japan with Glinda. In New York the Security Council had already called for a cease-fire, but correspondents there were not sure the North Koreans had yet invented the radio and so it was unclear whether they would get the call. As far as I could tell we were in for a high old time.

I somehow consumed orange juice and eggs as I absorbed all this information. Bartoldi and I, with coffee cups at our elbows, were both reading the paper when Mrs. Bartoldi eased into the room, drawn thither perhaps by a maternal desire to see more of her son.

"Oh, so you've seen the crazy thing Truman's getting us into now?" she said. "This'll really send the market down."

Bartoldi said, "You'll survive."

"Sure I'll survive," Mrs. Bartoldi said, "but do you think it's fun watching the market take a skid?"

"It'll rise again." It was hard to tell whether this was said on the basis of some inside knowledge of market behavior, or merely to cheer up a temporarily discouraged Mom.

Mrs. Bartoldi said, "I'm glad you know so much. Anne thinks I ought to sell."

"She's a dope," Bartoldi said. "Buy U.S. Steel. It always rises during wars."

"I don't know. I'm thinking of bonds," Mrs. Bartoldi said. "And don't talk that way about your aunt." She looked at me. "I guess you didn't expect this when you joined the army?"

"No," I said.

"That Truman!"

Bartoldi rose with the sports section in his hand. "Going to the can," he explained.

89

He was regularity itself. I sometimes imagined a professor of internal medicine pointing with his lecture rod at an enlarged X-ray of Bartoldi's interior. "Now, students," he was saying, "here you see a normal digestive tract at work . . ."

Mrs. Bartoldi looked after her son with an enigmatic expression on her features. Then she said to me, "You have everything you want?"

"Yes, thank you."

"Okay," she said, and I was left alone with the coffee cups and the news.

Since all thought that morning seemed more or less futile, I allowed myself to start thinking about Martha. I took it for granted that she was overwhelmed with shame, guilt, and remorse. I was even generous enough to assume that she was suffering more than I was, since my conscience at least was clear. I had heard often enough (from Father) that a clear conscience was a precious possession, and I was willing to accept the proposition when it worked in my favor. So there we were: she suffering and I with my clear conscience. I was somewhat hurt—numbed here and there—but otherwise intact and ready to do battle with the whole Korean army. The question seemed to be, what happens now? Aside, of course, from the war. Should I telephone her?

Looked at one way, the answer was *no.* Looked at in another way, the answer was still *no.* Why should *I* telephone *her?* If anyone was going to do any telephoning, it was certainly Martha's role to initiate things by making a humble call to me. A small, humble, crushed little plea for me to see her one last time so that she could explain (though no explanation could ever explain) just how it happened she had gone to bed with a Shuttleworth on the very night I had come to see her. Or any night. Or day, for that matter.

The only trouble was that she didn't know I was at the Bartoldis.

Perhaps already she had made several calls to the suite, listening to the phone ring a dozen times, and then creeping —well, hurrying—back to her dark room and the gnawing pangs of conscience. It was pitiful. I could almost feel sorry for her, especially now that she must know there was a war on and I would shortly die a hero's death defending the Han River line. (I was not quite certain how I felt about the war, but I was temporarily willing to face a hero's death provided Martha knew I was facing it.) In fact, the more I thought about my hero's death, the more I felt it would be cruel to depart without first giving Martha a chance to atone. (How?) If she hadn't atoned (How? How?), would not my death saddle her with a really unbearable sense of guilt?

Feeling, therefore, almost like a Christian, I left the breakfast table and found the Bartoldi's telephone. It was installed not far from the ticker tape (silent on Sunday) in a closet which was more or less fitted up as a deluxe telephone booth. An ample chair fitted to Mrs. Bartoldi's specifications, a pad of paper, ashtray, cigarettes, and matches, provided all the appurtenances for long, comfortable chats with one's broker or one's faithless girlfriend. I dialed the Sears' number.

At first I thought no one would answer. Then came Martha's voice saying, "I can't stop it, you'll have to send a man."

What was this? What fresh abandonment was this?

"Hello?" I said.

"Hello?" she said. "Isn't this Mr. Forbes?"

"I'm Samuel."

"Oh, Samuel." She spoke with no trace of anguish I could detect. "I can't talk to you now. I'm expecting a call from Mr. Forbes. There's a pipe broken."

"Look, Martha . . ." I began.

"Where are you anyway? I've already called Leverett House."

"I'm at the Bartoldis."

"Well, give me the number. I'll call you back."

91

So I gave her the number and hung up, flummoxed. Sitting in the booth for a while, I toyed with the idea of undermining my health by smoking a cigarette. My first. Perhaps it would induce a Keatsian decline.

10

Martha and I finally met toward the middle of that Sunday afternoon in front of the Boston Museum of Fine Arts, a suitable backdrop for the scene we had in hand. In justice to the occasion she arrived almost on time, wearing a white summer dress with a string of coral beads. Her expression was serious but not, I would say, apprehensive or guilt-ridden, and among the first things she said was, "Now I'm not going to listen to a lot of your arguments and criticisms. I'm sorry it happened, but it's your own fault for not writing sooner. By the time I got your letter I couldn't get out of that date."

"That date!" I said.

"Yes. He'd asked me weeks ago, and it was a big dance. I couldn't stand him up."

Reason tottered. I put my hand on the head of one of the stone lions that overlooked the steps on which we were standing.

"Martha," I said, "that wasn't just a date. I'm not complaining about your going out with him on a date." So far I hadn't had time to complain about anything, but I was too flabbergasted to point that out. "I hope you don't call that just a date?"

"Well, I let him come into the house, afterwards." She shrugged slightly. "You've been in the house."

"He was in your bedroom."

"You've been there too."

Did that have anything to do with it? Was that the point?

"Martha . . ." I said.

"I told you," she said. "I'm not going to listen to a lot of criticism. This is my life I'm living."

I made a tactical error at that point. "Hitler could have said the same."

"Hitler has nothing to do with it, and you know it." Then her manner softened perceptibly. "I'm sorry, Samuel. I know you come from a religious family and you're easily shocked, but it just isn't the Middle Ages any more and there's no use pretending."

"The Middle Ages!" My hand was still on the lion's head. Now I felt like leaning on its neck. I remember wondering how she could possibly be so confused about things, and in the intellectual chaos that seemed to be opening up around me I grasped for solid ground. "You think Blake is medieval?" I asked.

"Blake?"

"William Blake," I said, feeling some ground coming back under my feet. Blake is always a useful person to have on your side. "Blake didn't believe in chastity, but he certainly didn't believe in casual fornication either."

Martha's face closed slightly. "We just have different attitudes toward sex."

I hastened to apologize. "Martha, I didn't mean to insult you, but after all, you'd just called me medieval."

"Well, maybe not medieval," she said. "It's just you're very old-fashioned. It's not your fault."

I didn't understand and still don't understand why fleets of North Korean dive bombers didn't appear at that moment to blast us and destroy the museum we were standing in front of. The only possible explanation is that for some dispassionate and I'm afraid not very nice Oriental motive they preferred to stand by and watch Western civilization stew in its own juices. At any rate the moment passed, and I found myself looking at Martha with new eyes. There she was, dressed in white with coral beads around her neck, educated at Radcliffe, taken to concerts and plays all her life, and now standing there in her open-toed shoes under the gray-blue skies of Boston saying that it was old-fashioned of me to be upset that she'd screwed with Shuttleworth the night before. I felt like writing a letter to the *Christian Science Monitor* about her. I felt about a million and a half years old, and I found myself spontaneously inventing an old folk saying to the effect that "One has never really plumbed the depths of a woman one loves, until one has plumbed her depths."

"Martha," I said, "you can't mean that."

"What?"

"That I'm old-fashioned."

"Well, you are, Sammy. I like it, except when you get like this."

"Like what?" I asked, feeling in need of information about myself.

Which was not forthcoming. "Like this . . ." She gestured vaguely. That's the trouble with women. Just when you think you're going to find out something, they gesture vaguely.

I took her arm. "Martha, let's go sit down somewhere." In a deep hole and pull the earth in over us, I thought.

She acceded to this reasonable suggestion, so off we went. When finally we were sitting together over cups of coffee, I said, "How do you really feel about me?" During our walk I had come to the conclusion that the complicated moral, spiritual drama of her repentance and my forgiveness, the drama I had promised myself in my musings of the morning, that particular drama would have to be postponed to some other lifetime. "How do you really feel about me?" I asked.

"I like you."

"We can do better than that," I said. "You like your mother and father and roommate, but you don't go to bed with them." Her delay in answering gave me the chance to add, "I hope."

"Not very funny, Sammy."

"Well, answer my question."

She hedged. "It's hard to say how you feel about anyone."

"It is not," I said. "I've told you often enough how I love you."

The careful reader of this confession will probably spot the same flaw in that statement toward which Martha now directed my attention. "You have not."

"I've certainly told you I love you."

"Maybe once or twice. But I don't know *how* you love me."

"Anyway, you know I do love you."

"I'm not even sure of that."

"Oh, Martha . . ."

"Sammy, why don't you just accept things the way they are?"

"Never!" I felt the word sounding like a trumpet within me. "But I can see it would be convenient for you if I did." I leaned forward. "Martha, I've got to know whether you care for me at all, or whether I'm just another Shuttleworth to you." She didn't answer. "Am I?"

"No, you're not like Richard," she said.

"Do you care for me more than you care for him?"

"Well . . ."

I was tempted to shake my finger like a district attorney warning a witness: Be very careful how you answer that question, Madame. I had time to do it, too, since she drew things out until I thought she wasn't really going to answer at all. "I guess . . ." she looked at me in an appraising way. "I guess I like you more than I like Richard."

I was absurdly glad to hear it, though I couldn't be sure I believed her. "How long have you known him?" I asked.

"Oh, we've met lots of times. We only started dating in March."

"Immediately after I left?"

"Yes."

"And how long have you been letting him into the house?"

"That's not your business."

"I want to know."

"Well, you won't find out from me."

I sat back in my chair. "And don't you feel any compunction about carrying on with two different men at the same time?"

"I have not been carrying on with two men at the same time," Martha said. "*You* have been away, in case you've forgotten. And anyway, I told you earlier that this is my own business."

Her own business! How I despised that phrase. There is scarcely a criminal, a pervert, or a lunatic in the entire world who has not at one time or another said, "What I do is my own business." Well, I knew better. The Bishop's theological ideas might be quaintly old-fashioned—that was the phrase which somehow popped into my mind—but I thanked him and his Lord that together they had brought me up with a firm grasp of the fact that *no one* can be allowed to go through life thinking what he does is his own business. Her own business, indeed! I had arguments and quotations aplenty to refute *that* idea, and I was about to tumble a few of them over her smoothly combed head when, looking at her across the table from me, I suddenly realized she believed what she had said. She thought it was her own business! That was what she actually thought, sitting there as cool as a cucumber, calmly prepared to defeat my attempts at moral browbeating.

I felt suddenly lost. I thought, What amazing people women are. "You're amazing," I said.

She smiled.

"I didn't mean it as a compliment."

"Thank you, anyway."

I shook my head in disbelief. "I really believe you don't feel guilty." It was like discovering the Pythagorean Theorem. In a right-angle triangle, the square of the hypotenuse is equal to the sum of the squares of the other two sides, and Martha doesn't feel guilty.

"Well, why should I?" she asked.

"And what do you think your parents would say if they knew you've been sleeping with Shuttleworth?"

"What do you think they would say if they knew I'd slept with you?"

That's different! I wanted to shout. "That's different," I said. Why couldn't she see it? What deep moral obtuseness, what paralysis of soul prevented her from seeing the difference?

"What is the difference?" she asked.

"The difference is that when we . . . The difference is that you and I are two people. Not *three*."

"Well, last winter I told you about the others," she said. She had, of course. I'd been trying to forget them ever since, and I wasn't going to start thinking about them. "Martha," I said, "are you going to go on seeing Shuttleworth?"

"Probably."

"And are you going to go on seeing me?"

"I'm seeing you now."

"I mean more than that. Are you going to go on having an affair with both of us?"

It was a good question, I thought. Martha apparently thought so, too. She looked at her watch. "I think I'll go home now," she said. "Someone's coming at four-thirty to fix the pipes."

"Martha, it was a simple question."

She got to her feet. "Well, you shouldn't have asked it."

But I had. I looked up at her. "Could I come back to the house with you?"

"Do you want to?"

"No."

She pursed her lips. I think, at least I like to think, she felt bad for that moment. She put out her hand. "Then, good-bye, Sammy. Thanks for the coffee."

"Good-bye," I said.

So we had parted forever. I sat on over the coffee cups savoring the pathos of the moment until it occurred to me that there was a lot more to say. I paid the check and hurried out onto the sidewalk just in time to hop into the cab Martha had hailed.

"Do you realize," I asked her, "that a war's beginning?"

"What are you talking about now?"

"North Korea has invaded South Korea."

"Well, what of it?"

"But don't you see? This could involve us in war with Russia."

At that point the cab driver intervened, precipitating one of those human-interest episodes that do so much to enrich urban life. "Ahhh," he said, "we've got the Bomb, don't we? They've got to do what we say."

"Will you shut up?" I said.

Immediately the driver pulled into the curb and turned to look over the seat at me. A large-shouldered, black-haired fellow, he struck me as being essentially the kind of man who values his own dignity and opinions. One of the fighting Irish, perhaps. "No one tells me to shut up in my own cab," he said.

"I'm trying to talk to the lady here."

"Yeah? Well, you can apologize or just get out. I didn't pick you up anyways. I picked her up."

Anyone can pick her up, I thought. And then, "All right, I apologize, you jerk. Now will you drive on?"

"Go on, get out of here," he said. His manner seemed threatening.

99

"Okay, here's your fare. We'll walk." I tossed him a dollar and pulled Martha out of the cab. The driver leaned across the front seat and threw my dollar on the sidewalk. "Keep your goddam money, you bastard." Then he drove off.

"Martha," I said, "I've got to talk to you some more."

"Are you going to pick up that dollar?" she asked.

"No."

So we walked on. In silence for a while. I was trying to frame a speech that would skirt the Charybdis of anger without absolutely flying into the Siren arms of self-pity. Martha, I wanted to say, I will shortly be sent overseas to fight the entire Russian and North Korean armies single-handedly. I do not say this to rouse your admiration, but simply to point out that I shall shortly die. And what I ask of you during these few remaining months of my life is that you refrain from cohabiting with Shuttleworth. Is that too much to ask? Is it too much to expect, while I am overseas engaged in a dangerous and in many ways admirable resistance to naked Communist agression, that you attempt to observe one of the simplest, most elementary moral codes known to our race? Remember, it is only for a few months I ask this. When I am dead, do what you like with your life, but at least honor me now by a temporary fidelity.

When I had that all worked out in my mind, I said, "Martha, I don't want you to see Shuttleworth any more."

"He doesn't want me to see you."

That enraged me. The thought of that civilian with his overweight problem and his flat feet acting as if he had rights in this matter was just too much. "If you ever see him again, I'll never forgive you," I said. It was doubtful I would ever forgive her anyway, but I wanted to retain some leverage.

"I can't break off with Richard just because you're jealous, Sammy. Anyway, it isn't civilized."

What did she know about civilization? I took hold of her

100

arm to emphasize my point. "Martha," I said, "it isn't a question of jealousy. There's a principle involved here."

"What principle?"

"Faithfulness!" That was what civilization was based on, if she wanted to know. Faithfulness. Keeping the faith. Could I tell *her* something about civilization!

"I've said I like you as much as I ever did. Isn't that enough?"

"*No!*"

"Well, I'm sorry."

"That isn't good enough. *I am a jealous God, saith the Lord.*"

"You just said you weren't jealous."

"I was quoting the Bible." I looked at her. "Martha, haven't you ever heard of the idea that people commit themselves with all their heart, with all their mind, with all their soul? Don't you know when a woman marries a man she gives herself to him and he gives himself to her and they *stay that way*? They do not go sleeping around with every Tom, Dick, and Harry." Or Richard.

"We're not married," Martha said.

"We were going to be married."

"We were not. We're not even engaged."

I tried to control myself. "Martha, use your reason. Would I ever have asked you to go to bed with me if I hadn't intended to marry you?"

"You never mentioned marriage that night."

"I didn't think, between us, it needed to be mentioned."

"Oh, *didn't* you?"

"It's just assumed when people of our sort sleep together they are married in the eyes of God. I planned for us to marry when I'd settled on a career."

"Did you?"

"Yes. I knew your father would want to know how I was going to support you."

101

"Very considerate. I don't believe any of this."

"Well, some of it's true. I did propose last February."

"It still doesn't change the situation."

"You mean you are going to go on seeing Shuttleworth?"

"I like him."

Like, like, like, like, like! "Martha," I said, "will you marry me?"

"No."

I stopped walking with her. "Very well, this is probably the last time you will see me alive."

"You mean, if I signal that cab you won't get in with me?"

"I'm sorry we're parting this way," I said.

Some weekend pass that turned out to be.

11

It was lucky for me that the Korean war got going just when I most needed to kill someone. Things moved like clockwork. The Security Council, its cease-fire call unheeded, formally condemned North Korea for its unprovoked aggression. Then Truman ordered our air force and navy to aid the South Koreans, and Seoul fell. Stronger measures seemed to be called for, so next the Security Council solicited member states of the United Nations to support South Korea, and in response to this call Truman authorized General MacArthur to commit more American troops to action. What more could one ask for? We were at war. Not that those pusillanimous gents on Capitol Hill ever ratified hostilities; still, they had the sense to vote the funds and then get out of the way while Harry and we fighting men carried the ball.

Ah blessed, blessed anger! Properly nursed it can sustain one for months. On its viewless wings one can even soar to those dizzy heights that only poets inhabit.

All summer I was in a state of incandescence, aided perhaps by the fact that early in July I was shipped to Texas for advanced infantry training. There, under cloudless skies, in 100-degree heat, in a landscape of supernatural ugliness, I was one of a batch of rookies slowly baked to military perfection. It was a hot, hideous, beautiful summer of bayonet drill, M-1 firing, and bivouacs under starry skies. I didn't complain. Far from it. I knew exactly how that German general felt after listening to some Weimar idealists discuss a plan for universal peace and disarmament. *So geht das doch nicht, meinen Herren, mann muss einen Feind haben,* he said, which is being translated, It's no go, pals, men need enemies.

Throughout the summer news from the front continued

to be encouraging. As United Nations troops fell back, MacArthur announced that though there would be heartaches and new setbacks, he was never more confident of victory—ultimate victory—in his life. It sounded just great. A maximum of present suffering for our side with assurance of a final bloody triumph over the enemy. Everyone would get it, which sort of corresponded with my feeling of how things ought to be.

Though for a time "ultimate victory" looked remote. On the East Coast Samchok, Yongdok, and Pohang all fell. In the interior we lost Chungju, Chongju, and Chingju. But by September our lines were stabilized along the Naktong River, the Pusan bridgehead was safe, and shortly Mac would attack. By then I was trained, orders were cut, we were off to the East, and then: Kill, kill, kill, kill, kill. . . . Except that we were given seven-day furloughs to say good-bye to our families.

I thought of vacationing in sunny Mexico. I thought of exploring the romantic French Quarter of New Orleans. I even thought of going to Cambridge to see if Martha had become a good girl. In the event I took a slow train to Kansas City.

At the station—I hadn't let them know when I would arrive—I found myself a taxi. Then, on an impulse, two blocks from home, I told the driver to let me out. Carrying my kit bag, I walked slowly under the arched elms until, rounding a corner, I stopped to survey the house where we had lived since I was five.

There it was, surrounded by a sun-seared lawn, and wrapped by pinnacled porches that were hung with swings and dotted with wicker furniture. I had read Balzac and Dickens and played Parcheesi on those wide porches while the sun wheeled overhead and shadows from the profuse fretwork moved slowly across the gray boards. Looking higher—the eye was led upwards by ornamental lightning rods—I could see bedroom windows with their shutters wide open, white curtains billowing gently in the draft. Higher yet, the house culminated in its many gables and a red brick turret topped by a wrought-iron weathervane rusted into inaction, so that the wind, for us, came always from the north. There the house stood on its deep lot, making its reserved and ambiguous comment on the human search for beauty, truth, and justice.

I felt a sort of apprehension grip me. What was this kill, kill, kill, kill, kill business? We should do unto others as we would have others do unto us, and sad and uneasy as I felt looking at my home, I realized I had no particular desire to be killed. As I crossed the street I thought, Oh why did it all have to happen? Why couldn't we still be happy Neanderthalers, gamboling in the forests, sliding on glaciers, and biffing the bison with our clubs? As usual, the mere sight of home had unmanned me.

On the porch, I put down my kit bag and peered through the screen into the dark front hall. A door opened inside the house and then closed. Mother came down the staircase.

"Why Samuel!" she said. I was still peering through the screen. "Samuel." She opened the door of Father's study. "He's home," she said. And then she hurried to the front door. "Why you look so tanned and healthy," she said. "I was afraid all that army training wouldn't be good for you."

I kissed her. Then Father came into the hall and stood looking at me. "We expected you yesterday," he said.

A lot of water had flowed, nay, surged under the bridge since I'd last been home. I had been swept far downstream, and even the Episcopal stern-wheeler seemed to have lost ground and had its fires dampened a bit, as I discovered the next day when I had my inevitable talk with Father.

This was a talk I would have given a good deal to avoid, but short of fleeing home or stuffing a sock in Father's mouth I couldn't think of a way out, so down I went, down, down I went to Father's study, scene of many a memorable and distressing talk between us. I filed in, took a pew, and Father, sitting at his desk, put his fingers together and said, "Samuel, I have made an appointment for you with Father Groves at St. Stephen's. He is a new young priest. I think you might be able to talk more easily with him than you can talk with me."

"Talk with him about what?" I asked. Father frowned. "Are you hoping Father Groves will convert me?" I asked.

"Conversion is scarcely the word I would choose," Father said. "You are baptized. You have been confirmed. In most fundamental respects you are a Christian."

"Except that I don't believe in Jesus any more?"

"I presume that is what you and Father Groves will talk about. Your appointment is for ten o'clock tomorrow. I think you will find him a sympathetic young man."

"Father . . ."

He held up a hand. "You will do this for your mother and myself. It is all I ask."

"All right," I said, getting to my feet. It looked like an easy way out.

"Please sit down, Samuel. We will not discuss religion this morning, but there is another topic I wish to question you about."

So down I sat and squared my shoulders. I was dressed in suntans, with my Marksman First Class medal on my chest, every inch a soldier, and every foot this man's son.

Father said, "I would like to know, Samuel, whether you are still chaste?"

"Certainly I'm chaste," I said. Father didn't look convinced. "I'm probably the most chaste soldier in my entire company."

"Standards of chastity are not very high in the army," Father remarked.

"Well, if you mean *Am I a virgin?* No."

He nodded. It was what he expected to hear. "You have visited a prostitute?" he said.

I thought about Martha. "Well, her morals are certainly open to question, but I wouldn't call her a prostitute."

"B-girl?" Father suggested.

"She gets some A's, too. She goes to Radcliffe."

"Oh." You could see certain readjustments being made. "And what is your present relationship with her?"

"Anguishing," I said promptly.

Father looked as if he didn't believe that, either. Like my claim to chastity, it probably sounded too good to be true. "Anguishing?"

"Yes. She's involved with another fellow besides me."

"A girl of loose morals?" As Father advanced into the topic, bringing out his little phrases—B-girl, loose morals—I seemed to hear eggshells crushing underfoot. Yet one had to admire how Father went forward, firmly poising his shoe above each fact before smashing every nuance of meaning out of it. "Did you seduce her?" he asked.

"How do you mean?"

"I should think my meaning is clear."

"Well, yes, I suppose I seduced her. I mean I wanted it to happen." He nodded. "I wasn't the first," I added. Then, since that sounded like an excuse, "But when I seduced her I thought I was the first."

"And you have since discovered you were not?"

It was my turn to nod. "Neither first nor last."

He turned the thing over in his mind. "To some degree that mitigates your responsibility for her wrongdoing, though not for your own." He looked at me. "And she is the only girl you have known carnally?"

I saw myself moodily chewing on Martha's thighs. "Yes," I said.

Father paused to take stock. I continued to sit upright, though inwardly I had begun to sag. I was being eroded underwater, and shortly North Sea swells would break my dikes and like some modern city of the plain—Rotterdam, for instance—I would find myself lying under ten feet of salt water.

Father got up and went to the window. He did some looking into the side yard. His was the only downstairs room that looked into the yard. The others were as dark as caves because of those splendid, wide porches.

Over his shoulder Father said, "It's a great responsibility to be a father, Samuel. Some day, perhaps, you will feel it yourself."

I devoutly hoped not, but said nothing.

Father fastened his hands behind his back and went on contemplating the side yard. "It is a great responsibility," he said. He was never above repeating a good line. "And you have not been an easy son to raise."

He had not been an easy father to have raising one, but it was the sort of point that never got made during these talks. Still with his back to me, Father said, "I should perhaps say I am somewhat encouraged by what you have just told me. I feared that, in the army, surrounded by men of lax or no standards at all, you might be tempted to give way." It was a nice sidelight on his view of Harvard. I wondered if I should tell him about Bartoldi, but at that point he turned around and looked at me. "I do not know how best to advise you," he said. "If what you have just told me is true," (his remarks frequently contained that proviso) "you have already experienced the unhappiness that comes from yielding to impulse. Perhaps I do not need to point the moral."

He seemed to want some response, so I said, "I don't think you do."

He nodded, and for a while we had one of those silences that did so much to enliven these talks between us. At last Father sighed and went back to his desk. I started to rise, but he waved me back into place. There was more coming.

He gave me a brooding look. Then he said, "One can be unchaste alone, Samuel." I nodded. "Have you been touching yourself?" he asked. This was a little euphemism we used when we discussed sexual matters, for this was by no means the first time we'd waltzed together over these green fields.

I looked him in the eye. "No, Sir," I said.

He stared at me thoughtfully. There was always the possibility I was lying, of course. He had to take that into consideration. Then, rather dryly, he said, "I am glad to hear it."

The things that made him glad and drove me wild were legion. We were a good team. I couldn't have asked for a father more calculated to drive me up the wall, and he couldn't have gotten a son more eager to bring the roof down over his head. It was a great act. Too bad vaudeville was dead.

I must have missed one of his sentences about then, because when next I tuned in he was saying, "Your morals are not really bad, Samuel, though you are given to the expression of extravagant opinions which might naturally cast doubt on the integrity of your character." A pause here to give us both time to think about some of my extravagant opinions. Then, "What concerns me even more than your occasional moral lapses is your apparent unhappiness."

"Do you think I'm unhappy?" I asked.

His answer was a firm and prompt "Yes." And did I detect some relish there? Never mind, he was going right on. "I have given a great deal of thought to your actions last winter. The only conclusion I can come to is that you were motivated by some unhappy sense of desperation." He looked at me as if challenging me to deny it. "Blowing up the riverbank. Rushing into the army . . ." He shook his head. "I have been very worried about you, Samuel."

"I'm all right, really," I said.

"I do not agree."

109

And at that moment, neither did I. God, he could make me feel gloomy when he put his mind to it.

He said, "We are not going to discuss religion. I am persuaded that the root of your unhappiness and trouble lies in your loss of faith. I have hopes that your visit with Father Groves may have some results. It will always be my prayer that eventually you will recover what you have lost, but personally I shall no longer attempt to press upon you the faith you have rejected.

Press it upon me, I thought. Go on, do it.

> For I
> Except you enthrall me, never shall be free,
> Nor ever chaste except you ravish me.

If he'd gone on a little longer, he might have had me down on my knees. But he never fully pressed his advantages.

He said, "I have questioned you this morning because I am aware that deep feelings of sexual guilt in young," sniff, "men can often lead to the sort of despairing and reckless actions we have seen. And to some degree my suspicion has been confirmed. Your relationship with this rather abandoned young woman . . ."

Abandoned! Martha abandoned! With Shuttleworth on top of her and me waiting in the wings? Well, yes, perhaps that was abandonment. But these thoughts caused me to miss another couple of sentences, and when I was conscious again, Father was winding it up. With a new twist.

"I am aware," he was saying . . . He was always saying "I am aware" and "it appears." From listening to him one got the impression he saw everything, until one heard what he was actually saying. What he was actually saying on this occasion was, "Of course, legally, you are not yet an adult, but since you are in the army, and since you have already passed

110

your twentieth birthday, I feel that from now on I must treat you with a difference."

What was this? I pricked up my ears, fascinated to hear what would come next.

Father said, "I must face the fact that you are beyond any means of physical and moral control that I can exercise. Perhaps you have been for some years."

Don't you believe it, I thought. You're closing in all the time.

"From now on," he said, "I shall watch—and so will your mother—we shall watch you with the greatest concern and affection, but I shall not require an accounting from you." He looked at me almost sadly. "I have decided I must treat you as an adult henceforth."

An adult with some future! Oh melancholy manumission, yet sorting it out and reading the fine print, it seemed to me I had probably gained something. Not anything very good or worth having, but something.

Later, when Mother asked me what Father and I had talked about, I said, "He wanted to know whether I've been visiting prostitutes."

Mother shook her head. "What unhappy women they must be."

"I don't know. I've never visited any."

"Well, of course you haven't," Mother said. "I'm surprised he ever doubted you." Then she handed me a letter from Boston. "This came a few days ago," she said. "I put it on my desk to keep for you, and I found it just now when I was writing to Cousin Mary Crompton Shale."

"How's she?" I asked.

"Dying," Mother said.

I took the letter up to my room and sat down at my desk to study the postmark: Boston, Mass. P.M. 2 Sept. 1950. I gathered, then, that one of my Boston admirers had tripped down to the corner one afternoon twelve days before and with her own white hand had pushed this greenish-colored envelope into the red and blue mailbox. A pretty picture. I picked up the envelope and sniffed it.

After a bit I opened it.

Dear Sammy,

We're just back from Chatham. The weather was lousy most of the summer, and now I'm getting ready for school again.

Why haven't you written? Are you still angry?

Martha

That was all, there wasn't any more—as I ascertained by looking at the back of the sheet and peering into the empty envelope.

I sat for a little while with my eyes closed. Wasn't life hopeless enough without this? Cousin Mary Crompton Shale dying, the poor unhappy prostitutes, Father treating me as an adult . . . did I have to take this, too? Then I opened my eyes and reread the letter.

It made no better sense the second time round. I tried reading it backwards. ¿Angry still you are? ¿Written you haven't why? Then I translated it into French. *Nous venons de rentrer de Chatham. Le temps a été moche tout l'été, et maintenant je me prépare à nouveau pour l'université. Pourquoi tu n'écris pas? Tu es encore en colère?* . . . How would it sound in German? After a bit, I tore off a corner and chewed it meditatively while I studied the four sentences Martha had seen fit to compose. Somewhere, I was convinced, there was a message for me, if only I could get it.

That night I had another vision into Western civilization. I saw that happiness was the worst rationalization of all. How dared those miserable old Greeks and Hebrews with their lousy climate and incessant wars and atrocious dooms, how dared they even raise the possibility of men

112

being happy? Socrates talking about the good life! Isaiah putting specious words in the Lord's mouth! *Comfort ye, comfort ye saith the Lord. Speak ye comfortably to Jerusalem and cry unto her that her warfare is accomplished.* Ha! Jerusalem's warfare was just getting well under way when Isaiah wrote those words. And yet both Socrates and Isaiah paled into insignificance compared to the Christian message. What a flood of false expectations had been let loose there! I thought of the early Christians, their hearts reeling with love as the Empire collapsed around them and the aqueducts dried up. Ahead stretched more than a thousand years when no one could have even a decent bath, and all they talked about was being washed in the Blood of the Lamb. Well, thank God I'd seen through it all early enough so I could go through the rest of my life with a firm, sober, rational understanding that things were just going to get worse and worse.

12

The day I visited Father Groves was another day of newspaper apocalypse. We came down to breakfast to find that General of the Armies Douglas Arthur MacArthur had just executed the greatest military coup since Cannae. He had landed two American divisions at Inchon, the port of Seoul, thus threatening the communications of the North Korean army massed around our perimeter on the Naktong.

"You see?" Father said. Father regarded MacArthur as a Christian and a gentleman, while I thought of him as a joke. Neither of us had the General really taped.

"It was the obvious thing to do," I said. "He has complete control of the sea."

"It appears to be a brilliantly executed stroke," Father said. Then he hogged the front page, reading up on the details, leaving Mother and me to fill in the conversational vacuum.

"Perhaps this means the war will be over soon," Mother said.

"Don't you believe it," I told her. "MacArthur will louse things up yet."

Father raised his head. "Louse? What kind of language is that to use to your mother?" He had promoted me to adult the day before, but where verbal niceties were concerned he was still Captain of the Ship. Not for nothing was he a minister of The Word.

Mother said, "I know you hope the fighting won't end before you get there, Samuel, but I'm relieved."

"Don't you think someone in the family ought to get into this war?" I asked.

"I don't think that sort of tradition is so important any more," Mother said.

Father said, "Your cousin John Logan's regiment is in the Inchon landings."

"Well, isn't that nice?" Mother said. She smiled at me. "Maybe you'll meet him." So it was with this prospect of a peaceful family reunion in Korea that I went off an hour later to discuss my chances of eternal peace with Father Groves.

Father had spoken of Groves as a sympathetic young man; I was therefore prepared to meet a pious jerk. Groves seemed to be neither the one nor the other. He looked tough to me. One of those priests who played football until he got the Call. I hoped he wasn't going to scare me, and probably for that reason I was unusually cordial in my greetings. "It's awfully nice of you to talk to me," I said. "I've been needing help. I hope I'm not interrupting anything?" I put in that last because his desk looked as if he were in the process of composing about ten sermons at once.

"No," he said. "Sit down."

I sat and looked at his desk some more.

He waved a large hand over the mass of papers. "I've been working on a book," he explained, though that didn't seem to me to explain it. Here was a messy person or my eyes deceived me. And somehow that made me feel more at my ease and less likely to be intimidated by him, though at the same time I maintained my cordiality. It's always well to be cordial with the clergy, just in case.

"Well, it's certainly nice of you to take the time," I said. He made no answer, and I myself had begun to feel that we'd had about as much of that as we needed. "What's your book about?" I asked.

"The Kingdom of God," he said.

I waited hopefully, but he was not one of your talkative authors. Just what had Father found sympathetic about him?

115

His mass? His specific gravity? Not his looks, certainly. Father was a handsome man himself and preferred people to be good-looking rather than otherwise, if that could be arranged without any loss of spiritual values. Maybe he'd liked Groves' views on the Eucharist, whatever they might be? *What do you think of the Eucharist?* I was about to ask when the silence seemed to have been going on too long. Talks with Father were difficult enough, but a talk with Groves promised to be even more excruciating. Maybe that was what Father had found sympathetic about him?

He spoke at last. "You blew up the riverbank?"

"Oh, Father told you about that?"

His head moved.

"Yes, I did blow up a little bit of it." For some reason I felt the need to minimize the size of my explosion.

"Whereabouts?" he asked.

"Well, it happened where I was going to college . . . Harvard." I would have liked to minimize the Harvard note, too. I decided that in spite of his messiness, Groves definitely was going to scare me.

"Where on the riverbank?" he asked. Then he explained, "I went to Harvard too. I'm trying to visualize the thing."

"Oh! Well! In that case . . ." and then I told him all about it.

He nodded heavily when I'd put him in the picture. "And you didn't kill anyone?" he said.

"Oh, no."

"Then what's your father so worried about?" he asked.

"He always worries about me."

"Why?"

"*Why?*" I found that one of the strangest questions I'd ever heard. It was a self-evident, perhaps *the* self-evident proposition of my existence that I was the sort of person who ought to be worried about, if not by myself then by Father. Groves seemed to be upsetting the whole apple cart.

"Yes, what's he so worried about?"

"Well, I mean . . . everything. What I'm going to do. Whether I'm going to be killed. Why I don't believe in Jesus. Why I blew up the riverbank. I mean, there are things for him to worry about." I found it a little offensive that this rector should presume to question the validity of his bishop's worries. "I mean, I worry about myself."

Groves passed a hand over his cheek as if he were checking on whether he needed a shave. Then he said, "Well you ought to believe in Jesus, but other than that I don't see much to worry about."

"You don't?"

"There's the war," he conceded. "You may have something to worry about there." He grinned pleasantly. "I was in the Second War," he added. "Normandy."

His sympathetic quality suddenly came through to me. Blindingly, in fact. Real soldiers are usually the nicest of men. "What was it like?" I said.

He thought about it for a moment. "The thing to do," he said at last, "is just concentrate on what you're supposed to be doing and forget about the rest."

It sounded like good advice. I thanked him. "And you think I should believe in Jesus?"

"That's for sure," he said.

He even made that sound pretty authentic. What a treasure the church had picked up when Groves was ordained! "Where'd you do your seminary work?" I asked.

"Harvard," he said.

He pronounced it with the flat *a*. "You're from Massachusetts?" I asked.

"Cambridge," he said, and so for another ten or fifteen minutes we chatted happily about the familiar streets. Then I felt I was taking up time that might be better spent on the Kingdom of God, so I got to my feet. "It's been very nice meeting you, Father," I said. "I'll think over what you've told me."

"You do that," he said.

117

We shook hands, he saw me out, and then presumably went back to work on his manuscript. I floated home.

Father was lurking around. "You weren't gone very long," he said.

"We had a good talk."

"Yes?"

"Tell me, is Father Groves effective in pastoral work?"

"I have had very good reports of him," Father said.

"How's his theology?"

"Quite sound. Rather conservative, I believe. He has not shown me the manuscript on which he is working."

"I liked him," I said.

"I am glad to hear it."

He was obviously dying to hear more, but I went on upstairs. The moment was too precious to be spoiled in prolonged conversation with Father. I had just been told by a man in holy orders not patently out of his mind that all I had to do was concentrate on the thing before me in Korea, and believe in Jesus. And while that advice might not be particularly easy to carry out, nevertheless the simplifications and clarifications provided by the Groves formula were about the most luminous and welcome I'd received for a long time.

I looked around my old bedroom and felt a sharp need to throw things away and put things in order before I left for the war. So I went to work burning old poems and diaries, throwing out letters, and even getting rid of all my collections: stamps, coins, shells, butterflies, and gruesome old bubble gum cards with pictures of the Japanese rape of China. Mother took them off to some charitable organization of hers.

On my last night we had steak and baked potatoes and more beans than I can well enumerate. Mother had planned the meal for me. There was a fatted calf atmosphere in the air, if not a Last Supper mood. From time to time I looked up at Bishop Benedict with his hand on the globe, and thought to myself that pretty soon I would be on the other side of that globe, Samuel in Korealand, where I could run my legs off without bumping into anything or even getting anywhere. It was a comforting thought. Then a spice cake was brought in, decorated with twenty candles. For reasons of her own, Mother was celebrating my birthday five months late. I'm Taurus, and here we were in Scorpio. As I blew out the candles I felt I ought to make a Death Wish.

Afterwards we went out on the porch. It was a hot September night. The crops were in, the leaves were turning, and soon the hunting season would begin. We sat thinking of these things. To keep from attracting bugs, we sat in the dark, silent and rather logy from all the food we had eaten. I could smell Mother's geraniums that hung in pots along the side of the porch. I could smell Father's cigar, and see its glowing trajectory from mouth to armrest. The swing on which I sat squeaked from time to time. Bats shrilled as they circled the house, feeding on the bugs we weren't attracting. Along the horizon there was an occasional flicker of lightning.

"Now you will write regularly?" Mother said.

I promised.

Father cleared his throat but didn't speak, though I could imagine him saying, "Son, how about a fishing trip up Mount Moriah way?" He was still miffed that I'd refused to go to his cathedral that afternoon for a spot of quiet meditation, if not prayer. I'd refused because, although he'd promised to lay off the rough stuff and treat me as an adult, I wasn't sure I really trusted him. What if he'd mustered his canons and given them orders to frog-march me into confessional? After which a quick low mass, and then holy communion, a burly verger holding me down, while an altar boy pinched my nose to make me open my mouth for the wafer. Then the descent of the Dove and perhaps the gift of

119

tongues. I didn't think I could risk it, but Father had been miffed. I sensed it was pretty much touch and go whether he most wanted to sacrifice me to his God or save my soul.

So there we sat, a perfect example of what sociologists call the nuclear family unit: Father, Mother, and Son. Sociologists are not usually poets, but they couldn't have found a better term, since the nuclear American family produces mushroom clouds and fallout all its own, as I am here to tell you.

Presently Mother said, "There's some more lightning. I think we're going to have a storm."

We did. The heavens opened and thunder shook the windowpanes as we were getting ready for bed. Mother came to my room, ostensibly to see that I'd closed the windows, actually to say, "Now, Samuel, I don't ask you to be heroic. Just do your duty."

Five minutes later Father turned up in his dressing gown. "You do remember the Act of Contrition?" he said.

"Really," I told him, "both you and Mother behave as if I'm going to be killed."

"I am aware of no such premonition," Father said. I didn't believe him for a moment. A clean death in Korea with the Act of Contrition on my lips was just the thing his doctor would order.

"Well, then, what's this about the Act of Contrition?" I asked.

"It is perfectly reasonable and natural that I should wish to know whether you remember it."

"How could I forget it?" I asked.

"It seems to me you have forgotten a good deal of what you have been taught."

"You're wrong," I said. "I haven't forgotten a thing."

"In that case, I shall bid you good night," Father said.

Ah home, home, sweet home! Though a few days later, as we trundled across Colorado in a troop train, I decided that if Father didn't exist, I would have had to invent him, for I was feeling combative again. I had Martha's letter with me, and the more I read it, the more I felt I couldn't go off to war without doing something in that direction.

In Seattle I made my move. Before we sailed I got change for ten dollars. Then, my pockets obscenely distended with coins, I found an empty telephone booth and put in a call to Cambridge. Operator talked to operator. Routes and numbers were discussed, switches clicked, connections were made, Cambridge information provided the number of Radcliffe College, Radcliffe information provided the number of Miss Sears, and finally on the other side of the continent a telephone bell rang and presently I could hear Martha saying, "Hello?"

"This is Samuel," I said.

"Sammy! Where are you?" She sounded pleased.

"In Seattle. I sail for Korea tomorrow."

"I thought something like that might be happening. Why didn't you write?"

"Why did *you* write?" I asked. "Is Shuttleworth out of your life?"

"Are you still mad about that?" she asked.

"I asked you a question."

"I can tell you're still mad."

"All right, I am," I said.

"Poor Sammy," said Martha.

"And what about Shuttleworth?" I asked.

"Poor him, too. I haven't seen him since July."

"Then will you marry me?" I asked.

"How can I?" she said. "You're going to Korea."

"I'll be back," I said.

"Well ask me then."

She seemed very chirpy about it all.

121

"Martha," I said, "I don't trust you. I want it understood that we're to be married, or I don't want to have anything more to do with you."

"Oh, don't you?" she said, the chirpiness suddenly gone from her voice.

"Do you understand?" I asked. "I can forgive you once, but I couldn't forgive you again, so if you want to marry me, you better say *Yes* now."

There was a short silence. Then, enunciating her words very distinctly, Martha said, "Damn you, Samuel," and hung up on me.

I felt she had no call to take that tone, and so the next day I sailed off, smoldering, into the blue Pacific on my way to a war.

BOOK TWO

13

Now of arms and the man I must sing and of Korea and the fate that befell me there, for we have come to the predominately historical part of this confession and history is war. And war is a delicate topic. In a nineteenth-century story sex was unmentionable, while war was frankly accepted as part of life. Now the situation is almost reversed. The Mrs. Grundys of pacifism have taken over from the Anthony Comstocks of sex and we writer chaps are no better off than we were. We can write about war but we have to approach it very carefully for fear of offending the susceptibilities of our readers. And, of course, carefulness was notably lacking in my attitude in 1950. By the time I arrived in Korea I was rather looking forward to action. After all, the North Korean army was in full dissolution. The war seemed to be won— General MacArthur had recently said so—and I saw my Korean service as essentially a mopping-up exercise followed by a victory parade through Pyongyang. I felt fully equal to taking part in a victory parade. Indeed it sounded like fun. Doubtless there were beautiful, freedom-loving North Korean girls who would swarm into the streets to kiss us. It would be like the liberation of Paris, an event I was sorry I'd missed.

We debarked at night. I remember the sound of our clumsy boots clattering on the gangplank. The sweet menagerie smell of the troop ship was replaced by a bitter frostiness laced with underlying odors of dung. The sky was huge. On the horizon, flares. I was looking at the sky and so I bumped into the man ahead of me. "What's the effing hurry?" he asked. The familiar words made me laugh. "Montjoie St.

Denis!" I cried. "Christ!" said someone else. Then I heard the sharp word of command, "Shut up, Heather." It was Master Sergeant Simmons somewhere ahead of me. I stopped laughing. Order was restored. Ten days later we were in battle.

And now occurs one of those hitches that do so much to disturb the even flow of my narrative, for when I found myself in actual battle I discovered all at once that *Montjoie St. Denis* was not the right formula for the kind of thing that was shaping up around me. It's a great war cry, of course, the old war cry of the French monarchy, heard on every battlefield from Roncevalles to Fontenoy, but it does not apply to Korea. I might just as well have shouted *No Taxation Without Representation,* or *Remember the Maine!* Once again I had been misled by my books.

At that time I didn't know about Proust. Proust has one great war scene in which the Baron de Charlus is chained and flagellated in an upper room of Jupien's brothel while German zeppelins drop bombs on Paris. It is an obviously fruitful scene. Indeed, I consider it the necessary starting point for any serious attempt to get at the nature of modern war, but somehow the modern writers I'd read had not followed in Proust's trailblazing footsteps. I knew Hemingway, of course, but Hemingway was no help to me. He was as hopelessly out of date as I was. Indeed he was an admirer of Stendhal and Tolstoy, who were my teachers, too. Hemingway looked modern, but he smelled not exactly of the museums, as Gertrude Stein used to say, but of Captain George's shooting gallery in *Bleak House.* Hemingway was a sharpshooter and a big-game hunter in the age of the barrage, carpet-bombing, and the mushroom cloud. Don't talk to me about Hemingway. My advice to young men facing the draft is, Throw away your copies of *Farewell to Arms,* and shoulder *Remembrance of Things Past.* You may not finish it before the war is over, but it will give you something to think about and it may illuminate your experiences.

But as I say, I couldn't have given and wasn't in a position to take such advice twenty years ago when things began to get lively on the morning of November 26, 1950. Then I found myself high and dry on the seas of modern war with no literary guidelines as to what was happening or how I felt about it. We need another Homer, or at least a Tolstoy to describe modern war. The British lost fifty thousand men on the first day of the Somme offensive in 1916, and what's come out of that? Some Georgian poems, parts of Graves' autobiography, and a couple of lovely pages in *Tender is the Night*. Nothing else that I know of, and fifty thousand is a lot of men. More than were killed at Troy in ten years. And I calculate that in the Second World War fifty major cities were entirely wrecked, together with thousands of lesser places each the size of Priam's six-gated city, so to celebrate devastation on that scale we need perhaps five hundred Homers, together with corresponding numbers of Virgils, Chaucers, and Shakespeares to complete the story and fill in the details.

It's a little hard that a child of the century should be required to venture out onto the battlefield without the help of twentieth-century master poets and novelists capable of leading him through the crossfire, but I'm afraid that's what is about to happen. Our twentieth-century father artists, who should have been forging in the smithies of their souls the uncreated battles of the age, have—always excepting Proust —shirked their duty and devoted their great talents to piddling matters. Hence you see me, Reader, engaged in a doubly difficult task. At twenty I was fighting a war I didn't understand, and at forty I am obliged to write about it without being able to beg, borrow, or steal the correct style. Yet write I must, since if I wait around for a modern Homer to show me how to tell my story, I may never get it told.

So there I was on the morning of November 26, dug into the slope of a Korean hillside and looking down into a dark wood of scrub oak and screw pine. On my right Pfc. Winterode was dug into the same slope, and beyond Winterode the keen-eyed observer (for it was a dark night) might discern Private Dalbert in *his* hole. There we were like three characters in a Beckett play, or three musketeers in a Dumas novel, or three blind mice in a nursery rhyme, though none of the comparisons is really any good.

All three of us had our eyes on that wood. Mark those trees, stranger, for they shelter not so much the defeated remnants of the North Korean army as woodland folk of another stripe. We could hear them at their revels, playing on their shepherd's pipes, blowing their horns, and generally getting ready to come out of the wood and cast their spell upon us.

I will not speak for Winterode and Dalbert, but personally I felt threatened, for down below, not to make a secret of it any longer, the entire Chinese army was massing for an attack. An unexpected thing had happened. "We must face the fact," General MacArthur wrote, "that the situation has changed and this is now an entirely new war."

Later on I will have something to say about General MacArthur, but for the moment the situation is too tense for a digression on High Command. Let me only say that our company had jumped off on the morning of the twenty-fifth as MacArthur's great *On To the Yalu* offensive started, and now, less than twenty-four hours later, we were surrounded by the Chinese. First, Second, and Third Platoons were dug into the slopes in an all-around defense. Fourth Platoon, which had gotten lost during the day, might, or perhaps might not be encamped on a neighboring hilltop from which we could hear firing. For the time being all was silent on our front except for the shepherd's pipes and the bugle calls in the wood below. The rest of the United States Army—to give you a bird's-eye view of the situation—had gotten separated from our company. We didn't know where Generals Walker and Kaiser were, but we hoped they were safe. MacArthur

128

was in Tokyo, so his well-being didn't press on our mind.

And now I come to the first shot that was ever fired in anger against me, personally. It went *bang*, and Heather, who had been lying on his stomach, felt his stomach turn over, leaving him—if life were as literal as cliché—lying on his back. Actually, he continued to lie on his stomach, turned over though it was. His heart, which had suddenly enlarged and turned into a stone, pressed heavily into his chest, causing him such discomfort that he would have moved aside if he could have moved. He stared downhill through the night trying to discern his enemies. If he felt like saying, "Come out of those woods and fight like men," he didn't say it.

There was noise of some sort going on around him. He couldn't identify the harmony. It was not Mozart or anything like that, nor was it a subway train nor a pneumatic hammer. It was just noise of some loud variety going on around, above, and behind him. It was shooting, he presumed. It might be mortar shells exploding, he thought. Or someone could be dynamiting something in the vicinity. Whatever its source, the noise was loud, continuous, and subtly varied. One got the impression—this at least was the impression Heather got—that one was listening to the music of the future when woodwinds and strings have been definitely suppressed and all is percussion and racket.

In the midst of this racket, Heather was no longer certain that his enemies, if any, were going *bang* at him. He had not, so far as he could tell, been killed as yet, or even wounded. Nor had he seen anything to fire at, though of course, missing all the fingers on his right hand, he felt it would be a difficult job to pull the trigger of his M-1. He had never before noticed that all his fingers were missing, and he wondered how he had gotten into the army with such a handicap. An oversight of some sort. A great many oversights seemed to be taking place all around him.

All this that I have recorded took place in one or perhaps two seconds. We literary men clump along well to the rear of reality. Heather, whose age had been twenty when the firing broke out, had shot up to a paralyzing ninety and was now sinking rapidly toward three, traversing one hundred and fifty-seven years in a matter of seconds. This put him back in 1793 when General Washington was taking office for the second time as President of the United States, while in France Louis XVI was about to be guillotined, which showed that good republican virtue paid off every time when compared to foreign despotism. Or, if one counted forward, Heather was now living in the first decade of the twenty-second century, when demographers calculate that ten out of every nine people alive will be Chinese. So why, he wondered, were his own countrymen firing at him?

Time passed. Heather's rifle, which had been given to him by the United States Army and which he had cleaned many times and mantled and dismantled with admirable facility, lay now two or three inches just beyond the grip of the hand in which he clutched it. That was odd. He thought leisurely about the matter. What was this substance between his hand and the rifle? It could not be air. It could not be water. It could not be earth or fire, and those were the only four elements he knew about. It might, he supposed, be something discovered since Mendeleev had invented the table of the four elements, if indeed Mendeleev was the man he was thinking of. Heather was conscious that his knowledge of physical chemistry was shaky.

Taking a firmer grip of his rifle he found that whatever element had been between his hand and the stock had disappeared as mysteriously as it had appeared. The gun was in his hands, and, to his surprise, he noted that his fingers, which had not been there a while before, were now rigid and white with tension.

This is a gun I'm holding, he thought. It may not seem brilliant to the reader, but the idea presented itself to

Heather with a sort of Archimedean shock of recognition.

A gun. There was some idea connected with guns, some lingering memory in Heather's mind of something a sergeant had once said to him. He believed, though it seemed implausible, that he had once been lying on the ground somewhere in Texas or Massachusetts or one of those states with a gun in his hand. Yes. Yes, that was it. He had been lying on the ground with a gun in his hand, a gun very much like the one he could see he was now holding. And then, way back there in Texachusetts, he had done something with his gun. What?

Eons passed, fire was discovered, and the slingshot replaced the boomerang while Heather grappled with this problem. We are now at the fifth or sixth second of his actual experience of war, and so far we have seen how the mind and body of a trained soldier work under conditions of combat. There is first the tactical appreciation of the situation: someone is firing at me! There is then an instantaneous, very complex physical reaction. After all, a young man in good condition is a magnificent and complicated organism, capable of going through literally millions of reactions in no time at all. An old soldier might just have lain like a lump on that hillside and fired back at the Chinese without going through one quarter of the gymnastics Heather performed without even moving a finger.

This is impressive, but though we have seen Heather appreciate the situation and react to it physically, and though we have watched the orderly marshaling of his thoughts, we cannot help but notice that he has not yet begun to fight. We left him, if you remember, faced with the problem of what one does with a gun.

Heather in his younger manhood had known a girl, not Martha, who told him in all seriousness that she did not believe in war. He had been dancing with her at the time. In those days it was not enough for him to have his arms around a girl; he felt he should improve each shining hour with con-

131

versation, and so, for his pains, he had learned that his partner did not believe in war. He found that odd because the year was 1946 and the globe had just recently been convulsed by something remarkably *like* a war. Had his partner been on some other planet? Didn't she read the newspapers or go to the movies? Why didn't she believe in war? What would it take to convince her? Heather put the question to her. "My parents are Friends," she said. Heather, who felt his mother was friendly but not his father, remarked that he didn't see what that had to do with it. "We don't approve of killing," she told him.

It made sense, of course, and Heather saw the logic, for in war someone is bound to get killed, and if one disapproves of killing one must necessarily disapprove of war. Heather had been misled by the girl's use of the word *believe*. What she should have said was that she did not like war, or did not approve of war, but everyone, as Heather then argued, must believe in war because war is real.

How true, Heather thought, remembering the incident four years later. How well argued! He felt a surge of admiration for his younger self. What a bright, promising sixteen-year-old he had been! So able in argument, both on and off dance floors. And what a profound insight! War is real! With a good start like that, what had happened to arrest his development? For, as he lay in a real war with a real gun in his hands, he was conscious of a nagging sensation in the back of his mind that something else remained to be done. There was some conclusion which still eluded his intelligence. What could it be? It worried Heather that he didn't know the answer, because in spite of his father's opinion, Heather was a young man with a high sense of duty. If there was something more to be done he wanted to know what it was.

We have reached the tenth second of Heather's war, and notice what progress has been made. Heather has recovered from his low point of three and is now almost his own age. It is 1810. Madison is President, and shortly the War of 1812 will break out. Washington will burn, the Battle of Lake Erie will be fought, and Lafitte's pirates will help Andy Jackson win the battle of New Orleans. Oddly enough no Clay or Heather fell in that conflict, for though the young hawk Henry Clay had done much to precipitate the war, he survived his handiwork and lived to become the Great Compromiser.

But wait! There was the Jones connection. Heather had been forgetting Ezekiel Jones, who had been shot during the battle known as Dudley's Defeat. And that memory seemed to give Heather a line toward the solution of his present problem. People were killed in war by being shot with guns! That was why he had been remembering that Friend he once danced with. That was what they were doing when they were lying on the ground in Massatexas. They were *pulling the triggers* of their guns. They were shooting at targets. Yes, targets, whose black silhouettes he could dimly remember. He tried to picture them more clearly. They reminded him of something. In school—had it been first or second grade?— Teacher had brought in a slide projector one day, and each member of the class stood in profile in a beam of light while Teacher traced the outline of the child's head onto a sheet of black paper. Then the class snipped around the outlined heads, pasted them onto large sheets of white paper, and took the results home to Mother and Father. Those had been silhouettes, human silhouettes. And the Marquis de Silhouette—let's get it all in because it's there in the head just waiting to come out whether it's useful or not—the Marquis de Silhouette was finance minister under Louis XV. His taxes threatened to reduce Frenchmen to silhouettes of themselves, which is how we get the word. It was all falling into place. On the firing range during training one shot at outlines of the human form divine, while in real war—his mind leaping ahead now, tumbling downhill to hard conclusions—in real war one shot at real men. Heather had arrived. He looked downhill where there were now Chinese soldiers pointing their guns at him. He pointed his gun at them and fired.

Computers! Give me the human mind any day. It took only fourteen or fifteen seconds for Heather's brain to discover he was being fired at, that he had a gun in his hand, and that in war one fired one's gun at the enemy. What prodigies of memory, thought, and feeling compressed into a small space of time! Computers are nowhere, though they have one advantage over us: they don't grow tired, whereas I have somewhat fatigued myself in reconstructing this occasion, the first on which I seriously tried to kill a man. I believe I will knock off for the day and begin a new chapter tomorrow when I will be feeling fresh.

14

These chapters are necessarily different in tone and style from my earlier ones because I have grown a bit older, and I had no one to talk to except Winterode, and he was dead, as you shall see.

The first Chinese attack lasted about thirty minutes, a rather important half hour in my life. It is perhaps wicked to point guns at other people, but when they are being as wicked as you, then you must face the problem of whether the world will be better off if you kill them or they kill you. I solved that problem on the morning of November 26. It was the first major problem in my life which I did solve, and I worked my way through it in fifteen seconds, which is about par for the solution of major problems. Trivial matters take a lot of thought, but basic decisions are quick. I had such a deep and intimate conviction that my life was more valuable than the lives of the men trying to kill me that when I finally understood the situation I fired and went on firing until the attack ceased as abruptly as it had begun.

I was exhausted when it was over. I felt heavy, as if I had been absorbing lead rather than firing it. I wanted to sleep, but there was something I wanted even more than sleep if only I could think what it was. What was it?

The silence which succeeded the attack bothered me and hampered my thinking. It was very ominous, that silence. I would have preferred noise just then, for at times the noise had been a positive comfort. There was something huge, ungainly, and even playful about the noise, as if a pod of whales were cavorting in an ocean of tin pans. Now the leviathans had sounded. They were somewhere fathoms deep in the seas of the night, and rather than think about what I wanted before I slept, I found myself listening for some sound.

It came. On the hillside to my right I heard an American voice call out softly, "You okay?" Wonderful syllables. The first GI's into Dachau probably looked around at the starving heaps of what had been human beings and said, with real concern in their voices, "Hey, you guys okay?" thus starting the world on its slow process of recovery from the frozen madness into which Hitler had plunged it. An evil as complicated as Dachau can only be defeated by a simplicity as uncomplicated as asking a starving man if he's okay. There's no point in trying to understand Dachau; in fact, you're lucky if you don't. But I digress.

Across the ravine I heard Wolfson call out to Smith. Further up the hill I heard another voice. Buddy was checking with buddy. Their voices were like pinpoints of light in the darkness. I had been shown what I wanted. I called out to Winterode.

He didn't answer. I lay for a bit, still feeling heavier than I had ever felt. It was as if the weight of a whole other body had been added to the one I already had, making me twice as large and vulnerable as I had been before. How could Chinese bullets have missed this mountain of flesh I had become? But they had missed. I lay there on the side of the hill, enormous, heavy, and exhausted, but unable to go to sleep until I had checked with Winterode. So hoisting myself up—I needed a derrick really—I crawled across the intervening yards that separated our holes.

I had never before felt the force of that phrase *earthly remains,* but it is exactly right. It was as if some robust but sloppy feeder—Death, for instance—had started to chew Winterode's head and then dropped the whole thing to go off in search of a fresher morsel, leaving Winterode's body and legs perfectly intact.

I lay on the ground for a while looking at the results.

One hears a lot about the waste of war, and I suppose that was what I was thinking about, though not quite in the sense that pacifists mean the phrase. Winterode's shattered head did not move me nearly so much as his legs and feet which were still perfectly usable if only Winterode had been around to use them. I was outraged by those untouched legs. What I felt was, *Why didn't they finish the job?* I wanted Winterode to have been totally consumed by war, his whole body volatilized by high explosives so that nothing whatever remained, not even the kind of human orts and scraps they dug out of the trenches in the First World War and put together and called *The Unknown Soldier.*

One hopes at least to die beautifully even if one cannot live beautifully. At Harvard I had known a veteran of the Second War who told me about what might have been a great death. He was wounded in Italy at the crossing of the Garigliano, and when he came to himself he was lying on a hillside beneath a flowering almond tree. He was on his back, looking up through the branches of the tree at a cloudless blue sky as lofty and pure as the sky Prince André saw when he lay on the battlefield of Austerlitz. My friend knew he was badly wounded. Indeed, he felt sure he was dying, but he wasn't afraid or even sad. Looking up through the flowering almond to the heaven beyond, he simply felt how wonderful it was to have lived in such a beautiful world. Then the sky began to darken, which he took as a sign of failing sight. *It* had come. Life was over, and he felt a moment of impersonal pity for himself. "Then," he told me, "I saw a cloud and I realized the sun was not going out, and I was just wounded and there were no goddam medics around to do their stuff. I started hollering like hell."

It was a funny story in its way, though nothing is ever completely funny or even completely sad, not even Winterode's body. Still a body is a solemn object, and looking at Winterode's I didn't feel like laughing.

"Hey," I called to Dalbert, "Winterode's dead."

"We're all gonna die," Dalbert said.

There was so much in that speech I didn't like that I decided not to answer it. I looked back at Winterode's remains.

He had been a gloomy fellow, much given to a sort of growling *weltschmerz*. He and I had been dug in side by side because he was the one fellow in the company I could talk to. He was educated. He read books. He had read Spengler's *Decline of the West*, and it had impressed him favorably and profoundly. My more hopeful outlook on life struck him as frivolous and dangerously irresponsible. Now the irresponsible one was alive and Winterode, who prided himself on foreseeing the worst, was in no position to triumph over being right. For he had expected disaster to come from General MacArthur's offensive. Just the morning before he had been walking beside me, his chin dug into a long khaki scarf and a scowl on his face. We were about to cross the Chongchon River. "What's the matter?" I asked him. "Afraid of getting your feet wet?" His only answer was a scathing look.

Now there were his reproachful feet looking me in the face, so to speak, and it was his head that was wet with blood. I felt something had to be done. Winterode had been gloomy, but he cared about himself. He wouldn't want to have his body left lying in that uncomfortable position. The spirit was gone, but certain decencies had to be respected.

Reluctantly I approached the body and arranged it as well as I could, getting myself rather bloody in the process. Touching him—it—I felt a comradely sensation. In its heaviness and inertness the body had a quite human feel, as of someone who had fainted or fallen. I had once (age sixteen or so) been called next door in an emergency created by the fact that a heavy old lady with a heart condition had fallen out of her bed and couldn't be gotten up from the floor by the combined efforts of her maid and her chauffeur. I remember heaving at her body just as I heaved Winterode around so that he could lie with his head uphill, his arms at his sides, and his legs straight.

It was a clumsy process, and as I pulled and tugged at him, I felt sure he would wake up and say something sarcastic. It was just the sort of scene which would bring out his sarcasm. He disliked ineptness of all sorts. That was why he disliked the army, and General MacArthur, and Truman, and the United Nations, and the Koreans, and bad acting, and bad writing, and bad food, and bad movies, and bad weather (God's fault), and bad teaching (he had been at the U. of Chicago). He hated realistic novels, all poetry, every politician I had heard him talk about, and every scientist whose name he knew. He disliked postmen because they were too slow on their rounds, and milkmen because they woke him up in the morning. He hated hatcheck girls, doorkeepers, cops, waiters in good restaurants, most bus drivers, and all people who laughed at the wrong spots in funny movies. He was in most ways the perfect urban citizen, and there he was, lying on the soil of Korea with only a few of his gripes given permanent expression in the form of Letters-to-the-Editor, clippings of which he kept on his person and had allowed me to read. They were probably there now, I thought, buttoned inside his bloodstained battle jacket, all beginning *Sir!* and ending with resounding flourishes.

If you start thinking about dead people you find yourself bringing them back to life and reacting to them as if they are alive. When I had gotten as far as remembering Winterode's Letters-to-the-Editor, I felt like saying something to him, if only I could find him. I looked down at his body.

Should I unbutton the jacket and remove his letters and papers? Should I take his identity disc? Or wind his watch for him so that he could go on ticking for a while longer? I didn't know the answer. If only he had managed to get blown to smithereens so that none of those questions arose.

Better to die completely and be instantaneously consumed in the heat of the sun than be briefly munched, then dropped as Death shambles off into the darkness to search for other tidbits. I thought of that Japanese workman standing on a scaffold beside the concrete dome of the courthouse in Hiroshima. There, at the center of the explosion, his body had absorbed the light and heat of a thousand suns, then disappeared, leaving only a raised outline against the dome it had so briefly shielded from the full glare. His presence among us left behind a permanent shadow on that dome, a shadow on history itself. Winterode's presence had left behind just another bloody corpse.

In the end I didn't touch him again. I left him lying with his letters, his photographs, and his identity disc (Type O blood, now congealing) and whatever else he was carrying on his person when he stopped being a person. I did find his muffler, which I used to cover up his ruined head.

Sometimes I've wondered if I really thought and felt all those things at the time, or whether I've added and embroidered the experience during the last twenty years. I don't think it makes much difference one way or another. Experience is never just what happened at a particular moment, it's what you make of it after it's happened, and what you go on making of it to the very end of your life. I thought something that night. I felt something as I looked at Winterode's body. This is how I remember it now. Thirty years hence at the moment I myself die, I may remember it another way in that last instant when all our experience is gathered into one great whole and we see at last what we have truly done with our lives.

Back in my own foxhole, I found myself regretting I had not thought to take Winterode's remaining ammunition. He had no need of it now, whereas—checking—I found my supplies were low. I couldn't go back, however. Let Winterode lie there with the gun (of which he had never been proud) and the ammunition he hadn't used. It was not a Viking's death with all the trophies of war arranged around the corpse, but whatever Winterode had been he had been a reluctant soldier too and he should be left with a few last bullets. Besides, another Chinese attack was shaping up. They were blowing their bugles in the wood below.

At the thought that it was all going to happen over again I almost gave up and despaired. I couldn't go on. I had to get away somewhere to rest and think. I hadn't talked to anyone for days, it seemed, or years even. No one had said anything nice to me recently. I hadn't seen my King or Emperor to take courage from the manna of his presence. Henry V mixed with his English troops on the evening before Agincourt, just as Napoleon visited his encampments the night before Austerlitz when the French lit straw torches and shouted *Vive l'Empereur.* Tolstoy makes fun of the episode, but Tolstoy becomes just another old grouch whenever he has to describe battles the Russians didn't win. (Hey, Lev— if you're tuned in on this—you can't win them all!) Great generals *should* visit their troops and give them something to shout about. I was prepared to fight again, yes, but not the same night. Not just then. Not without some encouragement. How I would have shouted for MacArthur if he had suddenly materialized at my side.

But he didn't come and the Chinese did. From their point of view it was reasonable. They had us surrounded and outnumbered. With another attack, or another one after that, they could carry the top of the hill before dawn came and American fighter planes were able to intervene.

I estimated the number of bullets I had left. I forget now, but it was some frighteningly low number. If I fired as I had fired during the first attack I would have nothing left in a few minutes. Then the Chinese would come uphill and shoot me or bayonet me, and that would be that. Another Heather would have bitten the dust in his country's wars. As I thought of the possibility I was conscious of a certain diminution of feeling. It didn't really make that much difference, did it? A few minutes earlier I had been prepared to weep over Winterode; now I could hardly care about myself. I seemed to be going downhill spiritually. I even used a bad word. "Fuck it," I said to myself.

As a child I never swore at all. I never heard Father swear either, even when he spilled hot coffee on his lap one morning at breakfast. "I've scalded myself," he said to Mother, and hurried upstairs to change clothes. The look on his face had been impressive, but he had not sworn.

In school and at Harvard I had occasionally used a big big D, but I was an unusually clean-mouthed student at a time when standards were already beginning to go to pot. (Pot came later.) I think I had scarcely ever used the word I had just used, but with a sort of defiance I repeated the ugly syllables: "Fuck it," I said again.

My body still felt very heavy, but it seemed to have shriveled and condensed like a dwarf star. I was no longer enormous. I was no longer even sleepy. I listened to the Chinese bugling away in the woods, and said, "Okay, damn it, we'll do it again." Obviously it was going to be a long night. I hoped I would be killed soon.

The second attack found me feeling like a hard-bitten, disenchanted veteran, hopeless in his basic attitude and perfunctory in his responses. I aimed—I had not really aimed during the first attack—and fired, and aimed, and fired, and so on as if it were just something that had to be done. Bang. Bang. Bang. And around me and over me the familiar cushion of racket swelled until I couldn't hear myself go bang and wasn't even sure there were bullets left in my gun. All the earlier tumult and excitement of battle was missing, and even my tiredness had changed and gone inward until I felt my bones were old. My body remained that of a twenty-year-old, but now it was the body of an unsentimental slum kid. "Fuck 'em all," I might have said, except that one doesn't really talk while firing.

This phase of things lasted for five or ten minutes. Then, abruptly, everything changed once more and I found I was again a well-brought-up young man, and terribly afraid. I had run out of ammunition. And now that I was no longer firing, I could hear and see things I hadn't really heard or seen before. I could hear good old Dalbert still plugging away. How I liked him at the moment! And from the other side of the ravine, I could hear Smith or Wolfson firing. Further off a light machine gun was at work, so Abernathy or someone was alive there and still provided with ammunition. I wished them all well, for I could see the Chinese in a way I hadn't seen them before, and they were closer than I would have believed possible given the fact that East is East and West is West and never the twain shall meet. The Chinamen —Chinese?—were crouched in the ravine just below me firing at Smith or Wolfson, or both. I could have killed either one of them or both if I had had any bullets left.

Watching them was fascinating, and also terrible. They were masked from Wolfson or Smith by a rock. First one of them would pop out and shoot, then pop back. Then the other would do the same. They used different sides of the rock, so it was like watching one of those Swiss clocks with a fair weather and a foul weather figure that come out on either side of the base. Only instead of seeing it from the front, I was seeing it from the back, as if I were inside the clock. Then Foul Weather, instead of shooting, pulled the pin of a grenade and lofted it over the rock onto the lip of the ravine across from me. It burst, scattering fragments as far as where I lay. After that Smith or Wolfson stopped firing back, and presently both Fair and Foul Weather climbed out of

143

the ravine and moved upward across the face of the hill until I could no longer see them.

I could see other Chinese, however. There were at least five of them down below, lying on the ground partly screened by rocks. Their fire was concentrated on Dalbert. Every now and then one would rise and move forward quickly until he had found new cover. They were still out of grenade range. They fired at Dalbert and Dalbert fired back. I was beginning to think of him as a hero.

. . . the only one around, since I had become a spectator. I didn't even have grenades to throw when the Chinese should be close enough. Grenades had always struck me as heavy to carry and doubtfully useful. Now my opinion of them had gone up, and I wished that, like Winterode, I had trudged forward from the Chongchon festooned with grenades and spare ammunition. For Winterode, though unwarlike and essentially defeatist in his attitude like the French army in 1939, had believed in preparedness. He moved under a load of high explosives that other men in the company shunned. South Korean bearers were supposed to supply us when we needed such things. Winterode, not trusting Koreans of any sort, had carried his own grenades and there they lay in the hole next to mine. Along with the ammunition I had sentimentally left in place. Obviously it was time to be practical.

I leaped from my hole and jumped ten yards in one bound, tumbling down into Winterode's shelter, bumping against his dead body, and coming to rest behind the solid little parapet of stone and earth he had erected. He had worked much harder at his foxhole than I had worked at mine. Digging in the half-frozen soil had been difficult, but Winterode had nevertheless built himself if not a mighty fortress, at least a fortress of some sort. It hadn't done him much good, but it came in handy for me. I gathered in his grenades as a shipwrecked mariner might gather coconuts on

144

an atoll, and then I loaded my M-1 with one of Winterode's spare clips. I was prepared to rejoin the war. Together Dalbert and I would hold our front until dawn came and squadrons of jets screamed in from the south like the American eagle aroused and defending its young from predators. My whole mood had changed, and for the first time that morning I felt nimble and free. A kind of lighthearted alacrity came over me. When Dalbert and I had won our battle, I would take him in hand and educate him and teach him the poetry and other good things I knew. We were going to be lifelong friends, I was sure of it.

Meanwhile there were the Chinese to be taken care of. They were still firing only at Dalbert. My dash for Winterode's bunker—*festung Winterode*, I baptized it—had either escaped their attention, or else they failed to realize its extreme significance for their fate. I could get them with a grenade if they came much closer. In fact, I decided I could get them then. It was a downhill heave, though from my new position I couldn't exactly see any of them. Still, I knew approximately where they were. I pulled the pin from one of Winterode's grenades and threw it downhill with all my might. It exploded with a glorious bang, like my stick of dynamite going off on the Charles riverbank.

I shouted to Dalbert that I was with him.

But I am tired again. I'm forty-one years old now, and it takes it out of me remembering all this. I'll have to finish tomorrow. It's taken two days of hard work for a middle-aged man to reconstruct an hour of the life he lived twenty years ago. And people expect kids to go to school quietly until they're twenty-two or even older. And then settle down to a job! What a farce.

15

It is eight A.M. and I am at my typewriter again. In Korea it is four in the morning and dawn is still a long way off. The situation is the same as in the last chapter, except that the cast of characters has narrowed again. Dalbert is dead, or at least I think he is dead because he has stopped firing. The Chinese have not stopped, but now they are firing at me. If my grenade disturbed them, it has not silenced them, and at this point the war seems to be a straight proposition between Private Samuel Heather representing the Free World, and the Chinese army representing Asiatic communism.

The odds were uneven, but I was used to that. Besides, I had never been able to understand how an odd could be even, and I wasn't in the mood to give the matter any thought. I had been through a lot of ups and downs and I didn't want to puzzle or disturb the balance of my mind, for at the moment I was locked into a mood of crazy confidence. I suspected, in fact, that I had gone mad in some new, unexpected way. During certain periods of my adolescence I had sometimes expected to go mad with melancholy. Now the god had descended in another form, and I felt exhilarated. Crazy, but exhilarated. I would defend *festung Winterode*—accent on the final *e*—to my last grenade and my last bullet. Then I would order all German industry to be blown up. I would have my horses shot and my harem poisoned, and like Sardanapalus in Babylon or Hitler in Berlin I would go down in universal ruin. *Weltmacht oder neidergang* was the motto.

Below me crouched a Swarm of blue-clad soldiers. Beyond them, massed in blindly obedient ranks, stood Hordes of Communist fanatics. And my keen nostrils detected further back, in deep echelon, the presence of the Inexhaustible Pool of Chinese Manpower from which these Hordes and Swarms emerged. I decided I would sweep them all in front of me until I reached the Pool, pulled its plug, and let its waters drain out into the (Yellow) sea. With my seven grenades, a few clips of ammunition, my bowie knife, and my Yankee ingenuity I could end the war that very morning.

Here's what actually happened:

On my front the second attack petered out at four-thirty or so, but from other places on the hill I could hear firing. The Chinese below me stopped advancing, and except for an occasional shot to keep me in place, they lay still. Perhaps they were conserving ammunition too. If so, I understood their necessity, for by then I had thrown all my grenades and fired off half my bullets. The grenades were what I most regretted. I felt I had let them go too enthusiastically. I should have husbanded them. They were precious. Winterode had carried them ten miles. They were drenched in his sacred sweat and his holy blood, and I had thrown them away at a reckless rate. I blamed myself. And there were Winterode's feet right beside my head, and I could feel . . . Well, let's not talk about his body any more. I tried to ignore it as much as I could, given the fact that it and I occupied almost the same patch of ground. We were like those figures you see in Romanesque tympanums of the Last Judgment all coming up out of the same tomb. Or we were like a crowd of circus clowns bulging out of the same Volkswagen. There were so many of us in that foxhole that there was no room for a fox, and not even a mouse could stir. I felt terribly crowded by Winterode's unmoving form, but having arranged his body where it lay I couldn't disarrange it. I couldn't push him out of his own fortress. Luckily his head was where my feet lay and his feet were beside my head. We were like canned sardines, only I was alive.

The Chinese were making no immediate attempts to kill

me or occupy my position, and how could they have done that? The position was already thoroughly occupied. *No room*, I felt like shouting. *No room!*

"Why, there's lots of room," said Alice, taking her seat and staring at me through her slanted eyes.

Something seemed to be going wrong with my head again. It occurred to me to shout downhill, "Do you surrender?" After all, the Chinese had been going through battle, too; it might have confused them as much as it had confused me. Suppose they thought I outnumbered them and was about to charge?

Other things were on my mind. Dalbert. Was he dead or only asleep, or merely out of ammunition, or just taking a short cigarette break? Could he possibly be goofing off? My admiration for him, my deep feeling of friendship suffered a momentary lapse. And where were all the others? Where was Captain Spaulding, for instance, and why didn't I hear him leading his men downhill to join me in my charge?

And this is the point, Reader, where I should perhaps put you into the big picture.

High Command, we know, is an exacting art, the practice of which removes a man from the judgment of his military subordinates. Still, I have always ventured to think there was something radically unsound about MacArthur's *On To The Yalu* offensive of November 1950.

On paper it probably looked good. On the west coast of Korea the Eighth Army with some ROK divisions was to move north from the Chongchon, while on the east coast Tenth Corps (First Marines) was to fan out from Hamhung onto the North Korean plateau. To be sure there was a gap of some 120 miles between these two forces, but it was mountainous terrain where nothing much could be expected to happen. So, as I say, the operation must have looked golden in Tokyo, because after all it had been planned by Julius

Caesar von Rundstedt MacArthur. All that MacArthur had overlooked were six hundred thousand Chinese soldiers poised in that gap between his two small American forces. A man can't be expected to notice everything even when he's a military genius of MacArthur's rank (five stars).

MacArthur knew the Korean war was won. He had his own word for that. He knew, moreover, that the Chinese would not dare to intervene in the conflict. You see he was an admitted expert in Oriental psychology (self-admitted, Reader, self-admitted) and his textbooks had shown him that no Oriental ever dared to upset *his* plans. MacArthur intended to conquer Korea up to the Yalu, and that was what he would do. The North Korean army was shattered after the ever-brilliant landing at Inchon. All that was required was one last push and then Victory, Peace, and Promotions all around. MacArthur would receive a sixth star, thus making him exactly twice as bright as the Trinity, while others would be rewarded in strict accordance with rank and seniority.

Only it didn't happen that way. On the Eighth Army front where I found myself, the order of battle went like this: Ninth Division was along the coast. Inland a bit, Second Division was poised along the Chongchon, and still further inland some ROK divisions were supposed to be guarding our flank. I belonged to the Thirty-eighth (Rock of the Marne) Regiment of the Second Division. But the Rock of the Marne was the sponge of the Chongchon. On the very first day of our great leap forward, we set off into the hills where presently we found ourselves trapped in steep little valleys, lost in culverts, and isolated on hilltops while the Chinese flowed in around, behind, and finally over us. It was a shambles. And meanwhile, far to the East, the Marine prong of MacArthur's great offensive had its tines bent back at Koto-ri. The Chinese simply swept down the center of the peninsula and fanned out around the two isolated halves of MacArthur's

149

forces. Within twenty-four hours of the jump-off it was a question of whether there would be anything left to jump back onto. Opinions may vary, but I think MacArthur's Thanksgiving offensive of 1950 was the worst planned, most stupid offensive in the entire history of the United States Army, and I speak as an amateur historian who has made a considerable study of stupid offensives.

These, of course, are the statements of a child of the century, not to be compared in their weight and seriousness with MacArthur's explanation of the fiasco he had produced. He said, when he had time to figure out what was happening, that his offensive was not *meant* to succeed. It was merely a spoiling attack designed to trip the Chinese trap. Well the trap was tripped all right, and I was inside it feeling rather cheesy.

I was beginning to think I ought to be doing something other than what I had been doing, whatever that was. I should perhaps leave the spot I was lying on. One can't lie on the same spot throughout a war, however familiar and comfortable that spot has become. One must move around a bit if only to restore the circulation. I was conscious too that I had become even more surrounded than before since there were now Chinese soldiers further up the hillside than I was. I'd seen two climb out of that ravine, and now there seemed to be a battle going on at the *top* of the hill. I couldn't see anything, but you can't make a secret out of mortar shells and grenade bursts and automatic weapons firing. They were fighting up there right where Captain Spaulding had established his command post.

I listened to the sounds. I lay in my hole and kept a weather eye on the Chinese below me. I glanced occasionally at Winterode's feet. I wished passionately I had someone to talk to. I like talking, and there was so much to talk about. I wanted some very long-winded old Nestor of a fellow, deeply versed in life and war, with whom I could discuss the current

situation. I suddenly understand all the *talking* in *The Iliad.*
God, how I wanted to talk. I knew, too, that Nestor was not
the comic figure I had sometimes thought him. He was a life-
line ninety years long. Every time he opened his mouth you
could count on him to go on and on, gradually reducing the
situation to humdrum normality, blurring its sharper features, and merging it into a panoramic vision of human life.
How one needs Nestors! How I wished Winterode's feet
could speak.

My mood was changing again, this time because the war
had changed. Before it had been just a question of lying
where I had been told to lie and firing at the Chinese when
they fired at me. Now we seemed to be entering a war of
movement, and I had to decide which way to move—up,
down, or sideways. I could go uphill to join the battle, or I
could run downhill and either capture the Chinese there or
burst through them and hide in the wood from which they
had come. Or I could move sideways and try to connect up
with other Americans who were still in their original positions and wondering like myself what to do. I went sideways.

Dalbert wasn't dead after all, or if he was I didn't see his
body. He was gone. Vanished. Had he ascended? I looked
upwards. Nothing. Had he been blown up the way I'd
wanted Winterode to go? Hastily I began revising my ideas.
I'd gotten comfort of a sort from Winterode's body; the absence of Dalbert's left me with nothing to do, clutching at
empty air. If I ever encountered Dalbert again I'd certainly
let him know what I thought about his disappearing act.
Meanwhile what did I do?

Beyond Dalbert, if one moved laterally, the hill fell
away where a steep-sided bowl had been gouged out, evidence of ancient glacial activity, no doubt. But just as there
was no Nestor around, so I had no geologist friend to explain
the situation to me. I peered into the declivity. It had taken
some ice cream scoop to make that bowl, and I didn't fancy

151

climbing down into it in the dark. So I was stopped in that direction unless I went uphill and skirted the bowl from above. Uphill. Yes. They were still fighting up there. Some of them, at least. I could hear them. And now Nature and Nature's God seemed to have arranged the hill in such a way that I was led upward to duty. There is design in the fall of a sparrow, friends. I started up. If I had gone sideways in the other direction I would only have come to that ravine, and beyond it I was pretty sure Wolfson and Smith would be in no position to welcome my arrival. I was so alone at that point that I really preferred to do what was probably the correct thing. At almost any cost I wanted to get in touch with other Americans, other living Americans. I had had enough touch with dead ones.

The hill in those parts was steeply pitched and liberally equipped with boulders to thread one's way through and climb over. The vegetation was predominately of the low, scratchy sort. A botanist could probably be more precise about it. And the top of the hill seemed very far away. I remember thinking as I climbed that Captain Spaulding had staked out too large a claim the night before when he posted us along the lower slopes. He should have kept us all massed together around him at the top of the hill like Harold Godwinson's housecarls at the battle of Hastings. They were defeated, too, but it must have been chummier.

When I had climbed for a few minutes I began to feel my legs going. And I was curiously winded. I couldn't understand it. I had scrambled up hills like this many times in the Ozarks without any physical difficulty. Was I getting old? Out of condition? Something was wrong, anyway. I decided to pause for a rest.

I sat down on a convenient boulder, leaned my M-1 against the rock, and breathed deeply a few times. The war was still going on. I could hear firing above me, and now that I was higher on the hill, I could see flashes of light and hear dull explosions from farther off where other units of the good old Thirty-eighth were getting it that night. However—and this was an insight that would have been well worth avoiding—it suddenly struck me as a peaceful scene. The rumbling and flashing along the horizon was like a thunderstorm at home, and the firing from above had a sharp, brisk autumnal quality, like a big turkey hunt. I was pleased with these comparisons.

Then Stendhal, my old guide, philosopher and friend, came to my aid once more, and I remembered his wonderful description of Fabrice del Dongo wandering around the field of Waterloo hunting for the battle. Battlegrounds were like that, I suddenly saw. They contained little pockets of peace and quiet where a chap could sit on a rock and enjoy the night air and the view. And refresh himself. I was thirsty and it suddenly struck me that I had a canteen of water attached to my person somewhere. I routed it out, took a drink, and then I unpeeled a Hershey bar I had been saving up for an emergency. No point in arriving at the battle all hungry and thirsty and tired out.

So I was sitting there munching my Hershey bar and thinking of Stendhal and enjoying the sensation of being outdoors and alive when three Chinese soldiers materialized in front of me. You might call it a dialectical materialization. Thesis pointed his tommy gun at my navel, Antithesis picked up my M-1, while Synthesis stood by watching proceedings with what struck me as an inscrutable expression. And there I was, the son of the Bishop of Kansas City, partly a Clay, surrounded by the Red Chinese on a dark Korean night. Beat that for color.

16

At this point the assumption will be that I surrendered. At least that was my assumption. What else could I do? Throw rocks? Tackle them? Levitate? None of those alternatives occurred to me, although I had "Death Before Dishonor" pricked out on my wishbone, a decoration I had acquired by sitting around in Father's tattoo parlor. Also I was named for Samuel who once took an ax and hewed King Agag in pieces before Jehovah in Gilgal, but since I could neither see my chest nor remember my own name those high reminders did me no good as I stared, stupefied, at my three Oriental visitants. I just assumed I was going to surrender, and yet, thinking things over, I now believe it was an unworthy assumption. Why couldn't I have been like that harebrained French knight on the Sixth Crusade? This is the story.

Saint Louis landed his army at Damietta on the coast of Egypt, and then marched inland until he was well and truly surrounded on a hilltop, the plains below packed solid with Moslem warriors. As the King consulted with his barons about what to do next, up spoke that young knight. "Sire," he said, "let us all charge them together and tomorrow we will meet again in Paradise." *Mais nous ne le crûmes pas,* writes Joinville, who was there. We didn't believe him, and so they surrendered just as I did. I didn't believe in Paradise and I'd gotten myself into so isolated a position that I had no one to charge with. Sad. And yet this is not a sad story. Really, I think the time has come for me to define my genre.

The style of a comical historical pastoral should be a mixed style, both high and low, banal and eloquent, witty and sloppy. Indeed the more mixed the better, for what we aim at in works of this sort is to be all-inclusive. That is why the hero of a comical historical pastoral should have a character that is both better and worse than average as well as being average. Though highly intelligent, he should display great stupidity and make disastrous errors of judgment that lead to no harm. His passions should be simple and natural, yet give rise to actions and opinions so erratic as to be incomprehensible to most observers. He should be serious and silly, noble and vulgar, tender and cold. In short he should be a perfect mine of contradictions.

The plot of a comical historical pastoral should be made up of one whole and complete action which appears episodic and wayward. The action, though set in remote times and distant lands, should be described as if it happened yesterday in the backyard. And when we have said that the plot of a comical historical pastoral should arouse feelings of horror and joy we have said all and rather more than all that should be said of this genre.

And now back to the front.

The Chinese waggled their guns in a suggestive manner. I rose to my feet and went on rising until my hands were fully extended overhead. We posed that way just long enough for the muse of comical historical pastorals to get a snapshot for her album, and then we started downhill toward that wood at which I'd done so much staring.

Once among the trees we began to encounter more Chinese soldiers. My captors led me up to an officer. Should I salute him? Did captured privates salute enemy officers? I didn't know, and anyway my hands were still in the air. I tried to look *correct,* if that concept had any meaning at such a moment. Then the officer gave an order. I was led aside and presently found myself being trussed up like a chicken, after which my friends considerately propped my back against a tree trunk. They went off rejoicing in work well done, leaving me to digest the situation on an empty stomach.

There was another American prisoner, named Corman,

155

propped against the other side of the tree. As soon as we were alone he said, "What do we do now?"

Do? It was as if I'd never heard the verb. Do? To do? I do, you do, he does. What does he do? Do you do anything? Do we do something? What could they do? I said, "What do you think we ought to do?"

"You got a knife?" he asked.

"No." I'd left my knife stuck into the chest of that sawdust bear and never bothered to replace it. (N.B. boys, never part with your scout knives.)

"I got one," he said, "but I can't get at it. How you tied?"

"My hands behind my back and my ankles together."

"Same here. You figure if we wiggle back to back you could get your hands in my pocket?"

"I don't know." The whole thing struck me as so essentially hopeless I didn't care one way or another, but since he seemed to like his own idea, we wiggled until we were back to back and then I started worming my tied hands into his pocket.

Well, that did begin to intrigue me. It was rather queer to be forcing my way into another man's pocket, but as I've said, war is queer. We were like two camels copulating backwards, which is how camels do it in case you've wondered. I had the tips of my fingers on his knife when some Chinese noticed the funny business going on. They came over to put a stop to *that*. And, just to make sure, they searched us and took away Corman's knife, after which they banged us over the head because we'd been naughty.

So that was that.

Corman said, "Maybe we could roll along the ground until we get away from them."

The man was an absolute genius of improvisation and fantasy and hopefulness. I could see us rolling south in front of the Red Army shouting the news that the Chinese were coming. Modern Paul Reveres. "Listen!" I said, "the Chinese are all over the place. We're surrounded." Then I added, "We're captured." Didn't he realize it? After all, you couldn't just surrender and go right on as if nothing had happened. Obviously it was a grave event that had to be pondered. The Kansas City angle would have to be worked out by sextant. I foresaw many profitable months of mental hassle ahead of me. It would be irresponsible, almost anarchic to escape before I'd even decided whether my surrender was morally justified.

Later on, perhaps when we were properly installed in a prison camp, we would go about things in the right way, by forming an Escape Committee which would draw up plans. Then we'd all begin to tunnel and presently we'd escape. I'd read about it in a book and knew just how the thing worked. Corman's idea was all wet. You didn't just go rolling away without any plans. I told Corman that.

"Yeah? Well, here goes," he said. He toppled sideways and began rolling home. I watched him go and realized I'd feel rather foolish if he made it. He didn't, however. The Chinese caught sight of him, dragged him back, and after that they posted guards over us. Things were beginning to take shape. Two more prisoners were brought in, both wounded, one severely. So we were gathering a nucleus. I asked the less severely wounded fellow—his name was Humphreys—how things were going up there.

"Where?" he said.

"At the top of the hill," I said.

"How the eff should I know?" As you may gather, *eff* was not the word he used, but thank God this is not a naturalistic story where I'm obliged to quote other people's obscenity. My own is enough.

I turned back to Corman. "How do you think things are going up there?"

"I don't know," he said. "They jumped me from behind."

Whereat I began to feel guilty. Maybe he'd been cap-

157

tured by Fair and Foul Weather who had gotten through our
lines because I had no ammunition to shoot them. Because
I'd wasted a lot of ammo firing into the dark. Dear me, I
thought. In war you not only had to decide your life was
worth preserving, you had to make the same decision about
the lives of your buddies. And they had to make the same
decision about themselves and about you. In fact you sort of
had to love and trust each other and work together. Otherwise things would just fall apart. One guy would get captured from behind, another would vanish, while a third
would go mooning off alone to eat candy bars and think
about Stendhal. And before we knew where we were we'd be
where we were.

Reader, are you bored, amused, or angry to watch a
Harvard man discover an army is a team rather than a group
of virtuoso soloists playing different tunes on their magic
M-1's? Well, I'll never know how you feel. I felt rather elated,
as if I'd made a wonderful discovery. Though, as I thought it
over, I realized we'd studied the matter way back in prep
school when we translated Caesar's Commentaries. Mr.
Whibly had described the way Roman legionnaires used to
fight in close formation, the shield of Julius Nemo partly protecting Gaius Gracchus on his left, while Nemo in turn was
partly protected by Publius Semper Virus on his right. In
fact Mr. Whibly acted it out, showing that in close order a
soldier with a shield on his left arm and a sword in his right
hand could fight more effectively and safely by attacking to
the right. Hence old Nemo was supposed to kill the enemy in
front of Publius, while Gaius killed the enemy who was trying to kill Nemo. It took a lot of trust to rely on your neighbors to that extent, which must be why the Roman legions
made such a mark in history.

And actually war really hadn't changed so much, I decided, even though modern armies were spaced out and
modern soldiers were a bit more on their own—like the
Greeks in *The Iliad*. But even in *The Iliad* you could see—I

could see (who's talking here anyway, and to whom?)—*we* could see a sense of mutuality emerging from more primitive fighting conditions. Patroclus would not have been killed if Achilles had been where he ought to have been.

I was fascinated by my conclusions. I was part of a team —which was getting clobbered.

"I wonder what's happening?" I said to no one in particular.

Then a whistle was blown in our immediate neighborhood. The guards cut loose Corman and myself, someone shouted an order, and we were marched off down a forest trail. "I wonder where we're going?" I said.

After a dozen steps Montgomery, the badly wounded man, began to sag on his feet. Corman stepped up and supported him on one side. Then, after a few more steps, I moved in on his other side. He threw his arms over our shoulders and we proceeded that way.

It was dawn before we reached a Chinese camp. There were more prisoners there, some of whose faces looked white in contrast with the blood-soaked bandages around their heads. We slumped to the ground among them, and at that point I frankly lost interest in what was going to happen next to me or anyone else. I fell asleep.

The sun was well up when I woke. We were in a forest glade. Across from me there was a grove of aspens, their branches bare of leaves, their trunks white against the brown hillside. I could see Chinese soldiers in their quilted blue uniforms lounging under the aspens, smoking and talking. At the head of the glade there was a tent with some coming and going of messengers. Nearby the tent was a neat pile of ammunition cases. More Chinese soldiers were sitting on the ground there, chattering and laughing. Closer to hand there were six alert, confident-looking Chinese guards watching us.

The contrast between the cheerful Chinese and our tatterdemalion crew was rather painful. We were sprawled out

159

in various attitudes of woe and dejection. I looked around for Corman. He was cleaning his fingernails with a stick. I got out my comb and began combing my hair. After a bit I said, "I wonder when they're going to feed us?" No one answered.

A while later we were moved on again. So far there had been no signs of the elaborate hodgepodge of military equipment I was used to seeing in our army. But when we came out of the next wood we were on a road where six Chinese trucks were parked under some trees. Probably Russian-made, I thought. The drivers looked at us with interest but said nothing.

"I wonder where this road goes?" I said.

"North," said Corman.

He and I were again supporting Montgomery, who by then was not at all well. He had been bandaged around the chest and given some aspirin, but otherwise nature was taking its course.

In half an hour we came to a village where we halted. We were allowed to draw water from the village well, and those of us who still had our canteens could fill them up. The windlass creaked as we wound it. The bucket proved to be wooden with a furry growth on it. "Do you think this water is safe to drink?" I asked Corman.

"I guess so," he said, drinking some.

We were in a mud hut village with frozen rice paddies around it. Some small Korean children whose sex I couldn't tell watched us solemnly as we drew water from their well. Two old men bowed politely to our guards, who nodded in a friendly if patronizing way. The old men ignored us. I saw no women. Then we moved on.

It was eleven o'clock when we arrived at a village larger than the first. I knew it was eleven because I still had my watch. The Chinese hadn't fed us, but they hadn't robbed us either. I was beginning to find them rather impressive. In the

160

village where we halted for our noon break there seemed to be several companies of Chinese soldiers, sturdy-looking, smooth-faced, frequently grinning when they caught sight of us. And there was bustle and activity around the principal building in the village. It seemed to house a Chinese head-quarters of some sort. I saw more trucks and other signs of mechanization, but my principal impression was simply of men. Here were a lot of men (in blue uniforms) going about things in a rather elementary but effective way. They looked Oriental, of course, but they struck me as being more American than we were, at least at the moment. Some of us looked scarcely human by then.

We were fed rice with some fish chopped up in it. I looked at my small portion. I smelled it. Then I tasted it. It was ghastly. When I finished eating it I felt like vomiting. One man did vomit. Others simply didn't eat all of their portions. One fellow handed me his mess kit. "You want to finish this?" he asked.

"Isn't it terrible?" I said, finishing it.

Then, around one o'clock we moved on again. At three our day's march ended in yet another village where for the first time the wounded got some medical attention from an American doctor who was part of another P.O.W. contingent already gathered in that village. He had no morphine or penicillin or sulfa left, but he had needle and thread and he was busy sewing people up, fixing splints, and bandaging wounds.

He was furious. "This fellow should be in the hospital," he said when Corman and I deposited Montgomery in front of him. He bent over and began to examine the situation. "God damn it!" he said.

"Attaboy, Doc," someone said.

"Jesus Christ in hell," the doctor said, looking at the mess in front of him. Then he looked up at me. "Give me your undershirt."

"My undershirt?"

"Yes, your undershirt."

"But it's dirty."

"Not as dirty as this rag," the doctor said, throwing away the old bandage he'd removed. "Hell!" he remarked again as he started swabbing, snipping, and sewing. I, meanwhile, was removing my coat and shirt. When I got my undershirt off I smelled it briefly before handing it over. It had been liberally soaked in sweat the night before and now it gave off the pure essence of fear.

"Tear it in strips," the doctor said crossly. "I can't use it that way." So I began tearing it in strips, at which point, Reader, I think we may as well close this episode. We fade out as Samuel Heather, his stomach already yearning for more of that good old rice and fish, stands bare-chested in the November cold, tearing his undershirt into bandages. I was not really much of a soldier, as you've perhaps seen, but my little bout with war had had a more civilizing effect on me than life at Harvard. Perhaps becoming a prisoner would give me a chance for real spiritual development. Who knows? I thought, I may become an angel of mercy.

17

There were certainly opportunities during the next month, but . . . well. Look down and don't be too harsh on poor Samuel Heather as he trudges, footsore and weary, up the main street of Pyot Lon, a village on the banks of the Yalu. I got to the Yalu after all, though not as a conquering hero.

Pyot Lon proved to be an ordinary North Korean village which the Chinese had turned into a prison camp by the simple expedient of removing the indigenous peasants and installing us. We do not have record of what happened to the natives, but let us hope they were relocated in some model commune with indoor plumbing. They left none behind. They left only their huts, their stoves, their sleeping shelves and a faint personal aroma soon overlaid by the more robust smell of unwashed American prisoners, many of whom suffered from diarrhea.

Yet unattractive as it seemed at first glance, Pyot Lon was a haven, a refuge, a bourn toward which we had been struggling for a whole month. It was a permanent prison camp. Once there we could relax and begin to pick up the pieces. No more marches. No more uncertainty. And no more separations and departures, for in the month that has elapsed since the end of the last chapter I have become separated from all the men with whom I was captured. Montgomery did not survive, Humphreys was hospitalized, and Corman escaped, of all things. Without taking me with him! I felt abandoned. Later I learned that he was in another camp along the Yalu, so I felt slightly better about it all. Still I wish he'd stuck with me. I needed inspiring examples around me during those first months at Pyot Lon.

It was blizzarding as we marched in. Into each life some

blizzards must blow, and this one blew right into my face. I was front man on a litter team. Friend Hubler, a stumblebum if I ever met one, supported the rear, and between us reclined a young pasha named Hollins who claimed he couldn't walk any more. Hubler and I had been carrying him for the last few miles, though personally I was ready to dump him in the Yalu if only someone would give me the word. Hubler wouldn't. He was one of those trudging Good Samaritans who can never rise to the Nietzschean heights that are sometimes necessary in life. Nietzsche, as you all know, has written, "When you see a man stumbling, push." And there we were, not only supporting Hollins but carrying him grandly forward. It just goes to show how unphilosophic soldiers can get.

The Chinese prison administration met us with tommy guns, mildewed barley soup (a *spécialité de la maison*), and a doctor, whom Hubler and I enticed forward while Hollins rolled up his trousers. Hollins was always rolling up his trousers. Then we all had a good look at his suppurating sores. Doc shook his head dismissively, as if to say he'd seen sores compared with which Hollins' were mere skin eruptions. He murmured something and went off to look at the walking wounded.

"What did he say?" Hollins asked. He was always asking me to translate Chinese.

"E say e ope you leg well soon."

"Christ!" said Hollins. "I need zinc oxide."

Frankly I felt zinc oxide would only touch the surface of his problems. The man was singularly unaware Hubler and I were killing ourselves carrying him. But what can one do?

Then we were lined up and sorted out, and presently I found myself bearing my burden toward Hut 12, which was to be our happy home. It proved to be a small, smoking structure of wood and clay and perhaps a wattle or two. I was again front man on the litter, my hands occupied, so I kicked at the door which fell open disclosing a foul, fetid, and dark den into which I led my little procession. The Prince and his wise men had arrived all together and off schedule. "Watch out how you put me down," Hollins said, as Hubler and I dumped him in front of the stove.

There was a tall corporal lying on the floor watching us like the bricklayer in *Bleak House*. "What's that smell in here?" I said.

"B.O.," he answered.

"Close the door!" someone shouted from an even darker, more fetid region behind the stove.

"This place needs to be aired out," I said.

The tall corporal got up and closed the door himself. "Welcome to Pyot Lon," he said. "My name's Matthew."

"I'm Private Samuel Heather of the Thirty-eighth Regiment," I said.

He seemed impressed. "What's your service number?" he asked.

But this exchange of confidences was interrupted by characters emerging from the deeper dark, eager for news from the outside world. They'd been in Pyot Lon for some time and were as anxious to get away from it as we had been to get to it. The conversation that ensued is best rendered in song. Besides we need some song now. Life is too dreary without an occasional soft shoe routine.

> "Where'd they get ya?
> What's the dope?
> Where's the marines?
> 'S there any hope?" they said.

We answered:

> "They caught us on the Chongchon
> We never had a prayer

165

We don't know where the corps is
Nor do we really care."

They came right back at us:

"Where's the army?
'S Mac attackin'?
Where's the air force?
News is lackin'."

Hubler and I harmonized in response:

"The army's to the south of us,
The air force up above
MacArthur's off in Tokyo
So send him all your love."

Then we had a sort of tenor solo with **reprises and**
choric interludes as a young Italian took the floor.

TENOR: You know what I think Mac should do?
ALL: No, tell us what you think Mac should do.
TENOR: Land the marines at Sinanju.
            Yes, land the marines at Sinanju.
            And send them up the old Yalu
            To rescue him and me and you.
            That's what *I* think Mac should do.
ALL: That's what I think Mac should do
TENOR: Yes, that's what I think Mac should do.
TOGETHER: Just land the marines at Sinanju
            And send them up the old Yalu
            To rescue him and me and you
            Fa la lala la.

Then a Bass interrupted this feast of reason:

BASS: That won't work, but I'll tell you how
            Mac could win this war right now.

ALL:	"Tell us, tell us," we all said.
BASS:	Just drop the Bomb and kill them dead.
	Yes, drop the Bomb and kill them dead.
	That's what he'd do if he'd use his head.
	Just drop the bomb and kill the Chinks
	And rescue us from these old clinks.
ALL:	(*Doubtfully*) Drop the Bomb!
BASS:	Yes, drop the Bomb.
ALL:	What? Drop the Bomb?
BASS:	Yes, drop the Bomb.
	(*Recitativo*) You see, I don't say it's moral
	And I don't say it's sweet,
	But I do say it's simple,
	And I do say it's neat.
	Mac drops the Bomb and ends the fuss
	And sends some trucks to rescue us.
TENOR:	Don't listen to him. He's a nut.
BASS:	What? Me a nut?
TENOR:	Yes, a nut.
	(*Sings*)
	Don't you know,
	What the Bomb can do?
	The Bomb can kill
	Both them and you.
	Don't you know,
	You stupid clown
	If we bomb them
	They'll shoot us down?
BASS:	Listen! How can they shoot us down if they're all dead?
TENOR:	You want to know how they can shoot us down if they're all dead?
BASS:	Yes, that's what I want to know.
TENOR:	I'll tell you: (*Chants*)
	Seven hundred million people can't all die
	In the merest twinkling of an eye.
	Some will be left! Some will be left! to shoot you and I.
HEATHER:	Me.

167

MATTHEW:	What's your name again?
HEATHER:	I'm Private Samuel Heather of the U.S.A.
	Came to Korea on a black, black day
	Got myself caught in the very worst way
	Ain't God's chillun got fun?
BASS:	*He's* a nut. We shouldn't have let him in.
HEATHER:	Watch who you're callin' a nut.
	I got a right to be in this hut.
	Though I'd love to be out of it, but
	There ain't no way to go home.
ALL:	Oh there ain't no way,
	There ain't no way
	There ain't no way
	To go home
	O'er land or sea or foam,
	You can't get back
	By path or track
	Or call by telephoam. (*Sorry about that*)
HEATHER:	Thomas Wolfe was right!
TENOR:	Is that Sergeant Thomas Wolfe, B Company, 1st Battalion, 38th Regiment?
HEATHER:	Were you in the 38th Regiment, too, old buddy?
TENOR:	Naw, I was in the Artillery.
	(*Sings "The Caissons Go Rolling Along"*)
HEATHER:	Throw him out, he's a spy!
BASS:	And they call *me* a nut.
HEATHER:	All together, fellows!
	Give me an H for heroism.
	Give me an E for endurance.
	Give me an L for liberty
	Give me a P for pity.
	Help! Help! Help!
HOLLINS:	I'm a Seventh Day Adventist from Boise, Idaho, and I need zinc oxide for my legs.
HUBLER:	I don't see where we're going to sleep.
MATTHEW:	I sleep on the floor.
HEATHER:	I can't stand this. I'm going outside to freeze in peace. (*Opens the door.*)

168

MATTHEW: (*Closing the door*) Never leave that door open again.

HEATHER: I need air. Let's all escape.

VOICE OF P. CORNELIUS TACITUS: *Impunitatis cupido magnis semper conatibus adversa.* *

CURTAINS.

Faith, Hope, and Charity visited our hut the next day in the person of Chaplain Miller, still on duty as an officer and Christian. He blew in during the morning, rosy-cheeked and covered with snow like a belated Santa Claus without gifts. Not this too, I thought, as I watched him stamp off the snow.

He advanced to greet us with the straightforward manly lack of resonance one associates with FBI men and YMCA directors. "Fellows!" he said, "we're in a tight spot here and we'll all have to stick together and help each other if we want to pull through." Which was true enough, though it didn't require Divine Revelation to tell us so. I began to feel a little less threatened.

"Now I know we're of different faiths here," Miller said, "but I think we all ought to get down on our knees and pray to Gaud. You with me, fellows?"

It seemed we were more or less with him.

"Oh Gaud," said Miller, piping it up. "Look down upon us in our trials and extend Thy mercy to us as we kneel here before Thee confident of Thy eternal justice and love. Give us the courage to do what we must do. Lift up our hearts to Thee. And now boys, let's all pray silently for a little while."

That was not too bad, if you could forgive the mangled pronunciation of God's holy name. Miller actually won my respect when he announced that we would sing "Onward Christian Soldiers." He said, "You Jewish fellows just think

* Means, "The desire of escape—that foe to all great enterprises." What a life! You have to learn Latin to interpret your heavenly voices and Assyrian to read the writing on the wall.

about Joshua and the Ark of the Covenant of the Lord." That solved everything. Then we opened wide our mouths and treated the valley of the Yalu to some unfamiliar lyrics. When it was over, Miller made the rounds. He looked long and thoughtfully at Hollins' bared legs, patted the dispirited, and shook hands with me.

"Are you a Presbyterian?" I asked.

"That's right. You one too?"

"Not exactly," I said.

He nodded agreeably. "Well, it's all one big Faith," he said, and so passed out of the hut and out of my life, since the Chinese thereafter confined him to the officers' compound where I'm sure he did his best with the captains and colonels. Still, they are tougher nuts than we enlisted men, and I feel if Miller had been allowed to roam he might have sowed the seed and reaped the harvest, for we had theologically inclined men in that hut. Besides myself.

As soon as Miller was gone a thin, intense fellow named Rubecker pounced on Matthew. "How come you didn't kneel?" he asked.

Matthew just shook his head.

"Don't you believe in God?" Rubecker said.

"Do you?" Matthew asked.

"Of course I do," said Rubecker. "If God don't exist, what holds the world together?"

"Gravity," said Matthew.

"What's Gravity?" cried Rubecker, in tones of one about to explode an intellectual bomb.

"Gravity's . . ."

"Gravity's God!" Rubecker declared. "Gravity's God!"

Come, this is better, I thought. Argument on the high themes of existence was meat and drink to me, the only meat I seemed likely to get at Pyot Lon.

I said, "You've got to distinguish between the natural and . . . "

"Then pray to Gravity to get you out of here," said Matthew.

That silenced Rubecker momentarily, though it occurred to me that if he knelt in one spot long enough as he prayed he might sink out of sight, though more likely he'd be drifted over and so rapt from our view by the great god Blizzard, a big deity in North Korea. "You've got to distinguish," I said again.

Rubecker turned on me. "Don't you think God exists?"

"I'm trying to explain," I said.

Rubecker pointed at Matthew. "He says God don't exist."

"Well, He doesn't," I said. "Existence is for created things."

"Aw shit," said a growling voice from the back of the hut. "I hate atheists."

This, I knew, was Novotny. One does not live twenty-four hours in a small hut without becoming aware one has a Novotny in one's midst. Some of my hutmates were still mere faces, but Novotny's personality had already come across like a bullet between the eyes or a baseball bat over the head. The minute I saw him I knew we would never become quiet, thoughtful, considerate friends. We might eventually grow to love one another, but we would always fight.

"I'm not an atheist," I said into the darkness where Novotny dwelt.

"You just said God don't exist," he answered from his penumbra.

And at that point a well-brought-up young man like myself with half a Harvard education should doubtless have explained matters in terms suitable to Novotny's intelligence. Instead of which I said, "If you had brains instead of ball bearings in your head, you'd know the difference between essence and existence."

There were sounds of stirring in the cave and presently

171

Novotny emerged, sniffing the air to see if summer had come and the blueberries were ripe. How the Koreans ever caught him, I don't know. He must have been netted while he dozed in the sun.

"Wudge you say?" he said.

"I said essence is different from existence."

"You said I'm dumb."

I shook my head. "No, you said that."

At which point Matthew got up from the floor. It was a thoughtful move. It left a clear space in front of the stove where I could fall if—as seemed likely—I was going to do any falling.

Meanwhile Novotny and I were still at the talking stage. "Listen!" he said. In that hut people were always telling other people to listen, though no one had anything to say. "Listen!" said Novotny again. Then silence fell while we all listened. What were we going to hear, I wondered. The music of the spheres?

"I don't think we should fight each other just after we've been praying," Hubler said. He was really rather sweet, and a model of lucidity compared to the others, particularly Novotny.

Who said, "He was insulting my religion."

I really cannot bear intellectual confusion in others. "I was insulting you, not your religion," I said. "You're a dope, but there is a God, so cheer up."

"See?" Novotny said to Hubler. "He insulted me again."

I expected the fight to start right away, since at that time I was judging Novotny by Bartoldiesque standards. I was wrong, however; Bartoldi moved into action with Achillean rapidity compared to Novotny, who really took us back. Novotny, I decided, was Early Bronze Age. I dated him roughly as 1600 B.C. Those ears, those characteristic markings on the brow, that jaw . . . they told their story to the experienced eye. If I lived I could write a monograph enti-

tled "Early Bronze Age Survivals in the Valley of the Yalu."
The American Archaeological Society might be interested.

"Listen," said Novotny for the third time.

This was getting us nowhere. I said, "You're a Catholic,
I suppose?"

He swelled a bit, if that were possible. "God damn right
I'm a Catholic."

"Fine," I said, "but you're a stupid Catholic. You don't
know what your faith is all about."

I wasn't really angry with him, and I didn't want to get
hurt, but I knew if I didn't fight Novotny right away I might
become more and more reluctant to be hit by him. Call it
reasoned bellicosity or anticipatory rage, because I could
feel that eventually I'd be angry enough to want to fight him,
only by then I might be too sunk in cowardice to do anything
about it.

And now, observe Novotny. His eyes have brightened,
his chest heaves, and his fists clench. Altogether he is feeling
a lot better and more alert, for he was not entirely sure of
himself before. We come from different rites, and Novotny
was a ritualist of the most profound sort who had so far
missed fire because our conversation had not had quite the
proper tone and style. He'd been badly put off his paces by
that business of essence and existence. Now he knew what he
had to do.

Our fight had two rounds. At the end of Round One I
was upset by a sidewise blow. I sat down, striking my head
smartly against the stove. When the sickening stars had
faded off th' ethereal plain I saw Novotny standing over me.
"That will teach ya," he said. Education by being hit on the
head. It was a theory all right.

Round Two ended with me on the floor again and Novotny looking down with a satisfied expression on his face.
"Had enough?" he asked.

"No," I said.

173

But public opinion was against Round Three. Hollins, that leader of men, raised his complaining voice to observe that with us guys knocking each other around someone was going to bump against his (Hollins') legs and then there'd be hell to pay. I had done precious little knocking around of Novotny, but I rather liked the sound of Hollins' voice just then. Others associated themselves with his position. Matthew was the only one in favor of another round. "Let them fight," he said. "It's something to watch."

"Yeah!" said Hollins bitterly. "It's okay for you. You can get out of the way. But what about me?"

So the fight ended. That fight, at least, because the struggle never ends. I don't know what made me think my surrender meant a farewell to arms. I wish one could say farewell to arms, but it's like trying to say good-bye to one's feet.

18

Now my narrative breaks down a bit, and in place of the highly consecutive storytelling to which you've become accustomed, I intend to serve you up some scrappy vignettes of Pyot Lon life during that winter and spring of 1951.

[1]

Night. Darkness. The sound of breathing. The bitter, dense smell of my camerados presses in on me until I feel I am stifling. I turn to find a more comfortable position on the floor. Matthew, who sleeps next to me, mutters, "Why can't you settle down? What's eating you?"

"Eating!" I say. "Don't talk to me about eating." I am ready to take a bite out of him on the spot. I've had my eye on his rump for days. Eating, forsooth! I could eat Hollins' scabby leg with pleasure, and that is odd because I am normally delicate about my food. I like to be tempted by goodies and coddled with chicken, but a diet, and an inadequate diet of boiled millet and cracked corn, has changed all that. I am ravenous. "Just shut up!" I tell Matthew.

"Well, quit rolling around," he says.

"Quit telling me what to quit doing," I say.

From the back of the hut we hear Novotny's voice. "Shut up, Heather!" He feels he has Authority. After all, he has knocked me down.

"Yes, Arnold," I call back. He hates to be called Arnold.

Then I turn in the other direction, disturbing Hubler who sleeps on my other side. We have slung Hollins aloft to keep him out of harm's way. Feeling mean, I raise my leg and prod the bottom of his litter with the toe of my boot.

"Hey! Cut that out," Hollins says. "Was that you, Heather?"

I don't answer. Silence of a sort falls. Inside the stove two burning logs settle together. Outdoors, the wind whistles around the eaves and moans over the stovepipe. I think of sausages for a while. They give me no comfort. Then I begin to speak:

> O rose thou art sick
> Th' invisible worm
> That flies through the night
> In the howling storm
> Has found out thy bed
> Of crimson joy
> His dark secret love
> Does thy life destroy

Around me in the dark I can feel a sort of ringing silence, an almost palpable wave of shock, as the forces of chaos and old night gather themselves to resist this intrusion of poetry.

"Heather!" C'est Novotny qui parle.

"Novotny!" I call back.

"I'm gonna toss you out of this hut."

"If you lay a hand on me I'll bite Hollins' leg," I say.

"For Christ's sake!" says Hollins, slightly alarmed.

"*Will* you guys keep quiet?" someone asks.

"We want to sleep," says someone else.

"This is the worst hut in the compound," a third voice observes.

[2]

I am outdoors. It is a dim morning in late January. The temperature is 12° and I feel forty. I am pondering my alternatives: suicide, or starvation. Or possibly escape, which in this weather would seem to combine the advantages of both alternatives. Then I notice some Turkish prisoners in the next compound digging in the snow. I watch them for a while and presently dig on my own, coming up with dead dandelions or something which I promptly swallow and go looking for more. Hunger is my one reliable sensation. Sometimes anger fails me. On occasions I don't even feel guilty or ashamed of myself, but always right there at the center of things I can count on good old hunger.

I am first on the chow line and last to give up scraping an empty bowl. I am wearing that bowl thin with my scraping, and every day in every way I feel more and more like Oliver Twist in the poorhouse.

My bones have begun to appear, and I am getting onto quite familiar terms with my skeleton. Every week there is a new rib to admire or a fresh joint that has surfaced. I had no idea the human body contained so many bones, and I resolve that I will study anatomy if ever I get back to Harvard. It will satisfy the Natural Science requirement I have shirked for two and a half years. Also I feel I should know more about this remarkable framework that is starting forth through every tatter in my mortal dress.

Hubler comes walking through the snow toward me. He is carrying a familiar object: Hollins' pants.

"What, again!" I say.

Hubler nods. Diarrhea has struck like a dagger in the night, and now we must wash up the traces.

"I'll do it," I say. "You did it last time." He does not protest, and I spend the next hour in the primitive laundry, scrubbing, scrubbing, scrubbing.

[3]

We are standing around a grave one afternoon in February. Rubecker is no more. Gravity has called to him and he has harkened to its voice, and now I am intoning fragments of the Episcopal burial service over his remains. Is there a special rap for impersonating a priest? Never mind. I am in a grim, gay mood in which I don't much care what is going to happen next to me or anyone else. On the way back to the hut I fall into step with Matthew. "Who'll be next?" I say.

He shakes his head.

"Poniatowski, I think. Or maybe Williams."

He just shakes his head.

"I'll lay you two to one it's Poniatowski."

"Two to one what?"

"You're right," I say. "There's nothing to bet with."

[4]

Novotny and I are lying in the snow at dusk. He has seen a rabbit, or at least he claims he has seen a rabbit. I am not sure whether I believe him. I haven't seen anything, but that means little, since I am afflicted with acute night blindness. As soon as the sun goes down I can't see a thing. I have to be led to the latrine. So, on the way there, Novotny has seen this alleged rabbit and we are now lying down waiting for it to hop closer so Novotny can bean it with a rock he is holding in his hand. I have no confidence in any part of the scheme, which is strictly Novotnyesque. But I wait patiently beside him, the snow gradually melting into my clothes. At last there is a flurry of activity, a fresh spatter of snow in my face, and then Novotny says, "Missed!"

"Of course you missed," I say, getting up and beginning to brush snow from my garments.

"What do you mean of course I missed?"

"I've never heard of anyone hitting a rabbit with a stone, especially from a prone position."

"Yeah?"

178

"Yeah. And if you were from a decent part of the country instead of Whiting, Indiana, you'd know that's not the way to get rabbits."

"Oh yeah?"

"Yeah."

"*If* there was a rabbit there," I add. "Which I doubt."

"Listen!"

"Whiting!" I say with scorn. I have been through the town on the way to Boston and I know what I am talking about.

"I'd punch you for that, Heather, if you weren't blind."

"Don't let that stop you."

"Just don't push your luck," he tells me.

Then he leads me onward to the latrine.

[5]

We are having another fight inside the hut. The Chinese prohibit fighting, but they can't see what goes on indoors, so our brawls are all *in camera,* which is confining but relatively safe. So far no one has killed anyone, and gradually a feeling has developed that so long as we have the energy to hit each other we're still safely on this side of the grave.

This fight is about nothing in particular. I remember it only because of its bizarre and heartwarming ending. "Stop it! Stop it!" I am shouting in my most authoritative way. I like breaking up fights in which I am not personally involved. I step between the two antagonists—O'Higgins and Ramirez—and get hit simultaneously from both sides. Staggering backwards I bump against Hollins' swinging litter, which comes down with a crash on top of Hubler. Hollins screams with surprise and pain. Hubler groans, and suddenly Poniatowski leaps from the back of the hut and begins to hit *me.*

179

We are amazed. For two days he has scarcely spoken. We are convinced he is sinking into the sort of coma which preceded Rubecker's end. Now there he is hitting me. The sight cheers us all up. Someone leads him away. That evening he eats his cracked corn with appetite. We begin to be rather proud of our hut. So far we have only lost one man whereas other huts have buried two and even three and four. To keep up our superiority we become rather solicitous about Williams. "Here, you bastard," I hear Novotny say to him, "eat this." Novotny, the altruist, is actually giving some of his own food to Williams.

[6]

March. Williams has died after all and we are back in the hut after burying him. Heather speaks. "I say we ought to write a protest to the camp commander."

"Yeah?" Matthew says.

"I'll write it," I say. "Anyone have any paper?" While we are hunting around for paper the sentences begin to form in my mind. They have the high, Winterode ring to them. *Sir!* I intend to write. *We wish to express our most solemn and energetic disapprobation of the food and medical services in this camp.* I intend to hint that unless he improves things he may find himself charged with crimes against humanity. The phrase *Tribunal of Mankind* is going to be worked in somehow. And why have we not received Red Cross packages, or mail?

Then I am presented with a dirty blue piece of paper, an unfolded overseas envelope provided by Poniatowski (who is getting better, amazingly enough). On the back I can see female writing. Sometime last August, sitting in her home in Detroit, Poniatowski's mother had seen fit to pen the news that Anna is engaged to a fellow with a good job at Ford.

180

Who is Anna? Poniatowski's sister, or his girlfriend? It makes a lot of difference. Also it convinces me reality is not going to be altered by my indignant sentences. I hand back the envelope. "We can't send in our protest on this kind of paper."

[7]

April. The snows begin to melt. Like a thunderclap news comes that Truman has canned MacArthur. The fall of that great prince has a depressing effect on me. I realize I have been harboring the totally irrational hope that Mac will somehow pull the chestnuts out of the fire and rescue us from Pyot Lon. Now he is gone and where is help and why wasn't I warned that life could be like this?

That was the day I tried to eat a worm. Walking outdoors that afternoon I saw a robin with its head cocked to the ground. He pounced, found his food, and went flying off. After a bit I took a stick and prodded the earth. I found a worm of my own. Should I? I did. Down it went and up it came just as quickly, apparently none the worse for its adventure. I left it to crawl away and think things over. I'd learned *my* lesson.

[8]

And as if to reward me for holding out and not eating vile and prohibited foods, the Chinese issue us meat for the first time. Meat! Real Meat. Meat to eat. We argue about it as we look at our morsels, and resume the argument as soon as we have downed them. I maintain, and still do maintain, that the viand in question originated on a superannuated water buffalo. Novotny holds it was horsemeat.

"It was water buffalo," I say.

"What the hell do you know about it, Heather? My father's a butcher and I know horsemeat when I see it."

Fresh light on Novotny. "Your father sells horsemeat?" I ask.

"The hell he does. He sells good meat."

"Then how do you know what horsemeat looks like if your father doesn't sell it?"

"I know meat," Novotny says. "That was horsemeat."

"It was water buffalo."

I turn away from him. He grabs my collar to arrest my movement. The rotted fabric tears. I turn back to see Novotny standing with a stupid expression on his face, my collar dangling from his fist. Quick as a wink I slug him in the stomach. I have a theory. There is a lot of good clay in Novotny's composition. The Chinese have hollowed him out a bit. Now is the time to give him a quick spin on the potter's wheel to see if he can't be shaped up into a thing of beauty and a joy forever.

He clutches his stomach. "Wudge ya hit me for?" he says. The fact that he doesn't attack me at once is some mark of the ascendancy I have gained in that hut.

"Why'd you tear my collar?" I ask.

"I didn't tear it. It just came loose."

"Will you guys knock it off?" Hollins asks. Since the deaths of Williams and Rubecker there is room on the sleeping shelf for Hollins. He is therefore a less prominent eyesore than he has been, though he still emerges from the dark every morning to lower his trousers and get a good look at his sores. It is a regular after-breakfast feature of life in Pyot Lon —like reading Walter Lippmann or the Alsop brothers at home.

"Be quiet," I tell him.

Novotny, having had time to consider my provocation, says, "Listen, Heather! We're getting tired of you."

"Yeah!" says Hollins.

So it has come to this! I turn on Hollins. "Who saved your life? Who carried you here? Who's washed your pants? Who's kept this hut going all winter?"

Novotny, his wits sharpened by hunger and outrage, says, "Not you! I've done a hell of a lot more than you have, Heather."

"You! You couldn't even kill a rabbit."

"And what have you done?" he asks.

"I cleaned up this whole hut last week while you just loafed around."

"You cleaned it up!" Hollins says. "Hubler did most of the work."

"And who's chopped more wood than anyone else?" I say.

"You haven't chopped any more than I have," says Novotny.

"And who fixed the stovepipe?"

"Who broke it?" Poniatowski asks.

"It just broke," I say.

"Listen, Heather!" says Novotny. He has stopped massaging his stomach. "Listen . . ."

"And who's slept on the floor all winter while you've had a good place on the sleeping shelf?" I ask him.

"I have," says Matthew.

"Listen!" Novotny says again.

"I've done more than anyone in this hut," I say.

"You never shared your food with anyone," says Novotny. "What did you ever do for Williams?"

"I brought in sassafras bark," I say. "Don't forget that."

"And what a treat that was," Matthew remarks.

They're all against me! I look down at Matthew sitting on the floor. "And who had the idea of hanging Hollins' litter so we'd have room to stretch out?"

"And who knocked it down?" someone says.

183

"And who was trying to stop a fight?"

"And who's started most of them?" Hollins asks.

"All right!" I say. "All right!" I stare around the hut. "All right!" I say one last time, and then I grasp the door handle and stalk out into the compound where the late afternoon sun, declining in the west, has begun to gild the clouds a glorious pink. I would show them! I would do such things—I knew not what—but I would do such things as would astonish us all.

19

And thinking back I am still astonished by what I did. I read
Capital by Karl Marx. It happened this way: in May, prepar-
atory to their brainwashing program, the Chinese opened a
library at Pyot Lon and, of course, I fell in with the door.

Anyone who is a book-lover himself will understand my
emotions upon first looking into the Pyot Lon library. Much
had I traveled in the realms of gold and oft of one wide ex-
panse had I been told, yet never did I breathe its air serene
until I stepped across that charmed threshold. There in front
of eyes deprived for months of any reading matter worth the
name, there under my rapid and delighted scrutiny stood
whole shelves filled with the works of Marx and Engels and
Lenin and Stalin and Mao, together with many an odd and
rich volume by lesser luminaries in the pantheon. There were
also novels by Howard Fast, Jack London, Maxim Gorky,
Emile Zola, and Albert Maltz, to say nothing of Dickens, Balzac, and Tolstoy. On one table, arranged in chronological
order, lay issue after issue of *Soviet Life, Russia Today,* and
The New China, their covers bright with pictures of happy
Comrades gathering hay and building hydroelectric stations.
I was dazzled.

The librarian, one Chou, beamed his welcome. "You
read?" he asked, much as early Western missionaries must
once have asked his countrymen, *You pray?*

"I read," I said.

"Want to read book now?"

"Yes, now."

"Which book? Many books here to read."

"Have you got *The Eighteenth Brumaire of Louis Napoleon,* by Karl Marx?"

Something rather hard to describe happened to Chou's smile. It neither diminished nor did it increase in intensity. Rather as I stared deeply into its central radiance I seemed to discern another smile as if the Platonic idea of smile were visible through the perishable actuality of Chou's flesh. "You are Marxist?" he asked.

"I respect Marx," I said, "but basically I think he underestimates the importance of weather in human history."

"Weather?" said *mon petit Chou.*

"Climate. After all, the climate is as important as the ownership of the means of production."

Chou shook his head. His smile was gone, alas, and yet one cannot stare forever into the essence of bright effluence increate. "That is old-fashioned idea, not believed in now," he said.

"I believe in it," I said.

"No, it is not believed in," he said. He went to a bookshelf and came back with a volume open in his hands. "Here," he said, "you can see for yourself," and I found I was staring at a page from Mao's *On Contradiction.* There, just above Chou's scholarly forefinger, I saw the following sentences:

Many countries exist under almost the same geographical and climatic conditions, yet they are extremely different and uneven in their development. Tremendous social changes take place even in one and the same country while no change has occurred in its geography and climate. Imperialist Russia changed into the socialist Soviet Union and feudal, insulated Japan changed into imperialist Japan, while no change has occurred in the geography and climate of those two countries . . .

"That's interesting," I said.

Chou nodded vigorously. "Climate unimportant. You read this, not *Eighteenth Brumaire.*"

So I sat down to read Mao, whose prose, at least in English, had a plain, curiously simple sincerity which appealed

186

to me, although he was obviously wrong about the climate. I quickly spotted the fallacy in his argument—the socialist Soviet Union was just as imperialistic as Tsarist Russia (*plus ça change, plus c'est la même chose*) but I liked the essay "On Contradiction," and as I read it the conviction grew on me that my troubles might stem from the fact that I had never taken philosophy seriously enough. Maybe it was time to cut the comedy and buckle down to some serious reading. I'd asked for *The Eighteenth Brumaire* because the title had a fine, eccentric ring to it. Reading Mao I began to blush inwardly over my dilettante intellectualism, and when I finished the essay I looked Chou straight in the eyes and announced that now I would like to begin on *Capital.*

He was obviously impressed by the rapidity of my conversion and yet he was wise enough to suggest that something shorter and less arduous might be in order. He suggested Engels. I shook my head. He tried to interest me in an interesting work by Plekhanov. I would have none of it. I wanted the meaty word or nothing, and so Chou delivered into my waiting hands a Modern Library edition of *Capital.* I sat myself down to read the American editor's preface, the two Author's Prefaces, and the two Prefaces by Friedrich Engels (to the first English translation and the fourth German edition respectively), for this was to be no cursory reading. I had a lot of slipshod studying at Harvard to atone for. I intended to give Marx the full treatment.

And then began a strange, confused period in my life. It was not that I didn't understand it all; it was not even that I was bored. Or, rather, I was frequently bored by what was on the page in front of me, but never by the experience of myself reading *Capital,* if one can make that distinction. Sometimes, falling upon a sentence like "The two metamorphoses constituting the circuit are at the same time two inverse partial metamorphoses of two other commodities," I would feel a momentary itch to strangle Marx, but basically

187

my opinion of him went up and up. Imagine writing a book like this, I would say to myself, adding immediately, and imagine me reading it. It was thrilling. The heroic myth dies slowly; in fact it wasn't even ailing when I grew up in Kansas City. Pioneering . . . bigness . . . energy . . . persistence . . . they were in the air I breathed. And *Capital* fitted right into that framework, its sentences rolling ahead like the prairies, crisscrossed by watercourses all draining inevitably into the Mississippi of surplus value. I set out like a second Lewis and Clark expedition.

From time to time the Indians would try to bar my path and share my commodities. I got scarred beating my way out of ambushes, but by June I was approaching the continental divide where the waters separate into relative and absolute surplus value. Outside the library summer came to the valley of the Yalu, but up at my altitude we were involved in the changes of magnitude in the price of labor power. My thinking was haunted by images of Russian revolutionaries studying this book in Siberian exile and actually *making use* of it. The full heroism of the Marxist revolutionary tradition began to come home to me. What a dilettante Jefferson seemed, taking only five pages to prove King George was a tyrant unfit to rule. I was by then on page 568 of *Capital* and Marx was far from finished with his demonstration of the tyranny of capitalism. The whole American Revolution began to seem an impromptu, harum-scarum, ad hoc kind of affair, and George III was coming out smelling of roses compared to capitalism.

By late June I was in the midst of The Separation of Surplus Value into Capital and Revenue. I was no longer enjoying any part of the exercise, but I was going to finish if it killed me. During the first week in July I did finish. I closed the book and heaved a sigh and dust came out of my mouth. Still, it was a great book, and what was even more significant, *I had read it.* I wished Father were there to see me. Let

188

us hear no more about my lack of discipline and will power, I thought. Then I rose from my chair and went to the library window.

Outside the boys were playing softball. While I watched the game Novotny hit a long fly which Hubler muffed in the outfield, allowing Novotny to score. I felt a momentary twinge of annoyance. There was Novotny hitting things again and running around the bases while I . . . While *I* had just finished *Capital!* That was what really separated the men from the boys: those who had and those who had not finished *Capital.*

I looked around for Chou. Perhaps we could sit down together now and talk things over, one Marxist scholar to another. He was not in sight. My glance fell on a shelf of novels. *David Copperfield* was there. If I wished I could reach out and take it. In five minutes I could be back in Blunderstone Rookery with the sinister Mr. Murdstone about to loom up on my horizon. But could Mr. Murdstone ever impress me again? Hadn't I outgrown Dickens? I stayed my hand. I reached instead for *War and Peace.* I felt I deserved a picnic, but an *adult* picnic with rum and caviar in it. So I smuggled the book out of the library and bore it off to the riverbank where I found a comfortable spot and began to read:

"Well, Prince," said Anna Pavlovna Scherer on that July day in 1805, "Genoa and Lucca are now no more than private estates of the Bonaparte family." I was off. Dolohov drank his bottle of rum sitting on the windowsill. Nikolay kissed Sonia in the conservatory. Anna Mihalovna's face drooped with melancholy sympathy. Natasha giggled. The old Count danced. On and on it went: Austerlitz, money, sturgeons, duels . . . Natasha at her bedroom window at Otradnoe, exclaiming, "Oh my God how beautiful! What does it all mean?" Julie Karagin's anxious and imploring eyes, Princess Marya's walk, Anatole's leg, the Rostov's rugs, Moscow burning, Prince Andrey dying . . . It was all there just as I remembered it, only better because I knew it better. I read for five days, and on the afternoon of the sixth I finished and sank back on the grass to stare up through the leaves of an oak tree.

Thank God for novelists, I thought. And then I began thinking about women.

One thing to be said for keeping your prisoners on a low diet is that you solve *that* problem for them. But by July the diet was improved. Life had improved. Indeed at Kaesong they had just begun to discuss an armistice. The war would end soon. I was a man at last—twenty-one years old, with a war *and* prison camp *and Capital* under my belt. I could relax. I could forgive. I could lie back and think fond thoughts of Martha.

She was not a bad sort after all. Not much worse than Natasha and Natasha was perfect as far as I was concerned, though she almost runs off with that cretinous wretch Anatole Kuragin. Only Sonia and Marya Dmitrevna prevent her. Yet how childishly Prince Andrey had behaved about it, breaking their engagement and trying to duel Anatole! A man his age should know better, since even at my age I had just seen that these small charming girls get carried away by their own provocative powers, and one can hardly blame them for that. After all, if they can turn men's heads so easily, think how their own must be spinning around!

Dear Martha! Who was she sleeping with now? I could never love her again, of course, but I didn't want her to miss out on life or pine with vain regrets for all she had lost by betraying me. . . . Would we ever meet again? If they hurried up and signed the Armistice, there was still a chance I could be back in the States, even back at Harvard for the fall term. Though, of course, Martha would have graduated in June. Still, we might meet one day quite by accident. Perhaps she would catch sight of me from a distance as I walked

190

very slowly toward Widener. Tall, cloaked in the aura of battle and the dark mysteries of imprisonment, I would strike her as changed, more mature, more purposeful. Perhaps she would even follow me and wonder what book I was holding under my arm. And what book would it be? *Capital?* No. It was not a book one immediately rereads. Perhaps Lenin's *What Is To Be Done*. Yes, that would be better. Then I would turn my head and catch sight of her just when she was about to turn away. My expression would change. In a kindly, straightforward way I would go up to her and shake her hand. We would talk. She would understand that marriage was now out of the question. I was committed to a greater cause than my own personal happiness, a cause that would involve the overthrow of her father's bank and the whole unjust system of society in which the surplus value produced by labor was frivolously consumed by people like herself and (for that matter) by people such as I had once been. "I have wasted years of my life," I would tell her, "but now I know what is to be done," and I would tap my volume of Lenin and then proceed on my way to Widener to pursue my disciplined and rigorous enquiry into the fundamental contradictions of capitalist society. My thoughts would be concentrated on the means by which the proletariat, led by its vanguard (of whom I would be one), could bring to birth (without killing too many people like Mr. Sears) a truly human society in which men are at last masters rather than victims of historical change.

I liked the picture. Much as I admired Marx it struck me that a sort of Byronic Leninism might suit my style better. I could even develop a limp, though could one limp and still be part of the vanguard of the proletariat? I tried to think of revolutionaries with canes. Probably Ferdinand Lassalle had carried one. And wasn't Jaurès brandishing a cane in that famous picture in which he is haranguing a socialist crowd, trying to rally the people against the madness of the First

191

World War? Poor Jaurès! Shot by some fascistic social patriot. How many of the great revolutionaries had suffered! But they had also dared to stand up and wave their canes as well as limp along on them! Canes were useful. They were like umbrellas. In fact, I didn't need to develop a limp. I could carry an umbrella. Indeed, now that I thought about it, that picture of Jaurès showed him gesturing vigorously with his arms while a follower held an umbrella over his head. That was nice. Martha might even come to listen to one of my fiery speeches as I stood on a rostrum in Roxbury or Mystic with the rain pouring down, a sea of faces tilted up listening to my impassioned flow of tensely logical argument while a young follower stood behind holding an umbrella over my bared head. I would not wear a hat. . . . Or was it a hat Jaurès was holding in his hand? No, that was Lenin in another picture gesturing to a Petrograd crowd with his funny cap clenched in his fist. It was just like the kind of golfing cap Bobby Jones and John D. Rockefeller used to wear. As a matter of fact, as a kid I had had a cap just like that. It had a stiff visor with a button.

My eyes closed. I seemed to be sinking into a rather disorderly reverie. Oh well. The next day, or the day after that, or perhaps the following day I would get back to work on some great task. Or the war might end and we'd all go home, so why bother too much about anything in such weather and after having survived such a winter and spring? We really deserved medals. I wondered if there was a P.O.W. medal, like a Purple Heart. There ought to be one. Perhaps we could get the army to recognize the remarkable endurance and fortitude we'd displayed. After all, it's a lot easier to be heroic with a gun in your hand surrounded by a lot of armed buddies than to do what we'd done. When the story of the Korean war was fully known it would turn out that we P.O.W.'s had really carried the ball and shown what Americans are made of.

I thought of the prisoner Platon Karataev in *War and Peace* and his cheerful cosmic acceptance of things. How Russian! We'd not been like that. We'd hated Pyot Lon. And we'd hated each other. And that's the way things ought to be. The army should strike a medal for us: Two Bitches Rampant with Worms Impaled on a Toasting Fork against a Field of Black. That would do it. When I got home I would join the American Legion, and if some thick-waisted, heavy-thighed veteran of one of our more successful wars should ever ask me where I'd served, I'd say *Pyot Lon!* Like *Guadalcanal!* Or *Agincourt!* We would all join the Legion and meet year after year at convention hotels, a happy band of brothers recalling how we had stood together in our darkest hour, bereft of support from the American army, oppressed by the Chinese, humiliated and forgotten and indomitable. We would rent our own ballroom in Atlantic City and allow no one to enter who had not been in Pyot Lon during the months of December to May. We would be exclusive and proud, a dwindling band exchanging reminiscences no one else could understand or appreciate. I saw myself twenty years hence pounding Novotny on the back. "Say, remember how we used to fight?"

He'd say, "Do I! Wow!"

"I didn't hurt you too much, did I?"

"Naw. I hardly felt it. I didn't hurt you, did I?"

"Yes, you bastard, you did."

"Good old Heather!"

The scene almost brought tears to my eyes.

Then I heard a heavy footfall and presently Novotny himself appeared, trampling the daisies underfoot and dropping to the ground beside me. "We've got another effing lecture scheduled tonight," he said.

"I wonder what it will be about?" I said.

"Who the eff gives an eff?"

He was not taking advantage of the educational opportunites at Pyot Lon. He liked his mind the way it was and he freely stated (out of Chinese hearing) that no Chink could tell him what to think.

"Eff all lectures," Novotny said, from the center of some private malaise.

I felt slightly discontented to have him settling down on the riverbank beside me. True, I had just been thinking fondly of him, but that was twenty years hence and in Atlantic City. Two Novotnys in the bush are worth one in the hand. I looked over at him, pondering the low forehead, the lowering expression, the heavy jaw. I wondered, not for the first time, why such a poetic and high-minded young man as myself should have spent so much of his life in college and now at Pyot Lon consorting with the Novotnys and Bartoldis of this world. Was it fate? Or was there an even more sinister explanation? Maybe I was a latent homosexual attracted to thugs of the Novotny type?

That was a scary idea. I closed my eyes and tried to imagine myself putting my arm around Arnold and kissing him. The picture thus formed had a very cheering effect on me. If ever Novotny and I fought again, I *would* kiss him. It was Christian to kiss your enemies, and since Novotny was waxing strong again under the effects of sunshine and better feeding, that might be the best tactic to use on him. A kiss on the cheek from me would really send him ass over backwards. I realized I had him in my power.

"Arnold," I said, "would you like me to help you understand the production of absolute surplus value?"

"Nobody's gonna make an effing Commie outta me," he said.

That was so indubitably true I couldn't argue about it. Besides, why argue? Why even think about the problem of becoming the vanguard of a proletariat composed of people like Novotny? Better not to convert him. A Novotny in the works could jam up the flow of the dialectical historical process itself. Much nicer to think about Martha out there in

194

my Mystic audience, looking and listening as I orated and gestured. Afterwards she would come forward and I would be able to see my words had touched her heart. All her coyness and sophistication would have melted away. She would stand in front of me, demure and maidenly, and then with a quick gesture she would slip out of her mink coat, allowing it to fall in the mud. "Take me with you wherever you are going," she would say.

"Boy, I wish I was back on Schragg Avenue," said Novotny.

Other people's reveries are less poetic than your own. I didn't want to hear about Schragg Avenue or any other part of Whiting. I knew that town. A big yellow factory topped by a giant Lux box gives the unwary traveler his first intimation of the horrors ahead. Then some streets of squalid bungalows, after which all hell breaks loose. On one side of the tracks there's a giant Union Carbide installation. On the other side: Standard Oil. Pipes writhe in frozen agony like the entrails of the damned. Ferocious cracking units loom over you. Then you fall among oil storage tanks, each squatting isolated in its earthen pen like so many bloated capitalist pigs. By day the town is marked by a pillar of smoke, at night by a pillar of fire. If Whiting is the beacon, we'll all be asphyxiated before we get our Pisgah sight of the new Promised Land. "You're better off here," I told Novotny. "At least you've got some nice mountains to look at," and I pointed across the river to the mountains of Manchuria.

"Eff the nice mountains," said Novotny. "I got a girl on Schragg."

Well, all the world loves a lover. "What's her name?" I asked.

"Mildred."

I nodded. Then Novotny said, "You got a girl, Heather?"

It was practically the first decent question he'd ever asked me, though it nearly broke my heart since I couldn't say *Martha* in the same confident voice he'd said *Mildred*.

"Rachel," I said.

The answer satisfied Novotny. So we continued to lie on the grass, he thinking of his Mildred and I thinking of my Rachel. Who was she? She sounded Jewish. I began to picture her: a long-haired Jewish princess descended from many generations of high-minded radicals, perhaps an Aveling, a great-great-granddaughter of Marx himself. *She* would have an even better grip on *Capital* than I had. In fact, why not put her up there on the rostrum? I transferred myself into the body of my Mystic audience and when her speech was over, I came forward and threw away my cane and golf hat. "All I want to do is serve you and the Revolution," I would say. I liked that picture better. Rather than a leader I was perhaps better suited as an acolyte of the dialectic, drinking tea in the company of venerable Marxists and letting their wisdom flow into me. Then when their words began to weary my brain, I could always turn my eyes onto the beauty of the Revolution incarnated in my Rachel. Leading a revolution could be a lot of trouble. Rachel and I would do our part, but basically we would live for each other. One doesn't really want power, one wants love.

"Jesus, I need a woman," Novotny said.

His presence was definitely disturbing. "Go away," I said.

"What do you mean, *go away?*" I saw he was looking at me with that magic blend of indignation, thick-headedness, and suspicion I knew so well. "This ain't your private spot."

"When someone asks you to go away, the polite thing to do is go away."

"Listen, Heather!"

"Think about it," I said. "Am I asking so much? All I want is to be left alone."

Novotny said, "You've got a lot of nerve."

"Okay, you asked for it," I said, and I kissed him. He cleared out after that.

20

There's more than one way to rule the roost. I had Novotny on the run for the next few weeks. I rank that peck right up there with my accidental knock-down of Bartoldi when we were both freshmen. Unhappily the Chinese didn't let me enjoy the triumph.

This brings us to the vexed subject of brainwashing. The Pyot Lon library was simply a service institution. No one becomes a Communist just by reading books, nor is the trick accomplished by listening to lectures. The Chinese forced us to attend political lectures, but they well understood that you can't alter people's minds by lecturing at them, unless you happen to have a spellbinder like I. A. Richards to put on the podium. Richards was the greatest teacher I had at Harvard and he was pure lecturer, yet his lectures weren't like any others. I shall never forget the day he started to act out the retreat of Abner son of Ner after the battle beside the pool of Gibeon. Before anyone knew what was happening, Richards had assumed Abner's identity. He began to run in place on the podium, holding his lecture rod balanced in his hand like a spear. Then he looked over his shoulder to warn Azahel son of Zeruiah (who was in pursuit) not to get any closer. But Azahel, fleet of foot, ignored the warning, and with one mighty backhand thrust Richards rammed his lecture rod through Azahel's midriff. It was electrifying. I had thought I understood the Old Testament; Richards showed me I still had a lot to learn. His course alone was worth the price of admission to Harvard.

The Chinese, since they had no one of Richards' stature to lecture to us, fell back on what (in the absence of inspiration) seems to be the standby of modern education: the group discussion. The heart, core, center, linchpin, capstone, and pivot of brainwashing was what the Chinese called criticism/self-criticism, and what would probably be called group therapy in this country. The mechanics were simple. Groups of ten to twenty prisoners met outdoors in the best Socratic tradition to talk about their lives and hard times under the general supervision of a smart young Chinese political instructor.

In the middle of July I joined one such group because a) it was something to do, and b) Father had taught me never to miss a chance to improve myself. Comrade Liu was in charge of the group I joined. He was a dapper young man in his early thirties who had studied at Stanford. His English was good (better than that of most P.O.W.'s) and what was more he knew something about American life. I became quite attached to him, and some members of my group— Poniatowski, for instance—developed a real transference.

The object of the exercise was to make us critically aware of how a competitive capitalist economic system distorts human relationships and destroys social values. We were not encouraged to attack the system directly, which would have required an intellectual apparatus and a Marxist training which none of us had. I was in some ways the least useful and most disruptive member of my group, just because I was more prepared than the others to attack the system at an abstract intellectual level. Liu had to warn me in private not to generalize and conceptualize but to stick more to my own experiences. "You more than anyone here have been damaged by capitalist competitiveness. Do not try always to be first to speak. Do not try to dominate the discussion. Be more honest."

"Sir!" I said. (This was before we were on more intimate terms.) "I *am* honest. It's just that they're so slow-witted I can't help dominating."

"There!" Liu said. "Is that not a perfect illustration of

198

what is wrong with you? You have no comradely feelings. For you life is a continuous combat to prove your own superiority."

"That's not the whole story."

"We would like to hear your story, not your general reflections on life. It would be most valuable for the others to understand how even a privileged young man like yourself is ruined as a human being by the very system that rewards him in other ways."

"I don't think I'm ruined as a human being."

Liu smiled. He had a quite nice smile with strong, even teeth. He was from the North of China and had the sort of manly-jawed handsomeness of Chou En-lai rather than the dumpling looks of Chairman Mao. Except for the need to wear glasses, Liu was a rather unblemished specimen, though his smiles, his calm assumption that I was a human wreck, and most of all his coddling of the other members of the group got onto my nerves to a very considerable extent.

"What are you smiling about?" I asked.

"At the way you hug your own chains," he said. "For you life could be much happier if you could drop your aggressiveness and ruthless competitiveness as well as your crippling feelings of superiority."

"Oh, is that so?" I said.

There was no smile in response to that. "One other thing. You must drop this insolent attitude toward those in authority."

His warning came early in August when my insolence was fanned to white heat by a temporary halt in the truce talks, which had not been making quite so much progress as I had hoped for in early July. The U.N. negotiators had broken off the talks because some Communist patrols had entered the demilitarized zone around Kaesong where meetings were then held. (Later the meetings were transferred to Pan-

199

munjon.) We were all sore about the matter, but I feel I was the sorest person in Pyot Lon. At this rate we wouldn't be home before Halloween.

Still I stuck to the criticism/self-criticism sessions because I was fascinated by what was happening as a result of Liu's skillful handling of the discussions. Characters like Poniatowski and Hollins and Ramirez were actually developing a social conscience! I had lived with them for months without suspecting that anything so encouraging could take place in their psychologies. Lying around in the hut during the winter and spring we'd had the usual nauseating kind of dormitory bull sessions in which the point is to brag about how bad you've been. You know the conversation. It takes place in locker rooms and the library of the Harvard Club and wherever men get together and feel unrestrained by the presence of some morally superior individual. Then the stockbrokers start telling each other what sharks they've been and the jocks start telling each other what whoremongers they've been, and so it goes. I've even heard the conversation in mixed company when groups of liberals brag about their helplessness in the face of some fresh assault on decency. I think what I dislike most about the conversation is the tacit assumption that everyone present is essentially a rogue, a libertine, and a weakling. I may be all those things, but I don't like others to assume I am until I've proved it.

But as Liu remarked, we would like to hear your story not your general reflections on life, and my story at this point illustrates the astonishing point that self-pity can be a morally regenerative force. During the winter I'd heard Ramirez blandly describe his career in crime from thefts of penny candy at the age of four up to his arrest in a hot Pontiac at seventeen, an event which nearly prevented him from enlisting in the army to get away from a drunken father who used to beat him every Saturday night.

Liu was marvelous with him. He encouraged Ramirez to

200

talk about the hardships his family had undergone, and believe me they were something. "Let me tell you," Ramirez told us, "it was a good deal for me, getting into the army."

"Well, it was a good deal for me, too," I said.

"Yeah? You never had to worry about a thing."

"That's all you know."

"You went to college. You never had to work in your life." He tapped himself on the chest. "Maybe some of us had the brains to go to college, but we never had a chance."

"Listen!" I said.

"You listen. Poor people have it rough."

"I'm not saying they don't. I'm just saying middle-class people have it rough too."

"You're not middle class," Hollins said. "My family was middle class and we sure couldn't afford Harvard."

"The tuition at Harvard was only four hundred dollars. It doesn't take money to get in, it takes brains."

"Only four hundred dollars!" said Ramirez. "And where was I going to get that?"

"Steal it," I said.

"You calling me a thief?" he asked.

I looked at him, astonished. "Well you are one, aren't you?"

"I ought to pop you for that," he told me.

He was absolutely swelling with moral sensitivity and intellectual aspiration. And so were the others. Class consciousness was developing, too. Poniatowski, who was Liu's ablest product, remarked that one reason I'd been able to get into Harvard because of my brains was that I'd never had to work. "You had time to read and all."

"Also I had brains," I said.

"Don't you think we have some, too?" Hollins asked.

His leg was healed by then. I felt he was strong enough to take it. "You're not particularly intelligent," I told him. Occasionally the truth must out.

201

He flushed clear to the tips of his ears. He was getting to his feet when Liu intervened. He encouraged a spirit of vigorous criticism and self-criticism, but he did not permit fighting. "And what does this conversation prove?" he asked.

"It proves Heather's a bastard," Ramirez said.

Hollins, still incandescent at my insult to his intelligence, said, "You think you're so great because your father's a bishop."

This was news to some members of the group, and excited the particular attention of one O'Brien from South Boston. "Hey!" he said, "are you really a bastard?"

"In *our* church," I told him, "bishops can marry."

"Are we not getting away from the point?" Liu asked.

Poniatowski came through like a trooper. "The conversation proves that Heather can use his brain to insult people and express his antisocial instincts, while workers just get drunk and fight, and then they're picked up by the police."

"I fight too," I said.

Hollins said, "You're the lousiest guy I know, Heather."

"But what is wrong with him?" Liu asked.

"Look, why are we talking about me?" I said.

Ramirez said, "Poniatowski's right. He's antisocial."

These guardians and keepers of the social virtues! I looked around the group, my gaze coming to rest on Poniatowski. "And I suppose you're a model citizen?"

"I'm better than you, anyway."

"We all are," Ramirez said.

"You are not!" I said. "I don't lie or cheat or steal. Look, I've never stolen anything in my life."

"I don't believe it," Poniatowski said.

"All right, once. I stole an ornamental button when I was five years old and anyway it was for my mother, it wasn't for me."

"You didn't need to steal," Ramirez said.

"You want to know what my allowance was until I was ten? A dime a week. You think I lived it up on that?"

"A tough life," Ramirez said.

"Well it was a tough life. A dime a week and the weight of all past generations weighing on my brain like a nightmare."

Liu grinned, recognizing the source of my comment.

Poniatowski said, "And how come you never stole more than a button?"

Stealing was one of the main topics of discussion at these sinister brainwashing sessions. Liu and his Comrades were trying to instill some elementary concepts of social responsibility into the P.O.W.'s. They were very down on stealing. The problem was to get the P.O.W.'s to recognize it as a grave moral and social wrong.

"The reason I never stole again was that Father found out I'd taken that button." And then I told them about the scene that had followed; a genuine old-fashioned spanking and then a trip downtown to the Woolworth store where I was made to apologize and hand over my ill-gotten gains to an astonished store manager, who said, "I'm sure you'll never do this again." With Father looming behind me, my bottom still tingling, my system emptied of tears, and humiliation and disgrace turning my hair prematurely gray, I assured him I never would. I was five then. "And I've never stolen anything since," I concluded sixteen years later to my deeply impressed audience at Pyot Lon. "So don't call me a bad citizen," I said to Poniatowski.

Liu had been highly amused by my account of the button. He said, "Such terroristic Puritan methods as your father used may succeed in preventing the repetition of a crime, but do they lead to a love of the community and a real sense of social values?"

"No," said Poniatowski.

"And why is that?"

"What's wrong with stealing," said old teacher's pet, "is that it destroys trust between people. Everyone goes around locking up and suspecting others. Just scaring people out of stealing doesn't create trust and respect for others. Look at Heather."

"Why are we always looking at me?" I said.

"You ask for it," someone said.

"Yeah!" said Hollins.

"I hate you all," I said.

"There!" said Poniatowski.

I stayed afterwards to talk with Liu on a man-to-man basis. "Do you really think this is doing them any good?" I asked. "I mean, I can see how they're developing certain basic notions of the communal good, and they're becoming sensitive to moral and intellectual values, but don't you think by encouraging them to pick me apart you'll just weaken their respect for the virtues I do have?"

"What virtues do you have?" Liu asked.

"Well, really!" I said. "I am honest."

Liu gave me a straight look. "You are perhaps the greatest thief in the whole group."

"Now just a minute . . ."

"Today, for instance, you said the weight of all past generations weighs on your brain like a nightmare."

"Well it does."

"That is a phrase you have stolen from Karl Marx. It occurs near the beginning of the Eighteenth Brumaire of Louis Napoleon."

Feeling, and probably looking very innocent, I said, "Well I don't consider that *theft*. Everyone quotes famous authors."

"You were not *quoting*."

"Maybe not, but it certainly doesn't do anybody any harm. It's not antisocial to quote Marx." I felt like a worldly burglar explaining to a wide-eyed naïf that banks were insured and anyway the money didn't really belong to anyone.

Liu was unimpressed. "It is quite antisocial to abuse intellectual property by misusing other people's words and applying serious ideas in a half-serious manner."

"I . . ."

"Such conduct cheapens and damages the intellectual property that belongs to the whole community and at the same time it destroys our respect for you, just as you show your disrespect for Marx by using him without acknowledgment.

"Surely this is a rather strained view of things?" I said.

"You have much to learn about yourself," Liu said.

"I admit I'm not perfect."

"Already you have earned the dislike of most of the members of your group, but this does not bother you because you feel superior to them and able to take what you want from life. Yet one day you will find that without a true sense of social values, without respect for others and a feeling of responsibility toward the community, you will be isolated from all your fellow men and truly hating them and being hated in return."

Where had I heard cadences like those before?

21

It has been my fate to be well ground between the upper and nether millstones of two different systems of moral coerciveness: Father's and the system represented by Liu. That neither Father nor Liu completely succeeded with me should not be taken as a sign that the systems are at fault. We must never allow ourselves to be discouraged about the possibilities of human perfectibility. Think of all the great Christian saints and Marxist heroes and the host of faithful, cheerful, dutiful, hard-working men and women who actually care about the world around them and the way their societies are developing. Really, one can only admire good Communists and good Christians.

I think what went wrong in my case is that neither Father nor Liu had sufficient control over me. Father subjected me to a Christian upbringing in what is after all a non-Christian world, while Liu's Communist reforms were applied in what is after all a non-Communist world. But, who knows? Even the Russian Revolution might have turned out better if the whole world, or at least all Europe, had gone Communist in 1917. The isolated and threatened position of the Bolshevik régime certainly accounts for much of the moral and bureaucratic deterioration of the Soviet state. And comparable disasters have overtaken Christianity in the past. The Mohammedan irruption broke up the unity of the Mediterranean world and inaugurated the Christian Dark Ages. Perhaps without the Mohammedans around the Christian Empire of Rome could have held together and the great Papal-Imperial conflict which rent the high Middle Ages would not have occurred. Dante's Ghibelline dreams might have been actualized and we could have had a high Catholic

Imperial civilization to this very day. The point is that neither Christianity nor communism has had a real chance to show what could be done with men, but in both I see great possibilities. Both have shown an amazing ability to recover from their own mistakes and defeats and put forth new, creative life. For instance Protestantism arose out of the Christian failure to achieve what Dante hoped for, while Maoist communism has arisen out of the failure to achieve what Lenin and Trotsky hoped for.

The Chinese Revolution is really a new departure and basically different from the Russian. The Bolsheviks simply shot the Tsar and Tsarina and Tsarevitch and all the poor Tsarevnas (plus their dogs). The Chinese Communists would not have done that because they believe there is hope for everyone. And they have the time, the patience, and the manpower to put such a belief into practice. Thus when Henry Pu-Yi, the last Manchu emperor, fell into their hands, they stuck him into prison for ten years where they struggled with him, worked over him, and finally got him to make his own bed, wash his own clothes, shake hands, speak politely to others, and show a little elementary trust in and respect for other men. Theoretically an ex-Son of Heaven like Pu-Yi should be utterly incorrigible, but the Communists did succeed in reforming him. Then he was released. He got himself elected to the Red Congress (you can't keep an emperor down) and when last heard from he was standing on Prospect Hill in Peking looking out over the golden rooftops of the Forbidden City where he grew up. As the sun set in the West he found himself repeating the first lines of the *Three Word Primer* which he had been taught as a boy but never understood until he had learned what it is like to be a man:

Jen chih chu   When man is born
hsing pen shan   His nature is basically good

| hsing hsiang chin | Human nature is similar |
| hsi hsiang yuan | Only environment makes it diverse. |

Read about it in his autobiography, *The Last Manchu,* edited by Paul Kramer of the CIA. It's a great story, but it's Henry Pu-Yi's. This is mine, and I had better get back to it.

Late in August a dreadful thing happened. An American plane bombed the Chinese truce delegation at Kaesong, and so the Communists broke off negotiations.

"Isn't that just what you'd expect of the air force?" I said to Matthew. He was one of the few people I could talk to in those days.

"So they'll start up the talks again," Matthew said.

"How can you be so relaxed about it? Don't you realize this could mean we won't be home till Thanksgiving?"

"Stewing about it won't do any good," Matthew said. He had developed quite a fund of philosophy since the food had improved.

"What's your secret?" I asked. We were sitting side by side on a log in the warm sun. Below us the broad and majestic Yalu flowed toward the sea. Matthew needed only a whittle stick and a knife to be a picture of the perfect American sage, full of deep, inarticulate wisdom. "What are you so calm about?"

"What are you so jumpy about?" he asked.

"Listen! If you were taking part in these criticism/self-criticism sessions you'd be jumpy too."

"So drop out of them. You don't have to go."

"Well, but I'm learning about myself."

"Is that so good?" he asked.

"Good? It's terrible. Self-knowledge is mainly bad news."

"So drop out."

I gave him a scornful look. "You can't just drop out of things when the going gets bad." He shrugged. Neither of us spoke for a while. Then I said, "Human life is too much. I'd like to be a protozoa just dividing and multiplying without a care in the world."

"I'd like to own my own garage," Matthew said. I felt defeated by such an essentially reasonable ambition.

"Is that all?" I asked.

"I guess so." He yawned. The sun made him sleepy, also the moon and stars. He was getting a lot of sleep in those days. He grinned. "And I will own that baby yet." He'd worked as a mechanic in Racine, Wisconsin, and he was married to a local girl. Part of his general contentment in those days was that we'd at last had some mail from home. His news was good. Mine was just so-so. The Bishop had written a deeply felt, touching letter about the long period of anxiety he and Mother had passed through, their profound relief and gratitude to God when they learned I was alive, and now their deep concern for my moral and spiritual welfare as a prisoner. It seemed I was enthroned in their hearts, mentioned in their prayers, and never far from their thoughts. P.S. They were both in good health, Kansas City hadn't burned down in my absence, and the cathedral was at last getting its new roof. Somehow the Bishop's letters, even when well meant, had a dampening effect on my spirits.

Which had been dampened enough by *szu-hsiang kai-tsao,* which seems to me a more elegant phrase than brainwashing, or criticism/self-criticism. By late August we were onto the subject of vandalism. Not only was I a great thief of other people's intellectual property, but I was a vandal damaging the poetry and ideas I touched, to say nothing of blowing up riverbanks and sticking knives into sawdust bears. I could see just where I was heading: murder. For that matter I probably was guilty of killing some Chinese during my couple of hours of battle. It takes a lot of sinning to make a Heather whole. Oddly enough Liu was keeping us off the subject of sex, probably for compassionate reasons. Sex was becoming an unendurable subject even to think about, which (since I was thinking about it all the time) gives you some notion of just how carefree I felt as we slid into the autumn of 1951.

"I realize I'm antisocial," I said to Liu in private one day, "but I don't see what I can do about it. That's just the way I am."

"Are you not ashamed of yourself?" he asked.

"Of course I'm ashamed of myself. But at my age it's just too late to change. I'm twenty-one years old."

"That is not such a great age."

"I feel older than the rocks which surround me." There were some small rocks on the ground. "That's a quotation from Walter Pater," I added.

"It is this eclectic and aesthetic attitude toward life which hampers you," Liu said. "You pick and choose according to your own taste without consulting any general principles."

"I know," I said, "but to have general principles you've got be convinced about things. I just don't have any faith."

"It is the great fault of all the prisoners here. America has given them no faith in Man, and the decadent Christianity in which they have been raised has given them no faith in God."

"The Christianity in which I was raised wasn't very decadent," I said.

"That is the chief of your problems," Liu said. "Your father has crippled you as a human being, and yet you will not repudiate him or attack his whole system of values."

"Actually, he's a pretty good man," I said. "He's not antisocial. He believes in holding society together and making people feel part of some congregation."

"But like all modern Christians he is powerless against the humanly divisive and selfishly competitive tendencies of capitalism."

I sighed. "I suppose so. Kansas City isn't a very Christian city in spite of Father's work."

"Naturally not. He is working in the wrong way. It is only by abandoning his unreal idealistic metaphysics and looking at society in a truly dialectical way that one arrives at a correct understanding of the situation and of what is to be done." When the dialectic came into our conversations my thoughts always flew out the window. I nodded vaguely. "Your father is a failure," Liu said.

"Not entirely. He's just put a new roof on his cathedral."

Liu smiled. "Always you will find some way to make a joke."

I apologized. "It's just I get too depressed to do anything else."

And there was no joy in Mudville (get the allusion, Reader?) throughout the early part of the autumn. The truce talks did not resume until October. I was beginning to think we wouldn't be home until Christmas, and meanwhile I was being *szu-hsiang kai-tsaoed* right off my feet. Inevitably we had gotten onto the subject of war. Everyone in the group frankly admitted he'd come to Korea with absolutely no idea of what the war was about and no feelings one way or another concerning the Korean struggle for unification and national independence.

"I never even heard of Korea," Poniatowski said.

Liu said, "And yet at the bidding of your government you came to kill Koreans and prevent the unification of this country."

We all nodded. Those were the facts all right.

Liu said, "Is this not the height of antisocial irresponsibility?"

"Maybe," I said, "but the truth is fighting had a civilizing effect on me. I bet soldiers in an average combat platoon feel a lot closer to each other than neighbors on an average city

211

block." This was a conviction that had been growing on me ever since I'd been captured. I'd really cared about Winterode more deeply than I'd ever cared about another guy my own age—though he had to be dead before I could give way to my tenderness.

"But is that not the height of shame?" Liu asked. "That only in militaristic and imperialistic adventures abroad does American society provide its young men with the feeling of working and fighting together?"

Hollins said, "Whaddya mean, *civilizing*, Heather? War's murder, that's all it is."

"Oh put your head in the oven," I told him, and then they all jumped on me like trained fleas and before very long I was made to feel like a bloody-handed militarist.

At the Battle of Fredericksburg, as he watched his Army of Northern Virginia mop up on the hapless Army of the Potomac, Robert E. Lee, that great man, remarked that it is good war is so terrible otherwise we would love it so much we would always be fighting. That was basically how I felt about the matter, though admittedly war had become even worse since Lee's day. Still I had a remedy for that: dynamite, the old Heather solution to complex problems. Blow up the Pentagon, hang all the unchivalric generals, and then set to work designing a prettier uniform for the troops. No one wants to fight or die dressed like a slob in olive drab. At the Battle of Balaklava the Eleventh Light Dragoons charged up the Valley of Death tightly encased in cherry-colored trousers, and if you've got to go it seemed obvious to me you ought to go dressed up like that. It was hard, however, to put this point of view across to my fellow P.O.W.'s, and more often than not they succeeded in putting their point of view across to me. I was probably a murderer. "Alas, My God," I might have said, stealing and vandalizing Candide's line, "I am the mildest man in the world and already I have killed eleven months here in Korea, ten and a half of them in prison." For though I might be a murderer and was certainly rather rude and domineering in my ways, I was perfectly convinced I was a good and mild man and that all I needed was some freedom in order to become the sunny and entirely likable person I'd been back in the sweet old days at Harvard. One of the funniest and perhaps most encouraging things about life is that everyone secretly believes he is good. Our natures are so ineradicably moral that no one can honestly want to be a bad man. Even the topsy-turvy moralists who laud corruption and the crazy tyrants who kill millions of people think of themselves as doing good work.

Well, I was eventually going to do some good work in this world, though as we got into the month of November I realized I wouldn't be home by Christmas after all. I set my sights on Epiphany and gritted my teeth through the *szu-hsiang kai-tsao,* which went on in its endless, dripping way.

I said to Liu, "I admit I've learned a lot about myself, and I can see that I have serious antisocial traits, but I think being cooped up in Pyot Lon is partly responsible. I never used to hate people this much."

He nodded sagely. "I agree. It is wearisome here, but the news from Panmunjon is encouraging."

"Ah, fine."

He smiled. "And perhaps we will send you and some others back to America improved and made into better citizens."

"You know?" I said. "It's really very remarkable that you're taking this kind of trouble with us."

"We wish to help all men."

"Very benevolent, I'm sure."

I got his *no insolence* look. Then I went back to the hut where Novotny, leader of the local reactionaries, was sitting beside the stove picking his nose.

"Arnold," I said to him, "you are about the ugliest, least hopeful sight I've laid eyes on all day."

For a miracle we were alone in the hut. He got up. "I've

been waiting for this," he said, and we had what amounted to a formal fist fight. I lasted surprisingly well, everything considered. When I felt I was bruised enough I dropped my arms. "All right," I said, "you're stronger than I am."

Then that night, lying awake fingering the sore spots, I had a little insight. The blows we invite from life are a test of our strength, which is why people like Novotny are so valuable. They're strong and they're willing to hit you. The attack of a person like Hollins proves nothing one way or another, but if you can last out a few rounds with Novotny then maybe you're not quite as weak as you feel.

22

We come now to the most fabulous period of my life, though the real drama took place not at Pyot Lon but all over the map through time and space and involves such outstanding figures of our times as Stalin, Hitler, Truman, and Dean Acheson, to mention only a few of the remarkable characters who now enter my story to play their allotted roles. True, I was not present at any scenes described in this chapter, but I have read some of the books and meditated on the history of our times. With the aid of my visionary powers plus my basic grip of reality, I think I can convey the higher truth of the great voluntary repatriation controversy. It is so crucial a part of my story that I must convey it in some manner, so you will have to permit me every kind of dramatic license while I whisk you through some stirring scenes.

First a few facts. The Armistice negotiators toiled their way along the demarcation line, sticking pins in the map and taping things out until by the end of 1951 all was ready for a cease-fire and an exchange of prisoners. Then, as soon as the two sides began to discuss prisoner exchange, a whole new continent of controversy emerged from the waters. The upheaval began when Admiral Libby introduced the idea of voluntary repatriation. The Chinese listened with frozen incredulity, rejected the idea out of hand, and the talks became stalled for the next eighteen months over that single issue. But to understand matters we must shift our sights from Panmunjon to Washington where the idea originated, for voluntary repatriation was a play sent in by the old haberdasher himself. And to explain where Truman got the idea we must zoom backwards in time from 1951 to 1941–42 when hundreds of thousands of Russians were surrendering to the Wehrmacht. I told you this was a fabulous episode. Sit tight.

So now we are back in 1942 and the spotlight falls on one General Vlasov, a hotshot of the Russian *stavka,* chosen by Marshal Stalin for the difficult task of commanding the crack Second Striking Army which has somehow gotten itself isolated behind the German lines in the region between Nijhni Novgorod and Chudovo. You get the picture? Said army had started off in January under orders from Stalin to break through the German position, relieve Leningrad, and roll up the flank of the German central army group. Those orders proved a trifle unrealistic, but in fact the army did break through, moving fifty-five miles into the icebound, godforsaken wilderness beyond, where it stopped, its communication with Moscow having been cut by the Germans who closed in behind it. When it radioed back for advice, word duly came that Marshal Stalin had the situation in hand and was planning fresh military miracles that would free the land from the fascist invaders and set the Volga flowing backwards. Meanwhile he sent Vlasov to take over the Second Striking Army, clear its rearward communications, and carry on the attack toward Leningrad.

Vlasov arrived in the Russian pocket sometime in March. He did reopen communications with the Russian front, but he found it somewhat difficult to carry on toward Leningrad or anywhere else since the spring thaws presently began. As the ice underfoot melted it was revealed to Vlasov and his army that they were not on land but at sea in a swamp of mud. As tanks and artillery and other heavy equipment disappeared into the ooze, Vlasov and his men climbed aboard the few firm tussocks and scanned the horizon for help. Vlasov was a general not an admiral, and radioed back to Moscow that relief ships were now necessary. Stalin's reply to *that* was a furious rebuke for the equipment that had been sunk and the ooze that had been abandoned and left vulnerable for occupation by the beastly fascist invader. Moreover, why had not Vlasov advanced another hundred and fifty *versts* to relieve Leningrad?

I think it was at that point Vlasov began to wonder if Stalin's grasp of the situation was quite as masterly as advertised. These thoughts must have deepened during the ensuing weeks as the Germans gradually closed in around his bebogged, bedraggled, and bewildered army. During the winter the Germans had watched with considerable admiration as the Second Striking Army dashed gaily through their position and into the frozen swamp. During the spring they had reason to admire the desperation and courage with which Vlasov and his men tried to fight their way out. It was a ferocious battle even by Eastern Front standards, and on Vlasov's side of the affair, the German attacks were counterpointed by increasingly menacing messages from the Kremlin. Instead of relieving Leningrad, liberating Poland and Czechoslovakia, and perhaps capturing Hitler as he sunbathed in Berchtesgaden, Vlasov was trying to save his men from capture, defeat, and imprisonment. What was this? Intelligence? Concern for lives? A feeling of responsibility for those one leads? Off with his head! Vlasov would certainly have been punished by Stalin if he had not been captured first by the Germans.

In his German prison camp, whose miserableness may be imagined without my having to evoke it, Vlasov pondered the lessons he had recently learned and came to the conclusion, I don't know how quickly, that Stalin was not perhaps an adequate expression of the finer qualities of the Russian people. Stalin could produce sacrifice in great quantity, and sacrifice is Russian and noble, but Stalin lacked a certain generosity of spirit. One did not find in him that instinct of trust which is the reciprocal obligation great men owe to those who have been loyal. Stalin was a moral mess, Vlasov decided, and he had gotten Russia into a gigantic jam, and at that moment Vlasov made a fateful decision. He would fight against Stalin.

No one but the most narrow-minded patriot can blame him, but what he did was rather perplexing. He took arms from the Nazis and used his considerable personality to organize anti-Stalinist prisoners of war into a series of adjunct divisions of the Wehrmacht. Vlasov and his new army wanted to fight against the Red Army and help the Germans overthrow Stalin. Then, who knows? they might have fought against their German allies in order to liberate Holy Mother Russia from the Germans. In any case they were doomed men, surrounded by doomed people, for in deciding to fight against Stalin, Vlasov had somehow failed to reckon with Hitler, that other great genius of the age.

By the time Vlasov's new army was in being, Der Führer had more or less gone underground where he spent his nights popping pills and rhapsodizing to his female secretaries and vegetarian cook about his great plans for the German people once this cruel war was over. Aboveground, those Germans who were still attempting to carry on under the rain of Allied bombs got from Goebbels such encouragement as was available. The Reichsleiter used to broadcast deeply touching descriptions of how war had affected their beloved Adolph. "Ah, my people," he used to say, "if only you could see Our Führer, aged and saddened by the tremendous burdens he carries on his shoulders . . ." And who can say that his misfortunes didn't actually work some good even on a soul as hardened as Hitler's? He was certainly in a self-pitying mood those days, complaining that he hadn't been able to see a movie in years. Then to add to his burdens came news that there were now Russian soldiers in German uniforms. "Imagine," he exclaimed to his girls, "Russians in our army! You have no idea what's floating around out there now." *Out there now* was his term for the aboveground world where things were cracking up apace.

Hitler did not feel quite up to leading his people any more, but he was still capable of sending out orders to prevent others from doing useful things, so among the directives that flowed from the *Führerbunker* came word that it was *streng verboten* to employ *untermensch* Slavs in defense of the *Vaterland* and the Master Race. This order was partly ignored. Some of Vlasov's new divisions were shipped off to Normandy to oppose the British and Americans who had landed there, but the bulk of Vlasov's army was kept in the East where it was shunted around behind the crumbling Eastern Front, underarmed and distrusted by its German allies. Vlasov never got a chance to fight against Stalin, and when the Eastern Front finally broke up, he and his men were swept like flotsam and jetsam right into the lap of General Patton's Third Army, where they offered, eagerly, to surrender. For Russians of that sort it was better to be in American hands than in the hands of their own countrymen.

General Patton, however, didn't quite know what to do. He was okay when it came to treating shellshocked soldiers or facing bullets, but the subtler, more inward aspects of action and policy eluded him, and Vlasov's men posed some very inward and subtle problems. What were they? Liberated Allied prisoners-of-war? Captured enemy soldiers? Or just soldiers who were trying to fight a war that hadn't gotten itself onto the official record books? Patton scratched his head with his pearl-handled revolver and fired off a telegram to Eisenhower, headquartered in the cathedral city of Rheims, to ask Ike what he would do with some Russians in German uniform who wanted to surrender to the American army. Patton had a touching belief in Ike's wisdom, but of course, Ike was the last man in the world to be able to answer Patton's question. Eisenhower's instinct was to save life when it was possible, but you need brains to work your way through a problem like that posed by Vlasov's men. And meanwhile the Russians, our great allies, were clamoring for the return of all liberated Russian prisoners, most especially including Vlasov's army, for which they had plans. Telegrams flew around, Washington was consulted, and before we all knew where we were, the decision had been taken that

Vlasov and his men were the property of the Red Army and should be handed over to it. This was done. Some of Vlasov's men committed suicide rather than go home, others went and were shot, while General Vlasov was flown off to Moscow to receive special attention. Exit General Vlasov.

Enter now Harry S Truman who became President shortly before these dire events took place. When he learned what had happened he was shocked, and with a moral sensitivity that seems to have been rare with him that summer (the same in which he ordered the atom bomb dropped), he resolved that such a thing would never happen again if he could prevent it, and as things turned out he did have a chance to prevent it, for history repeats itself—once as tragedy and again as farce. ("I can't help myself," as the pickpocket said, helping himself to another Marxian phrase.)

I was lucky enough to be in on the farce, and thanks to my penetrating vision and acute hearing, you too, Reader, can enjoy the scene. This time we are in the Presidential bathroom in the White House where Truman was taking his bath early one morning in December 1951. The tub is an important feature of the scene since Truman had been sitting in that same tub several years earlier when the bathroom floor gave way. After the plaster stopped falling and the waters had subsided, the President climbed out and found himself on the first, not the second floor of the White House where he had begun to wash. He gazed up at the hole through which he had descended and came to one of those snap judgments which were to make him so famous. He decided the White House was just too dangerous to live in, so he took Bess and daughter and moved across the street to Blair House while architects and workmen strengthened and rebuilt the interior of the Presidential mansion making it stronger and finer than it had been at any time since the British wantonly burned it in 1814. The architects even added a new balcony on the South Front, and when all was done Harry came across the street to check the work and prod the floors with his cane. He was a shrewd Missouri gent and he wasn't going to be taken in with any shoddy workmanship. Also he didn't care for another magic ride in his tub. After all, he was plain American President, not some crazy near-Eastern sultan.

Satisfied that the place was sound and the floors firmed up, he moved back in and the years passed and we find him sitting once more in his tub. "Here I am in the same old tub," he said to himself, remembering his great fall. "How time has passed!" And these reflections led him to muse on his early years in the White House. His mind then drifted to the subject of Vlasov's men, whose fate had been on his conscience for six years. "I really *must* do something about those fellows," he thought. He was in that balmy, early morning mood when everything seems possible to a Chief Executive. Briefly he considered resurrecting Vlasov's men, and then rejected the idea because it might cause complications with the Vatican. Then one of those creative fusions took place, and in a flash Truman connected the fate of Vlasov's men with the problem of prisoner exchange which was up for discussion at Panmunjon. "By the Lord, Harry!" he exclaimed, "what if we send back our Korean and Chinese prisoners and they are killed by being run over by trains or falling into wells? Then their blood will be on my conscience, too." He felt a chill of horror. He squeezed a spongeful of warm water onto his head. Then his thoughts darkened. "Or suppose those prisoners of ours are shot by their governments? Can such things be allowed?" He squeezed another spongeful of water over himself. "No, by God," he exclaimed, "such things cannot be. I will prevent it!" And, being a man of action, he hopped out of the tub, threw something loose and absorbent around his body, and headed for the phone which kept him plugged into the State Department.

221

The wires of that phone were made of special alloy guaranteed not to melt or fuse as they transmitted the hot creative energy that flowed from the State Department during Acheson's tenure. Indeed, Acheson's book on the period called *Present at the Creation* is recommended reading for anyone interested in this story. But back to Truman, whose eager finger has by now spun the dial and composed the mystic number which always brought him into contact with his Secretary of State.

"Speaking," said Acheson from the pregnant void at the other end of the line. It was five-thirty A.M. but Acheson rose as early as his Chief and worked just as hard. In those days he had already created the Free World and he was now further reducing chaos by inventing the Neutral Nations. Just that very morning he had started at the southern tip of Ceylon and was planning to work his way up the east coast of the subcontinent to the Bay of Bengal. When the phone rang he suspended operations at Trincomalee on the coast of Coromandel in order to listen to his big Chief.

"Acheson," Truman said, "I've just decided we cannot force our Korean and Chinese prisoners to go home. Suppose something bad happened to them there? We could never live with ourselves afterwards."

"Yes?" said Acheson.

"Of course," said Truman, "if some reckless prisoners insist on going home, we will let them. You can't stop people from committing suicide. But we will definitely not force anyone to go back to North Korea or China. It must be a voluntary decision on the prisoner's part. . . . You getting all this down?"

"Yes," said Acheson, who kept a recording angel on another extension.

"I have just invented the doctrine of voluntary repatriation," Truman said. The heavy work of creation was done in the State Department, but Truman was allowed to make up mottoes and slogans.

"Very well," said Acheson. "You realize, of course, that the Communists will never accept this. It will prolong the war, perhaps indefinitely."

"That can't be helped," said Truman. "There's a principle involved here. We cannot force any of those poor, brave, freedom-loving prisoners to go home against their will. If the Communists won't accept our principle of voluntary repatriation, then we'll just keep our prisoners on Koje Island until hell freezes over." The Chief Executive sometimes expressed himself in such colorful terms.

"And the Communists will keep their prisoners," Acheson pointed out.

"I've thought of that too," said Truman. "I've thought of everything, but there's just no other way. I'm very sorry for our boys in Communist prison camps because I know how eager they are to come home, but they're fine, idealistic American boys, and they'll accept the situation when they understand there's a moral principle involved here."

"Yes," said Acheson. One of the Dean's salient characteristics was that he supported his Chief even when he knew that Chief was talking out of the back of his head.

"It's a terrible decision we've had to make," Truman went on, "but I know it's the right one."

"The Generals won't like it," said Acheson. "They'd like to get their men out of Communist prison camps as soon as possible."

Truman's face darkened. He had been an artillery captain in the First World War and he knew what to do with generals. "If any General comes around to complain to you about this, just send him over here." Then Truman hung up, finished drying himself, dressed, took a ten-mile walk, ate breakfast, and began his day's work.

He was a simple citizen of Missouri, just like myself. He could recognize a moral principle when he saw one and a

223

weak floor when he fell through it. And, like me, he was an amateur historian capable of constructing faulty historical analogies with the best of us. There was absolutely no connection between Vlasov's men, who had after all taken arms against their own government, and the Chinese and Koreans we had captured, but Harry never seemed to realize the fact. The subtler minds in the State Department may have spotted the flaw in Harry's premises, but if so they didn't point it out, because a preliminary survey of our prisoners indicated that a substantial percentage would rather *not* return to North Korea or China. Why anyone would ever want to return to North Korea is a mystery to me. That some North Koreans chose their homeland over the temptations of the Free World is startling evidence of the mysterious popularity of Communist government among Asians.

Nevertheless the State Department was deeply impressed by the results of its survey. It seems we had actually captured some Chinese and Koreans who preferred to be taken care of by Uncle Sam rather than go home to struggle to build socialism in their own countries. Clearly this proved, or could be made to prove to the entire world, that all a free man really needs or desires is government by Chiang Kai-shek or Syngman Rhee, plus, of course, an American pension. Shouting *Excelsior!* the State Department swung into line behind Harry, who was by then far up the mountainside bearing aloft his banner with a strange device: *Voluntary Repatriation.*

This *anschluss* between the White House and the State Department left the Pentagon outnumbered but not surrounded, since only the Pentagon surrounds itself. The Generals caucused and selected the Chief of Staff Omar Bradley to drive over to the White House to salt Truman's tail and bring him down to earth. I think I can reconstruct that interview along Thucydidean lines. The talk began pleasantly enough in the Oval Room of the White House.

"Take a load off your feet, Omar," Truman said to Bradley. "How's the wife?" he asked.

"She's fine," said the General. "How's yours?"

"Just fine," said Truman. "And how's your daughter?"

"Fine," said Bradley. "And yours?"

"Just fine. Her voice gets better and better all the time."

These preliminaries over, the two men got down to business. "Frankly, Mr. President," General Bradley said, "we don't like this principle of voluntary repatriation."

"Oh, don't you?" said Truman.

"Well, it's something new, isn't it?" Bradley said. "Offhand none of us in the big P can remember a single war in history where this kind of principle has been written into the Armistice."

"We live in new times," Truman said, "and in new times you have to invent new principles to cover the new situations that crop up."

Bradley nodded. "We can see that, it's just that we can't see how this principle will work out in practice."

"It will work out just fine," said Truman.

So Bradley dropped that point for a while and switched to another. "We're also afraid it's going to delay prisoner exchange for quite a while."

"Let it," said Truman. It was spring by then, and his will had swollen as the sap ran upwards.

"And meanwhile," said Bradley, "our prisoners on Koje Island are beginning to give us a lot of trouble. General Dean doesn't know what to do with them."

"He'll keep them there until we exchange them," Truman said, "and we'll exchange them when the Commies agree to voluntary repatriation."

General Bradley fingered one of his campaign ribbons. "There's another problem," he said. "We would like to get our boys back."

"So would I," said Truman.

"We've been getting very funny reports out of those camps up on the Yalu. It sounds as if some of our men are turning Communist themselves. We want them back so we can feed them up and put them on the right track again."

Truman listened until he was sure the General had finished speaking. Then he said, "Our boys will come home just as soon as the Communists accept the principle of voluntary repatriation. Do you have anything more to say, General?"

The two men looked at each other. Truman was a tough cookie, but the General was no doughnut himself. He coughed mildly, and said, "Yes, Mr. President, I would like to speak a little more if your time is available."

"General Bradley," Truman said, "my time is always available whenever you want to speak to me." Truman had the ready and generous courtesy that we Missouri gentlefolk always display when we're in positions of power and know that nothing the other person can say will have the slightest effect on our minds.

Bradley could feel this—he was from Missouri himself —but he was also a West Pointer and a veteran and he had to go on. "Sir," he said, "touching on this principle of voluntary repatriation again. . . . There are some of us on the other side of the river who don't see why it's necessary. They want their men back and we want ours. Why don't we just exchange?"

Truman looked Bradley in the eyes. "General, aren't you forgetting what happened to Vlasov's men?"

Bradley had been mixed up in that one, too, and so he knew the facts. "No, Mr. President, I don't think I am. General Vlasov's men were traitors to their country. If any American prisoner of war took arms to fight the United States Army, I would recommend he be shot."

"Would you?" Truman said.

"Yes sir. And I would keep on recommending it until you, as Commander in Chief, signed the order of execution. And if you refused, it would be my plain duty to resign."

"Oh would it?" said Truman.

"Yes. The idea of a prisoner accepting arms from his captors and fighting against his own army violates every rule of war and discipline and loyalty I know about. I could not let such conduct go unpunished."

Truman leaned forward. "General Bradley, Vlasov's men were true Russian patriots, fighting against Communist totalitarianism. I cannot see them punished, and I will not allow such punishment to be meted out to the prisoners we have captured in Korea."

"None of the prisoners we've captured have taken arms against their governments," Bradley said. "We wouldn't *give* them arms," he added, with some energy.

"Listen!" said Truman. "We know there are anti-Communist, freedom-loving Chinese and Koreans on Koje Island. Are you going to ship those men home and let them perish?"

"We don't *know* they will perish," Bradley said.

"We can guess," said Truman.

"But it's just a guess," said Bradley.

There was a brief silence while two strong men wrestled with their tempers. Then Truman said, "General, I appreciate your concern for our boys in prison camps over there, but the issue we're dealing with transcends their fate. It transcends my fate and yours. We are dealing here with the principle of free choice. Do men have the right to choose the kind of government under which they want to live, or don't they?"

Bradley was an American and a Republican or a Democrat, and appealed to in that way all he could think to say was, "I appreciate that issue, Mr. President," and as I heard him say that, I despaired for a while. Once two adversaries have begun to appreciate each other's position all is lost. I knew I was going to be stuck at Pyot Lon for a good long while. I suppose I'd known it from the moment I first spotted Harry in his tub inventing the doctrine of voluntary repatriation. One of the disadvantages of living in the twentieth cen-

227

tury with all our marvelous communications is that you often know ahead of time just how badly things are going to work out. In the Middle Ages you often didn't know how a crusade would end until the survivors came limping home with the bad news.

Still, Bradley didn't give up without making a last try. "Sir," he said, "what if the Chinese who don't want to go back to Red China don't want to go to Formosa either? What happens then?"

"Our plan," Truman said, "is that all prisoners on both sides shall be turned over to a Neutral Nations Prisoner Custodian and Repatriation Commission, which will then interview each prisoner to establish whether or not he wants to go home. Such prisoners as do not wish to go home will be given a perfectly free choice to go wherever they choose, and it will be the duty of the Commission to help them gain entry to the country of their choice."

Bradley blanched. "You mean they can choose any country in the world?"

Truman reflected a moment. "Well, of course, in practice the anti-Communist Chinese will choose Formosa and the anti-Communist North Koreans will choose South Korea."

"And the Communist South Koreans will choose North Korea," said Bradley, picking up the ball, "but what about other United Nations prisoners in North Korea? There are a lot of different nationalities there and not all of them come from divided countries."

"We don't anticipate any problem," Truman said. "The British, Australians, Dutch, French, Swedes, Canadians, Turks, and Americans will naturally choose their own countries."

"But there might be problems," said Bradley, who was inclined to look on the gloomy side of the picture.

"We'll meet those problems when they come," Truman said. He added, "Anyway, it won't be our problem. The Neutral Nations Commission will handle it." And then he explained that India would chair the Commission.

Bradley was naturally relieved things would be in such capable hands. He didn't ask *why* the Indians had agreed to chair the commission since he knew their record of helpfulness and general all-round benevolence. They were, after all, a young people, fresh from the hands of their creator, Acheson, who was even then at work raising the Himalayas to create a barrier between China and India so that his new Indian people could not be overrun by the Chinese when he got around to creating *them*. Acheson was troubled by Russia and China. It was his duty to bring them into existence—after all, the world wouldn't be complete without totalitarian nations on it—but Acheson was saving the Communists for last and creating wide oceans and high mountains to keep them away from his Free World and his Neutral Nations. Really Reader, you must get yourself a copy of *Present at the Creation*, the most revealing book since Genesis. You probably think, as I used to think, that Acheson was something of a hawk, but now we know he was that dovelike presence who sat brooding on the vast abyss. And what eggs he laid! We've been hatching them for the last twenty years.

So that is how voluntary repatriation became the policy of the American government. Truman rallied his State Department, subdued his generals, and led his team in the great fight for voluntary repatriation. There is nothing in nature so impressive as an American President (or bishop) with a moral bee in his bonnet. I'm convinced Truman's concern for those Korean and Chinese prisoners was utterly sincere. They rioted on Koje Island. They captured General Dean and held him for ransom, but nothing they did and nothing the Communist negotiators at Panmunjon said could change Truman's opinion that he was protecting those prisoners from the fate of Vlasov's men. There was a humanitarian

229

principle involved, and for months Truman confronted the Chinese on the mountaintop, eyeball to eyeball, while below him demons capered and criticized and called it Truman's war. Harry ignored them. He allowed nothing to distract him, and at last the Communists caved in. "By the dragon's tail," they said to each other, "these Americans have a tiger in their tank. We better sign." And so they signed.

Eisenhower was President by then and got credit for the Armistice, but he didn't deserve it. He was a cheerful, bustling, helpful soul who would have made a good male nurse. He could never have outstared the Chinese the way Truman did. Ike would have grinned or dozed off during that staring match because he didn't have a very long attention span.

And now it is altogether fitting and proper that we end this chapter on a more bucolic note:

It is the summer of 1953 and prisoner exchange is finally under way, but a snag has shown up, for here is a group of South Koreans who do not want to live either in North *or* South Korea. General Bradley's forebodings have been realized and we are faced with the sort of inconvenience that disturbs even the mighty flow of modern history. People are troublesome and difficult to satisfy. Even if you divide every country in the world into Manichean halves—Nationalist and Red China, North and South Korea, East and West Germany, Moslem and Hindu India, Arab and Jewish Palestine —there will always be some duds and grumblers who refuse to be satisfied by such a wealth of choices. And, as I say, here they are: some eighty or ninety Koreans who have consulted among themselves and allow as how they would like to live in Switzerland, a country of which they have heard good reports.

Clearly it is a case for invoking higher aid, so the Indians flash the word to Trygvie Lie in the United Nations who then approaches the ministers and plenipotentiaries of the Helvetic Republic to ask if they would like to welcome some Korean immigrants? Swiss eyebrows are raised, Swiss mouths are pursed, and presently the answer can be heard. It is No. This response is duly transmitted to Panmunjon where the Neutral Nations Prisoner Custodian and Repatriation Commission breaks the bad news to the Koreans, who take it stolidly as Koreans tend to take most bad news, they having had a lot of experience along those lines. They consult afresh and announce that since the Alps are out, they'd like to try the Andes. Will Chile admit them? Same routine, same response, for Harry, in giving everyone the right to choose what kind of government he wants to live under, had somehow failed to nail down the responsibility of governments to let people live under them.

If I remember correctly the Koreans next tried Australia or New Zealand, but by then all the other prisoners had been disposed of and the Commission was breaking up housekeeping in the DMZ. The Indians, left holding the kitty, or Koreans, decided to take them back to New Delhi and when last heard from those sons of old Chosen were somewhere in Uttar Pradesh petitioning Dag Hammarskjöld to ask if the Canadian government would like to have them? About that time Hammarskjöld crashed in the Congo where he'd gone to solve some problems *there,* and a great darkness descends on the scene. I presume by now those Koreans have been absorbed into India's heterogeneous population, but I wish they'd been allowed into Switzerland. That's the picture I want to leave you with, Reader. Imagine them settled happily atop some unoccupied alp so that mountain climbers making their arduous way from *piton* to *piton* could be confronted at the summit by the little Korean village of their dreams, another Shangri-la.

23

So that's voluntary repatriation in a nutshell—a coconut shell. And where did it leave me? Exactly where I'd been all along, moldering in Pyot Lon. On June 10, 1953, I had reached a thrilling point in *Germinal*. Etienne, Catherine, and Chaval were trapped together in a half-flooded gallery of Le Voreux mine. Etienne had just killed Chaval, whose dead body was floating in the water. Etienne and Catherine were themselves slowly starving to death, though they were not in the least tempted to eat Chaval. Indeed, as the floating body occasionally bumped against Etienne's legs (he was sitting on a ledge with his feet dangling into the cold water) he felt a horrible suspicion that Chaval was still alive and perhaps about to bite him. He was also obsessed by his desire for Catherine, who was just lapsing into a coma when I heard a great shout go up outside the library window. I raised my head, frowning. Why couldn't everyone sit around quietly and read good books? Real life was obviously too screwed up to be enjoyed, but one could still have fun reading.

I turned back to my book. Catherine was coming to. Etienne gathered her into his arms. A spark of life was generated between them, and there on the brink of death in eternal blackness she gave up her virginity and her life at almost the same moment. And damn those fellows outside who had begun to sing! I went to the window to shout at them.

Outside Poniatowski and Hollins were frisking about on the grass, chanting, "They've signed, they've signed, they've signed."

"Signed what?" I yelled.

"The Armistice!" Poniatowski yelled back.

"We're going home!" Hollins screamed.

Then they grabbed each other and began to waltz. This will turn out to be just another false alarm, I thought, as I went outdoors leaving Etienne still trapped in the mine with Catherine's cooling body in his arms.

Matthew arrived, rubbing sleep out of his eyes. I estimate by then he was getting eighteen hours of sleep a day. He and I watched Hollins and Poniatowski, who continued to waltz. At last Matthew turned to me. "May I have this dance?" he said.

"I'll believe this when I'm back in Kansas City," I said.

But I was already beginning to believe. The Turks in the next compound had begun to celebrate in their own Turkish way, and then Novotny came lumbering up. "Hey!" he said. "You heard they signed the Armistice?"

Matthew said, "You don't say?"

"Yeah. They signed it. It was just announced."

Matthew looked at me. "You've got to believe it now."

I found I did believe. It was all ending. I tried to feel happy, but actually I was scared. One of the finer mysteries of life is that prisoners are frightened of being released, though they don't always admit it. The mood was ostensibly joyous that evening as we sat around the hut talking about the pleasures of the future, though even the most enthusiastic of us admitted there would be problems. One gathered, for instance, that faced with the choice between a cheeseburger and a piece of gash, Novotny's powers of decision were going to be sorely tried.

"Couldn't you eat and screw at the same time?" I asked. "Flaubert is supposed to have smoked a cigar while copulating, which sounds harder than munching a cheeseburger."

Novotny stared at me. Two and a half years had not inured him to my presence. "Now what's the matter with you?" he asked.

"Nothing."

"Why can't you be happy like the rest of us?"

"I am happy."

He looked at me suspiciously. "Go ahead," I said. "Tell us how you're going to eat scrambled eggs off some girl's stomach."

"Listen, Heather!" he said.

"Let's not fight tonight," Hubler remarked.

Novotny was still staring at me. "I suppose you're going to go to the library when you're home?"

"I might."

"And read some effing book?"

"Don't knock books until you've read one."

"Listen, Heather," he said again.

"Let's make them kiss each other," said Matthew.

I got up. "I'm going out," I said.

"Yeah?" said Novotny. "Well why don't you jump in the river while you're out there?"

"I'll think it over," I said.

Outside things were a little better, though not much. My night blindness was cured by then so I could see the old stars up there winking away, but down on earth where I seemed to be living (if you could call it that) things weren't really so very gay. I was feeling supersaturated. World-weary. It may have come from reading too much Zola recently, or it may have been due to spending too many years in prison, or there could be some unknown cause. If I was going to cry, as seemed likely, my tears might be genuinely Tennysonian, welling up from some divine despair.

But never mind them, the thing to do was think about the future. I would go home, kiss Mother, give Father the big Hello, and when the first dizzy rapture of feeling had subsided he and I could have one of our Father and Son talks about what I did next. "I've been thinking about finishing my education," I would say. "I've learned a lot of Marxism;

234

maybe I could become a political scientist?" How would that strike him? How would it strike me? Did I really see myself back at Harvard as a Social Relations major?

No. But what did I see myself as, besides the aging prisoner at the bar? I was twenty-three incredible years old. My age struck me as one of the most preposterous facts of what was turning into a fairly preposterous life. Twenty-three! In a few more years I'd be thirty, which is to say no age at all: timeless, immemorial, like a rock, a pre-Cambrian rock. Already I could feel calcification setting in. Senility was around the corner and I hadn't yet decided on my major at Harvard. Let this be a lesson to me, I thought. If I am ever reborn into a new and better world, or even if get shunted back to this one, let me remember to come out of the womb firmly decided on what I will major in. One must not let these decisions slide until there is time to think about them, otherwise all is lost.

I was wandering down toward the river as I made these good resolutions about my next life. Meanwhile I could either end this one by jumping in the river as Novotny had suggested, or I could take the bull by the tail and solve my dilemma by letting him drag me along. Where would that lead?

Obviously, to cows, to heifers, to girls.

"Father," I would say, "I need lots of girls. I think I'm old enough now to make up my own mind about these matters, and I have decided I believe in polygamy. Moreover I have found these Twelve Wise Virgins who say they want to marry me because I am the only man they have ever met who can wiggle his ears this well. So please don't let's have any argument about it. I'm going out now to buy a baker's dozen of rings, and we'll see you in the cathedral anon."

That would fix things, and probably in the most felicitous way they could be fixed. Twelve virgins would probably restore me to my old sense of virgin power. When it came right down to it, one really pure girl could probably do the trick if I could just find her and bundle her off to church and bed quickly enough.

Though, of course, I didn't really deserve a virgin any more since I wasn't one myself. What an incredibly stupid business that had been with Martha! To have thrown away all the possibilities of pure love on the off-chance of finding out in bed that sex was really that thing called love. Madness. I should have known. What sort of girl would go to bed with a man she didn't think loved her? Right there I'd known it was all wrong, but then, though sex might not be love it was certainly something pretty powerful in its own right.

I was thinking about sex when my profound meditations were interrupted by an alien footfall. I was down by the river, standing above the tangled bank, when Comrade Liu hoved into view, two crescent moons reflected from his glasses.

"Ah, you are alone, too," he said. "What have you been thinking on this night when the war is coming to an end?"

"I've been thinking that God or Nature didn't need to provide men with quite such strong sexual drives just to ensure the reproduction of the species. It's like giving men Howitzers to shoot pigeons."

"Yes. It is very strange," he said.

"Men would be willing to beget children if the drive were only one quarter or one tenth as strong."

"The sexual drive is part of the general excessiveness of life," Liu said. "Think of the cerebral cortex. Fantastically complicated, and most people have no use for their intellectual capacity."

"I know."

Together we brooded on these matters. I felt it was a nice meeting, and that we had struck up a fortunate comradely note on which to end our relationship, which had had its ups and downs.

"I'm glad we've met," I said.

"I too." We turned toward each other and made dry little mock bows. I saw the moons dance on his glasses again.

"It's possible for us to be friendly even though you're an officer and I'm a prisoner."

"Of course. These differences are superficial. We are both intelligent men, which means we have more in common than most people."

I felt thrilled as if I were a girl and he'd just told me he loved me. "You think I'm intelligent?" I said.

"Certainly. Very intelligent. Indeed, that is why I am willing to make a proposal to you. Since our side has agreed to voluntary repatriation we must be prepared for the fact that many silly Chinese prisoners will choose to go to Taiwan rather than return to the People's Republic. I do not envy them though they are not of much importance. Still for propaganda purposes it will look better if some American prisoners choose not to return to the United States. We will offer them a place in China. They will be trained; they will learn the language; they will see what the Revolution is really like; and, of course, if they do not like our ways they can always leave. However they must expect to work and study and do their best while they are in China. Do you understand?"

"Yes."

"Not only because of your intelligence, but because of the propaganda value of your family background, you would make a very suitable person for us to accept. Would you like to come to China?"

"Yes," I said.

And now the Home Front. Scarcely had I arrived in the Demilitarized Zone to be quartered in a special tent with my fellow defectors when I was presented with a cablegram from Kansas City. INFORMED YOUR NAME LIST PRISONERS GOING CHINA. ASSUME ERROR. CLARIFY IMMEDIATELIEST. Facilities were available. I cabled back: NO ERROR. GOING CHINA.

LETTER FOLLOWS. The gong had struck. Father and I emerged from our corners and the letters began to fly, though in presenting this as a set battle from the beginning I do myself a real injustice. For once in my life I'd taken a major step without thinking about Father's reaction. Standing there in the moonlight I'd said *yes* without any calculations or *arrière pensées,* and indeed my first letter home was a chatty, enthusiastic description of the wonderful chance I had to see China. I knew Father was a moderately bigoted anti-Communist, so I expressed myself carefully, pointing out that seven hundred million people couldn't be all bad, and that I was bound to *learn* a lot in China. (Learning was the King of Trumps in Father's deck; Faith, of course, was the Ace.) I concluded my first letter by saying I knew he and Mother would be sorry I wasn't coming home right away, but having been *invited* to China I just didn't see how I was justified in passing up such a rare, extraordinary, once-in-a-lifetime opportunity.

I felt very satisfied with my composition and stepped back to await results. Which were not long in coming. Father must have sat down to write the minute he received my cablegram. He certainly didn't wait to hear what I thought I was doing. Our letters crossed (our letters always crossed), and while I was waiting for a riposte to my lead, he came at me from an angle all his own and landed quite a blow before I had adjusted myself to his style of fighting. I'd been out of training for too long.

Dear Samuel, he wrote. (I think we'll quote Father at least selectively—he's quotable.) *I cannot sufficiently express my shock at what I have just learned from your cable.* Then he expressed it pretty sufficiently, going on to a vigorous and juicy summary of his idea of the trials through which I had just passed. Finally he got down to business:

But those trials are past, Samuel. The path to freedom is now open to you. You have but to say the word and you will be received with the respect due to those who have suffered in the cause of their country and with the honor that attaches to soldiers, who through misfortune, not dereliction of duty, have been forced to surrender themselves to the enemy.

I beg you, therefore, not to close the door, not to throw away what you have earned by so many months of captivity. It breaks my heart to think that for some fanciful or mistaken reason of your own you should now choose to bring dishonor on your name. Though you are my son and the name you bear is my own, I write to you as I would write to any young man in your position. Draw back from this unnatural choice. Return. Think of what you are about. On the one side stands your country, your family, and all the habits, thoughts, and ways of life you understand. On the other side stands an alien people, a violent, harsh, suspicious creed, and a way of life incalculably different from any you have known before. Can there be a moment of hesitation between such alternatives?

There it was, there it all was just the way it had always been. Two and a half years of my life casually dismissed as a trial I had nobly borne in order to earn the right to return to my dearly loved Father and Mother. Anger overcame me, especially when I began to react to that delicate (and charitable) playing on my old sense of guilt at having surrendered in the first place. How did Father know I had been forced to surrender through misfortune and not a dereliction of duty? I still didn't know that much myself (and still don't know to this day). But he understood that I must feel uneasy about having surrendered, and so he'd gone out of his way to let me know he wasn't going to blame me for letting myself be captured.

I sat down and wrote him an angry letter in which I asserted that life at Pyot Lon had not been a trial at all. I'd enjoyed myself some of the time and felt I'd profited in many ways and learned much about Marxism and done a lot of serious reading. Moreover the valley of the Yalu was rather pretty in certain seasons, so please stop thinking of me as having just passed through Purgatory on the way back to the Heaven of Kansas City. And, incidentally, write to me not as you would write to any young man, because I am not any young man, I am myself. Furthermore, my surrender *was* a dubious business about which I felt uneasy and I would thank him not to absolve me before I'd confessed and asked for absolution. I went so far as to remind him that priests have responsibilities in these matters. They cannot go around handing out free pardons any more than they can presume to sell them in order to collect money to build St. Peter's. I worked myself up into an almost Lutheran rage against his cavalier attempt to smooth over my own moral life. I even asserted that no soldier has the right to surrender while his comrades are still battling it out on the hilltop, and his assumption that I would accept his pardon just showed that he had no idea and never had had any clear idea about how I felt or what sort of a person I was.

It was a terrible letter to write him. I could never have said such things to him face to face, nor would I have dared (or perhaps even wished) to write them if he had been more present to my imagination, but we had been out of touch for so long that he had receded from the center of my thoughts, though once I'd sent off the letter I began to feel ashamed of it. Hence his second letter was a positive relief to me.

By then he'd received my Cook's-Tour-of-the-Revolution, learning-about-China letter. Evidently he decided I was out of my mind.

Please make no mistake on this matter. The step you now contemplate will irretrievably ruin you. By this act you will cut yourself off forever from the respect and trust of all honorable men. You write as if going to China were the most ordinary kind of foreign travel. Can it be that your long, unfortunate imprisonment has led you to lose touch with the way the world views turncoats and traitors?

240

This was war! I lost my diffidence and feeling of shame and wrote back that honorable men did not wrap themselves in the flag and do a dance around the teepee as if America were still in its tribal or Indian stage of development. We were supposed to be a civilized, Christian country at the moment (at least I had always supposed that was his view of the matter), and Christian gentlemen did not call each other traitors and turncoats. Doctor Johnson, I reminded him, had defined patriotism as the last refuge of a scoundrel, and I for one wished to associate myself with Johnson's position. No one ever questioned Johnson's loyalty, and I saw no reason why anyone should question mine. And P.S., What is a turncoat?

In answer to that I got his reply to my second angry letter.

My Dear Son,

You say I have never understood you though you must know in your heart that is not true. We have not always agreed. There have been periods before this present one in which I have seriously disapproved of your actions (or contemplated actions, for I will not believe that your mind is set on going to China). Yet in spite of our disagreements, I have always felt we understood one another and that under the occasional anger or resentment which flared up between us there has been an abiding love on your part as I know there is on mine. I cannot believe you are so changed as to deny this, or to accuse me in all seriousness of neglecting my priestly or my fatherly duties toward you. It has always been my dearest wish that you would make a sincere act of contrition and absolve yourself from the acts of disobedience and willfulness and dereliction of duty which necessarily accumulate in the souls of those who do not confess themselves and seek His pardon and grace.

I will ignore the studied anger in your letter and continue to believe that between us there can be no doubting or questioning of the deep love and respect we hold for each other. Your mother

241

joins me in wishing you well and wishing for your speedy return to us. This separation, which has been such a grief to us, will be mended once we have you here. I cannot doubt that. I write to you as my own dearly loved son, for though I am a priest with fatherly duties to many, you have and always will have a special place in my heart and in my thoughts and in my prayers.

Shortly after composing that, he must have received my letter quoting Dr. Johnson and heaping scorn on flag-wavers and loud-mouthed patriots. If this correspondence is difficult to follow, it is because we were always responding to the wrong letters. While I was answering his loving letter, just quoted, with a fairly loving letter of my own, he was busily composing the following remarks:

You say that Christian gentlemen do not call each other traitors and turncoats. I agree, but let me point out that for some eight years now you have by your own actions repudiated Christianity. Samuel, I must tell you frankly, though it gives me pain to say it, that you have betrayed your Lord Jesus Christ, and from that first great betrayal and dislocation of loyalties all your subsequent acts of disobedience and disloyalty can be traced. I do indeed think that in proposing to go to China you are acting in a traitorous manner. And you ask what is a turncoat? Need I explain such an elementary thing to you? You are an American citizen born and bred, descended from ancestors who have ever held up their heads among their neighbors and often played an honorable part in the public life of their country. Yet you propose to ignore all that and make yourself a pauper and parasite, living on the bounty of a people lately at war with your country and still hostile and implacably opposed to all the values your country is based upon. They will feed and clothe you, and what will you do in return for their bread which you will eat and their clothes which you will wear? How can you doubt that you are turning your coat and throwing in your lot with the enemies of your country?

By then my anger was tempered. Father was very real once more, but I was puzzled. Why was he so upset? Did he

242

really think the Chinese were fiends and that communism was a devilish affair? Was there perhaps a touch of racism in his apparent horror at the fact that I was going to China? If I passed his letters over a candle would I see the words ASIATIC COMMUNISM written in the invisible ink of his most private juices? Or was he more thin-skinned than I assumed, and seriously upset by what the morons and the pusillanimous *canaille* would say about me for choosing to visit China at this particular moment in history? Evidently I would have to take thought. It never occurred to me, of course, to change my mind about going to China.

While I was taking thought, the other American prisoners left the DMZ zone. I waved good-bye to them. Matthew and Hubler and some of the others waved back. That jerk Novotny refused even to look at me. I was blotted out of his book forever, the way some people imagine that at the Last Judgment the wicked will be erased from the Book of Life so that the story of mankind will be as purged and purified as a Stalinist history of the Russian Revolution.

The departure of the returnees left the camp pretty empty. There was my little band of American defectors, plus one Englishman, and there was that group of South Koreans I've already referred to. We were guarded from the press and from other interference by some splendid Sikh warriors with moustaches and beards that I envied. Indeed, I began to wish I'd used my time in Pyot Lon to greater advantage by growing an enormous beard which might give me an air of authority. I needed authority, and there's no doubt that lots of hair helps a man look prophetic or wise or strong. While puzzling out the sources of Father's agitation, I gave a good deal of irrelevant thought as to whether I'd earned the right to let my hair grow. I finally decided I hadn't.

At last, when I felt I'd delayed long enough in answering his last letter, I sat down and composed a reasonable epistle setting forth the doctrines that, socially speaking, communism was rather like the early Christian communes, and morally speaking it was rather like Puritanism, and intellectually speaking it was rather like a secularized form of the Augustinian view of history. It was a serious if half-baked argument designed to set Father's mind at rest about the real value of going to China to watch such an interesting phenomenon at work on a large scale in the oldest, most deeply civilized country in the world.

But I had waited too long, and Father had grown impatient. He suddenly took to the air and when next heard from he was in Tokyo writing me daily. Between polishing his periods and agitating for a pass to visit me in the DMZ he must have led a full life. It was a busman's holiday in all respects, since he also found time to inspect some church missions and firm up the spiritual life of the Japanese Episcopalians.

We did not meet, however, for which I'm sorry. It would have made a good scene for this book and might actually have changed the course of my life, which has been a happy one though admittedly full of complexities. If Father had appeared in person in the tent where defectors were supposed to be wrestled with by official army explainers, I don't see how I could have resisted him. But according to the terms of the Armistice, only authorized army personnel were to have access to us. All others were barred by those splendid Sikhs. So Father and I didn't meet.

Mother, whom we must not neglect, came into her own as the result of Father's self-removal to Tokyo. Some army psychologist conceived the brilliant idea that if only the defectors could hear the voices of their loved ones their hearts would be changed. So tapes were prepared in the States and flown to Panmunjon, and one fine day Major William van Pappenhacker strode into the tent listing slightly to the right under the weight of a heavy tape recorder he was carrying. The tape had been made while Father was in Tokyo, so Mother played a stellar role on it. She had written, of course, but I felt it was appropriate that hers should be the actual voice I heard.

"Samuel?" she said, her voice sounding curiously muffled and unlike itself. "We're having very nice autumn weather here. The leaves are turning and they're perfectly beautiful . . . Oh!" Then, much louder and clearer for she was now speaking into the microphone, she went on to say that I was continually on her thoughts and that she was sure I would change my mind and come home where she was sure I would be happy. There was talk of Thanksgiving. Turkey, cranberry sauce, and pumpkin pie drifted into and out of her discourse. Then I would go back to college and all my old friends would be so glad to see me and so many people had given her nice messages for me so I mustn't think people would be unkind when I got home because everyone understood I'd been brainwashed and wasn't really responsible for anything I'd ever said or done.

I summarize all that part because it sounded like a public relations officer's idea of what a Mom should say to her Son. Toward the end Mother herself surfaced for a while:

"Your Father is very upset and angry," she said, "but I've told him I'm sure it's all a mistake. After all, Samuel, your ancestors have fought in every war this country's been in and I know how proud you are of that and that you'd never think of doing anything unpatriotic. It's just silly how people don't understand. Your father wants the telephone number changed because of all the calls we get about you, but I told him I thought we should answer people and talk to them so that they can see what sort of family you come from and what sort of person you really are. You know I've always been proud of you and I still am because I know this is just a misunderstanding, and I must say I'm getting angry at the sort of thing people write about you in the newspapers and even say to me on the phone. I'll be very glad when you come home so that we can show them how wrong they are."

245

Thus Mother, but the tape was not done. It whirred silently and then, wonder of wonders, I heard an unfamiliar male voice saying, "This is Mr. Miggs, Samuel. I taught you Civics and I must have taught badly if you're really going to go ahead and do this thing." Miggs? I thought. Miggs? Who's Miggs? Then I remembered him—an unremarkable *privatdozent* who held forth at St. Stephen's, my Midwestern prep school. But the hour throws up its hero, and Miggs had evidently risen to the occasion when the army visited my school looking for some deeply loved old Chipps of a character whose honeyed voice might lure me back to the Republic. "Samuel," Miggs told me, "the Communists have gotten into your mind. You've got to throw them out, and you can do it if you *will* it . . ." Evidently he'd been reading or watching science fiction. There's a British TV program called *The Quatermass Experiment* in which three astronauts who have been out in space have had their bodies invaded by a Thing which upon their return slowly amalgamates them into a single pullulating sponge which begins to ooze around London and drip from the triforium of Westminster Cathedral. Just as the sponge is about to cast out millions of spores which will invade and infect everyone, a bold Miggs steps forward and summons the consciences of the sponged astronauts to resist what has happened to them. Expunge it, as it were. "You can do it," he tells them, adding that if they withdraw their wills then the Thing will have no earthly foothold and will be forced to return to outer space from whence it came. There is a breathless pause while the spore pods pulse and threaten to burst. Then at the last possible moment one hears an unearthly screeching sound as the Thing flees back to where it came from and the sponge collapses into bits of dry vegetable matter. The story was made into a low-budget movie called *The Creeping Unknown* which you can still see in certain New York movie houses and which was evidently making the rounds in 1953 when Miggs recorded his message.

And scarcely had I recovered from Miggs when who should pipe up but my old roomy Morrison! Would wonders never cease, and where had they found him? And how had they overlooked Martha? Her explanation of why I should return to the land where my fathers died, land of the Pilgrim's pride, would have been interesting to say the least.

The Major played me this tape and when it had left me visibly unmoved, he prepared to do his own duty. He was a well-set-up specimen who squared his shoulders and set to work with a will, but by the time he entered the fray the waters were thoroughly darkened with ink and like a cuttlefish I had anchored myself to the rock of my decision. The major plunged in and yanked, but he did not dislodge me from the pool of Marxism and the only thing I learned from him was that I would be dishonorably discharged from the army if I went to China, whereas I would be given approximately five thousand dollars if I returned home. The latter sum represented my accumulated back pay and P.O.W. allowance.

"That's real money," the major said, putting a new string in his lute and twanging it with his strong thumb.

"Why don't you pay me now if I've earned the money?"

"You won't see a penny of it if you go to China."

"All right, then, keep it," I said. I wasn't going to squabble with the likes of van Pappenhacker over a sordid matter of five thousand dollars. I was very unworldly in those days.

That, I think, was the whole problem. I simply could not understand that the opinion of the world counted in any way. Father's opinions counted. Mother's feelings counted. My own opinions counted very much indeed, but I felt, if anything, a certain contempt for the world's opinions. Please note the irony. My reasons for going to China were essentially private, but I was at least sympathetic to the idea that the world needs to be changed and reformed. And, as everyone knows, the best way to influence the world is to show your contempt and disrespect for it. As a reformer I was straight out of a Dickens novel.

In Tokyo, however, Father was beginning to think I was straight out of Marx. Reading the letters I sent him and meditating on the whole situation, he came to the conclusion that I was really changed. His son, a believer in World Revolution and the Dictatorship of the Proletariat! Then he made the mistake of deploying his own political and social views, which I fell upon with glee. Our letters became more controversial and politicized and hence lost their value, at least from the point of view of this story.

Father stayed on in Tokyo well into the autumn, camped in Frank Lloyd Wright's Imperial Hotel. On gray days when romance seems to have drizzled out of the modern world, I can still get a *frisson* as I picture him there attempting to influence my mind during the ninety cooling-off days we defectors were held at Panmunjon. But why didn't he make the whole matter a simple test of love? "If you love your mother and myself, you must come home whether or not you think we are right in demanding this of you." He never quite said that. He had to *prove* he was right in demanding what he wanted, and that's just what no one can prove even if he happens to be a bishop of the Protestant Episcopal Church of the United States of America. They can make mistakes too.

INTERLUDE

Liu had led or perhaps even misled me into thinking we would go straight to Peking. Shortly after he rejoined the troupe he let us know that our ultimate destination in China would be the city of Taiyuan.

"Taiyuan?" I said.

"It is the provincial capital of Shansi Province," Liu told me.

"Where is that?"

"It is in the northwest. It is a mountainous region." He gave me a rather bland look. "I have never been there myself," he added.

"Has anyone you know ever been there?"

"It is a large city. The capital of an important province. Naturally many people go there."

"But no one *you* know?"

"I think you will find it agreeable," he said. "In any case, that is where you are going. The authorities have decided that in a city like Peking there would be too many distractions. What this group needs is a quiet period of study and more intensive *szu-hsiang kai-tsao*. Taiyuan is a very suitable place for such purposes."

"I see." Apparently Taiyuan, except for the mountains, was another Kansas City. I had been conned, but at least for the moment I could enjoy the first fruits of my defection. There were speeches and banquets and head-turning receptions in Kaesong and Pyongyang and other way-stops on our slow journey into China. Red carpets were unrolled, and it had been so long since I'd trodden on a rug of any sort that I was rather uncritical of the warp and woof of those welcome mats. The general atmosphere was triumphant and victorious. In the ruins of Pyongyang we were treated as heroes who had done something great and magnificent. There was a Sino-American-Korean Friendship Banquet in a patched-up government building where we were actually toasted by some of the leading personalities of the North Korean régime. Yet—heartbreak—looking around their capital I couldn't understand why they wanted to toast any American, pro-Communist or otherwise. Twice our army had taken their capital, twice it had made strategic demolitions as it retreated. For years our planes had dumped high explosives on the city, and now here were these much pulverized people actually staging a Friendship Banquet amid the debris. It was tragic, especially since the Americans they were toasting had done nothing to deserve their friendship. We were a tiny, unrepresentative band who had come to Korea for our own foolish reasons, spent most of our time there in prison, and were now leaving that torn country in our own foolish way, totally unaware of what Korean life was all about. Yet here was this banquet full of soaring rhetoric referring to friendship between peoples and the victorious march of the progressive and peace-loving forces in the world. I had once imagined I would take part in an American victory parade through the streets of Pyongyang. Now I was participating in this banquet. Life seems always to provide us with strangely transformed and more meaningful versions of our crude dreams.

Liu was with us on the train, though *he* was not going all the way to Taiyuan. He got off at Kalgan, a border city at the Great Wall separating China from Inner Mongolia. He was going to get a connection there to Peking.

We spent almost a whole day while our train sat in the station at Kalgan. Liu's train was not due to leave for thirty-six hours, so we had time to talk and even make an expedition to look at the Great Wall. From its ramparts I could see the Inner Mongolian steppe. Here civilization ended. "Not very attractive scenery," I said. Liu was noncommittal. It wasn't his cup of tea either. I said, "I think of myself as essentially an urban personality. I like river valleys. That's where civilization started and that's where it still is."

"Taiyuan is near a river," Liu remarked. He, too, seemed daunted by the sight of Inner Mongolia.

"A smooth, placid river?" I asked. "That's the kind I like best." Kansas City is at the junction of the Kansas and Missouri rivers, neither of which were exactly to my taste.

"I do not know how placid a river it is," Liu said. "You must just make the best of the situation."

"It's awfully nice of you to say that."

He then assumed his Commissar role. "It is important that you approach this experience in the right frame of mind. We have talked before about your habit of expecting life to suit your private tastes. It is a very bad habit."

"Comrade Liu . . ." we called each other *Comrade* now that I was no longer an official prisoner . . . "Comrade Liu, I don't think I'm being arbitrary or willfully aesthetic when I say that smooth rivers bordered by grassy banks, cultivated fields, nice pastures with sheep and horses and cows in them, and neat houses surrounded by trees are to be preferred to this kind of landscape."

"Much can be done even with this," said Liu turning away from the sight.

I turned away too and we walked back toward the station.

When we parted that evening we saluted each other with clenched fists, and then Liu shook hands with each of us. "I wish you all a very prosperous and happy time in Taiyuan," he said. Then we climbed aboard our train, which presently steamed out of the station. Liu waved from the platform with another officer who was also leaving us. We were going on accompanied only by two officers, neither of

251

whom I knew because they had served in another camp along the Yalu. I waved good-bye to Liu, who waved to me before turning away to enter the station.

I'd had too many partings. I felt as torn up as Korea and as barren as Inner Mongolia. I felt as if I might never see a familiar face again. My friends in America had all graduated from college and scattered God knew where, I didn't. (How on earth had the Army contacted Morrison?) Winterode was dead; Dalbert had disappeared; Novotny and Matthew and Hubler and even Poniatowski, Ramirez, and Hollins were all gone. I had just left Liu. Father would probably want to kill me if we ever met again. Mother was inseparable from him. Really, I was rather alone out there in Inner Mongolia. From Kalgan to Taiyuan was a bad trip, as they say now. We were getting deeper into the mountains all the time. I sat at the window with another defector named Herbie Smith, about the only one I liked, and looked at the scenery, telling myself that I was seeing part of the world and that eventually some connections would be established between this part of the world, whatever it was, and the part I really wanted to live in.

Taiyuan confirmed my worst expectations. It was a dark, shuttered city. We arrived in the dead of winter, just the worst time of year, when snow lay on the surrounding mountains and accumulated on the rooftops and in the streets. A cold wind blew from the west laden with dust from the Gobi desert. Walking in the streets I could see old snow-piles evenly striped with clean and dark snow like gigantic slabs of bacon only less appetizing. The citizens were unfriendly. Westerners were unknown there. Our height, our big noses, everything about us struck them as strange and barbaric, while they struck us as being cruel and savage. Once, while walking alone in the city, one of our number was set upon by the townspeople and beaten up. We were

252

thrown together, willy-nilly, and even so there was little comfort. One of us died that winter and lies buried there in Shansi Province. How strange it is that we are born in some ordinary American town and raised amid familiar sights and then die on the other side of the world, scarcely knowing how we got there.

We might have been more comfort to each other if we had not been going through so much criticism/self-criticism which made us critical of each other as well as ourselves. And there was certainly a lot of criticize, though at some stages of life what one wants is comrades, not critics.

I thought a lot about God, which is probably the best thing to do in a place like Taiyuan. All the Marxian dialectics which I had by then absorbed made me more receptive to the idea of the Trinity. Life is contradictory. There must be some opposition, or at least tightly poised tension in the very source of things. If God were really unitary, then the world would not be quite as dramatic as it is. I began to think that God as Unmoved Mover might very well require a different mode of being in order to effect His operations. Christ, then, as First Efficient Cause, the creative and active principle of reality. And once you had Father and Son, obviously you needed something to keep them from falling apart into mere opposites. The Holy Spirit became for me the synthesizing and linking principle, and I even began to understand why, in the Creed, it was so confidently asserted that Mary was fructified through the Holy Spirit. The Holy Family in which there was supposed to be no natural connection between Joseph and Jesus was nevertheless brought into being and made a family through the operations of the Holy Spirit.

It was, of course, unthinkable that Jesus could have been the Christ. If any part of the Godhead actually entered the world I felt the result would have been some sort of catastrophic explosion, as in the meeting of matter and anti-matter. God had soiled His hands with matter once at the beginning of time when the universe came into being, and would soil Himself once again at the end of time when the universe was unmade and the story finally completed. Yet meanwhile in such paradigmatic formulations as the Holy Family and the Marxian Thesis, Antithesis, Synthesis, we had been given a way to understand the ultimate configuration of the Godhead. I saw the dialectic and the Holy Family as symbols of the ultimate triune reality, and of the two I found that the Holy Family made more sense to me. Marx seemed to have put the terms of the dialectic into the wrong order. It should be Synthesis, Thesis, Antithesis. In the material world we were moving *away from* the perfect integration of the Godhead into mere opposition and fragmentation. The Christian formula was superior because it showed the Holy Spirit, the very essence of the unity of the Godhead, giving rise to the strangely disunited family of Man in which the son Jesus was not related to his father Joseph and even went so far as to deny his mother at the wedding feast in Cana of Galilee.

Naturally these were not thoughts I could very well express to my fellow defectors or our Chinese instructors. That is why this little chapter is a sort of strange interlude in my story because for once I was truly alone, unable to find anyone to argue with or love or hate. I seemed to have dropped right out of life into some never-never land of inward meditation and external chatter that didn't make much difference to me. I mean, our criticism/self-criticism sessions were lively, but they didn't get at what I was interested in. We were also studying Chinese and learning something of the history of China, which was fine, but it was just schoolwork. At times, in Taiyuan, I began to think I'd made a very great mistake in going to China, but it is always darkest before the dawn. In the summer of 1954 our life in Taiyuan was broken up. Half of us were assigned work on state farms and pulp mills; the luckier half was sent to Peking University for further study and training. I felt life was beginning to move again as I settled into a top-floor dormitory room that fall. Not only was I back in circulation, but Peking was the first truly royal capital I had ever seen. Also, as some faint intimation of the possible harmony of life, I found I was living on the campus of the former Harvard-Yenching Institute, which had been taken over by Peking U. As for what happened to me there: Behold and see.

BOOK THREE

24

I rose with the sun. There was the usual splashing around the sink, then tea, porridge, and dried bananas for breakfast. The bus was already waiting when Herbie and I left the dormitory. The girls were sitting up front. We took a vacant seat halfway down. Gradually the bus filled with students and presently we were off. The sky was turning a deeper blue as we left Peking through the Chao Yang Men. Our destination, State Farm 7, was half an hour away in the direction of Tungchow.

I could see May, in her workclothes, sitting up front with another girl whose name, Su-An Tu Tit Won, would have been recommendation enough for me even if she hadn't also happened to be May's roommate. They kept their eyes on the wide, empty road. I stared at the back of May's neck. Beside me Herbie settled himself and closed his eyes. He had been out late the night before at a bar frequented by the foreign element in Peking. I shunned such places.

We turned off the Tungchow highway and took a winding road between duck farms and vegetable gardens. The land was flat. Brown walls, ditches, ponds, and farm compounds gave the countryside an organized, *used* look, very different from the land around Kansas City. Even if I hadn't known I was in China I would have known I was there. Where else do you see so many Chinese-looking sights? May's hair, for instance, was the same color as Martha's, but the texture seemed to be quite different though I had not actually touched her hair yet, or any part of her.

The bus parked in the compound of State Farm 7. We climbed out, Herbie rubbing his eyes. A smiling farm official shepherded us along a narrow lane between two long sheds or barns, past an apple orchard and a duck pond, out into a wide field where familiar-looking crinkly green leaves edged with purple told me that on this work holiday we would be harvesting beets.

They are very simple little plants. You grab them and yank and up they come, beet and all. It's not like digging potatoes.

We fanned out along the rows, bending and yanking, then beating the dirt off our beets before dropping them into sacks which had been given us. The girls tended to stick together, Herbie and I tended to stick together, but I managed things so that I could see May and Su-An as they moved down a row a little ahead of us. May was wearing trousers so there was no chance to catch a glimpse of her calves. I was inclined toward idolatry. I wanted a good look at those golden calves.

And now who is May and what is she that all the swains do love her? That's the problem. I don't know who she is. I saw her first sitting in Changshan Park reading a book. A few days later I spotted her in a university dining hall. I sat down at the same table and asked her to pass the mustard, which she did. On that occasion I discovered she knew English. Then I saw her in company with Su-An signing up for something at a booth. I asked what they were doing, and found out they were volunteering their services for a harvest holiday. As soon as they moved off I volunteered my own services, and then, thinking things over, volunteered Herbie's as well. Herbie had socially useful instincts. All he needed was a little prodding. That, briefly, is the history of my relationship with May up to the time you find me admiring her in a beet field.

Ah though! She was lovely, even in her clumsy work clothes. Impossible to apply the word *rump* to what I could see of her when she bent over. What word did apply? I ran over the possibilities and found none of them satisfactory.

We need a better vocabulary to deal with the female form.

When she straightened up there was a faint suggestion of swelling under her work jacket. What was the word for that, or them? *Orbs* was too fancy, and the other terms struck me as too anatomical. I felt dissatisfied. I didn't know May and couldn't even think about her in language that suited me. What frustrations life imposes on the would-be lover!

Then Herbie remarked that his back was killing him.

"If you took better care of yourself and didn't hang around bars you might be in better shape," I said. One must not palter with these night owls.

"Doesn't your back ache?" he asked.

It did, but the logic of my position would be destroyed by admitting the fact. "No," I said.

So we went on harvesting beets.

Did May and Su-An complain, and put each other down, and lie the way Herbie and I did? Probably not. So was that the secret? Was that why women are more attractive than men? They have nicer characters? Maybe it was not really May's body I ought to be thinking about so much as her soul. Well, it was a theory anyway, though I knew as little about her soul as her body. Damn clothes and conventions! Why couldn't we just meet in primal nudity to talk about grave and eternal subjects?

That was a large beet field. Even with twenty intellectuals—well, students—at work it took us an hour and a half to clear it. During the rest that followed two farm women brought us hot tea. We sat on the grass near the duck pond and I managed to drop into position next to May. "It's a beautiful day," I told her. This was a classical remark but I really couldn't think of anything better. And besides it was a nice day. No one could argue about it. Comrade Lee (May's name was May Lee) acknowledged the profound truth of my observation. It established another of those tenuous bonds between us. Fabricating such bonds kept me as busy as a spider throwing out filaments of silk in a high wind. A smile here, a comment on the weather there, a well-placed look: it would all add up in time, but meanwhile I felt how very difficult it was in socialist China to get things started with a girl and then keep them going in the right direction.

Indeed scarcely had May and I come to a good understanding about the weather when Su-An finished her tea and rose to her feet. May showed signs of rising, so quickly I said, "Are you studying English?"

"I learned it as a child," she said.

"You speak it very well."

She acknowledged my compliment. Then she rose and joined Su-An. Together they strolled down to the pond to admire the ducks. I watched them, discontented by these developments. Herbie came over to me. "Why don't you ask her for a date?"

"I haven't had a chance yet."

"Just ask her."

"Listen," I said, "you're used to dealing with *déclassée* foreign girls." There was a very mixed bunch at the Purple Rickshaw where Herbie hung out: Eurasians, Russians of various vintages and hues (Red, White, Blue), and European and American Communists resident in Peking—a very mixed bunch indeed. "She's pure Chinese," I said.

"What's so special about that?" Herbie asked. "There are about three hundred million pure Chinese girls."

If he couldn't understand, I wasn't going to explain things to him. Herbie was from West Virginia and had rather blunt conceptions of class and rank and even ideological purity. He was currently seeing a Russian girl of Menshevik origins.

After the beets we picked apples. All that reaching and stretching would have been wonderful for May-watching except she was up a different tree. Herbie and I picked with a businesslike silence. Once he said, "I wonder how Barber and those guys are doing at the pulp mill?"

I didn't wonder. I'd never liked Barber, and I considered the others who had gotten the pulp mill treatment more or less deserved their fates. Not a real ideologue among them. You couldn't count on Hopkins to know the difference between a left-wing deviation and out-and-out social fascism. When he and Barber were sent to the mills it proved to me the Chinese really knew what they were doing.

"You wait and see," I said. "Those guys will be screaming to go home in a couple of months."

He said, "Do you ever think about it?"

"Going home?"

"Yes."

"Never," I said.

Another lie. Would May like a liar? "I think about it sometimes," I said.

He nodded, and we let the matter drop. I began wondering about May's ideological purity. I took it for granted she was a virgin, but was she a good Communist as well? How could I ask her that? How could I ask anything of real importance? Suddenly I was overwhelmed by the shame and disgrace of my position. Here at twenty-four I was an alien interloper looking at girls from a distance, unable to make any sort of natural contact with them. I was a failure as a man.

For lunch we were invited into the communal dining hall to break bread with the farm workers. The dining hall was new and clean and decorated with highly encouraging posters about rising agricultural productivity. There was also a big, beaming portrait of Guess Who, together with some of his thoughts on the relationship between Agriculture and Patriotism. These decorations, however, bulked less large in my mind than the sight of May seated next to Su-An on a long bench. There was another student (male) seated near but not next to May. It seemed to me a moment of crisis. Either I inserted myself between May and her compatriot and tried to improve our acquaintance, or I accepted the natural course of things which would place me with Herbie. And really there was more involved than that. If I accepted the natural course of things it meant never getting into close contact with pure young Chinese girls, for they are not easy to know. I had found that out. It was much simpler to go out to bars as Herbie did and meet the mixed company one found there. Girls like May were embedded deeper than beets in their society. It seemed almost impossible to get at them in a way that was neither violent nor hopelessly polite. They couldn't be yanked up, or plucked from a bough. How did one get at them? By sitting down beside them?

There was just enough space for me to crowd in between her and that fellow who had obviously put himself next to her because she was the most attractive young woman in the room. *He* felt he had the right to sit next to her, whereas I was very unsure of my rights in the matter. It was that thought which spurred me to action. I might not have any rights, but I certainly had needs. Besides, why shouldn't I hope? I had some things going for me: desperation, nerve, and a nice smile.

So I wedged myself between the pure Chinese girl on my right and her pure young compatriot on my left. "I'm surprised you studied English as a girl," I said.

"It was an English-speaking school I went to," she said.

Then our conversation had to end while the farm manager rose to welcome the Comrade Students to State Farm 7. He talked and talked about the indissoluble bonds between farm and intellectual workers. He took notice of the presence of the two Comrade Americans. This led him into a none-too-brief recapitulation of the Korean war, which had proved to the world that China, united at last and inspired by the teachings of Chairman Mao, had become the second pillar (the first being Russia in those days) of the Victorious Advance of the Freedom-Loving Anti-Imperialist Progressive Forces of World Socialism. He got quite a hand when it was over. The appetite for that kind of speech never failed to amaze me. Then the real edibles were brought in, hot and tasty, and I said to May, "Was it a church school?" I had been dying to ask the question for the last fifteen minutes.

She looked rather grave. I had been speaking in English, which presumably no one around us understood, yet she hesitated for a moment before she allowed as how *yes*, it had been a church school.

I thought so. Indeed I had already worked out all the hopeful implications. Would peasants send their daughter to an English-speaking church school? Obviously not. Would small shopkeepers or artisans? Again, no. May, then, was the daughter of some educated professional or even higher. Her father might have been a landowner and magistrate, though in that case would May be the good Communist she had to be? Probably not. Therefore May came from the professional class, roughly the same class I came from if one ignored the Clays as one was entirely justified in doing. And couldn't we go further than that? A *church* school? Why not simply say a convent school and have done with it? If not a Christian upon arrival, May had undoubtedly been converted. And since she could not be a Christian now, clearly she had followed somewhat the same spiritual trajectory I myself had followed. It had landed her in dialectical materialism and me on the bench beside her, but we could alter that. I could convert, or take her on my lap.

"That's very interesting," I said. "I went to a church school, too."

At that point the boy on my left finally expressed his sense of displeasure at my intrusion. He said, "Paper tiger American imperialism has been taught a lesson."

Nodding vigorously, I said, "World imperialism must always fall back before the aroused conscience of mankind." That was how to handle that sort of thing.

He came right back at me. "It is impossible for American fascism to encircle the Chinese people."

I said, "The Chinese people will break through the encircling threat and establish comradely relations with all the world."

He scowled. I smiled and then turned back to May, my inquisitiveness temporarily distracted from religion to more mundane matters. "Have you always lived in Peking?"

"No," she said.

Hotspur on my left had found a new formula. "The poisonous Counterrevolutionary Reaction cannot have any effect on those whose minds have been formed by the thoughts of Chairman Mao."

I answered, "It is by correct thinking and determined action that we will sweep to victory." That fixed him. "Where did you live before that?" I asked May.

"In Paoting."

"I am from Kansas City."

On my left I heard a voice saying, "The lackeys of finance capitalism do not know which way to turn," but I felt he was temporarily a spent force. "Was your school in Paoting?" I asked.

She looked grave again. This school was a sensitive topic. Hastily I decided I should tell her about my life and wait for her to vouchsafe information about hers. Yet what, exactly, could I tell her? "Kansas City," I presently heard myself saying, "is in the Midwest of the United States. It is a railroad and meat-packing center and has the largest horse and mule market in the United States."

May didn't know what a mule was, and before I'd well considered the matter I plunged into an explanation of *that*. By the time the meal had ended I was pretty sure I had still not found the formula for making friends with Chinese girls.

266

After lunch it was apples until my arms ached. Then a rest break during which I finally popped the question. "If you went to a church school you must have been a Christian at one time."

May looked angry. "I was very young then."

"I was a Christian when I was young," I said. "It's remarkable how much we have in common."

Name one other thing, she didn't say, for which I thanked her mentally.

Su-An said, "Do you like Peking?"

Yes, I liked Peking. "When did you lose your faith?" I asked May. She seemed more real, more accessible as a fallen Christian than a pure Communist.

She said, "It is of no importance."

The answer was that everything concerning her was of extreme importance, but the time hadn't come to tell her so.

Su-An asked, "Have you seen the Monuments of the Past?"

Chinese public buildings are often rather oddly named, but I took it that she was referring to the temples and palaces generally, rather than some particular structure. It seemed too good an opportunity to lose. "I've seen some of them," I said, "but they make very little sense to me. It would be so much more interesting if I could visit them with some Chinese friends who could explain things."

Su-An looked at May who looked at Su-An. My suggestion seemed to be falling to the ground until I scooped it up and dangled it invitingly in front of them. "Would you be willing to accompany me one day on a sightseeing expedition?" The question was addressed to May, but it was Su-An who eventually said *yes.* So it was Victory of a sort, with only the usual amount of adulteration, and probably I could arrange for Su-An to get lost in the shuffle. We fixed it up that on the following Friday we would tour the Palace Museum together.

25

So we move now from State Farm 7 to the Court of the Golden River, and Su-An is saying, "Since the Liberation all this has been repaired and put in order." Something will have to be done about Su-An, but at the moment there seems to be no opportunity. We are in a large walled area facing the Gate of Supreme Harmony. In front of us the Golden River lies stretched across the courtyard like a bent bow, spanned by five white marble bridges, known as the Five Arrows. They are aimed at us. I said, "I've always wondered why Marxist revolutions are so tender toward royal palaces while French revolutions generally begin by sacking Versailles or burning the Tuileries."

May, to whom this was addressed, said, "This palace is a great work of art built by the Chinese people. Why should it not be preserved and opened to the people?"

"Oh, I'm for it," I said. "I just think it's odd. The Bolsheviks moved right into the Kremlin, and now Chairman Mao uses the Forbidden City for state banquets and receptions."

"That is quite proper," said May.

Something in her tone brought me up. This was not the sort of girl who was going to stand for a lot of razzle-dazzle from me. She was perhaps a *serious* girl. Just the kind I had always needed.

"Shall we go forward?" Su-An said.

Forward we went across the Third Arrow and through the Gate of Supreme Harmony into the next courtyard where visitors are confronted, or perhaps overwhelmed, by the Hall of Supreme Harmony where formerly the Celestial Monarch seated on his Dragon Throne received the kowtows of his most important subjects. It was the throne hall in which the

Emperor's identity as Son of Heaven was most emphatically asserted.

"What does your father do?" I asked May.

The question was not well received. "He is not here," she said.

We were speaking in Chinese and soon (but too late) I was to learn that the idiom *He is not here* meant he was dead. I said, "Naturally I didn't expect him to be here, I meant what does he do for a living?"

Su-An looked uncomfortable, May looked furious. "My father is not living," she said. Then she walked on ahead.

"I'm afraid I have offended her," I said to Su-An.

"It is possible," Su-An said. "She was devoted to her father."

"What did he do?" I asked.

"It is not nice to talk of these things," said Su-An.

We caught up with May. Then, in silence, the three of us climbed the marble terrace on which the Hall sits. At the top we admired the Imperial grain measure, the sundial, the cranes, and the bronze tortoises, after which we stepped into the Hall itself and stood looking up at the empty throne.

"I hope you are not angry," I said to May.

She hesitated for a moment, then she said, "To question people as you do is not respectful." She looked up at me and for a moment our eyes met. I felt myself shrinking. "Nor are you respectful to my friend," May added.

Su-An colored, and I had the decency to blush. May went on looking up at me. "To respect others it is necessary to respect oneself." Then she moved away to examine a bronze urn, leaving me feeling a good deal worse than I had any notion she could make me feel. Su-An, her eyes downcast, remained near me. Together we stood before the throne like unhappy children caught in the act.

After a while, when I had touched bottom, I began to get angry. What right, what possible right did *she* have to suggest I lacked respect for others and for myself? I looked over to where she was standing, still inspecting an urn. The nerve of these women! They sense you admire them, and then swift as rattlesnakes they strike you in some vulnerable spot. All right! I thought. I may not be perfect. There may be choked and unnavigable shallows among my depths, but what makes you think you're so perfect? With your back turned to me pretending to admire that hideous urn?

Su-An, trying to rescue things, said, "The Emperor was always screened from view when he sat upon this throne."

It was a moment of great intellectual clarity for me. This round-faced, agreeable, kind-hearted Su-An probably liked me, but it was my fate to be attracted to her touchy friend now examining a silk wall hanging. "Thank you," I said, as respectfully as I could. Then I gestured at May's back. "Tell her she misjudges me." Bowing slightly, I then withdrew from the throne hall.

They found me sitting on one of the bronze tortoises, outside, probably another act of *lèse majesté* on my part. May, however, took no notice of it. She inclined her head slightly though I had no idea whether this was to indicate I was forgiven or simply too unimportant to be taken seriously.

I rose and to my horror it appeared that our tour was to continue.

Behind the Hall of Supreme Harmony stands the Hall of the Happy Mean, a smaller throne hall consecrated to the pursuit of agriculture and used by the Emperor in his role of First Farmer of the Empire. The girls walked together, I brought up the rear of our little procession thinking *respect works both ways*. What sort of respect was I being shown in this country with the Korean war tossed in my face practically every day, and everyone ranting about the imperialistic foreign policy of my country. So American foreign policy wasn't perfect? Did these people think we'd invented imperialism? Ha! They'd been imperialists before America was even dreamed of. And for that matter what was so wrong with imperialism anyway? Were the Roman and Chinese Empires *more* or *less* civilized than the surrounding tribes? Answer me that, you . . . you . . . And is America *more* or *less* technologically advanced than the rest of the world?

I caught up with them and together we entered the Hall of the Happy Mean.

I said, "In my country it is not considered rude or disrespectful to ask questions."

May looked surprised.

"When we are interested in each other, we ask each other questions. That's perfectly natural." I was speaking in English; my feelings about the whole matter were too urgent for me to risk saying it badly in Chinese. "Besides," I added in what may have seemed a non sequitur to her, "in the present world conditions America is bound to be the most imperialistic country because everyone has to learn from us. We are simply farther ahead in the direction the whole world is going. You can't go on farming with implements like these . . ." and I gestured at the yellow plow and the gilded grain basket set out on the floor in front of the throne.

"I do not understand," she said.

"I am very sorry if I lacked respect," I said, "but frequently I feel that Chinese people lack respect for America." It was clearly a startling notion to her. "Think of the millions and billions of dollars worth of equipment we sent to China during the war."

Her eyes flashed. "That equipment was sent to the corrupt Nationalist government."

"Well, so what? It was sent so that the Chinese people would have modern equipment to fight the Japanese invaders with. Is it our fault China had a lousy government then which was unable to put the equipment to good use?"

Our voices were raised in an unseemly way, though as a matter of fact that particular throne hall had seen a fair

271

amount of unseemly violence. The Emperor Kuang Hsu was arrested there on orders from the Dowager Empress Tz'u Hsi, and for years there had been an arrow stuck in the ceiling, shot by the Emperor Tao Kuang when he was facing down some rebels who had broken into the Forbidden City, just as May was putting down my rebellion at the moment. Shifting to Chinese so that Su-An could get this, she looked at me with a sort of wondering pity. "Why do you speak of such aid which did the Chinese people no good whatsoever? Is it not you who should be grateful for what you have received from China?"

"Well, I'm naturally . . ."

"Have you not been invited here, and supported by the state, and educated at state expense when there are millions of Chinese people who are not so well cared for?"

"I'm sorry," I said, there being nothing else to say.

"It is very strange you should talk about the world learning from America. Have you not come here to learn from us?"

Su-An said, "We wish to share our new life with all comrades everywhere."

I said, "But . . ."

Abruptly, with an almost disdainful expression, May turned away and I trailed miserably after her with Su-An at my side.

May stopped at the third great throne hall, the Hall of Established Harmony where the Emperor received imperial scholars, foreign envoys, and tributary vassals. It was there that Lord George MacCartney, Ambassador of George III, refused to kowtow to the Emperor Ch'ien Lung, and it was there, one hundred and seventy years later, that Samuel Heather crooked a knee to the Chinese Revolution incarnated in the person of Comrade May Lee.

I had been having one of my visions as Su-An and I walked along the marble terrace in May's wake. A political revolution, I saw, was a sexual restoration in which the monopoly of royal sovereignty is broken and majesty descends to ordinary people who begin to feel as whole as the greatest potentates. Eunuchs disappear, concubines become women, harlots feel virginal again, and citizens walk through the streets of the liberated capital seeing it with fresh eyes. They visit the palaces from which the kings and emperors have fled and redeem those often tawdry dwellings by the genuineness of their belief in the sanctity of power, and the healing touch of revolutionary sovereignty. Trotsky describes how the crowds in St. Petersburg surrounded the Tsar's gendarmes with the timid confidence of virgins, summoning them to come over to the Revolution in order to be unmade as soldiers and remade as men. My God! I thought, thinking of May, she could make a man out of me.

Inside the Hall of Established Harmony I turned toward her and said, "Comrade Lee, you have made me feel very ungrateful. I wish you and Comrade Su-An would let me do something for you. Could I take you to an opera tomorrow?"

"Tomorrow is the fifth anniversary of the founding of the Republic," she said.

"Could I take you to that?" I asked.

We had a great time. If I've so far given the impression China is a sparsely inhabited country filled mainly with Su-An, May, and myself, let me here correct that impression. We three were part of an audience of two million people watching another million parade through Tien An Men Square, like a human Mississippi flowing past the great red bluff of the Gate of Heavenly Peace on which Chairman Mao himself could be seen beaming and waving.

New Yorkers in a subway or in Times Square on New Year's Eve never really have the experience of being surrounded and inundated in a joyous and totally sober crowd. I suppose it's rare anywhere, to find three million happy, civi-

273

cally aroused, patriotic citizens all shouting and waving flags and banging on drums and blowing whistles. The noise was Niagara-like, deafening, at times almost painful. The Chinese love noise. Noise seems to play about the same role in China that automobiles play in America. A Chinaman making a lot of noise apparently feels enhanced, powerful, transfigured by the racket he is creating. The great spirits of the air are being stirred; waves of life and sound are traveling at great speed in all directions. Heaven must take note of all this precious commotion. There is an almost religious meaning to noise in China.

And now the parade. There were workers, soldiers, mothers, gymnasts (male and female), students, miners, artisans, streetcleaners, and professors. Every national minority seemed to be on parade: mountain people, steppe people, nomads from the Central Asian deserts—Tibetans, Is, Miaos, Uighurs—on and on they came with a sort of controlled anarchy. There was some order in the different contingents of the parade, and the soldiers at least maintained formation fairly well, with dressed lines, but most of the other groups were pretty informal. Bystanders would step into the parade, carried away by enthusiasm, and then step out again when the rest of the family refused to join. There were children and grandparents everywhere. It wasn't like anything I'd ever seen before.

I had to shout to make myself heard by May and Su-An. "Would you like some litchi nuts?" I shouted. They nodded and smiled. Su-An had a flag to wave. May had a horn. May, I learned, loved litchi nuts, and rising as I did above the general level of the crowds, I was in an excellent position to spot the litchi vendors circulating around shouting out their wares. I could make purchases by passing my money to them through half a dozen intermediary hands, and receiving the litchis, also touched by half a dozen intermediaries. Luckily everyone seemed to have washed his hands that morning.

In the evening there was a fireworks display that made me think the war had begun again. We watched it from Prospect Hill. The rockets shot up and burst over Pei Hai Park, sometimes in such numbers that the sky was actually illuminated and we could see the great yellow tiled roofs of the Forbidden City looming below us. Military bands were still marching around the city deafening the deaf. Sparrows, swallows, and pigeons fluttered overhead, their sleep completely disturbed. Many of the pigeons had little whistles attached to their legs so that as they swept about overhead one had the impression Heaven itself was celebrating.

During a tiny lull Su-An shouted to me, "The last Ming emperor hung himself on a tree over there."

Poor Emperor! He'd probably never had any fun in his life, and the Chinese are a very fun-loving people, I was beginning to think. Two old gentlemen near us were almost hysterical with laughter over something they'd seen—which turned out to be me. I got down on my knees which made me the same height as May and Su-An. The old men thought that was even funnier. Then we all began to sing revolutionary songs.

At midnight things calmed down. We were surfeited by noise and crowds and starved for food. It had been impossible to get back to the university for our evening meal, so on the walk back to campus May and Su-An bought me a warm fried roll. I had spent all my money on litchis. When I left them at the door of their dormitory I tried to explain that this had been one of the happiest days of my life. I was so relaxed I didn't even try to arrange a further date. Then I walked to my dormitory and crawled into bed and fell asleep with my head still tingling with euphoria.

26

May and I were married on April 25, 1955.

I would dearly like to describe the ups and downs of our courtship, but at a certain point one's story is no longer one's own. Mrs. Heather must be listened to, and the word from her is *No.*

"I will not have you use the most sacred moments of our life together for commercial purposes."

"Commercial purposes!" I cried.

"I know you, Samuel. You will describe our first kiss. You will go on and on about it." This was an uncannily accurate prediction. I had plans for that kiss.

I looked at her reproachfully—we were sitting across the kitchen table from each other. "All I can say," I said, "is that you have a lot to answer for to your conscience, letting me get started on this confession and then ringing down the bamboo curtain at the most interesting moment."

"This confession was not my idea," she said.

"You know I've been writing it. Did you think I would just skip over my marriage?"

She finished her cup of oolong and got to her feet.

"I asked you a question," I said, but it was the old story. No one ever tries to answer inconvenient questions.

Over her shoulder (she was standing at the sink by then) Mrs. Heather said, "I would expect you to show respect for our privacy." Then she turned on the faucet, thus cutting off communications. I continued to drink my tea. After a while I came up to my study where I am working on this.

Life, or rather, literature is very unjust. In books one can describe sorrow and despair and struggle and all the more unpleasant features of life, but happiness falls flat. And while I naturally resent May's frightful curtailing of my artistic freedom, I have begun to see it may be for the best. Perhaps our first kiss would not have made such a great scene. Maybe our excursion to the valley of the Ming Tombs is more idyllic in my memory than I could make it sound on paper. After all, what is there to say? We went to the Ming Tombs and picnicked on a grassy slope near the Ting Ling. It was our first outing without Su-An and we were both rather quiet, even shy with each other. What was actually said? I can't quite remember.

The arguments we had stuck in my mind. I can remember a long, increasingly bitter quarrel that started in Changshan Park and culminated in a rowboat disaster. (Ladies should not rise indignantly while sitting in rowboats.) But such arguments are not at all the point. We would never have gotten married on the basis of those arguments. Indeed, considering how much we argued, it's a little mysterious just why we did get married. Basically I think it was because I fell in love with May and May fell in love with her idea of me.

I may not have her permission to explain her feelings toward me, but I will explain them anyway. In spite of my manners and looks, she began to see me in an heroic light. Don't laugh, she had grounds, however mistaken. In October two defectors who'd been sent to state farms came through Peking on their way back to America where they were eventually arrested by military police on their arrival in San Francisco. This was reported in the Peking press, and naturally all of us there followed the case with considerable interest.

It was an illegal arrest, of course. The army had no jurisdiction over us ever since our dishonorable discharge. I was very steamed up and indignant about the matter. "It is not what one would expect?" May asked at the time. (It was our Changshan Park date.) "It's certainly not what I expect when I go back," I said.

We quarreled then over whether it was right for me to benefit from my studies in China and then leave the country without contributing what I could to the advance of socialism. I argued that I could do more good in America than in China, and that in any case America was not nearly as bad as May seemed to think. There was, for instance, more intellectual freedom in America than in China, at which point she leaped angrily to her feet and fell into the water, as noted above.

The dousing did her no real harm, while my argument did me some good. May began thinking it over. She had already seen I was not such a disrespectful or selfish person as she had first assumed. ("I did not like you at all when we first met.") Next she began to think I had the makings of a real hero. I would go back to my country and face the persecution there and do what I could to educate and socialize my fellow citizens. She was first intrigued, then captured by the idea, much as Christians are captured by the heroism of missionary life.

There was something else at work in her, too.

Papa Lee, as I eventually found out, was no longer here because he had been shot by the Communists in 1949. It was a mistake, according to May. The village near Paoting where they were then living changed hands three times in as many months. During the second Communist occupation, Papa Lee, a liberal and a man of peace (a doctor, as a matter of fact), was summarily executed. Some low people with outstanding doctor's bills (which Papa Lee was not pressing them to pay) represented the good man as a tyrant and bloodsucking leech. It was a very confused and anarchic period, and so he had died.

The death of her father, whom she reverenced, had a curious effect on May. It became, in fact, the prop of her Communist faith. She could bear to think of him dying as part of a great historical transformation of Chinese society; she could not bear to think of him being stupidly killed in a squalid struggle for power between rival gangs. And since there was absolutely no way to idealize Chiang Kai-shek's gang, she began to believe more deeply in communism, toward which her sympathies were already inclined. The injustice of her father's death was swallowed up in the greater justice of the Revolution. She was even able to see the matter philosophically. Socially her father came from the landowning class, which had to go. Though the manner of his going was wrong, looked at in a larger perspective it could be seen as the will of Heaven.

But this introduced a certain tension into her Communist faith and also left her with a widowed mother in Paoting with whom she was not on good terms. "She thinks my feet are too big and that I am clumsy and stupid. She did not want my father to have me educated." Thus, when May became convinced I loved her, she was able to contemplate the possibility of going to America with me to carry on the revolutionary struggle at a conveniently enormous distance from her mother and from the painful reminders that in practice a revolution is not always as beautiful as it may seem in theory. She had her doubts about the executions that were occasionally reported from provincial centers. Maybe some of the victims were not really enemies of the people.

Yet when all this is explained, I must confess I am still puzzled as to why she married me. I think no man ever really understands what possesses a woman when she agrees to give herself to him. How can they possibly trust us to that extent? The whole thing still seems to me miraculous.

I believe Milton was right when he pictured the first instinct of Eve upon awakening in Eden. She comes to herself *"much wondering where and what I was,"* hears the sound of water, and follows a brook until she comes to a *"smooth lake that seemed to me another sky."*

> As I bent down to look, just opposite
> A shape within the watery gleam appeared

Bending to look on me: I started back,
It started back, but pleased I soon returned,
Pleased it returned as soon with answering looks
Of sympathy and love; there had I fixed
Mine eyes till now and pined with vain desire
Had not a voice thus warned me: What thou seest,
What there thou seest, fair creature, is thyself,
With thee it comes and goes; but follow me,
And I will bring thee where no shadow stays
Thy coming, and thy soft embraces. He
Whose image thou art, him thou shalt enjoy . . .

And so on, but notice that it takes divine intervention to turn her from her own beautiful world toward Adam, and she frankly admits when she first saw him she found him *"less winning soft and less amiably mild than that smooth watery image."* She turns back, and poor Adam has to follow along behind her crying out, *"Return, fair Eve, Whom fli'st thou? whom thou fli'st, of him thou art. . . ."* Critics claim Milton has no delicacy of psychological insight. They're wrong. Any fool of a litterateur can describe neurotic sensations; it takes real greatness to describe normal ones, which is one of the reasons I am giving in to Mrs. Heather's Chinese-Marxist sense of decorum and not really describing our courtship. Falling in love with and marrying May was the most normal thing I've done in my whole life. There's no mystery at all why I fell in love. May is the only human being besides Father who has always taken me seriously.

So we were married, and now another inhibition arises. How am I to describe my honeymoon? If my courtship was sacred and really too normal for me to be able to describe, my honeymoon was even more so. We were given two weeks at state expense at a holiday resort along the Gulf of Chihli. The flat land ran down to the flat sea as if the world thereabouts were pressed flat under the weight of sex in the atmosphere. To entertain the honeymooning couples, there was bathing, and Ping-Pong, and lectures on family planning, and even the caterwauling of an itinerant opera company, but one did not notice that these pastimes were very popular. The reason there are six or seven hundred million people in China is just as simple as you've always suspected, Reader, but modesty and taste forbids me to expatiate on this subject.

Picture me then, a bridegroom sitting beside my bride on a train going to Paoting. We are on our way to meet May's family. As a liberated girl she has taken the great step without introducing me to the old folks at home, but now the time has come.

We were met at the Paoting station by the Lees, a fairly numerous tribe who had given of their plenty in order to form a somewhat daunting reception committee, every member of which was eager to get a first look at this strange foreigner who had carried off their May.

First and foremost came Mama Lee, a balding little broad-shouldered lady who shuffled forward on lotus bud feet while the others hung back. She looked up to where my face was and decided kissing would present too many problems, so she took both my hands in hers and said, "We welcome you, my lord."

That was a hard one to answer. She may have known that in Europe bishops rank as noblemen and assumed I, as the son of a bishop, deserved a title. Or she may just have been being polite. Anyway, she put me off my paces. I fluffed the greeting I had arranged in my mind and then stood looming up crazily and feeling stupid while I was introduced to Younger Brother, Elder Brother's Widow, Younger Son, Younger Son's Wife, and various grandchildren and cousins. I tried to look attentive—these were, after all, my kin—but I was feeling fairly dazed by the time the presentations were over and we all left the station and went outside where up rolled a trolley that had Kansas City written all over it. Old

American streetcars don't die, they fade away to Brazil and China and places like that where they rattle through alien streets yearning for the sights and sounds of their youth. I gave this car a familiar nod, it nodded back, opened its door, and we all climbed aboard.

It was a full old streetcar. There were no seats for any of us. Mama Lee tolerated the situation for perhaps three seconds and then began to talk to us in clearly overhearable tones about the decay of manners and lack of respect for age one encountered in China these days. She developed it as a theme with variations in both major and minor key. Then she hit the dominant with a long account of a crippled old lady who had been forced to stand all the way from the Temple of Ten Thousand Beauties to the 13th Precinct Police station. This recital at last had its desired effect. A laborer who had had his eyes closed, pretending to sleep, got to his feet and offered Mama his place, which she took with many a thank-you and compliment on his manners, his intelligence, his good heart, and his manly bearing. She went on even after he had shouldered his way down the car to get out of range. "You can see," she said, "how our glorious revolution has given common people pride in their own strength and virtue." Then she smiled around at the common people nearest her. May, standing just under my left armpit, scowled out the window.

The Lees lived in a modern apartment building designed to last for all time like everything else in modern China. We passed through a street entrance amply provided with oak doors seven inches thick, climbed granite steps, and at last entered the Lees' apartment where I was confronted with a dainty Sèvres clock under a cloche and various other relics of the family's bourgeois fortunes. "You see our humble abode," said Mama, gesturing around. "These bandits have ruined us, ruined us!" By *bandits* she meant the Communist régime in all its myriad manifestations from Mao down to the cop on the local beat. *Chez elle* she felt no need to indulge in loose talk about *our glorious revolution.*

The first business was to get some idea of just how tall I was. The youngest grandchild was brought forth and put beside me. The family derived considerable amusement from that conjunction. Then Mama decided I should be welcomed once more. This time she took the plunge, or rather the reverse, by indicating I should bend down. We kissed formally, and when I straightened up she raised her arms to see if she could touch my shoulders. This got an appreciative laugh from the rest of the family, which prompted her to hug my waist and put her ear to my stomach. May stood watching these goings-on with a remote, quietly suffering expression like someone under a glass bell from which the oxygen is being pumped. I relaxed, however, and began to enjoy it. Mama had obviously taken a liking to me. I might be a scream to look at, but evidently she had decided I was a highborn holy idiot, a sort of Prince Myshkin, who was bringing luck to the family by marrying May, whom she had never liked anyway.

Next we sat down and began to go into things more seriously.

"Your father is a lord?" Mama asked.

"A bishop."

She nodded. "He owns land?"

"My mother's family owns land."

"Ah. How many *mou* of land?"

I had already worked out their acreage in terms of *mou*. The result was impressive, even startling. Mama raised her hands. "The land is rich?" she asked, a suspicion crossing her mind.

"Yes."

"What do they grow?"

"Well, tobacco," I began.

"Tobacco!" Again her hands went up. "The lord's family grows tobacco," she announced to the company, who had been listening anyway. She gave them a rapid, triumphant look as if to indicate what a good marriage this was turning out to be.

"And what else do they grow?"

"Corn." She nodded. "Some jute." Her lips pursed. "And timothy," I said, finding I'd about exhausted my knowledge of the subject.

There was a pause. Mama tried to help me out. "Beans?" No. "Millet?" I doubted it. "Wheat?" Possibly. "Rice?" No. Mama's face smoothed. "Peppers? Peanuts? Cloves? Bananas? Pineapples? . . ." Her guesses were getting wilder all the time. As I continued to shake my head Mama began to glance around the room seeking advice from the adults present. What kind of strange and possibly fatal diet was tobacco, corn, jute, and timothy?

While the interrogation went on, various women were setting the table for a feast which finally delivered me from Mama only to plunge me into a welter of jellied birds' nests and other delicacies. From time to time new dishes would be brought in from the kitchen. Mama ate sparingly and more out of politeness than hunger. She kept plying me with bits of ancient egg and so on and telling May to pay attention, the lord liked this dish and did not like another.

"I like them all," I kept saying.

"It is terrible cooking," Mama remarked, "but what can one do?"

Young Brother belched politely to indicate how excellent the food really was, and then I belched because I had to. This made us all feel better, and presently a sort of joking began which could not have occurred among polite and well-bred people in any other country than China. Elder Brother's Widow, a salty old lady, I suspect, began it, and thereafter it became the one steady undercurrent in the conversation, periodically rising to the surface in jokes that had a generally convulsive effect on everyone but May, who flushed, and I, who didn't get the puns and innuendoes. Mama waited until she had seen whether I was going to be offended, and when it was clear that I was not understanding enough to be either embarrassed or offended, she joined in with a will. I have the impression that many of her remarks were considered a little daring even by Elder Brother's Widow. However, they got a great reception.

And the funny thing is that though I was by training and instinct a natural and intense prude, I rather enjoyed the whole situation. What a relief to have one's sexuality joked about by Mama rather than worried over by Father. I even began joining in the laughter though I didn't understand what was funny. Indeed, I became hilarious after a while, just thinking of myself happily married and eating pickled pig's feet in Paoting, surrounded by all my Chinese family. Then I swallowed something the wrong way and had to be pounded on the back.

Speeches were next. Mama proposed a long life and incredible virility for me, an equally long life and astonishing fecundity to May resulting in numerous children who would respect us and support us in our old age. I think it was a traditional speech and had no particular reference to the fact that May and I were about to leave Mama in the lurch by decamping to America. Not that she was being left exactly alone.

Other speeches followed. Younger Son (May's brother) made a particular hit with me by boldly asserting that May had become yet more beautiful as the result of her most fortunate marriage with the tall and handsome foreigner whom to see was to admire.

Elder Brother's Widow then took the floor to compliment May on finding a man in whose height she could shelter, in whose strength she could rest secure, in whose

285

courage she could shield herself, and in whose good heart and kindness she would find solaces through all her days.

There's a good deal to be said for indulging in this kind of rhetoric from time to time. I clapped wildly at all the speeches, every one of which seemed to me both heartfelt and profound.

Then May was forced to rise and address me in my new character as her wedded husband. "O Samuel," she said (Mama frowned, this was too intimate a form of address), "O Samuel, we come to each other out of a past we do not share and go forward into a future we cannot foresee, so that what joins us now is a present we must make firm and bright by our faith."

The others, except Mama, found that a little modern-sounding, but well put. Then I had to rise and reply to everyone in my uncertain Chinese.

To Mama I said that I was a thief, stealing from her a daughter, and yet I knew she would forgive my theft for to be great-souled is to be generous; and to Younger Son I said that I was an ill-looking man much in need of nobility and purity and which I had found in his sister, who if she looked more beautiful now did so only because the good she had done me had already further illumined her soul; turning next to Elder Brother's Widow I told her in all honesty that she was a great flatterer and must have been describing some other man, her own husband perhaps or one of the many young men who had yearned for her, but as for myself I could only hope that May would prove as virtuous, as witty, and as full of character and fine thoughts as the honorable person I saw before me. And finally, to May, I said, "The blessing you have given me is yourself; the blessing I wish to give you in return is a man better than myself which I shall be because you are mine."

This was generally felt to be a very fine sentiment if a bit ungrammatical, and we concluded the feast by drinking some extremely strong brandy and singing a song or two.

27

Before we went to Paoting we had already applied for exit papers. When we came back to Peking I went to the Chinese Red Cross, which was the responsible authority for defectors, and found that my exit permit had been signed and stamped with an unflattering promptness. Didn't they want me? Didn't they feel I was necessary? Never mind. I'd asked to go and would have been outraged if they'd put impediments in my way. Then followed a very anxious six weeks while we waited for May to get papers. I am so grateful to the Chinese régime for the care and consideration they gave me while I was there that I hate to complain at all, but really young married people should not be put through the kind of uncertainty May and I experienced while we were waiting.

I kept saying to her, "It's all right. We'll just settle down here. We don't have to go to America." In Paoting I had begun to understand and appreciate the possibilities of domestic life in China, but May was less touched. If anything the trip had increased her desire to accept the great challenge of America rather than the even greater challenge of coming to some kind of terms with Mama.

"We will go," she said. "It is just a matter of waiting."

"Actually life might be easier and happier here," I said. Now that I was faced once again with the problem of doing something in America, I was beginning to get cold feet. Why *not* just find a niche in the New China Information Agency or something like that?

"It will be better for us to go," said May. "That is what we have made up our mind to do."

"Yes, of course," I said. "But if you don't get your exit permit, then we'll just accept the situation and settle down. I'm happy here, aren't you?"

Here, in those days, was a single room in a building for married students. It was really a cubicle more than a room, but at that stage of marriage one really doesn't need much space. Indeed, I found it distinctly convenient that without moving from the bed I could reach out and touch May in any part of the room. What she thought about the convenience we naturally don't know. Personally I was feeling more and more lordly and octopus-like all the time. There is really nothing like marriage.

Then her exit permit came in June, just as classes were ending anyway. The Red Cross bought me a ticket to Hong Kong; May purchased one for herself with her own money, and we set off after farewells with Su-An and such of my buddies as I was on speaking terms with in those days. The famous twenty-two defectors don't figure very prominently in this confession because the simple truth is that we got onto each other's nerves to a frightful extent. I've never spent a longer time with a group of men who influenced me less. Herbie was my favorite, but he'd already left in January, which brings up a point that needs explaining. Herbie had not been arrested upon his return and neither had two others who left together during the spring. Apparently some judge had explained to the army that it couldn't go around putting civilians into the stockade. Even the first pair of defectors had been released by then. This development was a decisive one as far as I was concerned. I was willing to return to the United States and do what I could to make the country a happy, lovable place, but I was not willing to start off by spending a term in jail separated from May. Such a sacrifice seemed to me well above and beyond the call of duty— whose notes were, in any case, a little faint and far away. I hoped May knew what we were doing by leaving a country where we had been happy in order to live in a country which (experience had shown me) was a pretty rough proposition happiness-wise. Father, for instance, was going to have to be confronted and that promised to be no great pleasure. Also, and already, the money problem was beginning to claim a good deal of my attention. How were we going to live? How were we even going to get to the U.S.?

In Hong Kong, that last problem was solved. The U.S. Consul there was a decent Harvard man (Eliot House '38) who lent me the money on the prospect of my inheritance, or the five thousand dollars that the army owed me, or perhaps just on my winning smile. I paid him back in installments over the next eighteen months.

We flew from Hong Kong with stopovers at Midway and Oahu. It was the first time either of us had flown, and May, for one, proved to be no swallow. Each time the plane dipped, she heaved. My memory of returning to the States is soured by the smell of vomit.

Then at San Francisco we encountered the Fourth Estate, out in force, and not to be denied. One reporter even climbed into the cab with us and rode into town collecting human interest material on the way.

"Well, how was China?" he asked.

"Great."

"Glad to be back?"

"Yes, sure."

"And eat some good American food at last?"

"Don't mention food, please." May had turned a delicate yellow-green at the sound of the word.

"Feel pretty sorry you ever defected?"

"It was the luckiest thing I've ever done. I met my wife in China."

The reporter tipped his hat to May who contained her joy at having him with us.

"But I bet you're sure glad to be back."

"I said I was."

"And what are you going to do now to make up for it?"

"Go back to Harvard, I guess."

He scribbled that down. "You think they'll let you in?"

"Why shouldn't they?" I asked.

He nodded. "I guess it's a pretty radical place, isn't it?"

"That's right."

"Ever thought of changing your name?" he asked.

"To what?"

"Well, so you won't be identified all your life as a defector."

"Oh, that won't bother me."

"It must have been a pretty big decision to make?"

"I did it on the spur of the moment."

"Well, you've certainly been lucky to be let back into the country, haven't you?"

"They couldn't keep me out. I'm a citizen."

"Didn't you expect to be arrested when you got back?"

"How could they arrest me?" I asked. "Our government bargained for eighteen months to give prisoners the right to choose what country they wanted to go to."

"And you chose wrong, didn't you?" he said.

That was his story line. We read his column on the train to Kansas City.

"I chose wrong," turncoat Samuel Heather said yesterday after returning from 18 months in Communist China. "I made the worst mistake a man can make, but I'm grateful to the Army and the American people for allowing me to change my mind and come home again." Asked whether he intended to change his name, Heather pondered the question and eventually said it might be a good idea. "I don't want to be tagged all my life as a defector, but I know the American people are forgiving and I'm sure I can contribute something to make up for what I've done."

Heather said his immediate plan is to finish his education at Harvard College, Cambridge, Mass., where Dean of Admissions

Kelmscott, contacted by this reporter yesterday, revealed that Heather's application for reinstatement has not reached his office. Asked whether it would be treated in the normal way, Kelmscott commented that "he didn't see why not." Harvard College has recently been the object of investigation by various committees of Congress seeking evidence of subversive activities. "We do not let that bother us," Kelmscott said.

Heather's father, The Right Reverend Samuel Heather, Bishop of Kansas City, was unavailable for comment on his son's dramatic return to the United States. . . .

The rest was recap. I read it aloud to May, who had no comment either. She was still feeling unwell, and a night on the train had done nothing to revive her. We arrived in Kansas City a somewhat bedraggled couple. Less than ninety-six hours before we had been in China.

Mother met us at the train station wearing one of her hats and the sort of vague, anxious look that came over her when she was looking for something that was lost—her garnet necklace or, in this case, her son. She brightened up when she saw me. "Your father isn't here," she said at once. "He's gone to the country."

"Oh?"

"We'll drive down there tomorrow." Then she explained that they'd bought a fishing lodge in the Ozarks. "We've used it quite a lot since you've been gone," she said.

There were pressmen at the station in Kansas City, but they got more of Mother than me. "Yes," she said for the benefit of the world at large. "Yes, I am very happy to welcome my son home. He has always been a very patriotic and loyal young man and I am very proud of him." Then, leaving them guessing, we got into the car and drove off to the palace where we put May to bed and then settled down for a reunion.

I was unambiguously glad to see Mother and she felt the

same way about me. Indeed if it were possible for a woman to bring up a son without a man around the house, that might be the solution to what otherwise seems a well-nigh insoluble problem. Mother and I never had any serious disagreements, though once we'd had time to relieve our feelings she did say, "Samuel, you shouldn't have done what you did."

"But I wouldn't have met May otherwise. Don't you think she's nice?"

"She's very pretty," Mother said.

"And she comes from a very good family."

"Yes, dear."

"Even older than the Clays."

"Really?"

"The Lees of Hopei province."

"It *is* a nice name," Mother said, visions of Lighthorse Harry, Marse Bob, Rooney, and Fitzhugh dancing through her head.

She patted my hand. There was a little pause. Then she said, "Dear, there's a question I want to ask. I hope you won't be angry?"

"Of course not."

"Well, dear, are you really married? I mean in a church?"

"It's a legal marriage," I said.

"But don't you think you should be married in church?"

"Well, maybe, but what church? May's a Communist and I'm certainly not a Christian."

Mother had obviously been thinking it over. "I believe the Unitarians would be the answer."

"But I'm a trinitarian."

"Are you?" This was not her department, but she'd been kept abreast of my theological ups and downs. When last heard from in 1950 I'd been a non-churchgoing theist, a sort of Voltairean, who occasionally snuck off to Episcopal churches to bellow "Onward Christian Soldiers" and other good tunes. I gave her a rundown of ideas I've expressed earlier, ending by patting her arm. "I think the Trinity makes a lot of sense."

"Your father will be so glad to hear this," she said, which brought up a little question that had been on my mind.

"How is he?"

"Your father?" She sounded surprised as if I'd suddenly suggested he was looking poorly.

"Why wasn't he at the station?"

"Oh." She sounded worried.

"Doesn't he want to see me?"

"Oh yes. He does, Samuel. You mustn't think that."

"Then why wasn't he there?" It wasn't at all like him not to be there.

"Well, I don't think he's really forgiven you," she said. "You mustn't blame him for that because it really was very terrible for him."

"I understand that."

"And I know when you see him tomorrow he'll be so happy to learn you're a trinitarian. Now maybe you could be married in our church."

"Without believing in the Incarnation?" I said.

"Oh. Well then, I suppose it will have to be a Unitarian marriage after all. They're very liberal, you know. I think a Unitarian minister would be willing to marry a trinitarian."

"To a Communist?"

Mother considered the matter. You could see she was trying to judge just how far the Unitarian clergy would go. Plumb their depths, as it were. At last, out of her general knowledge of Unitarianism plus her acquaintance with the local field, she nodded her head. "I believe I know a man who would do it." He sounded pretty disreputable to me—a sort of theological abortionist—but I nodded my head too. At least I wasn't threatened by a cathedral wedding with

293

Mendelssohn and Wagner and Father all doing their bits.

Upstairs May was awake. "How'd you like to marry me?" I asked her.

"I am feeling better, Samuel, but not that well."

I sat on the edge of her bed. "I mean in a Unitarian church. With a minister. So we can be joined by the laws of God as well as Man."

She removed her hand from my grasp. "You know I do not believe in God."

"Neither do most Unitarians. I think we ought to take the plunge. It will please Mother."

"Samuel!" said May, astonished by this evidence of backsliding.

"Think of it as a tribal custom," I told her. "After all I made speeches to your family."

"Oh, Samuel," she said. "I am not in the mood for this kind of talk."

My heart melted. I realized I would have to be strong and gentle if that were possible, given the fact that I was home again.

The following day we drove down to Father's fishing lodge on the Pomme de Terre River. I'm not making this up, check a map if you don't believe me. I drove. It was nice to have my hands on the wheel of a car after five years. In fact it was nice being back in Missouri, a beautiful state in my opinion, though I might have enjoyed the greenery and scenery more if I hadn't felt so nervous.

Father greeted us wearing a shirt open at the neck, a mode of dress which he may have chosen to help ease matters, but which in fact disconcerted me. He was informally garbed in other ways, from walking shoes to a straw hat. He met us on the porch of the cabin and shook my hand quite civilly. "Samuel," he said, that being my name.

"Hello, Father."

"And this is your wife?"

I presented May. Father bent down and kissed her on the cheek. It was well done and almost lured me into a sense of security. Then he greeted Mother. "Won't you come in?" he said to us all. His little flock, his family. "Samuel, leave the things in the car until later."

Inside he took off his straw hat and hung it on a peg. But why had he put it on just to go out on the front porch? Or had he been walking? But his shoes weren't dusty. The hat, I decided, was a prop, part of some interior scenario he'd worked out, an item in his picture of himself greeting an errant son. It alerted me to the fact that all would not be smooth sailing. One gets to know people one has known all one's life.

"Perhaps some refreshment?" Father said, looking around to see where the kitchen might be. "Are you thirsty, May?"

"I'm thirsty," I said. It seemed to me we might as well plunge ahead and get things going. "Then if you will sit down," said Father, "I will fix you all some lemonade." It couldn't have sounded more sinister if said by a Borgia Pope rather than a mere bishop of the Protestant Episcopal Church.

So we all sat down to await our potions. Mother looked as if she too thought things might not be quite as calm as they seemed. "Isn't it a nice cabin?" she said.

"Very nice."

"We've used it more than we expected."

I was sure they'd never expected to use it for this purpose. Even Father couldn't be quite that farsighted, could he? I mean how many fathers within a month of their son's defection to Red China would think to buy a quiet country retreat where revenge could take place without the interference of neighbors or the police? It was a very isolated spot, I realized.

295

Father returned and I watched his hands as he dealt out four dripping glasses of lemonade. I didn't learn anything, of course, beside what I already knew. He was a messy man in the kitchen. Came from lack of experience.

"And how was the drive down?" he asked.

"The traffic wasn't bad at all," said Mother.

I looked at May. *Well, here's my family,* I wanted to say. *Here they all are. Do you love them?*

Father observed the glance. "And what do you think of the countryside?" he asked May.

"It is more wooded than I expected," she said.

"This is the first time you have been in . . ." he hesitated. Would it come out *Western Hemisphere?* ". . . been in the United States?"

"Yes, it is."

"Of course, on your trip from San Francisco you will have seen the Rocky Mountains, which are quite impressive, but this area, which is known as the Ozarks, is considered by good judges to be rather favored in comparison with other regions of the country."

Was he talking that way because she was foreign, or because he talked almost like that most of the time? I decided I couldn't stand it any longer. "Father, why don't we look around the place? I'd like to stretch my legs."

He regarded me for a moment. "You wish to look around?"

"Yes. How many acres do you have?"

"Well . . ." He glanced at Mother, then at May. "Well, if Samuel wishes it, perhaps you will excuse us for a few minutes?" He got to his feet and reached for that straw hat. My heart sank. "If you will just accompany me," he said, and out we went into the favored Ozarks for a walk that took us over hill and dale, up theological byways and down side paths of guilt and repentance. Poison ivy, blackberry bushes, and wasp nests figured in the itinerary. The climax came on a

296

hilltop a mile or more from the cabin. We had been circling that hill for fifteen minutes, sometimes rising, sometimes descending slightly, until at last we made it to the top in one grand burst, the neatest allegorical climb since Petrarch's ascent of Mount Ventoux.

At the top Father paused for breath. By that time he was no longer pretending anything.

"The pain, the inconceivable pain we have suffered as a result of your action. It's monstrous, monstrous. Your mother weeping day after day. I feeling I could no longer hold up my head in public. It's inconceivable to me that you could bring that upon us. In the depths of my despair I seriously considered resigning my office. How could I presume to lead, to guide, to sustain others when I had failed so abysmally with my own son? Can you imagine how I felt?"

He stared at me, his face trembling. "That you, my only son, should be one of twenty-two miserable wretches out of thousands of prisoners, one of twenty-two, to reject his fatherland, his God, his family, everything . . ."

Then he simply broke down and cried.

"Well, then, hit me," I said.

His hands had been over his face. He parted them and looked at me with a kind of horror. "I have wanted to. Don't think I have not felt things for which I'm ashamed. Bitterly ashamed. I have hated you."

"I've hated you, too."

It was just too much for him. For a moment I thought he would strike me. He thought so himself. Then a complicated look of repulsion came over his face, he turned abruptly, and took a few staggering steps before he dropped joltingly to his knees. "Oh my God, my God," he cried out, "dost thou extend thy understanding even to these poor wretches?"

He began trembling all over. His head dropped forward with such violence that his straw hat fell off and came rolling gaily toward me. It wobbled twice and then fell flat at my feet. I couldn't have been more appalled if I'd seen Ezekiel's wheels.

Meanwhile the Bishop seemed to be coming asunder. His hands were clasped galvanically, his body shook, and I was afraid he was about to have a fit. I wanted to pat him on the back, but I felt my magic touch would only make things worse. Should I lay his hat on his head to keep off the sun? I bent down to pick it up. I was still holding it, wondering what to do, when he seemed to get control of himself by some sort of inner judo work. The trembling subsided, and after a minute or so he began praying silently.

I had to admire him—I had always had to admire him— in fact that's my whole story right there: he was an admirable man though I felt he had been killing me by inches all my life. Now that I seemed almost to have killed him, were we even? Though that wasn't the point. This wasn't a revenge story, it was a war story. I had fought him in Kansas City and in Cambridge; I had fought him in Korea and in China, and I was prepared to go on fighting him if it took me to the uttermost ends of the earth, only I'd made a slight miscalculation. I'd fallen in love and gotten married and allowed myself to forget what my life was all about. Coming home was not such a good idea, I saw, because the closer we got to each other, the more likely we were to provoke each other into scenes like this, which were better avoided. He'd been able to pull himself back from the edge of hysteria this time, but what about the next time and the time after that? As we get older we do not get any stronger, and eventually there would come a time when Father would simply let go.

Or if that didn't happen (and as I tried to picture it I saw it couldn't happen), something even worse might take place. For I had put him into as impossible a position as the one I was in. He was really a Christian. For him anger was a deadly sin. At that very moment he was probably praying for forgiveness. His flight to the country, his straw hat which I was holding, the whole setup he'd arranged were desperate, even pathetic expedients, very much—here was an insight!— very much like my own expedients of getting away from him and theatricalizing the situation in order to take some of the sting out of it. I'd driven him to become a kind of actor with a straw hat on his head, only he wasn't that sort of man. He ought to be in his study in his ordinary clothes, not kneeling here on a corny hilltop. If I went on treating him this way, our relationship might take on a sort of cat and mouse cartoon quality in which the antagonists, annihilated, stunned, squashed, and scorched in one sequence emerge fresh and ready to do it again in the next. Whatever dignity Father had been able to maintain in his dealings with me would be lost, and after all there was little enough dignity in the world that I should go about destroying Father's by providing him with unassimilable amounts of anger.

He prayed for some time. When he rose and turned toward me, his face seemed more or less normal. I said, "I shouldn't have come home."

"Please do not say such things, Samuel." He reached for his hat which I handed over. There was a little pause. "Naturally," he said, "I am disappointed that you do not seem penitent. Nevertheless, for your own sake and for your mother's I am glad you have come home."

"Thank you."

"Your life, however, will be very difficult here. You have done that which will not be understood or easily forgiven by your fellow citizens."

"I know."

"What are your plans?" he asked.

This was more like it! I almost smiled. "I don't have any," I said.

"You were quoted in the newspapers as saying you intended to go back to Harvard. I suppose that was as inaccurate as every other part of the article?"

"Well, actually, I have been thinking of going back to

299

school. I could major in Far Eastern Studies, and I guess Cambridge would be a simpler place for May and I to live than almost anywhere else. At least right now."

"That seems reasonable," he remarked.

"It'll take money," I pointed out. "The army really owes me about five thousand dollars, but I'll probably have to sue to get it."

"You cannot sue for your back pay after what you have done," Father said. "I will naturally advance you what money is necessary."

"Considering I've hurt you more than I've hurt the army, I think it would be more fitting for me to try to get the money from them."

"It is out of the question," Father said.

"I'll feel odd taking your money."

"It is perfectly reasonable that I should help my son finish his education," Father said. It was a formula that seemed to spread some decency over the thing. I felt grateful, and relieved.

"I wish things weren't like this between us."

He said, "It is a little late in the day now, Samuel. You are twenty-five."

I said, "I can't say I haven't wanted to hurt you because that wouldn't be true, but I haven't *just* wanted to hurt you. It's been more mixed-up than that."

He turned from me. "We will not reopen these matters, Samuel. I brought you up as I conceived a father should bring up his son. I have evidently failed, though I still do not understand how or why it happened."

"It happened because . . ."

Father swung back, angry again. "It is enough for me that the failure is so complete. Explanations will only lead to recriminations."

So I was not allowed to tell Father what I think accounts for three-quarters of the turmoil in Christian house-

300

holds like ours. A boy growing up loving a father who himself is in love with The Son gets into the curious position of having a sibling rivalry with Jesus Christ. In my case this was complicated by the fact that I was a pious little boy who really did love my Lord and wanted to be like Him. I couldn't account for the fact that I had these strange, jealous feelings of rivalry toward Him. I wanted to be the son my father admired the most. Then something even more peculiar started happening, for as I grew older I began to respond to Father in his role of bishop in which he was clearly (and dramatically) doing The Son's work as he celebrated Mass and preached in his cathedral. Father was installed in Kansas City when I was five; we had lived in Louisville, Kentucky, before then, and it seems to me I was never as completely happy in Kansas City as I had been in Louisville. Ours was a dull neighborhood for a child, and as I say I was beginning then to develop the disturbing feeling that *I* ought to be doing the work Father did while Father should stay more in the background looking down upon me from time to time merely to remark, "This is my beloved son with whom I am well pleased." I was beginning to feel sibling rivalry with Father as well as Jesus. Mercifully nothing ever happened to disturb my feelings of confidence and affection toward my Father in Heaven, but meanwhile I was beginning to be much troubled by these Fathers and Sons on earth with whom I felt bewildering complexities of identification, dependence, and competitiveness.

At which point adolescence arrived. I was standing naked one day in front of my mirror, admiring the goings-on and dreaming of the time when I would burst in all my glory upon a startled and grateful world, when Father opened the door. He looked me over, and said, "Put on your clothes and come down to my study." That was the beginning of our real Donnybrook. He convinced me that no one but Jesus Christ could or should dare to offer his body to all the world, and

301

that even Christ had suffered as a result. Fair enough. I was not Christ, but then neither was Father, yet he went on giving the Word, planting the seed, and offering the sacred Body with which by then he was emotionally identified in my mind. It didn't seem fair that he should be permitted to go merrily ahead taking on the whole world while I was not allowed to prove my virility with even one girl much less the fifty or a hundred I felt equal to. My mind was inflamed in those days with legends of the great crusaders—Bohemund, Tancred, Richard Coeur de Lion—who were supposed at Constantinople to have deflowered fifty Imperial virgins in one night. I wanted orgies, I got nothing. It was then I began to feel Father was killing me.

A palace conspiracy had taken place. I was being kept from the throne and slowly poisoned so that my rival could rule in my place. And moreover, an irony that made me want to scream, the King had no clothes, he had no body even. Christ wasn't really there in the person of Jesus. I had lost my faith. I felt people were communing with unreal flesh while my real flesh was rotting away in prison. But it took me several more years to work free from that prison, and even then I wasn't so very free and I promptly fell into another more real prison in Pyot Lon and so on up to the moment at which I would have liked to say some of these things to Father but didn't get the opportunity.

That confrontation in the Ozarks was the last serious talk Father and I ever had. We were never reconciled and we never fought again, since both of us seemed to realize that to draw closer would only stir up a deeper anger for which there could be no compensating love. I had hurt him too much, and been hurt too deeply by my own mistakes for the anger ever to disappear. It would have required a tremendous effort on his part to overcome the resentment he felt toward me, and he was too good and practical a man to waste his emotional resources that way. Though a Christian, he did not feel obliged to be saintly, for which I thank him. It would have been most uncomfortable if I had felt him wrestling with himself out there in Kansas City trying to squeeze out some compassion and understanding for the sort of son I had become. He was a man of the church with duties that kept him busy. From his point of view I was no longer worth the effort it would have taken to love me wholeheartedly. *When thine right eye offends thee, pluck it out*, though he was not really that stern. As I've shown, he offered me money and acknowledged his duties toward me, but he was not going to clutter up his life by fussing around internally over what he rightly regarded as a failed relationship. I needn't have worried about him losing his dignity where I was concerned.

I took my line from him, and in a way I was glad when I saw he was writing me off emotionally speaking. I assume he prayed for me as indeed I prayed for him from time to time, but it was impossible that we could ever approach each other as comrades or men. He was Father and Brother to me, and now I catch myself from time to time turning him into my son and worrying over his spiritual and moral life just as he used to worry over mine. Was he touched by grace? What were the secret vices with which he contended? How happy was he with Mother? Did he suffer from a feeling of failure that he could not redeem the times? And, of course, did he blame himself for what was my fault? Of all the questions, that last is the one that bothers me most.

28

May and I spent the rest of that summer alone in Father's cabin. It was felt everyone would be happier if the generations didn't mix too much, so Mother and Father went back to Kansas City leaving us Mother's car to drive, and we settled down to a curiously isolated vacation in the Ozarks. Our nearest neighbors were a family named Styles who had created a wasteland of rusting cars and farm equipment and dwelt in the center of it in an unpainted shack. There was an old lady always rocking herself on the front porch. She wore a curious headdress which I finally identified as a football helmet. This mystery was explained by a gas station attendant whom I questioned.

"Who are those people who live up on the side of the hill beyond the turn up there?"

"Oh that'll be the Styles," he said.

"Well, there's an old lady with a football helmet on her head."

He agreed with me. "Yeah. That'll be Grandma Styles."

"Well, why does she wear it?" I asked.

He thought for a moment. "She's got some sort of disease," he said. "I disremember the name of it, but she don't have her balance anymore. Ed Styles says that helmet's saved her many a nasty knock."

"Ah." There's a rationale for almost everything if you seek long enough. I was preparing to drive off when the man became confidential. He rested one arm on the car roof and bent down to look at me. "Say," he said, "you're the young fellow with the Chinese wife, ain't you?"

"That's right," I said, bracing myself for whatever was coming.

"Listen!" he said, "there's something I heard. Is it true they got different-shaped snatches?"

Now how can you either love, or not love, or be indifferent to a man who will ask a question like that? We need some new feeling to handle such people.

That was the sort of incident which made me decide I must get May established in Cambridge as soon as possible, so for a few days I left her in Kansas City with my parents while I hurried to Cambridge to see if I couldn't talk my way back into Harvard. Dean Kelmscott agreed with me that I'd probably matured a good deal since 1950 and that I wasn't necessarily a bad bet academically. "But there are still these basic undergraduate requirements," he said, looking at my transcript in the dissatisfied way that deans look at one's transcript.

"I'm going to take Anatomy as my science," I said.

"And major in Far Eastern Studies?"

"Yes."

"You didn't even have a major in 1950."

"No."

"Well . . ."

It wasn't the moment to ask him about transfer credits from Peking U. Instead I said, "I think after the kind of experiences I've had I can bring a certain point of view to bear on what I'll be studying. I hope to finish my B.A. quickly and maybe even go on for graduate study. I want to make something out of myself."

Luckily he didn't ask what. He did, however, readmit me, and encouraged by that I went right off and found a cheap apartment on Story Street where May and I could live. Then back home to Kansas City where in my absence the question of a church marriage had come up again.

"It won't hurt you," I said to May, "and it will please Mother and maybe even Father."

"It is the principle involved," said May.

305

"The principle involved is a very good one," I said. "Marriages ought to be sealed in every possible way. The only great political and social reform two people are capable of making on their own is to create an absolutely solid family." We knew by then (August) that May's airsickness was partly due to pregnancy.

She was not entirely convinced, but life was sweeping her along like everyone else, and before she could think out a really good reason for not going through with a Unitarian marriage, she was going through with it. Father and Mother were our principal witnesses, Mother smiling at this happy arrangement and Father looking professionally pained, like a distinguished undertaker at a mass burial of cholera victims.

Then another interlude along the Pomme de Terre during which I read English poetry to May and she tutored me in Chinese, and before we knew it Labor Day had come and it was Ho! for Cambridge and the life of reason and progress.

The apartment on Story Street came ready-furnished. That is, the furniture was ready for us but we weren't ready for it. Tables wobbled, chairs collapsed, and the bed sagged in the middle and squeaked with such vigor we had to put the mattress on the floor so we could make love without absolutely deafening the neighbors, a slightly sinister young couple named Waskom, of whom more anon. After a few days on Story Street, May went out one morning to buy us an inexpensive work of art to brighten things up. She came home with a reproduction of Picasso's *Repasseuse,* which we hung over the couch. The picture—I'm not sure if you remember it—is about the most lugubrious example known to us from the master's Blue Period. A haggard woman, her breasts sagging and askew, presses down in agony on an iron. She is trying to finish her husband's shirt, but it looks hopeless. The work will never get done before she drops dead from fatigue and malnutrition. A powerful composition, altogether. Too powerful for some tastes. I helped May hang it and made no comment about the subject. Either she was cockeyed where Western art was concerned, or that was how she felt about life those days. I didn't really want to know which.

Once settled on Story Street and enrolled in classes I made a few tentative efforts to pick up some threads from my old Cambridge life. I found Bartoldi—now hold your breath, Reader—in Tufts Medical School, *specializing in psychiatry.* Indeed, why torture you with suspense? As I write these pages Bartoldi is even now practicing his chosen profession in New York City. I think of him wielding his Freudian monkey wrench on the loose nuts who come rolling in to be tightened up, and I wonder if during the years we lived together I missed some nuance of his personality. Maybe. Anyway there he was in Tufts.

He came to dinner, our first dinner in our American love nest, bringing a blonde, a bottle of champagne, and a bottle of Scotch in about that order of importance. He was sort of off women that year and drinking to compensate. In private he told me he'd had an unhappy affair. "She was a real bitch," he said several times. "I almost had to marry her." That disaster had been averted by a timely operation, but the experience had sobered Bartoldi on women and turned him to drink, though the blonde that evening, a comely Tufts undergraduate, seemed to be more and more on his mind and under his arm as the evening progressed. Of course they sat on our couch which tended to throw them together. Still sex was in the air when they left rather early in the evening.

After the door closed behind them May said, "And those were your friends?"

"I never saw her before in my life."

"And he drinks so much!"

"I never claimed he was an ideal character."

307

"But he was your friend!"

"Yes," I said. I couldn't deny it.

May shook her head. "The more I see of what life is like here, the more I wonder about things." I attributed her doubts to her delicate condition.

After that we saw less of Bartoldi than I might have liked and more of the Waskoms than either of us would have chosen if there had been other dishes available that season on the table of life's feast.

The difference between the Waskoms and Bartoldi can best be illustrated by their reactions to the Picasso on our wall. Bartoldi glanced at it in passing and remarked to May, "Christ! The things they hang on the walls of these furnished dumps." Whereas neither of the Waskoms saw anything odd or unusual about the choice of a famine victim to brighten up our happy home. You see, their own rooms downstairs were decorated with a series of Kathe Kollwitz prints that could break your heart if it weren't already broken.

They were Leftists, which meant they took to us like ducks to water. Had they been herring we might have trapped them in our weirs and eaten them fresh for dinner, but as it was they paddled securely on our surface, bobbing their heads occasionally to look for watercress. Patricia was an ordinary graduate student, but Joe was a Junior Fellow or Senior Guy, or he held some bourse or had won a prize or sat in an endowed carrel at Widener. I never quite got it straight, but whatever the distinction it gave them both a sense of wealth and accomplishment which they were glad to share with us.

They had us to dinner frequently to fill us with good red meatloaf, though with their social consciences I never understood how they had the heart to fill their bellies while those Kollwitz waifs hung around, their poor little noses pressed to the glass. And along with the vittles we got news about what the Waskoms referred to as the McCarthy era. May and I

308

had heard about the man from Appleton—the Chinese press was full of picturesque denunciations of him and his work —but since you can't always believe everything you read in Chinese (or American) newspapers, we listened attentively.

It seemed that the Junior Senator from Wisconsin had been trampling on the Constitution, goring the Bill of Rights, and tossing every liberal matador who ventured to engage him in the ring. He was still around and occasionally one saw pictures of him in the papers. I could not see what the fuss had been about. He needed a shave and toupé, but otherwise his looks and bearing did not seem noticeably below the Senatorial average. Nevertheless I gathered from the Waskoms that he was an *ur*-demagogue and reactionary hetman of considerable if waning powers. One chief topic of Waskom conversation was whether McCarthy could stage a comeback after being censured by the Senate. They talked about a possible McCarthy comeback the way citizens of the late Roman Empire must have talked about a return visit from Attila or Genseric.

"You just can't imagine what things have been like," Patricia frequently assured me. "I just can't describe it." Then she would try. "It was fantastic."

"Fantastic?"

"Simply fantastic."

"Tell him about the Perez case," Joe would say. He seemed to admire Patricia's narrative gift. He was always asking her to tell me about the Perez case, or the Lattimore case, or about two unter-fiends named Cohn and Schine, subluminaries in the McCarthy demonology. Thus encouraged Patricia would strike her lyre and launch into an epic recital from the hash of which would emerge the fact that things had been simply fantastic.

Nevertheless her recitals did partly explain to me why I got dirty looks from time to time when it came out that I was a returned turncoat. The political atmosphere had changed, and a certain light had gone out of Cambridge with the destruction of the tower of Memorial Hall. I used to gaze sadly at that vast bulk now topped by a mere ort and relic of its once crowning glory. Then I'd heave a sigh and go on to my Anatomy class.

May got a job as waitress in Chez Dreyfuss, a French restaurant on Mass. Avenue, and after a bit I found work as a dishwasher in the same joint, the advantage being that we could eat cheaply there. Our grand aim was to make ourselves independent of Father's bourgeois benevolence, but neither of us could disguise the fact that though we had successfully sunk out of our own class we were not exactly emancipating the proletariat or doing much to set the world on fire. I was getting dishpan hands while May was developing a streak of grimness which I didn't like to see. She wouldn't come right out and say we'd made a mistake in leaving China, but her homesickness was evident, especially on those happy occasions when we blew ourselves to a Chinese meal in Boston or went to look at the Ming ceramics in the Fine Arts Museum.

"Don't worry," I would tell her. "We'll be independent yet. Things are going to work out."

"But what good are we doing?" she'd say. "We have no comrades here."

"Don't forget the Waskoms," I once said, which made her cry.

Other things happened to draw the bow across my strings. One November afternoon, walking up Brattle Street I encountered Miss Martha Sears coming toward me in a fall ensemble with hat and gloves to match, looking quite the little lady. And pushing a baby carriage. I was wearing unpressed suntans and an army surplus jacket.

She recognized me at the moment I recognized her. We stopped. We looked. And then we approached each other. Martha put out her gloved pinky and prodded my chest.

"Samuel T. Heather," she said, spacing them out and getting the most from the syllables.

"Hello, Martha," I said. Then I stared into the carriage. "Is this yours?"

"Absolutely. I'm married now."

As a matter of fact that was no surprise, since I'd gone to the trouble of checking with the Radcliffe Alumnae Office to see what dope they had on one of their old lags named Sears. Which is how I happened to know that Martha was no longer Miss Sears but none other than Mrs. Caleb Green of Newton and Ipswich. So what was she doing on Brattle Street in my path?

But you don't walk around a chunk of your past when it gets in your way. You stop and chat with it as if . . . as if life were less linear than it is. We always go on, though we carry everything with us, so that when you meet a person like Martha you are dating her and hating her and chatting with her all at once. It's a curious sensation.

She seemed to find it interesting herself. I think we both considered going somewhere to sit down and talk it over, but neither of us suggested it. There was, after all, the heir of the Greens to be considered. So we stood on the pavement blocking traffic and talked for about five minutes. And since it was the last time we ever spoke to each other, I should perhaps let Martha say her final lines in these pages.

"And so how's life treating you?" she said.

"Fine," I said. "Is that a boy or a girl?"

"Boy, stupid. Can't you see it's in blue?"

"You have a boy?" Something was not right about that, though I couldn't put my finger on the spot. Given the fact that she was married, a child was in the cards, and given a child there was roughly a fifty percent chance of it being a boy. Still the whole thing was obviously phony and preposterous. "What do you call it?" I asked.

"Chum," she said.

I winced. "Motherhood is a serious business, Martha."

"When you're a mother we'll talk it over."

"I'm going to be a father."

"Congratulations."

She was altogether too bright for my taste. "Are you sure you're prepared to bring up a boy?" I asked. "What's his real name?"

"Cal."

"That's a bit better." I peered into the carriage to get a closer view.

The child was asleep, his mouth plugged with a pacifier, which gave him a dopey look. "Cal," I said. "Well, well, well."

Martha said, "What made you come back?"

"I don't know. I must have been out of my mind."

"What made you defect?"

"I was out of my mind then, too. Aren't you supposed to take out the pacifier when they're asleep?"

"No," said Martha.

"What if they choke on it?"

"They can't."

"Well, I suppose you know what you're doing." I looked at her again. "What does your husband do?"

She grinned. "He's a stockbroker."

"I suspected something like that."

"You still way up there with God and all?" she asked.

"Martha," I said, "the revolution is coming. I don't want to scare you, but I think you ought to know so you can prepare for it."

She looked a little uncertain, as if she thought I might have gone crazy. "Do you believe that?" she asked.

"I wish I did. My wife does."

She nodded sympathetically. "Cal's worried about the revolution, too," she said. "Cal Senior," she added.

I asked, "Does Caleb (Why can't people pronounce a

whole name?) does Caleb think there's a big Communist conspiracy?"

"Well, maybe a little Communist conspiracy."

"I'll tell May that," I said. "About the only encouragement Communists have in this country is knowing how worried stockbrokers can get." And then, having said that, I immediately felt ashamed of myself. It was as if I'd betrayed May by talking about her to Martha. I could even—such is life—feel most of the old attraction Martha had once had for me. She really looked very nice. And as that sort of thought began to take shape in my mind, I said to myself, *Elle le trompe, j'en suis sûr.* I generally use French when I'm thinking along those lines.

Martha may have divined it all—she was a person of quick perceptions. Anyway she suddenly tapped me on the chest again. "I've got to be going," she said. "I'm glad we met." She paused. "Look, I hope things work out."

"Thanks," I said.

"Well, so long." And off she went with Cal Jr. and whatever secrets she may have had those days. Thinking her over, once and for all, I decided she was not really very much like Natasha Rostov. She made me feel weary somehow. I abandoned the idea of going to class and went back to the apartment.

May was having one of her afternoon naps. I paced restlessly around looking at the closed bedroom door. I briefly considered throwing my Anatomy text out the window, but it had cost eight-fifty and I wasn't in a financial position to express myself to that extent. Finally I tapped at the bedroom door.

"I am awake, Samuel," May said.

It was dark in the bedroom. I knelt on the floor beside the mattress. "May," I said, "would you think it awful of me if I got a job and earned some real money?"

"What sort of job?" May asked.

313

"That's the hell of it," I said. "I'm not trained to do anything."

"When your studies are finished," May said, "you will be able to find work, teaching perhaps."

"But when will they ever be finished? And anyway, what sort of work's teaching?"

"Is that not what we have come to the United States for?" May said. "To teach and influence people?"

"Yes," I said. "Yes."

"We must not be discouraged," May said. "When I feel better I will make contacts. There must be comrades somewhere in this country."

"Yes."

"And then we will both work for what we believe in."

"Yes."

"It is just a question of time, Samuel."

"I'm twenty-five going on twenty-six," I said, "and I have an Anatomy test coming up next week. What sort of life is that? Besides, questioning is not the mode of conversation between gentlemen. Doctor Johnson said that."

"We must just go ahead," said May.

"Yes, but where?" I asked.

29

That spring I dropped out of Harvard for the second and last time. I felt taking exams derogated from my dignity as a father-to-be and a potential revolutionary messiah. Also, and perhaps more importantly, Morrison visited our apartment one afternoon.

He looked prosperous and well-kept in a light gray topcoat, gray suit, white shirt, and dark necktie with a thin red stripe in it. Quite one of the boys. We hadn't seen each other in six years.

"Hello, Heather," he said.

"Hello yourself," I said.

He came in, removed the topcoat, shook hands with May, and looked around our little home. "Well, you seem to be settling down."

"And what are you doing?" I asked.

"Oh, I work in Washington."

"What kind of work?"

"You know," he said, "they were quite interested when they found out I knew you."

"Who's *they?*"

"You've had some unusual experiences, haven't you?"

"Do you work for a publisher?" I asked. "Does someone want me to write my memoirs?"

"No, it's not that," he said. He glanced around the room. His eye rested a moment on the Picasso. Then he said, "The real problem is whether you're reliable enough."

"Am I being approached?" I asked.

"In a way."

May looked puzzled. She asked if we would like tea or coffee. Morrison refused both. "Why don't we take a walk?" he said.

"Don't worry about me," I told May. "I'll get back in my basket when this snake charmer stops blowing his pipe." Then I held Morrison's topcoat while he slipped back into it. It was from J. Press. I put on my surplus army jacket and we strolled out into the town.

"How well do you know Chinese?" Morrison asked.

"I'm still studying it," I said. "It's a complicated language, especially to read."

"I know. Of course I'm not in that department."

"What department are you in?"

"We don't say," he said.

"And have you no shame?" I asked.

"You'd find it interesting work," he said.

"Spying!"

"What do you mean, *spying*?" Morrison asked. Who's a spy? You don't think I'm a spy, do you?"

"You are certainly spying out the ground around here, but you're not going to recruit me for the CIA."

"We call it The Firm."

"There! If that isn't spy talk, what is it?"

"It's just security," said Morrison. "And anyway, there's no need for you to get onto your high horse. With a Communist wife and your past, you'll be lucky if they hire you at all."

"You think I'd take such a job if it were offered on bended knee? I'm a progressive. I believe in progress, not reaction."

Morrison had paused to peer into the excavation for Holyoke House.

"Actually, I believe in the revolution," I announced. "A Second American Revolution, in which God's young heroes shoulder their way out through the hanging chains of the world's bordello into the sunlight and grass of freedom."

Morrison wasn't listening. Having satisfied himself with the state of things in the bowels of the earth he took my arm

316

and began leading me along Mass. Avenue towards Plympton Street. "I want to see if they've changed any of the books in the window of the Grolier," he said.

"Listen," I told him. "I'm telling you that if I had my way we'd take down the Washington Monument and the Lincoln and Jefferson Memorials and use the stone to cover up those ghastly faces on Mount Rushmore."

"Not a bad idea," he remarked.

"And then I'd blow up the White House and Congress."

"Where'd the President live then? We've got to house him somewhere."

"I'd put up a log cabin. Then we could brag that our Presidents, though often born to great wealth, have succeeded in making it to the Whitewashed Cabin. And we could find some old shoes worn by Washington and Jefferson and Lincoln and make impressions in the cement outside the White Cabin—like the impressions in front of the Graumman's Chinese Theater in Los Angeles—and put up a plaque saying, "Friends, these Great Men walked here, put your foot where theirs trod.""

"Inspirational," Morrison agreed.

"I am definitely not spy material," I said.

"The place is filled with inspirational moralists like you," he said, "but we'll talk about it later."

We had arrived in front of the Grolier Bookshop. Morrison studied the books in the window. "What do you suppose keeps it going?" he asked. "I know for a fact that copy of Theodore Spencer's poems has been lying right there since 1948."

"It's a notorious CIA front."

"Possibly," he said. "Let's go look at Leverett."

We went and looked at Leverett. I even had to dissuade Morrison from climbing the stairs to knock on the door of our old suite. "You'll scare the boys," I said. "They don't want revenants dropping in on them."

Morrison said, "It's only after you've graduated you realize how much you enjoyed yourself here."

"Speak for yourself," I said. "I haven't graduated yet."

"Well, come on. Let's talk," and he took my arm and led me down to the river. All his touching of me was beginning to have an effect I couldn't quite identify and didn't think I liked very much.

"In the first place," he said, "you're obviously unchanged, which means you're an old-fashioned Puritan moralist just like the Dulles brothers."

"With different opinions," I pointed out.

"And secondly you have practically no chance of getting a decent or interesting job except with The Firm, so I think you ought to listen to me."

"I'm listening," I said.

"Now what's your relationship with your wife?"

"We're married."

"It's a real impediment," he said.

"Would you like to be pushed in the river?" I asked.

"I'm serious, Sammy. I'm the one who persuaded them to let me come up here and talk to you."

"I'm serious too."

"If you'd make the effort to talk sensibly to them, they might see the point of hiring you. After all, you've had some first-hand experience there, and you know the language. They have lots of researchers with less brains than you have. It's mainly a question of your reliability."

"Talk sensibly yourself," I said. "Why would a person like me want to work for the CIA?"

"You're ambitious, you want to have some influence in the world, and you like getting into things. I thought of you the minute I heard you'd redefected."

"You did?"

"I've always thought you were smart. It's just a question of getting you in."

"I don't want to be gotten in." I drew myself up. "I'm really quite opposed to what the CIA is doing."

"You have no idea what the CIA is doing," he told me, "and in any case you'll have nothing to do with Operations. What I'm talking about is simply an intelligence job where you'd use your brains and understanding of China to explain what's going on and what's likely to happen next. It's essentially like a teaching position at a university, only you'll have the attention of people who really count instead of dopey students."

"Oh." Then I said, "Is that what you are? An intelligence specialist influencing people who count?"

"We don't say what we do," he said.

"You know," I told him, "I'm going to worry about you from now on—down there in Washington not saying what you do."

"All right," said Morrison.

"Do you do what you say?"

"Very amusing."

"Well, really," I said, "it's an insult for you to think I might fit into such a framework, to say nothing of your hideous and futile attempt to break up my marriage."

"Isn't she going to get homesick eventually?" Morrison asked.

"She already is."

"Well!"

"Well, nothing. I'll make that up to her somehow."

He shrugged. "If you don't want to help yourself . . ."

"How much is the salary?" I asked.

"It varies. It's not too bad."

"And they'd hire someone with my background?"

"That's the point. You have to show them what you really are."

"Long embarrassing conversations about how much I love America?"

319

"Not that exactly. Just don't talk about blowing up the White House."

"And what about the revolution?"

"That's all right. Show them you mean business morally."

"But I really do. I mean I try to."

"They'll love that. They're all frustrated moralists themselves. And stress God."

"This is obscene," I said.

"God's one of your best points. You do believe in Him still?"

"I really ought to push you in the river."

He patted me on the shoulder. "I can't promise anything, of course, but someone else will be getting in touch with you now that we know you're interested."

"But I haven't said I'm interested."

"I won't come back to the apartment with you," he said. "Now that I'm up here I want to look around some." He grinned. "First time I've been back in three years. I've really been working. It's a hell of a job, let me tell you."

"You have been," I said.

May asked, "Who was your friend?"

"He's a CIA spy. He wants me to work for the CIA."

She looked puzzled. "I'm sorry, Samuel, I do not understand the joke."

"It's not a joke. It's the truth."

When she finally believed it she was furious. Furious that I'd admitted Morrison to our house, furious I'd gone out for a walk with him, furious I had even listened to his infamous proposals, and finally furious I had not taken this heaven-sent opportunity to denounce a spy in Harvard Square.

"Yes, I know," I said, "but I am going to have to find a job, and Morrison says the pay is good."

"You are seriously thinking of it?" Her eyes opened to

their fullest extent. How I loved her when she was that angry! "Samuel, I will leave you. Yes, I will leave you. I will do that if you even consider such an idea."

"We have the baby to think of," I said.

"You cannot be serious," she said. "I do not think it is funny. Your sense of humor is no longer amusing to me."

"And then what if we have another baby? You know, as a defector I may have trouble getting good jobs. We have to consider that."

"We will not consider it," she said. "A spy? You want to be a filthy spy?"

"Intelligence work. That's what it's called."

"Spying," said May. "I am disillusioned with you, Samuel."

"Of course," I said, "I didn't commit myself with Morrison. Something else may turn up, but frankly I'm getting tired of school. I'm too old for it."

"This is quite definite," May said. "Quite definite. I will leave you if you even talk to another CIA man."

"You know, probably the CIA is full of interesting and civilized people. I mean, look at Morrison."

"Absolutely not. I will not look at such people. Our house is defiled . . ." she stared around the room. Perhaps she would pull down the Picasso print and stamp on it. I hoped so. I wanted something brighter, happier. A Klee, perhaps, or a Miró. With a good job in the CIA, I could afford to have nicer things around the house. Our couch was an absolute snare, a travesty of a couch, and God! was I getting tired of rice and spaghetti dishes. Looking at my May sparkling with anger I realized that there would be a good deal of love/hate work involved in reconciling her to the idea. But that would be pleasurable, too.

One evening ten days later a man wearing a raincoat knocked on our door.

"My name is Brown," he said. It sounded implausible.

321

"Heather," said I. "And this is Mrs. Heather."

Brown shook her hand. "Do you want to take a walk?" I asked.

"Oh no," said Brown. He seemed amused by the idea. "No indeed. Why don't we all sit down and have a chat?"

May suddenly stiffened. "Is this another one of them?" she asked. She sounded as if *I'd* invited him to come defile our home.

"I don't know," I said.

We were still standing. Brown said, "I understand Mrs. Heather has certain political objections?"

"I am Communist," May said, "and Samuel is not going to become an American spy."

"But you don't belong to the American Communist Party," Brown said.

May glared at him. "I can be a Communist without belonging to a party—which you are illegally suppressing in this country."

"There are publicly acknowledged Communists and Communist sympathizers in Cambridge, Mrs. Heather. They are not suppressed, but you haven't made any contact with them."

"Give us a list of them," I said. "We're lonely."

"So I am being spied upon?" May said.

"Shall we sit down?" I asked.

Brown said nothing. May said, "You may do what you want. I am going to our room where I will stay until this man leaves." She walked out, and Brown and I sat down.

"What *is* the state of your wife's political opinions?" Brown asked.

"She has a Constitutional right to think whatever she wants to think."

"Yes, of course."

"She's told you she's a Communist."

"But what sort of Communist?"

"Ask her."

"I would like to," said Brown.

"But she won't talk to you," I said.

"Apparently not."

Brown had not removed his raincoat, and he was sitting on our couch, which, as I have said, was a snare. He looked uncomfortable. "Would you like a beer?" I asked.

"Yes, thank you," he said. So I opened two cans of beer and Brown removed his raincoat.

"What *is* your name?" I asked.

"It's Brown," he said.

"Really Brown?"

"Yes, really Brown. My father was named William Brown. I'm John Brown."

It still didn't sound likely. "I'm Samuel Heather," I said.

"Yes, I know."

"Do you think I'd make a good spy?"

"I gather they're interested in you because of your recent experience of Red China. It would be some sort of intelligence work you'd do."

"Well, it's all spying of one sort or another, isn't it?"

"Oh, it varies a good deal," Brown said.

"Well I'm not interested," I said. "May's too opposed."

"Could you tell me something about her current political activities?"

"No, I couldn't."

"What about your own?"

"I'm a student," I said.

"Are you a Communist?" he asked.

"I'm a Platonic anarchist."

"I don't think I've met many of those," Brown said. He had a certain low-level charm. Also he was bearing up manfully on the couch. I sort of warmed to him.

"Actually, I'm really nothing. I would have liked to have been a Crusader."

"A crusader for what?"

"A Crusader. You know, the Crusades."

"Oh, the Crusades," Brown said.

"Yes. I've just been reading Runciman's *History of the Crusades*. Do you know anything about the battle of Dorylaeum?"

"No."

"Well, it was quite a battle."

"I expect it was. Did you enjoy your fighting in Korea?"

"Some. Yes. It's hard to explain. Look, why don't you take a more comfortable seat? That couch is murder."

"It's quite all right," Brown said. Probably they hardened their spies by special training methods I knew nothing about.

"You were captured during the retreat from the Yalu?" he said.

"During the advance," I said. "Do you want to hear about it?"

"If you want to tell me."

"I suppose you can read about it in my file. You do have a dossier on me?"

"We're building one up."

"Well, I think it's a waste of time. I wouldn't make a good spy. I don't know what I'd be good at, to tell you the truth." Brown nodded sympathetically. He was such an easy, nondescript fellow he made me feel like talking about myself. Maybe his name really was Brown. "My problem has always been that I don't know what to do."

"I see," said Brown.

"But people have to do something. I'm twenty-six years old."

"Well, there's always The Firm," Brown said.

"Yes, but you see how I'm fixed." I glanced at the closed bedroom door. "She'll give me hell if I tell you to go on investigating us."

"Oh, we'll go on anyway," Brown said.

They did. I was put in touch with a man named Morgan who was staked out in Boston, and from time to time I went into town to talk to him. And my! didn't that produce some stormy scenes on Story Street. One night May even started to pack her clothes. I followed her into the bedroom and took the suitcase away from her. "I forbid you to pack," I said. "You cannot leave me. We're married."

"It is not feudalism any more," she said. "We are not living in the Middle Ages. Women are free. I can do what I please." Where had I heard that sort of wild talk before?

"You cannot do what you please," I said. "There's me to consider. There's our Unitarian marriage sacrament. There's the child. It's quite impossible for you to do what you please."

"I shall. I will. I warned you, Samuel."

"I've explained why I'm doing it. I'm not going to go on being a student the rest of my life. Men have to get jobs and work to support their families."

"I will not let you support me by working as a spy. It's disgusting. Degrading. Secret. Everything is wrong with it."

"Naturally it has to be secret. A government can't tell the world everything it knows, or thinks it knows about other governments."

She put her hands over her ears. "Stop talking. And give me back my suitcase."

I was still holding it in my hand. "It's my suitcase," I said. "I bought it."

"I will leave with nothing. I will leave now," she said.

But, of course, being much bigger than she was, I could prevent that by simply standing in front of the door. "I hate you," she said after a little while. "I am sorry now I ever listened to you." Then she began to cry.

Soon I started to cry as well.

She was used to this. At first it had shocked her to see a man cry, but now that she was used to it she enjoyed it almost as much as I did. We wept and wept with our arms around each other—we always embraced as soon as we were both crying. After a bit she put her hand on my chest. "Samuel," she said, "for my sake, for the baby's sake, do not take this job." The baby, pressed between us, seemed to add infinite pathos to her appeal.

"You can't ask me not to, May, darling," I said. "After all, I'll be working for my government and for my country. I'm an American. You are, too, now."

"Oh Samuel!" Her weeping increased, and so did mine.

"We're both Americans, and our baby will be too. A fifteenth-generation American."

"A what?" she said.

"Counting from the Clays. Only eleventh on the Heather side."

Exhausted, May sat down on the couch and reached for a Kleenex. "What are we talking about?" she said sadly.

"And on your side of the family, a first-generation American." I took a Kleenex and blew my nose.

"You persist?" she asked me.

"I persist."

Oh, we had rational arguments as well. My basic point, a sound one I still think, was that if the CIA was going to make the mistake of recruiting me, then my obvious duty to humanity was to accept the call. "After all, the more people there are like me in the CIA, the less harm it can do."

"That is invalid," May said. "Think of the harm it will do you. And me. Think of us."

"And what about my duty to mankind?"

"I do not think you believe in it," she said.

Sometimes we even discussed it on a practical level.

"Do you realize my starting salary could be five thousand dollars a year? It took me two and one half years of prison to accumulate that much, and even then they didn't pay me."

"Money!" said May.

"We need money."

"I despise it." She glowered at me. "I admired you because I thought you were above such things. A free spirit."

"I am a free spirit. Free spirits need money as much as anyone else. Maybe even more than anyone else."

"Free! You are not free, Samuel. I find you are bound in a million ways—like a peasant."

"I thought you Communists admired peasants?"

"We love them," she said, "but we wish to liberate them so they will cease to be peasants." She shivered. "All this frightens me! The difference between us, Samuel!"

"We're bound to be different."

"I will hate your work," she said. "We will not be able to share each other's lives. I warn you, this is not good."

There was something to that. When Morgan came right out in the open and offered me the job I told him I would have to think it over.

30

I thought for quite a while—a full twenty-four hours. May was right, of course: spying *is* a distasteful business, and yet it was the only job anyone had thought to offer me. I simply could not go on studying and taking exams. Teaching had always struck me as the one honorable profession open to a person of my nature and talents, but I'd lost too many years and grown too restless to settle down and study. So I would take up spying. A shabbier profession, but one for which I was prepared by the life I'd led.

Well, no, there was another profession I could choose: preaching. Life had indeed prepared me to preach, and I could feel my sermons swelling within me the way my child was swelling within May. Why should we not both give birth at the same time, she to an heir, and I to the Word? I could announce *urbi et orbi* that I had become an unordained minister of the gospel. The age is rich in cuckoo sects, I didn't see why mine shouldn't prosper. Television was killing off the local movie houses, and as they fell I could gather one in and set up my altar where the silver screen had hung. The seats were in place, the air conditioning could be turned on, and I could collect offerings at the ticket window.

Earlier that spring, before Morrison's visit, I had actually inquired about the rental of an abandoned theater near Cambridge Square. A six-month lease was not beyond the realm of possibility. I felt equal to hustling the natives and proselytizing for my faith. It seemed possible I could collect a congregation capable of supporting me. After all, Cambridge was full of children crying in the night, children crying for the light. Why shouldn't I electrify them?

True, May would not like to see me spreading opium

among the people, but then a man must not allow himself to be deflected from his work in life by the idle fancies of his wife. Anyway I thought I could control her (where could she run off to?) and maybe even convert her and put her in the choir. So the idea was still simmering in my mind when Morgan made his indecent proposition.

As I say it took me fully twenty-four hours to consider the matter and I really tried to work things through to a logical conclusion. I took a long, almost endless walk down one bank of the Charles as far as the Basin, up the other side of the river clear around the bend beyond the Stadium and then back down again as far as MIT and so across and back up once more. I was going in tightening circles, but I was trying to be analytical.

On the one hand spying offered some security and an initial salary (six thousand dollars) which seemed like riches. On the other hand it was a profession of doubtful utility to the world at large and it might both damage my character and impair my relationship with my wife. And suppose I had a son? Would I want him to grow up and find out his father was a pipe-smoking spy like Morgan? Or a dandy like Morrison?

At that point it seemed clear to me I should take up preaching. It was a really useful profession for which my talents and disposition were suited. True, there would be no security in it. I would have to work very hard and make my sermons glow with faith, hope, and charity. Yet shouldn't one work hard and shouldn't one spread the Good Word? Even if one's wife didn't want to hear it? My son, at least, would be proud to see his father standing tall before the altar in his chasuble and dalmatics, then kneeling before his invisible sovereign. And how he would thrill when I mounted my pulpit and spread my arms to my people. Then when the lad was old enough I would make him altar boy, just as I had been, and there would be continuity in the generations, the family rift might even be healed, and we would be all in all. Obviously I should take up preaching even with all its insecurities. It was the nobler choice.

I was in front of Tech by that time on my first lap around the river. My mind was made up, but I kept walking because I was determined to really think it out and I'd decided after only twenty minutes.

So I strolled along, thinking. And the more I thought the decision over, the more I wondered what would be the exact form of my ceremonies and the name of my church. I was a trinitarian, yes, but could I mislead people by calling myself a Christian? There is something very literal at the heart of Christianity. The faith is pinned to that cross, and unless you can believe the man who died there was indeed the Christ, then for you the show is over and you must find another name for your church.

I began thinking up names. I would be a Samuelite, and my church would be the First Church of Samuel the Anointer. The syllables did not fall trippingly from the tongue, but after repeating them several times they began to seem sufficiently impressive until I was assailed by a Doubt. Did I have the right to invent names and ceremonies? There was religious freedom in the land, written into the Constitution itself, but just because the Constitution stipulated that there should be no state church, did that authorize every private individual to invent his own uncouth religion and inflict it on the public?

My mind hearkened back to William Blake, in whom I had never lost interest though I had begun to doubt his total sanity. I had been reading *The Four Zoas* that winter. Enitharmun, Rintrah, Vala, Theotormon . . . what kind of names were those? My First Church of Samuel the Anointer sounded like home, Mom, and apple pie compared to them. But however conventional my names and ceremonies might become, did I really think I had the right to set myself up in a church of my own, and by so doing join that endless host of religious cranks that plagued the Republic? I thought of the swamis and snake chunkers and table-turners and head-feelers and card-readers and all the other simple seers and prophets who pretended to Know Something and have Something to Say. I would be joining *them*, as well as Blake. And at that point I made a great decision. I would spy. I would forgo the pleasure of sounding off in public.

I was on a bridge then, crossing over to the Boston side of the river. I paused to look at the sailboats in the Basin. There they were, some anchored, some tacking around free and easy with the wind and sun on their sails while I, twenty-six years old, would retreat into the labyrinth of secrecy and lurk like a Minotaur in the dark. Also I would be joining the forces of reaction. I knew from reading the liberal press that the CIA was behind every wicked thing that happened in the world. It was hand-in-glove with all the counterrevolutionary forces in South America. Could I really bear the idea of blocking progress in those poor, priest-ridden lands where people called out *Father, Father* to childless men who knew nothing about raising families and making sons into citizens? I agreed one hundred percent with Dante that only the Monarch can rule. Priests were not even noblemen. I held that they were essentially common men whose real office was to perform the simple ceremonies and keep the faith clear and intact, though I was willing to allow that they could offer advice *when it was asked for*. As a child I'd had far too much unasked-for advice to think that priests, even priests with sons, are qualified to rule others.

By God! I thought, I *will* preach. My first sermon in the church of Samuel the Anointer would be on the subject of Samuel himself, the last of the Judges, the man who had anointed first King Saul and then King David. I would explain to my people the significance of that tremendous event, how it marked the moment at which God had moved mankind forward and upward from its priestly to its kingly stage of history. And then I would preach a great sermon on true kingliness. I would describe the Royal Soul, and present a dazzling picture of the monarch of men: debonair, handsome, and dignified, he carried his great power and responsibility with easy majesty. Or if he sagged and sweated, he did his sagging and sweating in the privacy of his study or chapel. When he was in public he greeted his people with frank and friendly grace, neither condescending to them nor flattering them. Above all, he did not go around grinning all the time.

I paused at that point to think of all the Presidential grinners we had been getting from the time Teddy Roosevelt first unleashed that heart-stopping rictus of his up to the present incumbent. Really, I thought, if you can't organize your face into some semblance of coherence, *wear a beard!* What we needed was a line of tall bearded, majestic Presidents, great-souled men, firm in their thoughts, eloquent in their words, clear in their acts, and kindly in their manner. Instead of which . . . and as I thought of poor Eisenhower the blood rushed to my head and I raised my hands, fists clenched. "If only he wouldn't *grin* at us," I cried out, much to the astonishment of Mrs. Sears, who was out walking along her side of the river checking on the weather.

Yes indeed, there she was, the Shepherdess herself. It's a small world.

"Why, it's Samuel Heather," she said.

"Hello, Mrs. Sears," I said. If I'd had a hat I would have raised it. I wished, even more keenly than during my encounter with her daughter, that I had been wearing something other than my rather beat-up army surplus clothing. Also I wished my hair were not quite so long and windblown as it was. I reached up to straighten my locks. I grinned sheepishly. Mrs. Sears looked concerned.

"Are you all right?"

"I'm fine," I said. "And how are you?"

"Very well."

"Mr. Sears all right?"

"Yes indeed." There was a little silence. I buttoned a button. Mrs. Sears said, "We haven't seen you for a long time, have we?"

"No," I said. I wondered if a dinner invitation were to be forthcoming. I hoped not, and trusted that the Shepherdess could see I was no longer a fit shepherd to romp with her on enameled lawns.

She seemed to be coming to that conclusion herself. Six years, you could see her thinking, had had a surprising effect on this nice-mannered and formerly nicely dressed young man who had once romanced her daughter and recited a poem at her table. "You seemed to be very excited just now," she said.

I blushed. "I was thinking about something."

She nodded. It confirmed her judgment. A little excitement in young shepherds is only to be expected, but they should not go on getting more excited as they grow older, nor should they think too much. "Well . . ." she said.

"I'm happy to see you again," I said.

"And I'm happy to see you, Samuel. It's a lovely day, isn't it?"

And so, agreeing on the weather, we parted. Life is partings—also comings together, and that particular coming together rather sobered me. I walked off thinking I really must do something about my clothes and my hair. I could feel Mrs. Sears taking a last look as I departed, though had we only known it she was in fact getting a sneak 1956 preview of coming attractions. My dear, young 1971 friends (it's 1971 now) slop, if you must, in your own pads, but please do not give public scandal to nice old shepherdesses like Mrs. Sears. They're poetry-lovers themselves.

Well, that's irrelevant, perhaps.

333

Meeting Mrs. Sears made me decide once and for all that I would definitely take up spying, a quiet background activity which would give free scope to the play of my intelligence as I digested the latest news from China and analyzed each shift and turn in Communist policy, putting everything into the broadest, most luminous perspective. My summaries and prognostications would impress the White House staff which would draw my reports to the attention of the President himself, who might very well call me in for private consultation. And then a job on the White House staff could lead almost anywhere. Except for a defector.

There was this strange prejudice against defectors! I'd encountered it here and there, and though it seemed most unreasonable, still I couldn't ignore the fact that it existed. My employment at the CIA was not going to lead me into the sun of Presidential approval. I would be kept in the background under wraps like all the other odds and sods they had on the payroll—half the American Communist party, by all accounts. I'd probably be forced to hobnob with people like Herbie and eat at a special table in the cafeteria. I'd never see the bright lights or hear the crowds cheering me.

By then I was opposite the Fenway where Ted Williams was still knocking them out of the park in those days. His career, too, had been interrupted by the Korean war, but he'd fought his way through and back into the limelight for those last great years of a great career. His example encouraged me. I could do that, too, but not at the CIA. I needed scope. . . . Now if I took up preaching and made a name for myself among the ranks of the holy men of our time, that would certainly erase the stain from my reputation.

I held that thought and caressed it until I was approaching Harvard again on the Business School side of the river, at which point I became—how shall I put it?—slightly disillusioned as I viewed myself messing around in front of my congregation with unconsecrated chalices and pyxes and whatever other altar furniture I should find useful for the ceremonies I would devise. I mean, could I perform a kind of symbolic parody of the Mass even in good faith?

And what was my faith, anyhow? It did seem to get back to that.

I lingered a moment to examine the spot where my stick of dynamite had gone off. No signs were left. The grass grew, the banks of the river were level, the disturbance I'd created was smoothed over and forgotten by everyone, and even I wasn't sure of the exact spot. Time erases all things—except the faith which must survive—only what was the faith? Or at least what was my faith? It did seem to come back to that.

I was sound on the Trinity, of course, but that didn't get me very far since none of its members had ever spoken to me or made any other special acknowledgment of my humble existence. The problem was to get onto more familiar terms with God, or rather with His will. And there I was stymied by the problem of revelation. Just how did you come to know God's will if you didn't believe in revelation or in the Incarnation or any of the other helps He was supposed to have given us?

I assumed in those days that the way to know God's will as it applied to man was through a study of history. History had a providential ring to it as far as I was concerned. It was too eccentric, too full of strange events and astoundingly original people to be explicable by any general laws, Marxist or otherwise. There had to be an X-factor at work—clearly providence.

Take Jesus, for example. So far as I could see there was no one the least bit like him in all history. Certainly there was no one else about whom that sort of claim had been made for so many centuries by highly educated and intelligent men, from Augustine through Aquinas and Pascal right up to the latest Jesuit prodigy. The Moslems didn't think Mohammed was anything more than a prophet, and the

Buddhists merely reverenced a saintly enlightened one. What other even moderately respectable higher religion made the same kind of extraordinary claim about its founder? Christianity was certainly unique, and while it was admittedly a very dubious matter when looked at skeptically, it was very much a part of the general extraordinariness of history.

And not only was human history extraordinary, but so far as we knew it was unique. We might not be the only men in the universe, but we were the only men we knew of, and our history was the only history we knew. I was convinced Toynbee and others were off on the wrong foot in splitting up human history into the history of different races or civilizations. The whole thing, from Pithecanthropus erectus up to Samuel Heather walking along the Charles, was one incredibly complicated but essentially unified story which included the Chinese, the Negroes, the Indians, and of course the good old Jews and Gentiles. If God created and ruled the world then obviously he dealt with all men, though in different ways. Yet his dealings with us could not be ad hoc or disjointed. A unity, a plan, a meaning, and a design had to exist within the apparent fragmentariness and chaos of history, just as it existed within the universe as a whole. Indeed, the more I thought about it, the more I realized that *for us* the universe and human history were rather alike. Both were unique phenomena, and still unfinished in their totality. History was still going on, and the universe (I had heard) was still in the process of creation. So really when it came right down to it, the problem of the providential meaning of history was of about the same order of difficulty as the problem of the meaning of the universe. And quite a problem it was, since neither history nor the universe were natural phenomena. Nature does not work in terms of single examples, but there was only one universe and (so far as we knew) one history. Moreover to get real scientific knowledge you have to form a theory, plan an experiment, predict the results, and then do the experiment to see if your prediction was accurate. But you couldn't experiment on history or the universe. To understand either, you had to fly to the mind of God. I was in a dilemma. To understand God I was studying history, but to understand history I had to understand the mind of God. So unless I was going to get a revelation of some sort, the whole business seemed hopeless and I might as well go to work for the CIA.

Besides, what was so wrong with the CIA? Admittedly it backed a lot of tinpot dictators and antique fascists, but with people like myself working within the organization we might be able to inaugurate a policy of true restoration. We could put the Count of Paris back on the throne of his ancestors, and slip a Habsburg into Vienna and a Hohenzollern into Berlin. We might even be able to find a young sprig of the Romanovs willing to parachute into Russia from one of our spy planes. He would descend among his people, landing gently in the courtyard of the Kremlin, where he would find that great bell (or was it a cannon?) cracked like our own Liberty Bell. Yet as he struck the bell (or cannon) it would give out a sweet note summoning the Russians to love and obedience. Then he would put his manly young shoulders to the great task of lifting the terrible weight of oppression under which the Russians had bowed for centuries. After which he could give them a true Constitution just like ours so that they would be free to select as his successor the most royal man in Russia. Inherited monarchy didn't work too well, since for some reason great kings and emperors often had lousy sons. Look at Marcus Aurelius' boy Commodus, a mere thug and dilettante gladiator who had to be strangled in his sleep.

I was around the bend above the stadium by that time. I crossed the river and started downstream, wondering how one went about producing good sons who would grow up to be great princes and kings. That would be the trouble with the CIA, I would be forced to work with defective human material instead of being out there preaching and exhorting young men to grow up into great-souled characters. Besides, could the CIA really restore royalty and loyalty where it had lapsed? A true prince advanced to his throne on his own two feet. He was not put on the potty of power by well-meaning Mommas in the CIA. *Do your duty, dear.* Anyway, I was not going to be a mother, I was going to be a Father.

I began thinking of fatherhood and was still thinking about it as I approached Leverett House, where I saw a young man lying on the grass *sunbathing*. Was that all right? Could we allow that?

I remembered the shock I'd first experienced back in 1947 when I steamed in from Kansas City for the first time and discovered the typical young man of Harvard owned and even used an umbrella. After a bit I'd bought one myself, and even carried it about though I never opened it. Still it was fun swinging it around and balancing it on my palm. Then one evening when Morrison and I were fencing my umbrella got broken and I'd never bothered to replace it. Young men *sheltering* under umbrellas always aroused my contempt. And now here we were nine years later with male sunbathers in our midst.

A bad sight, I thought. A young man could be permitted to lie on the grass and play a shepherd's pipe while he watched his sheep graze, but he could not loll about three-quarters naked with his eyes closed. You've got to keep alert, I thought, and felt like prodding that sunbather with the toe of my army boot. My son would never doze off into a sun-drugged sleep. But what would he do?

That set off a whole long train of meditations and speculations which occupied me until I was halfway to Boston again. As the Shepherdess had truly remarked, we were having lovely weather, and I was enjoying my walk even though

I was conscious by then that I wasn't getting anywhere in solving my problems. Still it was pleasant to pace the banks of the river, and why not pass the time thinking firm, pleasant thoughts about the future of my son?

To what heights would he rise with the help I could give him? He would have no problems about how to behave: no umbrellas, no sunbathing, drink in moderation, virginity until marriage, no smoking, courtesy to old ladies and gentlemen, clean clothes, neatly groomed hair, regularity, harmony, courage, alertness, good humor, ambition, and perhaps a swing like Ted Williams'. One wants one's son to be graceful as well as strong.

I would explain all those matters and help him with everything, except perhaps how to swing a bat. You see, Reader, I have an amblyopic eye and as a result my depth perception is poor. I can't judge where baseballs and footballs are going, hence the only sports I ever went out for were swimming and track. Still, I could teach my son how to run and swim, and perhaps his swing would come naturally as Ted Williams' had probably come.

So my son would move forward into life, balanced and strong, his mind and character tempered by discipline and fired with honorable ambitions and ardent, lawful love. A young prince. Indeed, why shouldn't he become exactly the kind of President we needed? Half Chinese and half Anglo-Saxon, in him would be united the best qualities of East and West: serene Confucian humanism and firm Western faith; Communist solidarity and Western competitiveness. Why shouldn't he save us all and bring peace to the world?

At which point a voice called me to order. "Heather," it said, "you are out here to make a practical decision, not to cuddle up in the lap of your unborn son who may be a daughter and in any case will need to be supported. So stop hallucinating and try to think."

"Yes Sir," I said.

I crossed the river and started upstream again. The problem, obviously, was that neither spying *nor* preaching was exactly suited to my needs or to my talents, such as they were. Yet if I waited around to find an ideal occupation I might die of old age before I'd embarked on a career. Hence I had to choose between these rough and ready alternatives thrown up by life. So which was it to be?

For a long time I tramped along the riverbank mulling it over and getting nowhere until at last, exasperated by my own indecisiveness, I said, "Oh to hell with it." I recrossed the river and headed straight for a grassy knoll, one of my favorite spots in Cambridge. On that knoll some good citizens full of equal parts of simple faith and Norman blood had caused to be erected a stone which proclaimed the stark fact: ON THIS SPOT IN THE YEAR 1000 LEIF ERICSON BUILT THE FIRST DWELLING IN THE NEW WORLD.

In a locale so charged with future potentialities (the Empire State Building came to mind) I might get supernatural aid. When thinking fails, pray. And since it was a place sacred to Norse Legend, I thought it well to pray in Old Norse, a language I had studied on my first time round at Harvard when I was anxious to learn things I was sure Father didn't know. He'd had a good education—Latin, Greek, the works—so my laudable ambition to dazzle him had driven me a bit off the map into the pagan intricacies of the *Voluspa*, whose opening lines I still remembered. I knelt, then, beside that sacred stone and gave the invocation:

> Hlyoths bithk allr, hellgr kindr
> Meirri ok minni, mogu Heimdallr.

Then, switching to the vernacular, I said very simply, "What shall I do?" and the Tempter answered in distinctively American tones saying, "Son, six thousand is good money for a fellow with your qualifications. Get off your knees and go get that job," which is what I did.

340

31

In late April we moved down to Washington. Two weeks later a child was born. A girl. Some benign presence was taking no chances by giving me a son to raise. I named the infant Anne, and recognized how lucky I was to have her. And also May. May had been threatening to desert the ship, but looking around her she could see no viable lifeboat to transfer into. So she settled down with me in the apartment I had found for us in that shabby district off Georgia Avenue.

My job—my first job—was rather exciting at first. I bought myself a three-piece suit and a briefcase and went to the office every morning just like everyone else where I read the Chinese newspapers (just like everyone else), cutting out the more interesting tidbits to paste in my scrap album. It was not highly responsible work, but it was work and I had begun to realize that work and routine are the great anodynes of modern life. They may not solve the problems, but they still the waters a bit, and we need still waters if we wish to run deep, or even just float along.

My immediate superior was a soft-spoken, scholarly man named X, a trained Sinologist who had gotten into bad company (the OSS) during the war. One thing led to another until there he was in ripe middle age cloaked in secrecy while his peers at Berkeley and Harvard published articles in the learned journals and acquired great reputations in the field. X was a nice man, but a little embittered by his lack of academic recognition. "This work has to be done," he told me, gesturing around his office, "but I could have written a good book on the Imperial Civil Service."

I sympathized with him, but his problems were not my problems. There is a time when one wants to be known, and a time when one wants to be invisible. Perhaps due to my height I have always felt too visible; in Washington, with a sigh of relief I began to discover the pleasures of anonymity.

I had a game I played as I rode to and from work on the bus. I assumed I was being shadowed to see if I made contact with any Russian or Chinese agents. The trick was to pick out the undercover operator watching me. One particular commuter attracted my attention. I saw him most mornings and evenings, generally reading the *Washington Times Herald,* then still in existence. It was such a vile newspaper it seemed only reasonable to assume no one could really be as deeply immersed in it as he seemed to be. Ergo he was the man, masquerading as Casper Milquetoast hiding behind a newspaper. So one morning I sat down beside him and said, "You don't have to pretend any more."

That startled him out of the editorial page. "I beg your pardon?" he said.

"I know who you are," I said.

He moved closer to the window. "I'm sorry . . ." he began.

"That's all right. You have your job to do, I have mine."

He gave me a terrified look and then raised the paper and for the next six blocks pretended to be reading something piped into the *Herald* straight from the *Chicago Tribune.* At my stop I got up and gave him the high sign. "Be seeing you around," I said.

That evening when I saw him again I gave him a big wink. He turned pale, and thereafter whenever I saw him I rather enjoyed subjecting him to a mild persecution. After being watched over for years by Father and by my own fairly powerful super-ego, I was really delighted by the sensation of having this rabbit on the run. Then he dropped out of my life and I took to reading the racing form on my bus rides. I have no interest in horses or betting, but I was trying to construct an image of myself as *l'homme moyen sensuel*

342

going about his life without too much interference from the higher powers. The racing form seemed to fit into the general picture, though I always left it on the bus. It wasn't something I wanted May to see.

Frequently when I was out walking the baby with her or shopping with her in the local supermarket, I could feel how fragile and threatened my anonymity really was. People tended to stare at us, and indeed we did make an oddly assorted couple. There was, I knew, a built-in oddity to my whole existence. I was marked off, we were marked off, and I could feel thunderheads building up in the West. I knew man is not judged by ordinary or even by human standards, but for the time being I enjoyed pretending that I was free to live my own life according to my own lights.

"Isn't this wonderful?" I said to May one evening. "We have a home, a child, a job, and I'm thinking of making a down payment on a car. We can take trips around Virginia to visit the battlefields. You really haven't seen enough of this country."

"I do not think our life is so wonderful," May said.

"But you're happy?" I asked.

She considered the matter. I waited rather anxiously. At last she said, "I am disappointed, Samuel."

"But the baby?" I said. It seemed to me the baby was one of our strong points. It was a very pretty, fat little thing, then six months old. May admitted she enjoyed it. "And me?" I said. "Don't you enjoy me?"

"I do not enjoy the work you are doing."

"Well you're not going to make me feel ashamed of myself," I said.

She gave me a dark look, and then announced she was pregnant again.

Mother came to Washington for the birth of our second daughter. She was happy to see me settling down and producing pretty Eurasian grandchildren she could knit for. I think she found Anne and Sarah a welcome relief after dealing for so many years with Father and myself. Also she struck up some sort of friendship with May. I used to overhear them talking about babies. Once Mother said, "I wish I'd known that when Samuel was young."

"Known what?" I asked, putting my head in the bedroom where they were washing Sarah.

"Never mind, dear," Mother said.

Father came to Washington on high ecclesiastical affairs from time to time. Generally we met downtown at the Cosmos Club for lunch, or occasionally dinner. He gave up eating with us early on, since for some reason May always went out of her way to fix something really Chinese when he was in town.

My lunches with Father were jolly affairs during which we discussed the hot topics of the hour—Tillich's theology, the problem of Bishop Pike, outbreaks of cannibalism in the Congo, and things like that. He did not inquire, and I couldn't have told him much about my work. It was just as well, since my job impressed him as little as it impressed May. When I got a raise and a slight promotion after a couple of years, Father seemed only mildly pleased. Soon after that I moved my family to Alexandria, Virginia, and even insisted on driving him out to show him our house. I had a car by then. Father looked the place over, regarded his grandchildren, spoke politely to May, and then glanced at his watch, so I drove him back to town, boiling with the familiar anger but feeling superficially philosophic about it all. I'd disappointed him so severely that it was only human he should get some revenge. Yet how odd I should be hurt that Father obviously didn't think much of the nice semi-detached brick house I'd found for my family! Was this the currency in which life was going to pay me off for my transgressions and eccentricities?

I worked for the CIA for six years. Figure that one out, taxpayer. I'm off your back now, profitably engaged in another racket, but you supported me when I needed it most, for which much thanks. The CIA was probably the wrong place for me to be, but there I was and there I stayed, rising —hear this!—to a position of responsibility with two subordinate spies under my direction.

At first power went to my head and I arrived early every morning to be at my desk glancing casually at the clock when my subordinates tooled in. I felt it would be good for them to know they were watched and continuously judged by the Boss. Later I treated them with a more democratic familiarity, without of course blurring the distinction in rank that existed between us. This treatment worked well and we became a happy, harmonious team. Every morning after I had read the Chinese newspapers I called my players together and we would toss the crystal ball back and forth until I felt loose and warm. Then I pricked my finger, put a spot of blood on my forehead, spun around seven times, and fell into an ecstasy. The words I then spoke were immediately transcribed and printed up to be rushed off to the Pentagon and the White House, where I'm sure they made all the difference. Once I even felt I had affected policy, but I cannot speak of this great triumph because when I signed on and again when I signed off I swore a great oath not to reveal the secrets of The Firm.

Yet I must attempt to convey what I learned from the surprisingly long time I spent fiddling around in the CIA while Rome burned. I learned, for instance, that we must not expect more from government than it can provide, nor should we think it can provide very much. I also learned that those who begin by flattering the power of government end up by flattering themselves. These deep truths I will now illustrate by telling the sad story of Morrison. He was a flatterer of power.

I saw him from time to time, though usually alone since May did not like him. She didn't like any of my old friends, not that one can blame her. Morrison was getting pretty hard to take even for me.

He had not married, for one thing, so that all his powers of affection, such as they were, had become concentrated on himself. He dressed with discreet splendor. He drove a Thunderbird, and then a Jag, and then some kind of car that had to be referred to by cryptic letters and numbers—an XYZ 747, or something like that. His girls were chosen with an eye for how they would look sitting beside him in his current car. They were incredible creatures with long legs and noses, rather like the Afghan hound with which Morrison eventually replaced them. He was obviously going to pot. When he bought the Afghan I felt it was my duty to remonstrate with him.

"Unless you pull yourself together," I told him, "next you'll start collecting something."

"Would you like to see my icons?" he asked.

He took me up to his fashionable apartment and showed me his icons. "This one comes from Azerbaijan," he said. "You see the Persian influences?"

"You didn't use to be like this," I said. I felt sad. Oh what a semi-noble mind was here o'erthrown!

He poured us some vile unblended Scotch called Laphraoig and we settled down for a talk. The Afghan went to sleep on a Bokhara rug. The Scotch made me feel like throwing up over both of them. "You must have some decent bourbon," I said.

He gave me a drink from the bottle he kept for his cleaning woman. Then he said, "I'm beginning to know myself."

I said, "People who specialize in knowing themselves make poor friends and bad citizens," but he had never been easy to insult and by then it was impossible. I'm not even sure he heard me.

"You know?" he said. "We were incredibly naïve back in college. Reading all kinds of crap that had nothing to do with what we really are."

"Please tell me what these horrible icons have to do with what you really are."

He paused in the act of sipping Scotch. "You never had any taste, Sammy. Even then."

"I suppose that's right," I said.

"You weren't insensitive," he explained, "but basically you lacked a sense of identity. All that Bunyan and Blake and Keats and Homer and so on."

"Well?"

He shook his head. "You were a million miles from being Homeric or Blakean or anything. What you really were and are is a provincial Midwestern Protestant, and probably they are the least artistic or spiritual people who have ever lived."

I said, "I'm flattered you've spent so much time thinking about me."

"It was easy," he said. "After all, my background isn't a whole lot different from yours. Chicago is more urban, of course, and at least my father was in business." He paused in the act of sipping again. "A Protestant bishop! My God! But aside from that we had roughly the same kind of handicaps to overcome."

"And you've succeeded where I've failed?" I said.

"Yes." He stared at his Scotch which he was sipping from a balloon glass that cried out to be stepped on. There was a significant pause. He said, "I'll tell you something, Sammy. I believe in God now."

"What's so remarkable about that? I always have."

He shook his head. "It's not your abstract, moralistic deity I believe in. I believe in a real, personal God."

"Have you seen a psychiatrist about it?" I asked. "Why not call up Bartoldi?"

"See?" he said. "You have no conception of what a re-

347

ally emotional and personal spiritual life can be like. Frankly I think most Protestants are without a sense of grace."

"You presume to slop around this apartment swilling your foul drinks and pretend you're in a state of grace?"

"I knew you wouldn't understand," he said.

"What church do you belong to?"

"That's typical. Churchgoing is synonymous in your mind with a religious life."

"You just commune with your icons?" I asked.

He sighed. "I suppose I shouldn't have told you this. It's like trying to discuss music with someone who's tone deaf."

"I'm worried about you," I said. "What you need is a wife."

"Sex is an elementary kind of experience," he said.

"You need some elementary experiences."

"This whole conversation has been a mistake. I was trying to help you."

"I was trying to help you, too."

"What you'll find," said Morrison, "is that life becomes more rich the further in you go."

"I would never have believed it."

"Depth," he said. "We must see our own depths."

"You're drowning in your brandy snifter," I told him.

He put it down and turned to look at me with a determined good temper that was somehow more trying than anything else. "How are you doing on the job?" he asked.

"Brilliantly."

"I've heard you were promoted?"

"I'll overtake you yet," I said. "What's your salary?"

He waved the question away. "I *am* glad you got a job with The Firm. It's a civilizing experience."

"I wouldn't say that."

"You begin to see into the real depths of government."

"Like your own real depths?"

He nodded seriously. "It's a valid analogy. We are extraordinarily complicated creatures, Heather. That's what I've been learning. And government is extraordinarily complicated. You think you know what's really going on and why, and then you see that under the surface there's a whole new set of motives and a completely different drama. Frankly, I think anyone who isn't close to the CIA has a pretty superficial and naïve view of what this government is really doing."

I felt genuinely sorry to see a once intelligent student turn into a profound boob. "You really ought to marry," I said. "You need another human being around here. I'd shoot that dog if I were you."

At the sound of the word *dog*, Hyder the hound opened one eye and thumped his tail on the Bokhara.

Morrison shook his head pityingly.

At home I told May, "My friend Morrison is going insane."

"I am not surprised," she said. "Everyone at the CIA seems to be going insane," and while I disputed that point with her, I did lie awake that night thinking how truly she had spoken. We had a high rate of mental breakdowns. Was I safe myself?

You see, knowing secrets, or rather knowing what are alleged to be secrets is a self-defeating business, since if you know something it isn't really so secret any more. There seems to be a Law of Secrecy according to which a piece of information declines in importance proportionately to the number of people who know it. Thus the fact that the earth circles the sun is almost wholly unimportant since practically everyone knows it, while the most important facts of existence are so secret as to be known to only two or three men. There is even the distinct possibility that *the most important piece of information is known to no one*. This accounts for the concerned looks you see on the faces of dedicated CIA men. What if the Russians (or the Chinese) find it out before we do? Though on the other hand, *if* they find it out it can't really be *the most important* piece of information after all. There is thus a sort of contradictory or dialectical tension within all intelligence services. On the one hand they strive to find things out, but on the other hand they recognize that as soon as they have found out something, it is not as important as it used to be before they knew it. This has the most serious psychological consequences for individual intelligence officers. They destroy the value of the information they transmit. Moreover, since one's prestige within the organization depends on one's nearness to the most secret bits of information, there is a phenomenon known as Heather's Law by which a lower-grade intelligence officer becoming aware of a highly important (therefore highly secret) bit of information feels a deep reluctance to acknowledge to himself that he knows what he knows. Because, you see, if *he* knows it, then it can't really be so important, but if he doesn't know it then it really is important and therefore (since he does know it after all) he must be further in or higher up in the organization than he thought he was. The potentialities for a nervous breakdown provided by this situation are too obvious to need underlining. Morrison did, in fact, crack up early in 1962.

I saw him shortly before his collapse. There were several new icons in his apartment and the Afghan had been joined by a second Afghan, making eight Afghans in all. "Down Hyder! Down Rollins!" Morrison said. "They'll leave you alone in a minute."

"Why don't you give these animals their freedom?" I asked. "Send them back to Afghanistan where they belong."

But Morrison was not interested in the Afghan menace. He talked continuously and obsessively about President and Mrs. Kennedy.

"I know for a fact," he said, "that they shuttle girls in and out of the White House for him."

"Come, come, this is prurient," I said.

"They bring them down from New York."

"Wrapped in Oriental carpets?" I asked.

"*She* knows it, of course. It hasn't been a real marriage in years."

"Then why do they keep having children?"

"It was never more than a marriage of convenience on both sides."

"Well, it seems to be a pretty good convenience for them both."

"She's bitterly unhappy. She'd leave him if they'd let her."

"*They* being the church?"

"The Kennedys," he said.

He was drinking another unblended Scotch, Glenmorangie, which was not quite so foul as Laphraoig. I was drinking it myself, which shows where I was heading.

"Let's talk shop," I said.

"This shake-up is just window-dressing," he said. "Kennedy knows the Bay of Pigs wasn't our fault. He's admitted it was all his fault for withdrawing the air cover."

"He's a fool if he admits it," I said.

"Besides," said Morrison, "he knows that without us he wouldn't be able to do half the things he wants. Actually the whole Bay of Pigs business may just have been a tactic to throw blame on The Firm in order to get a greater leverage over it. You wait and see."

"See what?"

"Anyway, he's dying," Morrison said. "He won't live out this term."

"How's your icon collection coming?" I asked. "How's your spiritual life?"

"*He's* a nominal Catholic if there ever was one. I doubt he even believes in God."

"Why this extraordinary hostility toward Kennedy?" I asked.

"Who's hostile?" Morrison said. "I think he's great."

"Oh. I thought you thought he was awful."

"A great man," he said. "He really knows what he's doing."

"What is he doing?" I asked.

"You mark my words," he said, "we're really in at the beginning of something."

What *he* was in for was the beginning of about six months' vacation. Rest leave, it was called. What the country was in for was an adventure in Southeast Asia. And what Kennedy himself was in for is also history. Morrison, at least, recovered. He came back pretty much restored to his 1956 level of mental health. But by then I'd resigned from The Firm, a swift turn of events which requires a new chapter.

32

Father died eight years ago.

Well, all flesh is grass. No man is immortal. Still I confess that after putting down the telephone receiver I slumped to the floor with my back to the wall and burst into tears. When I'd calmed down a little, May said, "But you didn't even like him."

"I didn't like him," I said, "but he was my father. I loved him." She didn't look as if she believed it. "Do you think I'm an unnatural son?" I asked. "All sons love their fathers."

May shook her head. "You haven't even seen him for a year."

"I have a good memory," I said.

I left her with the children and flew out to Kansas City where I discovered Father had one last little surprise in store for me. That old Episcopal fox left a great deal more money than anyone, especially myself, had given him credit for. Naturally it was all tied up in a complicated will. Nothing was ever to be made simple for those he loved.

He had set up a trust fund, three-quarters of the income of which was to go directly to Mother. The remaining quarter was reserved for my use should Mother feel I merited it. Otherwise it would accumulate to be used by my children when they reached the age of reason, defined with astonishing liberality as eighteen. On Mother's death one-half of the principal was to be distributed to ecclesiastical charities, specified by Father, the other half to be inherited by my girls who could then, if they wished, let me have an allowance out of their income. I may be omitting some of the details and technical niceties, but that sums it up pretty well. I was never to get my hands on any of Father's capital, and such income as I might receive would be doled out to me by female relatives and bank trustees, provided of course, I kept my hair combed and my face shaved. Any little irritation these provisions might have caused me was erased when I heard the size of Father's estate.

"That's wonderful," I said. "Now I can retire."

Mr. Smed, Father's lawyer, looked shocked. "The money is not yours," he said. "During your mother's lifetime whatever income you receive from the trust will be dependent on her judgment of your conduct and needs."

"Well, Mother's always trusted me," I said. "Haven't you?"

Mother, in black, smiled faintly. "Yes, dear, but . . ."

So I postponed the rejoicing until Smed scrammed. When Mother came back from seeing him to the door I said, "Where do you suppose he got all that? Could he have been embezzling church funds?"

"Well, dear, he always saved," Mother said. "He tithed and he saved a tenth."

"Mother," I said, "a tenth of what he earned over the last forty years wouldn't add up to that."

Mother looked vague. "Well, he invested it," she said. "I think he got very good advice from Mr. Abernathy." Said Abernathy was a vestryman and local tycoon, one of Father's few close friends. Mother sighed. "I suppose it just mounted up over the years."

The whole thing still sounded pretty fishy to me, but I had no cause to complain. The Republicans had prospered as usual and now the Samuelites entered on their inheritance. I knew Mother wouldn't hold out on me.

Father was laid to rest in Kansas City. It bothered Mother. She yearned for Kentucky. She had always wanted to be buried in limestone soil with good Bluegrass over her

354

head, but as a loyal wife she would stick by Father even in death. Besides, the family plot at Weatherly was full up, and even Weatherly had been sold by her cousins ten years before, a family disaster I now realized Father might have prevented if he'd thought it worthwhile. I wondered if Mother realized that?

We went out to the cemetery on my last afternoon in K. C. The flowers were still fresh on the grave, and already a big double headstone was in place. Death had come suddenly, but it had not caught Father unprepared. The Bishop had ordered his tomb in advance, and there it was, solid granite, a rock to resist the blazing sun of summer and the freezing cold of winter. And at the top I read: Bishop Samuel Heather 1900–1962. He had been an inhabitant of the century, too. Below: *Hic Ego Sum.* Here am I.

I knew the passage Father had been thinking about when he chose that epitaph. First Samuel, Chapter 3. When the Lord called to him three times in the night Samuel answered each time, Here am I. Still, it seemed a strange thing to cause to be carved on one's tombstone. He was a strange man. And yet that epitaph perfectly expressed his sense of pride, righteousness, and isolation.

Mother knelt to pray, and I knelt beside her. I was busy thinking of the Old Testament. Those fathers and sons had not been easy on each other. When Eli was Judge in Shiloh his sons oppressed the people in spite of his reproaches. Then the succession passed to Samuel, whose sons did not walk in the way of the Lord. Next came Saul, searching for his father's asses and finding instead a kingdom. He was an exception to the rule, and I had to skate quickly over the thought of Saul and Jonathan, who were very pleasant in their lives and in their deaths were not divided. Saul was a good father, but a bad king, so the Lord rejected him and the kingdom passed to David, who had a notably unsuccessful relationship with Absalom. Hophni, Phinehas, Joel, Abiah,

355

Absalom . . . I was in bad company, but then the Old Testament was on the side of fathers. It's the New Testament that is on the side of sons, though look what happens there to Jesus. We sons need a book in which we survive to live happily ever after. Kneeling at Father's grave I got the first idea of writing this confession.

Before I left Kansas City Mother and I had a little talk about the future. She would move back to Lexington, she thought. Weatherly was gone, but there were still friends and relatives in the Bluegrass. "And besides, it will be closer to Washington," she said.

"Well, don't count on us being in Washington much longer."

"Dear, you're not really thinking of retiring?"

"Certainly I am. Besides this business of spying on China is about finished. Don't spread it around but we have information Mao's converted to Christian Science so now all we'll have to do is call up Mary Baker Eddy in Boston to find out what's going to happen next in Peking."

"Mary Baker Eddy is dead, dear."

"Yes, but there's a telephone in her tomb and we know the number. We know everything."

She nodded. "But, dear, what would you live on?"

"I'll be getting five thousand a year from Father's estate."

"But can you raise a family on that?"

"No, but then you can help us out. You won't need fifteen thousand. What could you spend it on?"

Mother looked a little doubtful. "I'm not sure your father would like you to be idle."

"I won't be," I told her. "I've been thinking of going into the writing game. There's a lot of money to be made there."

"In writing?" Mother's conception of literature was based mainly on the productions of her various aunts and cousins, whose slim volumes of verse and fat historical novels had never caught on with the public. Her grandfather's majestic work, *The Bible In Condemnation of Woman's Suffrage*, had caused a stir in 1902, but even it had not sold really well. I decided she must be brought up-to-date.

"You don't know it," I said, "but Ian Fleming is making a fortune out of these James Bond stories."

"I don't believe I've heard of him," she said.

"Well, he's an English writer President Kennedy likes to read."

"Oh," Mother said.

"And what I say is that if a hard working ex-spy and Harvard dropout like myself can't do better than a Limey gentleman, then there's something seriously wrong with this world, which I don't for a moment believe."

Mother always had a way of hearing something other than one's words. She nodded thoughtfully. "Of course you were always very imaginative as a child."

"And I still am. How do you think I've kept a job all these years with the CIA?"

Mother didn't answer. She looked as if she were trying to remember something. Then she remembered it. "I read a mystery story once about Charlie Chan. I suppose you could write something like that."

"You wait and see," I told her.

Back in Washington, or rather Alexandria, I hugged May and the children. Then I said, "Well, we're all going to be rich." I looked at the girls. "And I won't have to go off to work any more. I can stay home and play Parcheesi with you all day."

"We'll be in school," Anne said.

"Well, when you come home I'll be here. Won't you like that?"

She sort of nodded.

May said, "You mean you will really leave this terrible work you are doing?"

"Yes. Spying is no profession for a gentleman. I'm going to write books."

I was very lucky. A lot has to do with the name, of course, but I think I can claim some credit for the plots. My hero, Dalton Smed, caught on at once. He was very tall, jug-eared, not conventionally handsome, but good-looking in his own way. Readers first encountered Smed standing in the Oval Room of the White House about to receive the Congressional Medal of Honor for conspicuous gallantry in action at Taejon during the early weeks of the Korean war. I borrowed one of Truman's lines for the scene. The President lays the medal around Smed's neck, shakes his hand, and then says, "Young man, I would rather be a Medal of Honor winner than President of the United States." Smed replies, "And I would rather be President of the United States than a Medal of Honor winner. Do you want to trade?"

His character thus established, Smed is quickly involved in a series of astonishing adventures that would tax the courage and physical resourcefulness of anyone but a Medal of Honor man. At his own request he is sent back to Korea where, during the march on Pyongyang, being far in advance of his unit, he is captured by some Koreans lagging far behind theirs. They carry him off and though he soon overpowers them, he is by then so far out of contact with the U.S. army that he takes to the hills where he encounters a group of displaced anti-Communist North Koreans. There is a brief and rather idyllic series of chapters in which Smed organizes these peasants into a guerilla band and leads them into action against the supply routes of the North Korean army. Then information brought by villagers reveals to Smed the gathering presence of substantial Chinese army forces somewhere to the North. He realizes at once the extreme significance of this information: MacArthur must be warned! So, bidding adieu to his devoted band, and in particular to a dark-haired, athletic Korean girl whom he admires, Smed sets out for the South. Unfortunately he is captured on the way—it is his one failing that he is frequently captured—and so ends up in a prisoner-of-war camp not entirely unlike Pyot Lon.

I deeply enjoyed Smed's reaction to *that* scene. Undismayed by the prevailing apathy and despair, Smed rouses his hutmates, organizes a prison break, and leads a dwindling band of American escapees toward freedom. When recapture and execution seem inevitable, they meet with the remnant of the old guerilla force Smed had organized in Chapter Six. There is a touching reunion with the Korean girl who nurses the Americans back to health. (Their feet are frostbitten.)

The climax comes as Smed guides this mixed band of Americans and Koreans to the fighting lines, now stalemated along the Thirty-eighth Parallel. Trying to cross the lines they are shot at by friend and foe alike, but Smed leads them on, carrying the wounded Wook Wong Toi in his arms. He has chosen a sector of the United Nations front held by the Gloucestershires, and just when death seems certain an astonished British sergeant shouts out, "Hold your fire, mates, they're Yanks." Smed, wounded himself, but still carrying Wook, walks forward. "Ah, our British allies," he says, and faints onto Wook's warm body.

It was not, of course, a spy story in the strict sense of the word, but it had plot, character, thought, and diction. And since it satisfied those simple but wholesome tastes for blood, bravery, and escape, it sold well in paperback. For Smed's next adventure, I made use of my CIA experience, and though in my opinion the moral quality of that book was somewhat more ambiguous than that of the first, *The Cross and the Double Cross* outsold *The Medal* by half a million copies. A third Smed story came out in 1969, but since everyone has read it, I won't bother to summarize the plot.

I take pride in the fact that almost alone among practitioners of my particular craft I make no appeal to prurient sexual tastes. Smed is of course a passionate man, but his attachment to the short dark-haired women who pop up with some frequency in his life has, with one exception, been deeply romantic and pure. The exception, which I regret, took place in my second book, and it was at my publisher's suggestion. They felt we would have the reading public at our feet if only Smed could make it with one of his girls, and in my youthful inexperience—it was only the second book I had written—I allowed myself to be persuaded. This is the explanation of Chapter Thirteen in *The Cross and the Double Cross*, the chapter in which Smed, deeply smitten by a petite charmer of pure Anglo-Saxon ancestry and impure morals, has the misfortune to have her shot out from under him much as the heroes of Westerns sometimes have the misfortune to lose their horses. After that débacle my publishers did not insist, and so in *An Army Without Banners*, my celebration of the Green Berets, Smed reverted to the platonism I have always felt best suits his particular style.

An Army Without Banners sold and is still selling so well that my literary agent and my publisher agreed there was no immediate need for a new Smed thriller, which is why I have had time to write this *Confession of a Child of the Century*.

And now as we enter the stretch and come down to the wire I must try to gather up the few remaining threads of my narrative. I began this book around Christmas 1970. It is now high summer 1971 and I must finish and pack because we are off to Paris for a year. It will be our first long stay. We have rented an apartment in the 14th arrondissement. We'll put the children into a public school and enjoy ourselves. In Paris May and I find an echo, a sort of Western image of Peking. Both are royal cities, and sometimes, standing in front of the Louvre looking up through the Tuileries gardens to where the obelisk in the Place de la Concorde pricks the belly of the Arc de Triomphe on its hill in the distance, I have caught a sense of urban majesty that I first encountered in the Forbidden City.

I am not sure what the future will be. Writing this confession has given me a taste for more serious work. May will be pleased. When I brought her the typescript of *The Medal* she read it with growing distaste. "This is terrible, Samuel," she told me. "It is not true. It is not serious. It appeals to chauvinistic anti-Communist patriotism. I dislike it very much."

All my arguments then and subsequently have done nothing to change her first opinion, though it seems to me any impartial critic ought to see that, politically speaking, *The Medal* and its successors are as innocent as soap suds. (As a matter of fact soap suds have begun to pollute the streams, but let it pass.)

May disliked my next book even more than she disliked *The Medal*, and she has not read *An Army Without Banners*. I, too, was not quite so happy about that book as I had been about its predecessors. I didn't believe in it as deeply as I believed in *The Medal*, and it lacked, I thought, the psychological nuances of *The Cross and the Double Cross*. Somehow a touch of commercialism had crept in, and, thinking it over, I am not sure I will ever write another thriller, which will solve a little problem that has arisen in Kansas City. Dalton Smed, Father's man-of-law, has brought suit against me and my publisher to prevent the further exploitation of his name. Of course a man's name can't be protected by copyright, but to some extent Mr. Smed has a case, since I did steal his name and I admit it. My publishers want to fight, but I'm for settling out of court. Yet with Smed lost to me I doubt I'm up to creating another hero to equal him. I couldn't care and I doubt Readers could be made to care about some short, plump CIA agent. And if I were to create another tall, jug-eared hero, wouldn't people find that rather facile? I could give him a dimple to differentiate him from Smed, but even so there is the problem of naming him. Besides, I have other literary projects in mind. I've long wanted to do a study of the social and psychological significance of the vocabulary of Communist invective. Also I've recently been reading Gregorovius' *History of Rome During the Dark Ages* and I think there's material there for a popularized historical study. Gregorovius has the facts, all right, all right, and they're fascinating, but he covers too much ground and no one but myself reads twelve-volume histories these days. It's struck me that I might quarry out of Gregorovius a sweet book focused on the life and particularly the death of Pope Formosus. Odd name for a Pope. It means beautiful in Latin, but his end was not all that pretty. His body was exhumed, tried for heresy, and found guilty. His ring finger was cut off, and the remains were then flung into the Tiber where they floated downstream until some pious monks fished them out. The good brothers recognized what they were dealing with, but nevertheless gave the body Christian burial. But still it was not the end. After a few years Formosus' heresy became Papal orthodoxy again, and so Formosus was dug up and reinterred in one of the major Basilicas where he remained for a few years until there was another political-theological swing. His body finally disappears from history, or at least from the pages of Gregorovius, heading in the general direction of the Apennines. I think something can be made out of a story like that, and I'd like to try my hand at it.

I do feel I will go on writing. It was a happy insight that finally led me to the typewriter, for in many ways writing solves all my problems and satisfies my needs. It's moderately respectable. I can earn money at it. I have an audience, and yet I am not visibly making a monkey out of myself in front of strangers. I feel both protected from my own absurdities, and yet free to horse around.

Naturally, writing the sort of stuff I write is no more

what I wanted to do with my life than spying was. What did I want? I think at bottom I would have liked to do something good, even noble. That was what May wanted me to do. I feel that is what my daughters would like. They see me around the house too much, disheveled, listening to music, banging away at my stories, swilling tea, and chatting with May. I have only one suit with a vest, and I seldom wear it now. Father never appeared without a vest or without his clerical rig. I feel I am not giving my girls a sufficiently impressive image of fatherhood to get through life with. And certainly they're not going to get much from the young men I see around these days, these barefooted urban rubes with their hair in a braid. One of the main reasons we're going to Paris is to get the girls away from American boys for a while. Keeping children virginal is a mighty task. I've begun to appreciate Father's efforts along these lines. His argument seems to me more and more irrefutable. One cannot offer oneself to everyone. It's both foolhardy and vain. A pimpled adolescent boy is not really God's gift to the world, and neither is a beautiful adolescent girl. And if the young make the gift of themselves, they'll just get chewed up, swallowed, and digested, for the world has a strong appetite for young flesh. I tell my girls this, but they're not completely convinced, so it's off to old-fashioned Paris for them. If you can't convince them, carry them off!

And now I suppose at the end of a book like this I should deliver my conclusions about life and about myself. These are not tremendous. If you love any part of life I think it takes hold of you and gradually corrects your imperfect taste and gives you something better than you had much right to expect. If I'd gotten the sort of passion I thought I wanted at nineteen, I'd be an aging libertine by now, and if I'd gotten the sort of glory I admired I'd probably be dead or ossified into a militaristic freak, a domestic Coriolanus. What most people desire for themselves is so dreadful or vulgar that they're lucky they don't get it. Being a hack writer is certainly not the noblest of destinies, and yet I think I've come out pretty well, everything considered.

And as for my character I'd say that the icy and propontic flow of a father conflict into a basically warm and sunny nature has set up the whirlpools, eddies, and fogs you may have observed in my behavior. I am a reasonably good and moral man by most standards, but obviously I would be better if I had not spent so much of my life bucking the Bishop. He was a good man, damn it. So that's what I'd say about myself if asked, only don't ask me. I don't seek self-knowledge. I am not even sure it's possible.

Nosce teipsum, Socrates used to say in his quaint Greek way. Know thyself, know thyself, but how, but how? Can the mind divide and contemplate its separate halves, and where is the mastermind to put the resultant pictures together? Or can the eyes swivel in their sockets to see the face? And your tongue, Reader, exploring your mouth discovers a great hole in your tooth which the probing light of the dentist reveals to be a cavity one millimeter in diameter. We are not made to know ourselves, and shouldn't bother about the matter. The proper study of mankind is God.

I wish I did know Him, but such knowledge is not given for mere wishing. Naturally I still wonder if it could be true that He has debased His majesty to take on our flesh? Did divinity come down to us since we could not rise to it? For a person of my sort that would be the only solution, for I do not have the soul of a saint or the brains of a philosopher. I can't think my way through to Him, and I can't seem to love my way through either. Yet I know it is my duty to love Him, and I do, though it is hard to love fully what you can't see or understand or touch. I do what I can. The point is you have to love something better than yourself or life is hell.

I don't mean to end sadly, and in fact I am a rather happy man. And for this peculiar happiness I enjoy and probably don't deserve, I thank my parents for the excellent upbringing they gave me, I thank the schools I attended for the substantial though incomplete education I got from them, and finally I thank my loving wife and children. I've been very lucky.

33

It appears I must go on a little further.

We flew off to Paris as advertised and settled into that apartment which was not as advertised. "We've been rooked," I told May. She admitted as much but argued it would do no good to complain to the rental agency, the owner, the U.S. Embassy, or President Pompidou. After complaining to the rental agency, the owner, and the U.S. Embassy, I saw her point. I searched in vain for a French Better Business Bureau to take my horror story to. None existed. "This is intolerable," I told May. "I want to go home."

Then she reminded me why we had fled the howling wilderness of Alexandria. In particular she evoked in my mind the picture of Young Lochinvar Brown in all his slack-jawed grandeur. Keeping Anne away from him for nine months would be worth any amount of personal discomfort, so I reconciled myself to the apartment. It may be ignominious to take flight from a young man who doesn't even have the energy to get up when an adult enters the room, but sometimes in life an ignominious retreat is the better part of valor. Though incidentally I'd like to know how fathers whose work keeps them tied to one spot handle this problem. I suspect much of the opposition to the gun laws comes from fathers with adolescent girls, and more power to them. The fathers, I mean.

Though that is not really the point of this chapter and may provide just the worst kind of introduction to my Christian conversion, which took place in October 1971. Surprised by joy is scarcely the phrase for it.

I was alone at the time. May and the girls had gone to London, which I didn't feel up to seeing, so I was slopping around in what M. Adolphe Le Corbeau wrongly described as an apartment well provided with *luxe, calme, et volupté.* I went out for meals, read Gregorovius during the day, and in the evening listened to clear and distinct discussions on French television. First they would show some old movie, for instance *Lady Hamilton* with Laurence Olivier as Admiral Nelson and Vivien Leigh in the title role. Then, when we'd all had a good cry, the screen cleared and there was Mr. Moderator flanked by a member of the Académie Française, a commander in the French navy, a commander in the British navy, a youngish historian bucking for the Académie, a descendant of the French admiral defeated at Trafalgar, and finally an impeccable Sir Somebody Nelson representing the late Horatio's family.

After a rundown of the historical errors in the film, and an analysis of the personalities of the dramatis personae, the charts were brought out and the Battle of Trafalgar was refought. Such programs always sent me to bed feeling there was hope for the Old World so long as the supply of good old battles didn't peter out. I am what is known in France as an *ancien combattant,* someone who spends his life refighting old battles, and I like to see the job well done. One may not be able to change the outcome, but at least one can probe the old wounds with civility.

So what with watching television and reading Gregorovius and not having any ladies to please I admit I wasn't as careful about bathing and shaving and changing my underwear as I might have been. It was during the third day of my solitude when I distinctly perceived I was smelling a bit, but the thought of coping with M. Le Corbeau's plumbing deterred me from doing anything about the matter until, as I was readying myself for bed, a voice spoke, saying, *You stink to high heaven.*

Offensive words you will agree.

It was not an audible voice. I tried to dismiss it as a projection of my own psyche like all the other voices and

367

visions that have come to me through the years, although this voice seemed subtly different from the rest principally because it wasn't saying the kind of thing I usually say to myself. Still, since the matter seemed urgent, I took a bath, and from that moment onward I was absolutely haunted by voices telling me to shave and to clean up and so on and so forth. I was harried right and left. I couldn't get into bed without praying or get out of it without immediately straightening the covers and praying some more. I was even being told to go to the pot immediately after breakfast. It was like being back in the nursery and the army at the same time. Really, I thought, am I an adult who has written three thrillers and a comical-historical-pastoral, or am I a child? *You're a child*, a voice said.

Basically, of course, I was thrilled by the sensation of being watched over and organized and whipped into shape. It was just what I've always wanted, though at the same time I was troubled by the fact that my plans for the book on Pope Formosus were not taking shape. Every time I tried to think about it I'd be interrupted by a very sharp-tongued Angel who ranks low in the angelic hierarchy, I'm convinced. (By then I was convinced the angels were at last getting through to me.)

Now this particular young Angel I'm complaining about simply would not let me lie down on a couch during the mornings or afternoons, and as it happens much of my more creative thinking has been done on my back. How was I to plan my book on Pope Formosus if this sort of thing were to keep up? One afternoon when I'd just stretched out and my invisible friend had ordered me up, I complained aloud. "Don't nag," I said.

That scared me. Hearing and obeying my voices was one thing, talking back to them was another. There was a hush for a moment. I feared my offended helpers would withdraw from me, so I immediately apologized. But really,

I asked, how am I to do this book? *It's not worth doing,* they answered in chorus. Well, what shall I do? I asked, and they said, *Write something that will make people better rather than worse.*

Good God! I thought, I now know the function of art.

That was how things went. I wandered around the apartment drinking coffee and sitting up in the chairs conversing toe to toe with my angelic voices, while periodically I would have an Insight into some deep problem about which I'd always been undecided. So the function of art was to make people better? Why had I never seen that? Why had I wasted my God-given talent by committing three trivial thrillers? How could I atone?

Then I began to worry about this comical-historical-pastoral which I had finished six weeks earlier. Was it the sort of book calculated to make people better? The Angels kept quiet even though I asked them specifically whether I ought to go ahead and publish this. So, left to my own lights, I began to examine the question of whether this is a good book, and I was sorry to find the answer was at best ambiguous. My story showed that even a son of a bishop can live happily ever after, which would perhaps encourage other young men to keep plugging away without giving up on life. On the other hand my story seemed to advocate and even justify conflict and disobedience. What was this comical-historical-pastoral except the record of my epic struggle with Father, now in its third invigorating decade? The Bishop was down, but not out as his son went on kicking the body now thinly disguised under the papal tiara and robes of Pope Formosus. Did I want readers to assume that was how I believed life should be lived?

I wept a little as I considered the wastefulness and futility of my whole life. Then, feeling that it was not too late to change, I decided I would strike a blow for goodness by revising my confession. I would resurrect Father and show us

369

gradually becoming reconciled. It would be a lie, but a Noble Lie and therefore justified morally.

I began to imagine the final scene between us in which I confessed to him, while he in turn confessed to me. For he was at fault, too. He had ignored Socrates' warning that the Guardians should not know their own sons. And he had ignored the precedent and wisdom of the Catholic church. Priests should not have sons. But just as he would absolve me, so I would absolve him, for after all I couldn't blame him for giving me life, "and anyway I've enjoyed living," I would tell him, "even if I have never done anything worthy of all the advantages you gave me."

Yes. That would fix things up.

Really? said a rather sarcastic-sounding Angel.

Well, what else can I do, I asked, but he didn't answer.

Two hours before May and the girls were due to arrive at the Gare du Nord I went out to dine quickly at a local brasserie. Then I got into the subway to go meet them. I was in a curious state of mind, half elated, half contrite. I was sorry I hadn't led a better, nobler life, but I felt confident that I could tinker with the truth, patch things up a bit, and perhaps my next book (not on Pope Formosus) would be a really good one. I would fudge up the past, and then set to work building a better future. Memo, I said to myself, cable publisher in New York telling him you want to revise the ending of *The Confession of a Child of the Century*. Then I sat back, feeling that everything would eventually work out for the best in this best of all possible worlds.

And at that point something rather curious happened. I felt a slight wrenching inside my head, and all at once my world changed. There was imprinted on my mind the image of a human form at whose face I could not really look, though I could plainly see His bare shoulder and a portion of His chest. The wounds were there, below my field of vision, just as the face was above it. I can't remember thinking anything while the vision lasted. I knew it was Christ, though to say *I knew* implies I made some act of identification which was not at all how it seemed to be. He was simply there, His physical reality proclaiming what I would never otherwise have believed. I didn't identify *Him*. If anything, it was the other way around. Then the vision ended and life just went on. Apparently in this existence there are no stopping points or way stations. We go straight on, straight on even when we are just sitting in a subway train that stops every few minutes.

I was not even surprised in the ordinary sense. So it's all really true, I thought. It was the only genuinely supernatural experience I'll probably ever have, but the whole thing seemed far simpler and more factual than anything else that has ever happened to me. I felt as if I had at last been made into myself, and though one might expect there would be thousands of questions I wanted to ask, in fact I had none. I felt single. The Angels had departed. Presumably their function had been to get me into some sort of decent condition for presentation to my Lord. Now I had met Him and that was that.

At the Gare du Nord I got out of the subway and went up into the station where I bought a ticket to the platform. I was calmly waiting there when the the train pulled in and May and the girls climbed down. "Hello," they said. "Hello," I said, and after we'd kissed I picked up their suitcases. Presently we were all back in the subway heading in the direction of the Porte d'Orléans.

May was pleased to find the apartment so neat. The girls had been charmed by London, while I . . . Well, for the next few days I was content just to let life happen. Then, as the immediate effects wore off, my willfulness began to reassert itself. There were Things To Be Done. I suppose that as long as we are on earth we will never really escape that sensation. It is the penalty we pay for the Fall.

So *I* began doing things again. One night in bed, feeling

371

very tender and close to May, I told her that I had become a Christian. It was a shock to her, but I'd put her through a fair number of shocks during our life together. "I guess I'll join the church," I said.

"You will not convert me," she said.

I had already begun to think about the possibility. It had struck me that our domestic situation might be simplified and improved if the Heathers became a totally Christian family. As she announced her resistance to this very natural desire of mine, I felt a certain tightening of the loins. Don't tempt me, I thought.

"How an intelligent person can believe in those things . . ." May said.

Watch out, I felt.

"It is ridiculous."

"You're asking for it," I told her.

"It would be quite impossible for me ever to become a Christian."

"I'm warning you, May. I'm only human."

Something in my voice apparently did convince her that she was flirting with theological rape. She calmed down, and in fact I have so far managed to control myself where she is concerned. I can feel it would be wrong and lustful to tamper with her soul, but the temptations stirred up where May was concerned did boil over in another direction. I fired off a cable to New York announcing my intention to rewrite *The Confession of a Child of the Century*. If a man can't violate his own creation, what can he violate? I had plans for this little old comical-historical-pastoral. When I was finished revising it, it wouldn't know itself, so clean and smiling and Christian it would have become. I was going to make this story submit to the crushing weight of Truth, and grin beatifically under the burden. My readers would be left in no doubt that I meant business as a Christian. With a little prayer and luck I felt I could turn out a confession which would set the clock back fifteen hundred years and make us all citizens of Hippo and brothers of Augustine. This was going to be a confession of faith, not a confession of my crimes, follies, and misfortunes.

Well, you can imagine what happened. I encountered reality in the shape of a publisher reluctant to see a moderately unregenerate story turned into an immoderately regenerate one. I wrote right back in hot haste, pointing out that I was now a new man and felt I simply could not publish an old confession. My publisher replied to that by congratulating me on my new-found peace of mind but reiterating his point that I would ruin what merits this book has if I adopted an aggressively Christian tone from the opening pages.

I accepted his advice partly because it was probably true, and partly because I was stymied stylistically whenever I tried to rewrite any section of this book. The life I had lived as a comical-historical-pastoral could not be written about except in the style of a comical-historical-pastoral, and while admittedly it was an impure, un-Christian style, there seemed no way to correct it.

Balked in that direction and forced to accept the ineffaceable traces of my comical, historical, pastoral past, I immediately turned my energies another way and began looking around Paris for a good church to join. There was Notre Dame, of course, and theoretically I felt I ought to become a Catholic, but in practice I found I couldn't do that to Mother and Father. So I started visiting the Anglican churches. They rather put me off. I have always been a mild Anglophobe (heritage of the Revolution and the War of 1812, plus my general Francophilia) and while I found these feelings silly, I couldn't get over the sensation of being out of place in an Anglican Church with British accents all around me. Then, happily, I discovered the American Church in

Paris on the Quai d'Orsay. Obviously I belonged there, even though it was an interdenominational Protestant congregation which didn't believe in transubstantiation. So I joined, and this has created a fresh complexity for me since I really do hunger for communion. I wish some kind reader would recommend a guidebook for recent converts. Our difficulty is that we feel so healthy, happy, and whole that we immediately rush out into the world to create new problems for ourselves.

Meanwhile, back on the domestic front, May began making contacts with a sect of French Maoists. I had no objections to this, per se, but I did feel it was thoughtless of May to let them into the apartment. The result is that Anne has stopped sulking about her separation from Boy Brown because he has been driven from front center in her thoughts by an even more hideous French youth. This goony bird hates the bourgeoisie root and branch—on which he is perched, being the son of a Deputy and a student in one of the Hautes Écoles. Still, if he threatens too hotly I decided I can always flee with my family to West Germany. Nevertheless the development adds a further unsettling note to my life, and raised in particularly acute form a question that has begun to bother me. Am I really much changed or improved by my new-found faith? Yet how else can I behave? Twenty minutes' conversation with that boy convinced me he was not a pure-minded young man. I didn't like his eyes or his voice or his smile, what there was of it. I am not going to sit idly by while he spreads his traps for my daughter.

I know perfectly well what I am doing. With a past like mine, how could I not know that moral and religious certainties can have a killing effect, especially on the young? I felt Father was murderous toward me, and possibly Anne and Sarah will come to feel I am murderous toward them. If so, they may choose to break my heart as I perhaps broke Father's, in which case I will be repaid for my transgressions.

374

But I cannot believe that will happen, or that life is so inexorable or justice so Hebraic. That is not the meaning of what I have seen. There is mercy, forgiveness, and healing. And meanwhile I will take care that my girls receive as little damage as possible even if it means that I must keep my family spinning around the globe until Anne and Sarah have grown wise enough to choose some true shepherd or princeling into whose care I am quite willing to deliver them once the moment comes. Who knows? In keeping them from the traps and fleshpots I may get to New Zealand yet, a land I have always loved with a distant and ineffectual passion.

It's curious how everything comes true in a slightly or greatly different form from what one once expected. I toyed at one time with the idea of becoming an archaeologist. Now I find I have unearthed the perfect vessel of faith from the debris and alluvial deposits of life. I dreamed, too, of running off to the South Pacific to escape the moral pressures of home, while now I dream of some happy island far away where it would be possible for my girls to come of age in a morally and civically healthy environment. And most of all I used to long for faith so that my life would be simple and uncomplicated. Now that I have faith, I find it has accentuated most of my problems. My lustful instincts, my willfulness, my vulgarity and my taste for violence are more offensive to me now then they have ever been, and if anything they seem stronger.

What can be the explanation of this? Why have I not been quieted by my Lord who has graciously made his reality known to me? Why am I not in the process of becoming a gentle and loving man? Is it because life on earth is really a scene of warfare and only in Heaven can we know the perfect peace of His love and His will? Or is it really possible to build a New Jerusalem on this old globe and live ever after in holy peacefulness? I wish I could answer my questions. I wish, too, I knew how to end this book, but I don't. And luckily I don't have to answer my questions or end my story because life has turned me into a sufficiently honest man that I can now make the one last and only true confession in all these pages. I am not real. I don't exist. Thomas Rogers *me fecit,* and I'll leave him the problem of finishing what he began.

No. I'm sorry, Samuel, but you must carry through to the end. There is no escape as you should know by this time. And though you are not real you are true enough to finish your own story.

Oh very well. If I must carry on then I will make my choice and announce my decision that life on earth is a conflict, a great war which we must prosecute joyously and lovingly until we are given our final rest. We must fear no one and hate no one, but we must fight all our days against sin and death which have found their way into this world and will never be expelled. We have immortal adversaries, greater and more powerful than we are, and yet we cannot lose our fight since on our side, surrounded by his archangels, stands Christ Triumphant, through whom we are made, by whom we live, and from whose sacrifice we are restored to life eternal.

I have nothing else to say. Who knows what will happen to me? I hope, of course, that instead of making a fighting retreat through life I shall be called to the front once more to serve with some comrades in the great war, where—God willing—I may at last acquit myself as a man rather than a child. And, really, why shouldn't I be lucky? For I have come to think that the luck that has always attended me is simply a pale image of that irresistible grace that floods the universe from its triune source.

So let me pray.

Almighty Father, into Thy hands I commit my soul that Thou mayest use me as Thou seest fit, for I know that Thou hast not made me for myself, but to do Thy work and be Thy witness among men. And though I have never done anything worthy of the great mercy Thou hast shown me, yet Thou hast preserved me all these days. Be yet more merciful, Heavenly Father, and teach me what I must do now. Show me the work for which I am fit so that I may not rest before my time nor waste the little good that is in me.

And after we pray, we sing. All together now, for the tune is your favorite and mine, Old Hundred:

> Praise God from whom all blessings flow,
> Praise Him above, ye creatures low.
> Praise Him above, ye heavenly host.
> Praise Father, Son, and Holy Ghost.

AMEN.